D0891815

Lost Souls

WEATHERHEAD BOOKS ON ASIA

WEATHERHEAD EAST ASIAN INSTITUTE, COLUMBIA UNIVERSITY

WEATHERHEAD BOOKS ON ASIA

WEATHERHEAD EAST ASIAN INSTITUTE,

COLUMBIA UNIVERSITY

LITERATURE

David Der-wei Wang, Editor

Ye Zhaoyan, *Nanjing 1937: A Love Story*, translated by Michael Berry (2003)

Oda Makato, *The Breaking Jewel*, translated by Donald Keene (2003)

Han Shaogong, *A Dictionary of Maqiao*, translated by Julia Lovell (2003)

Takahashi Takako, *Lonely Woman*, translated by Maryellen Toman Mori (2004)

Chen Ran, *A Private Life*, translated by John Howard-Gibbon (2004)

Eileen Chang, *Written on Water*, translated by Andrew F. Jones (2004)

Writing Women in Modern China: The Revolutionary Years, 1936–1976, edited by Amy D. Dooling (2005)

Han Bangqing, *The Sing-song Girls of Shanghai*, first translated by Eileen Chang, revised and edited by Eva Hung (2005)

Loud Sparrows: Contemporary Chinese Short-Shorts, translated and edited by Aili Mu, Julie Chiu, Howard Goldblatt (2006)

Hiratsuka Raichō, *In the Beginning, Woman Was the Sun*, translated by Teruko Craig (2006)

Zhu Wen, I Love Dollars *and Other Stories of China*, translated by Julia Lovell (2007)

Kim Sowŏl, *Azaleas: A Book of Poems*, translated by David McCann (2007)

Wang Anyi, *The Song of Everlasting Sorrow: A Novel of Shanghai*, translated by Michael Berry with Susan Chan Egan (2008)

Ch'oe Yun, *There a Petal Silently Falls: Three Stories by Ch'oe Yun*, translated by Bruce and Ju-Chan Fulton (2008)

Inoue Yasushi, *The Blue Wolf: A Novel of the Life of Chinggis Khan*, translated by Joshua A. Fogel (2009)

Anonymous, *Courtesans and Opium: Romantic Illusions of the Fool of Yangzhou*, translated by Patrick Hanan (2009)

Cao Naiqian, *There's Nothing I Can Do When I Think of You Late at Night*, translated by John Balcom (2009)

HISTORY, SOCIETY, AND CULTURE

Carol Gluck, Editor

Takeuchi Yoshimi, *What Is Modernity? Writings of Takeuchi Yoshimi*, edited and translated, with an introduction, by Richard F. Calichman (2005)

Contemporary Japanese Thought, edited and translated by Richard F. Calichman (2005)

Natsumi Sōseki, *Theory of Literature and Other Critical Writings*, edited and translated by Michael Bourdaghs, Atsuko Ueda, and Joseph A. Murphy (2009)

Lost Souls

stories

HWANG SUNWŎN

TRANSLATED FROM THE KOREAN BY
BRUCE AND JU-CHAN FULTON

COLUMBIA UNIVERSITY PRESS   NEW YORK

THE BRYANT LIBRARY
2 PAPER MILL ROAD
ROSLYN, NY 11576·

This publication has been supported by the Richard W. Weatherhead Publication Fund of the Weatherhead East Asian Institute, Columbia University.

This publication has been supported by the Korea Literature Translation Institute.

Columbia University Press
Publishers Since 1893
New York   Chichester, West Sussex

Library of Congress Cataloging-in-Publication Data

Hwang, Sun-wŏn, 1915–
[Short stories. English. Selections]
Lost souls : stories / Hwang Sunwŏn ; translated from the Korean by Bruce and Ju-Chan Fulton.
   p.   cm. — (Weatherhead books on Asia)
ISBN 978-0-231-14968-6 (cloth : alk. paper)
1. Short stories, Korean—Translations into English.   2. Hwang, Sun-wŏn, 1915—Translations into English.   2. Korea (South)—Fiction.   I. Fulton, Bruce.   II. Fulton, Ju-Chan.
III. Title.   IV. Series.
PL991.29.S9A24   2009
895.7′33—dc22
                                                           2008051527

Columbia University Press books are printed on permanent and durable acid-free paper.
This book was printed on paper with recycled content.
Printed in the United States of America

c 10 9 8 7 6 5 4 3 2 1

CONTENTS

The Pond

THE POND

It all began, this tutoring job of T'aesŏp's, when the wife of his college instructor friend introduced him to the girl's family. After the introductions were made and the friend's wife had departed, the first thing the girl's mother asked T'aesŏp was how long he had known the wife and how he had gotten to know her so well. When T'aesŏp responded that she was the wife of a friend, the girl's mother asked him what he thought of a woman with three children who wore her hair short and frizzy and went around in a jade-green jacket. T'aesŏp had always felt that the wife's short hair complemented her face, and he said as much, adding, though, that the jade green of the jacket didn't go well with her unnaturally dark complexion. As he said this he became aware of the filmy gaze of the girl's mother. He tried to make eye contact, but the girl's mother promptly lowered her eyes. Her face with its impassive expression looked a bit puffy. And her labored breathing gave him the impression that she had a weak heart.

In her breathless tone the girl's mother said that she and the wife had the same ancestral home and that their families were familiar with each other's circumstances, including the fact that the wife's family had voiced many complaints in opposition to her marriage, but ultimately she had shacked up with the man. The girl's mother blushed slightly when she said "shacked up," then related that the wife had not been able to return to her family and that all of this had come about because the wife had lost her mother when she was a child and had been raised instead by her stepmother.

T'aesŏp felt uneasy listening to the woman and prepared to leave, saying he would begin tutoring the girl the following day, but the woman said there was no time like the present and asked him to begin that day instead. And then she mumbled to herself that the girl had never been this late coming home from school before, and with a fretful motion she reached inside her skirt and produced a cigarette from the pocket of her bloomers. But no sooner had she taken a couple of puffs than she started. Extinguishing the cigarette, she strained to listen.

From outside the room where they sat came the sound of whistling. When the whistling, and the sound of footsteps that followed, trailed off toward the room across the veranda, the girl's mother shouted, "Come here, girl!" In a solemn tone she asked the girl to present herself, and then she proceeded to remove herself farther from T'aesŏp even though they were already far apart. The girl slid open the door to the room and entered. She was holding a pair of track shoes and it was evident from her flushed cheeks that she had just finished a workout. Her face was round and the eyes beneath the long, dark lashes were small but sparkling with life.

T'aesŏp flipped through the pages of her textbooks, familiarizing himself with her progress to date. He found himself lighting a cigarette to block out her scentless but overwhelming sweat smell, which hung in the air every time she leaned forward to indicate something in one of the books. The girl's mother sneaked looks at the two of them in turn and told the girl over and over again to pay attention.

The next day marked the beginning of the tutoring, which took place under the watchful eye of the girl's mother. The girl proved to be quick at memorizing her language lessons. But when it came to mathematics she was perversely stubborn; she seemed to consider herself innately incapable of solving the problems. T'aesŏp asked the girl if she had always disliked mathematics, and she vigorously nodded. And yet when she solved practice questions she did it without assistance and could explain her answers when asked to do so. And she understood perfectly the problem areas T'aesŏp explained to her— but only when she had made up her mind to. It occurred to T'aesŏp that he should make sure the girl understood the concepts underlying the math that he taught her. As he considered this he turned toward the girl. She was moistening the end of her pencil with the crimson tip of her tongue.

T'aesŏp hastened to find the easiest problem in the girl's homework and asked her to answer it. The girl looked at the problem, but all she did was continue to moisten the tip of the pencil with her tongue. T'aesŏp hinted at the underlying concept, but still the girl merely kept her tongue to the pencil. T'aesŏp realized he was devoting more attention to the tongue and lips of this healthy girl sitting in front of him than to the math problems, and he snatched the pencil from her. But before writing anything T'aesŏp likewise put the pencil to the tip of his tongue. He was surprised at his own action. His first attempt to solve the problem was incorrect. The girl's mother, seated on the warmest part of the heated floor, scolded the girl for having a silly smile on her face. T'aesŏp felt as if the girl's cold, playful smile was fixing itself on his forehead, and again he attempted in vain to solve the problem. Again the girl's mother scolded her to stop smiling. But now the girl laughed; it was funny having to study when her mother was paying closer attention to the instructor than she was, she told her, and then she laughed more loudly.

Again the next day the girl arrived home whistling and again her mother summoned her. And again the girl's mother moved as far from T'aesŏp as she could—but the girl didn't enter. The mother went out. When she returned a short time later, her body language said she had given up; she asked T'aesŏp to do his teaching in the room across the veranda.

In that room sat the girl, quite graceful in traditional clothing, her legs gathered to the side. On the wall behind her was a photograph of a sprinter poised for the start. As he viewed the sprinter—the taut balance of the torso leaning forward and the toes dug into the ground, the eyes focused in an intense gaze—T'aesŏp drew in his mind an image of the girl's hefty bosom hitting the finish-line tape, leaving the ends to flutter in the air, and instinctively his thin body shuddered. And when his gaze fell next on the girl's fleshy knees he hurriedly collected himself, picked up the nearest textbook, and began leafing through it.

The girl gathered her legs to the opposite side and abruptly spoke up: there was something in the eyes of others that made her feel there must be an emptiness in this house. T'aesŏp looked up from the textbook and asked what she meant, and the girl responded with a question of her own: did he think it strange that there was no father in this house? T'aesŏp replied that he was aware there was no father;

his friend's wife had told him so. The girl immediately responded that her mother told everyone her father had died, but in fact he was still alive. When she was old enough to know better, the girl continued, she learned that her father had taken a mistress and gone elsewhere to live, at which point he and her mother divided their assets equally and made a break with each other. Her father lived not far away but had lost all his assets and for some time had been laid up with rheumatism, and her mother had developed a case of heartburn that had led to heart disease. Instead of responding to this with comforting words, T'aesŏp opened the algebra book in front of the girl and told her she should study hard and try to make her mother happy, since it seemed her mother's one wish was for the girl to be a good student. No sooner had he said this than the girl produced a cynical smile and said she was sick of hearing her mother say that. And then she opened the sliding door to the room, as if she had noticed someone eavesdropping outside. The girl's mother was in the yard preparing ingredients for kimchi; she turned toward them, startled.

On days when T'aesŏp arrived before the girl had returned from school, her mother would carefully slide open the door, enter, and sit, and then ask him how much the girl had learned at school. There wasn't much T'aesŏp could say except that the girl was quite good at memorization. The girl's mother would remain silent for a time, then fix T'aesŏp with her filmy gaze and say in a soft voice that studying was all to the good, but the important thing was for T'aesŏp to teach the girl to keep her distance from men; was there any man in this day and age who wouldn't deceive a woman? T'aesŏp would avoid her gaze but at the same time, and without realizing it, nod in agreement.

On one such day the girl's mother seemed to realize it was time for the girl to return, and breathing heavily, she left. The girl arrived, and the first thing she did was suggest to T'aesŏp that they go on a picnic the following day, which was Sunday. Without waiting for T'aesŏp to answer, she slid open the inside door and called toward the kitchen that she and Teacher were going on an outing the following day. "Isn't that right?" she said, turning back to T'aesŏp. T'aesŏp pictured the girl running around the picnic area in her spiked track shoes, and nodded yes.

The following day was cloudy and the wind was blowing. Still, T'aesŏp went to the assigned meeting place—a road that branched off toward the outskirts of town—and waited for the girl. After a time she appeared. T'aesŏp started. Instead of the school uniform he had expected to see, she wore traditional clothing—a white jacket and a long blue skirt embroidered with pairs of mandarin ducks against a blue background. The skirt rippled and flapped in the wind. Skillfully gathering the hem, the girl smiled, looked T'aesŏp straight in the eye, and asked what he thought of her taste in clothing. Setting out on the road, T'aesŏp mumbled something about breaking the rules by not wearing the school uniform on an outing. The girl came up beside him and he discovered not a girl in a uniform with a rucksack and a pair of track shoes but instead a woman. All he could do was lift his gaze to the cloudy skies above.

Without looking skyward as T'aesŏp had, the girl remarked that some bad weather must have come in overnight; they would probably get rained on, she said; maybe they should give up on the idea of a picnic. When T'aesŏp said he was open to suggestions, the girl took a quick look behind her as if they were being followed, then said, "How about a movie?" Here too the girl seemed to have made up her mind in advance, and she set out in front of T'aesŏp, telling him that her mother had been standing in the alley next to the fruit shop behind them to the left, and then suggesting that they follow the road leading out of town for a short distance before turning back toward the theater.

T'aesŏp produced a cigarette and turned away from the wind to light it. Sure enough, there was the girl's mother, observing them. T'aesŏp lit his cigarette, and as he turned back to the girl there registered in his mind the image of the girl just now, looking behind her as if they were being followed, and also an image of their study session at the girl's home being interrupted by the sudden opening of the sliding door, as if someone had been eavesdropping outside. This realization sent a chill up his spine. T'aesŏp hastened to catch up to the girl, and remarked that it might be better if they went their separate ways. The girl produced a hearty smile and looked back once more, telling T'aesŏp that her mother had followed them to make sure her daughter wasn't with a man other than him, and would now return home with her mind at peace. She then turned left down a narrow alley that paralleled the road they had been walking. T'aesŏp followed, the path being too narrow for them to walk side by side.

As they walked the girl said that her mother was always cautioning her about men, and this was only natural if you considered the impact of her father's behavior on her mother; she was well aware that her father wasn't comfortable seeing other women outside and that's why he began bringing those women home, and every time this happened her mother would grit her teeth and spend a sleepless night weeping, and she herself would rise the next morning hoping against hope to find her father and the woman he had brought home both dead. At the end of the alley they came out onto a street. The girl's skirt with its pairs of mandarin ducks flapped in the wind.

This time the girl made no attempt to gather her skirt, and turned down another alley. She paused, and when T'aesŏp came up beside her she said that her mother's resentment was, if anything, stronger now and that her mother held a grudge against her father; that while she was cursing those women of his she invariably lectured her not even to think of men; that she had only her daughter to rely on and had borne all kinds of suffering till now; that the woman who had introduced them to T'aesŏp (who himself had grown up without a mother) had chosen her own husband in lieu of the traditional arranged marriage and as a result had found herself not welcomed by her natal family, the poor thing (she repeated this over and over); and that she had made the girl pledge unequivocally that mother and daughter would live together, just the two of them, till death. The girl walked silently for a short time, then added that back then she had been of one mind with her mother, had borne a grudge against her father, and had found his women hateful, and that she had made a sincere decision to spend the rest of her life with her pitiful mother. But almost imperceptibly over time she had grown opposed to that idea, and although her mother would harp on the heartbreak she had suffered and say she wanted to save the girl from the same tragedy, the girl no longer considered her mother pitiful and had simply lost all desire to follow her lead.

T'aesŏp used his cigarette butt to light a fresh cigarette. Whereupon the girl remarked that her mother smoked; she understood it was an ingrained habit, something her mother did when her feelings were hurt, but she was displeased that her mother even now attempted to conceal this habit from her. And then she said that something had happened a few days earlier—that her father's concubine had visited, saying that his rheumatism had worsened and asking for money to buy medicine for him; that her mother, hearing this, had jumped to her feet and in a choking voice had shouted that that was what the bitch deserved for sucking up all his money and was she now to harass them with the intent of seizing what was theirs as well? The concubine had told her mother that she had met her father after he and her mother had split their assets and that she was by then widowed with two children, that the father had continued to have relations with other women, and that even while undergoing various hardships she had put up with these women and stayed with him. Her mother had responded that a woman with two children who served as a concubine was worse than a bitch, and continued to curse the woman over and over. But she herself no longer considered the woman hateful, and when the concubine suggested that maybe it would be good for them to take back the sick father, her mother clutched her bosom, clenched her teeth, and screamed that it was his choice to shack up with this mongrel bitch, and even if he had lost all his money and was about to be driven out by the concubine, there was no way she would take him back. And with that her mother had collapsed in a faint. While relating this to T'aesŏp the girl had not so much as blushed at the vulgarity of "shacked up with this mongrel bitch." And when she mentioned that her mother had fainted, the girl had shown no more concern than she did when attempting to solve an algebra problem. Finally the girl added that although she had run out to call a doctor to attend to her mother, how could she not feel more kindly disposed toward this woman and her rheumatic father?

Not knowing what else to say, T'aesŏp merely observed that the mother's heart problem sounded serious as well. And then he wondered if on the basis of the girl's remarks her mother had assumed that his relationship with his friend's wife was something sordid, and when he recalled how obvious it was that the girl's mother had been keeping a close watch on him and her daughter, he instinctively shuddered.

The girl considered T'aesŏp and said she realized it was windy, but he must really be cold to be shivering like he was, and then her face was transformed into an innocent smile and she nodded toward an alley across the street where there was a movie theater. The smile brightened when the girl discovered a boy standing in front of a tearoom next to the alley. She quickly approached the boy; it was as if T'aesŏp were no longer there. T'aesŏp remained where he was. The boy had dark eyebrows. While the boy spoke with the girl, the darkness of his eyebrows appeared to give a reddish cast to his white face, but when the girl returned to T'aesŏp his face seemed to turn pale again. The boy, she told T'aesŏp, was the older brother of a school friend, and the friend was sick in bed and wanted to see her. *Don't lie to me,* T'aesŏp thought, but then he said to the girl that it was all right and she could go ahead. When the girl suggested that T'aesŏp might as well watch the movie now that he was here at the theater he heaved a violent shudder. Feeling an urge for a steaming cup of coffee, he escaped into the tearoom.

One day, as T'aesŏp was waiting for the girl to return home from school, her mother carefully slid open the door and entered. She sat silently for a time before telling T'aesŏp that she sensed the girl was seeing a man; didn't he feel the same way? She blushed as she said this. Without thinking, T'aesŏp shook his head no. The girl's mother lapsed back into silence, then mumbled that no matter what her daughter thought, she wasn't going to let her do as she pleased. Then she seemed to realize that it was time for the girl to return, and she hurriedly left.

The girl arrived. But no sooner had she opened her algebra book than she began talking about the boy, saying that he had been studying philosophy in Seoul but had suffered a nervous breakdown and returned home, and that there was something about him that reminded her of T'aesŏp. T'aesŏp, feeling his ears flush for no good reason, replied that he'd finally realized that the girl's rebellion against her mother must have started when she met the boy; that it didn't seem the boy's edgy expression would deceive anyone, but these days who could know what a man was thinking; and that he himself was having a difficult time fathoming his own thoughts. With a twinkle in her eye the girl said it was amazing: T'aesŏp was beginning to sound like her mother.

T'aesŏp pointed to a factoring problem in the algebra book. The girl produced her notebook, moistened the tip of her pencil with her tongue, and began to write. Immediately T'aesŏp found the notebook placed before him. Instead of an answer he saw written "scaredy-cat teacher." T'aesŏp snatched the pencil from her, crossed out her scrawl with two long strokes, and asked the girl what was to become of her if she couldn't solve such a simple problem. So saying, he looked up, and when the javelin standing in the far corner of the room caught his eye he told the girl that she ought to reduce the amount of time she spent training.

The girl rose, picked up the javelin, and said that she had recently started throwing but couldn't get the hang of the posture, and stretched out her left arm in front of her. T'aesŏp imagined the girl placing the javelin on her shoulder and breaking into a run, and then the sight of her hair flying and the vivid arc of the javelin, but in the meantime the girl replaced the javelin and found her discus. The girl swept the discus back and forth as if to throw it and said she found it absolutely thrilling when she released the discus or javelin right behind the line and then was able to keep her body from crossing the line, and that it was only then that she was able to forget her home life and things like math homework. She continued to sweep the discus back and forth, and began to pivot. T'aesŏp noticed the wrap around her right wrist, then found himself imagining the hooks of the training shirt across her taut bosom coming undone as she pivoted, and moved out of the way of the discus. But then she stumbled, and before T'aesŏp could reach out to catch her,

her ample form had tumbled into his lap, knocking his frail body over.

The first thing T'aesŏp did after raising himself to his feet was to slide open the door. The girl's mother was rinsing vegetables at the faucet in the yard. She turned to look at him and then the girl slid the door shut, saying the open door distracted her from studying. T'aesŏp picked up the girl's geometry notebook with its clumsily drawn circles and straight lines. But instead of opening her geometry book the girl said she had been feeling weak lately, and that must have been why she fell. And then she seemed to remember something and she herself slid open the door and told her mother, who was still rinsing vegetables at the faucet, that she had to go to school that evening for an assembly on self-improvement. Without waiting for an answer, she slid the door shut and said in an undertone to T'aesŏp that she had something to talk to him about and could she please see him at nine o'clock that evening at the pond to the right of the road that led out of town.

That night as he waited for the girl T'aesŏp walked around the oval-shaped pond. The clock tower in the distance showed that it was past the appointed hour of nine. He observed where the trees bordering the road came to an end, wondering whether the trees or the girl, when she appeared, would cast the darker shadow in the moonlight. On a sudden impulse he looked for his own shadow, but it was lost in the blackness of the pond.

T'aesŏp resumed his walk around the pond. As he looked down at the black surface his imagination went to work. Before he had completed a circuit of the pond the girl would burst out of hiding and playfully place her hands over his eyes, and then for the first time he would take her by the hand, and what the girl had in mind to tell him was that just as she was able to block everything out when she threw the javelin or the discus, they should do likewise now and jump into the pond together, and he would consent and she would take the hem of her skirt with its mandarin ducks and wrap it around both of them and they would jump into the water and sink to the bottom of the pond and feel the cold water of the stream that fed the pond flowing up their backs. Then they would suddenly realize they had to find their way to the surface; the girl would find him a burden and try to get free of him, at which point he would grab her hair so as not to sink farther, and the girl would then swim to the surface, holding him around the waist, and when the girl released him he would do nothing but shudder because of the cold—and in fact he now found himself shuddering.

He completed his circuit and inspected the trees lining the road, his body shuddering and shuddering in the chill wind. He tried to make out the clock tower in the distance but it was no longer lit— had the bulb gone out? Again he looked toward the trees but then noticed his own slender shadow cast by the moon, and for a moment he had the startling sensation that the shadow was not his. He had the illusion that the girl's mother was watching him, that she had placed the girl in his presence as a kind of experiment, and this thought occasioned yet another burst of shuddering. Finally he turned back toward town, and as he observed the setting moon he imagined the girl and the boy meeting not at the pond but in some dark alley, and then he had the illusion that his shadow was instead that of the girl's mother, or of the girl and the boy, and with each successive illusion he shuddered yet again.

T'aesŏp returned to his apartment and for several days was sick in bed with a fever. The day he awoke to find his fever and chills gone he undid the towel he had wrapped about his head and rose. For the first time in a while he watered his flowerpots. And then his absent gaze moved to the window, where he thought he could see the play of a butterfly's wings. Initially he passed it off as the reflection of his haggard face, but then the movement seemed to reappear. He looked more closely and saw a pattern of mandarin ducks. Startled, he turned to see the girl standing in his room. But instead of the duck pattern, her skirt had a pattern of wind and waves. T'aesŏp, suddenly dizzy, toppled down onto his bedding.

The girl played with the gas stove beside the bedding as she offered an excuse for not appearing at the pond that night: she had intended to meet the boy and go together to the pond, where they would explain to T'aesŏp a plan they had developed, but somehow that day she had felt sorry at the thought of leaving her mother alone and instead had ended up going to bed, telling her mother she had a headache. She added that the boy must have felt betrayed after waiting in vain to see her, because he had cut some of his hair and sent it to her. T'aesŏp shuddered, whether as an after-effect of his fever or from something else he couldn't have said, and then without realizing it he uttered a loud laugh. The girl's eyes widened in surprise. In a deliberately stern tone T'aesŏp told the girl that the more delinquent boys were like this clownish one. With a twinkle in her eye the girl said that she had never expected to hear him talking just like her mother.

T'aesŏp then asked, having noticed a new strength in the girl, what would happen to her mother—once her daughter was gone she might collapse, never to awaken. The girl produced a cynical smile and said in a fearless tone that it was none of her concern if her mother, who had never taken back her sick father, should collapse, and that she and the boy were going off together. T'aesŏp adopted a cold tone and said that they wouldn't get far before misfortune struck them. The girl's hand flew out and slapped him across the cheek. "Devil, you devil!" she screamed; no matter what happened they would be happy, she shouted, tears pooling in her sparkling eyes. The waves on her skirt rippled as she pushed open the door and disappeared. T'aesŏp could hear the girl descending the unusually shallow stairs of the apartment several steps at a time. Calmed by the sound, he took his sprinkling can and resumed watering the flowerpots.

SCARECROW

Chun'gŭn started down the sloping path to the village. Now that he was out of the shade, the crowing of the roosters made the village sound closer than it actually was. The astringent odor of the pines that curtained the village coursed deep into his lungs, and he felt a coughing fit coming on. When the coughs arrived he put down his walking stick, squatted, clutched a handful of earth, and spat out a great glob of mucus. He noticed that the earth in his hand was part of an anthill and the ants were red. Nearby some of the red ants were swarming over a pine caterpillar.

Chun'gŭn sat, taking care to avoid the mucus, and observed the caterpillar. It would curl itself almost into a circle and then straighten, dislodging the ants, which then used their feelers to relocate the caterpillar and crawl back onto it. The intervals between the curling episodes gradually lengthened, as did the gap between the ends of the curling caterpillar.

He wondered what would happen if he placed an earthworm among the ants. He recognized a modest slope covered with mossy soil, a place where he had dug earthworms as a boy. There he found a worm and lifted its elastic body with a stick. By now the pine caterpillar was only barely squirming—although the swarming of the ants made it seem to be moving more vigorously.

Chun'gŭn dropped the earthworm onto the anthill. The worm wriggled, scattering the ants. He pressed down with the stick, severing the worm into two segments, each of which became another crawling worm. Chun'gŭn watched the head and the tail segments move in separate directions, then severed one of the segments and placed the two pieces near the ants, before rising to return home.

The morning sun shone on the leaves of the aspens at the entrance to the village. The village dogs kept up a chorus of barking. Strangely, now that he was close he seemed to hear the barking as if from a distance. In the village he found Myŏngju lingering beside the road, baby on her back. The baby burst into tears, its cries drowning out the barking.

"All you do is cry," said Myŏngju as she gave the baby's bottom a good slap.

Chun'gŭn came to a stop.

"Remember me? I used to snatch the wild garlic you picked."

Nodding, Myŏngju turned her back to him. Chun'gŭn's eyes came to rest on her jet-black hair and he felt a sensation akin to dizziness.

During the day Chun'gŭn enjoyed resting in his family's ancestral burial ground on a hill behind the village. He could see, directly below the gentle slope where he lay, the man everyone called Chaedong using a broom to remove spiderwebs from the thatch of his hut.

"Miserable sonofabitchin' spiders!"

With every pass of the broom the threads of the webs glinted in the sunlight.

After he had finished this task, he stood the broom in the corner of his yard, sat down beside his beehive, and muttered, "Damn me if I don't get rid of every last one of those miserable sonofabitchin' spiders."

Chaedong turned his attention to the bees arriving at the hive. Every once in a while he would press down on one of them with his finger. When he removed his finger, the small dark object dropped to the ground.

Myŏngju, baby on her back, appeared at the birch trees near Chaedong's hut.

"What are you killing those bees for?"

"They're drones and all they do is eat up my honey."

Chun'gŭn kept a tally as the bees fell lifeless to the ground.

"Well, instead of the bees, we could eat that honey—why don't you give us some?" said Myŏngju.

"It ain't ready yet," said Chaedong. "How's the little fuss-budget?"

"Still fussy." Myŏngju peeled a strip of bark from one of the birches. "Can't say as I blame it when our mama can't give it milk. Anyway, we'd settle for some of last year's honey."

"Huh—supposing some of it was left."

Chaedong went around behind Myŏngju, took one of the baby's feet, and licked it. The baby began to cry. Chaedong chuckled, revealing dark, toothless gums. Myŏngju tossed the strip of birch bark at his face. Chaedong chuckled again.

"Look at these pretty little feet," he said, taking the baby's foot and licking it again.

"That's disgusting."

Chaedong's dark gums revealed themselves in a smile.

"That's why your wife ran off."

Instantly Chaedong's face hardened.

"You little twit," he muttered. "What do you mean, she ran off—I *ran* her off, that's what. Want to know why? She was wasteful."

Myŏngju placed her hands beneath the baby's bottom and gently rocked it up and down.

"Then why don't you get yourself another wife?" she asked, smirking.

Chaedong's bent frame disappeared into his yard. He returned with a shovel.

"What's that for?"

"I got more soil to dig up. You won't believe the size of the sweet potato crop I'm putting in next year."

Hearing this, Chun'gŭn was reminded of what his father had said a few days earlier as he squatted to attach a new rope to his plow: "I wish we could work that plot instead of Chaedong." To which Chun'gŭn's mother had replied: "Are you serious? We're barely keeping up as it is." "I know," his father had said, "but buckwheat, millet, you name it—once they catch the sun they grow like crazy." "And sweet potatoes too—the ones he grows are huge," muttered his mother. "You know, he's worked that land of ours for years all by himself." To which his father had replied, "Heck, it's time we worked that land ourselves—we wouldn't have to worry about trees and roots and such." And then he rose. At that point Chun'gŭn had said, "But there's the ancestral graves—is it all right to be planting so close by?"

Chaedong cleared spiderwebs from the birches with the blade of his shovel, then shouldered the tool.

"Why don't you give us a few sweet potatoes?" said Myŏngju.

"They're not big enough yet."

"You could always dig one up and take a look."

"Listen, you," said Chaedong, making as if to poke her cheek with his finger, "how about coming back later on, after the sun goes down?"

"You and your filthy mind! What do you think you can see at night?"

"So what if it's dark? The moon'll be up. If I dig 'em up in broad daylight, the word gets out—'Hey, Chaedong's got sweet potatoes!' But I'll bet I can find some that are ready to eat."

Myŏngju pretended to scowl at him. "I bet *all* of them are ready to eat."

Chaedong merely chuckled.

A slender layer of cloud broke off from the cloudbank above; its bluish shade, now thicker, now thinner, enveloped Chun'gŭn. His eyes focused on Myŏngju's hefty bosom and the outline of her swarthy face, and he rose to his feet. He made his way among the burial mounds dotting the sunny foot of the hill, anxious to leave before Chaedong and Myŏngju noticed him. Off to the left of the mounds the earth had recently been tilled, exposing furrows of reddish soil mixed with bits of sweet potato leaves.

Chun'gŭn decided to revisit the hill north of the village, where he had been that morning.

Uncultivated land spread out beyond the pines to a band of gray hills, tinged with azure blue, that creased the skyline.

Chun'gŭn, enveloped in the shade of the pine limbs, was watching a stream that sparkled like the scales of a fish. Closer by stood an oak, and from behind it there appeared, plodding upward, a young man.

"Well, you're over here today," the young man said by way of greeting.

"I kind of go where my thoughts lead me."

The young man followed Chun'gŭn's gaze, which had returned to the stream winding through the fields. "Might be nice to climb that hill over there."

Chun'gŭn, thinking the young man had misperceived the object of his attention, focused upstream where the bends in the stream disappeared and said, "Which one of those hills do you think that stream comes out of?"

"Hard to tell unless you follow the water all the way up. Isn't it the highest one?"

"No, it's the one next to it—the one with all the trees."

"It sure does have lots of trees, just like this one here—that's the way it ought to be."

"I think we'll have an early fall—look how blue the sky is. And that stream looks awful chilly."

Chun'gŭn rose and gave his sheltering pine a whack with his walking stick. The sound rippled through the hills.

Chun'gŭn set off, followed by the young man, whacking the oaks and pines with abandon, trying to strike a second tree before the previous whack came echoing back. With one last mighty whack he strode ahead, passing only a few trees before this last echo coursed among them.

Chun'gŭn and the young man came to a small, exposed dropoff. A rivulet clung to its base. Upstream flew a kingfisher.

"Nice if this hill was a little higher," said the young man. A grasshopper lit on his arm. Before it could escape he pincered its legs.

"It must have been high enough in the past, but then we lost most of the trees. . . . When that happens you get one mudslide after another, and this is how it ends up. When I was little I used to come here for wood, and then one year, I forget when exactly, there was a mudslide. For all I know, where we're standing now might have come down from up there on top."

"You know, your face has a good color, maybe because I'm seeing you out in the open like this."

"I'm not so sure about that. All I know is, I'm not throwing up blood like I was in Seoul."

"If I were you, I wouldn't always be looking for shade—just go where your feet lead you. And you know, the way you bang those trees, you look as healthy as anybody."

"You think so?"

"Of course your family must be awful worried."

"Well, they don't know I've got bad lungs."

"They don't?"

"You're the only one around here I've told."

"Well, that's hard to believe, but I appreciate it. And I want you to know that I've always been open with you too."

"Well, I have to confess, when I'm up in these hills I just want to be by myself. That's why I told you I was sick—so you'd keep your distance from me."

"Well, it doesn't scare me," the young man said, his large mouth opening in a chuckle. "No reason to be scared of life, long as you don't try to predict it—it just moves on its own, like a mudslide." This seemed to set the young man to thinking. "I take that back—actually life is very mysterious."

Here it comes again, Chun'gŭn told himself. *He needs to unburden himself.* Chun'gŭn saw the grasshopper, only one leg remaining, fly from the young man's hand.

"I kicked my wife in the stomach once—when she was pregnant."

"Really? What happened then?"

"I never meant to do it, and when I saw her go down, it really put a scare into me."

"Don't tell me you're breaking up with your wife?"

"That's about the size of it—I'll decide for sure by autumn." The young man briefly clamped his mouth shut, which made it seem even wider, then continued: "She was squirming around on the floor, holding her stomach and whimpering. I hated her just then and I kicked her in the stomach again, like I was taking an ax to her. And the damn woman asked me what the baby inside her had done to deserve this; for years she'd never looked me in the face, and here she was giving me a look that cut right into me." The young man's eyes lit up inside their thick lids.

"Must be maternal instinct."

"Who knows? If only she'd had a miscarriage. Truth is, I was hoping against hope not just for a miscarriage but that she'd drop dead herself. But as hard as I kicked her, that baby inside held on to life. I tell you, life is very mysterious. And when she finally had the baby, I hated my wife even more—but not the little one."

As Chun'gŭn was thinking that the relationship between the young man and his wife might one day be mended on account of their baby, he heard a village rooster crow. It occurred to him that Myŏngju

might go out to the sweet potato field that night, and he grabbed a
handful of wild chrysanthemums, though they hadn't blossomed yet.

Around sunset that evening the villagers gathered some hay and
made a fire in which the children could have fun burning their old,
worn-out straw sandals. The children set the sandals on fire and
tossed them into the air. Bats chased the falling embers.

The only light admitted by the small hole in the rice-paper window-
pane came from the stars. Chun'gŭn felt the beginnings of a slight
fever. In the gloom he managed to locate the lantern and place its
glass enclosure against his cheek.

The enclosure was a receptacle for Chun'gŭn's fever. When the
side touching his cheek lost its coolness, he turned the lantern to a
different side.

In the city, when Chun'gŭn's evening fever came up, Namsuk's
cold cheeks served the same purpose. Her cheeks were soon as warm
as Chun'gŭn's feverish ones, and took on more color. And when
Chun'gŭn was pulling away and she touched her cheeks again to his
and rubbed them, her tears would moisten his cheeks and lips.

Chun'gŭn's tears formed a single line as they flowed down the
lantern's enclosure.

Mechanically he repeated the words "happy man" to himself as
he set the lantern down. He lit the lantern with a match. The wick
produced a smoky odor.

The sooty ceiling struck him as emblematic of the life his parents
had led. He took a deep breath of the smoke, but it only made him
queasy. And when he discovered his shadow, cast by the flickering
light of the lantern, almost touching the ceiling and then shrinking
oddly, he threw open the window. A small fire of mugwort plants
had been lit in the yard to keep the mosquitoes away; it sent aloft a
fitful stream of smoke and then flared up. The soy crocks on their
terrace and the sunflower next to them looked more true to life in
the moonlight. The chickens on their perches in the shed poked
their heads out from beneath their folded wings and shook them
back and forth.

Chun'gŭn went out, tamped down the fire with his foot, then turned his back on the resulting stream of smoke.

His legs were wet before he knew it. He was traversing the upper reaches of the ancestral burial ground. From the dew-soaked grass came the incessant chirping of insects—except where Chun'gŭn's footsteps landed; there the chirping would die out one moment only to resume more loudly as soon as Chun'gŭn had passed.

He arrived at the burial mounds. The bluish-black leaves of the sweet potatoes in the field that angled down from the burial ground glinted in the moonlight. Chun'gŭn skirted the upper verge of the ground and spotted Myŏngju crouched in the field. He hid behind a large pine.

Myŏngju was scooping the earth with her bare hands, and the sweet potatoes, thick and thin alike, rolled out one after another. She was anxiously placing every last one of them in the folds of her skirt when at the far end of the field Chaedong's shadow arose. He stole up behind Myŏngju.

When she had all the potatoes gathered in her skirt, Myŏngju rose. Chaedong was standing there. Myŏngju backpedaled, some of the potatoes falling free. Chaedong seized her by the arm.

"Got you, bitch!"

Chaedong's lips were black in the moonlight.

Myŏngju tried to free her arm. Chaedong's shiny black tongue came into sight, licking Myŏngju's cheek. Myŏngju took a step back.

"I'll let you keep the ones you dug," Chaedong said before licking her cheek again. He released her arm.

Myŏngju frantically collected the scattered potatoes, then ran off. The dew, as abundant as the chirping of the insects beneath Myŏngju's feet, reflected the moonlight one moment, then seemed to absorb the light and could no longer be seen.

Myŏngju had passed the white birches in front of Chaedong's thatched hut when a shadow appeared before her. Even in the dark Chun'gŭn could clearly make out Kŭksŏ.

Myŏngju flinched, but recovered immediately: "Don't scare me like that!" She made her way past Kŭksŏ, then turned back, produced a few sweet potatoes from her skirt, and placed them in his hands before running off.

Only then did Chun'gŭn emerge from behind the pine. His face wore a satisfied smile in spite of his fever.

The following day Chun'gŭn was outside in the sun, shooing away the chickens with a stick as his father threshed the first crop of millet. Amid the flying grains Chun'gŭn allowed himself to soak in the fragrance produced by the threshing. He felt that there was little to connect him as he sat there, the stick now idle in his hands, with his father, whose wrinkled face sprayed perspiration with every whack of the flail. Chun'gŭn tossed the stick aside and went into the inner yard.

The fodder chopper, blade up, lay at the entrance to the shed. Chun'gŭn picked it up by its cord and hacked once at the air. He tried to balance himself on one foot but tottered. He looked for something to chop and his eyes came to rest on his walking stick.

He touched the stick to the blade of the chopper, then turned absently toward the interior of the shed. His eyes met those of the cow, chewing its cud. He put the chopper down.

How round a circle could he draw? Closing his eyes, he rotated in a full circuit, inscribing a circle on the ground with the tip of his walking stick. Dizzy, he opened his eyes and saw that the end of the circle had missed the starting point. Inside this imperfect circle hopped a toad.

With his walking stick Chun'gŭn tapped the ground in front of the crouching toad to make it go away. The toad's response was to work its head up and down. Chun'gŭn tapped the toad's back. The toad puffed itself up but showed no inclination to move. Chun'gŭn had an idea. He caught a cow fly in the shed, and returned to find the toad perched beneath the cockscombs next to the soy-crock terrace. Chun'gŭn dropped the dead fly in front of the toad. As before, the toad merely moved its head up and down.

Chun'gŭn turned and left, thinking the toad might eat if he were not there watching it.

His mother had brought out the straw mat they used for drying grain and was beating the dust out of it with a stick. Chun'gŭn began to tattoo the mat with his walking stick.

"Easy, child," said his mother. She peered at his face. "Are you all right?"

"Yes. Why do you ask?"

"Is there anything in particular you'd like to eat?"

"No."

His father approached and gathered up the mat.

His mother looked at them both. "You're not going off again, are you?" she asked Chun'gŭn.

His father then spoke: "You don't have to worry about the family graves as long as you're here to close our eyes when we die." So saying, he put the rolled-up mat under his arm and went back to the yard.

Chun'gŭn noticed that the toad hadn't eaten the fly.

"That Myŏngju's all grown up," his mother muttered. "She's going to make a fine wife for someone, and she's as hard-working as they come." She turned to Chun'gŭn. "You're old enough to be thinking about a family of your own now. And we won't be around forever. Your father sings Myŏngju's praises—what's your opinion? All we want to do now is sell what little land we have left and find you a wife. Myŏngju's a hard worker, and she'd make a good wife. There are several families knocking at her door, and Kŭksŏ's people are first in line." Her bleary eyes examined Chun'gŭn's face.

"Kŭksŏ will never be a match for her." Chun'gŭn's words, spoken before he realized it, surprised him.

Out in the yard, his father had resumed threshing.

Chun'gŭn turned back to the toad. The cow fly still lay untouched. But then another fly flew from a soy crock, and the instant it came within range, the toad snapped it up.

Chun'gŭn had a sudden urge to go out to where the frogs were hopping about in the fields.

By the time he arrived at the sorghum field his back felt prickly from the sunshine. Some children emerged from the field, their mouths black from the smutty grain they'd been eating.

Rounding the corner of the field, Chun'gŭn came upon Myŏngju on one of the raised paths. She was hurling a frog to the ground. Seeing

Chun'gŭn, she turned away, but not before he saw the array of frog legs she had skewered on a plantain stalk.

"You're having pretty good luck, aren't you?"

The frog Myŏngju had thrown to the ground was squirming near her foot.

"Can the baby eat them already?"

"Yes."

The frog managed to flip itself upright and hopped off into the grass.

Chun'gŭn had a close-up look at Myŏngju's swarthy face and ample bosom and then left, thinking he felt a dizzy spell coming on. Before he'd completed a circuit of the sorghum field he heard Myŏngju fling another frog to the ground.

From out of the field came another child with a blackened mouth, running past Chun'gŭn to join two other boys squatting on the raised path. Chun'gŭn approached. The boys were gathered around a buzzard hole waiting for its occupant to crawl out. Another boy returned from the stream with a mouthful of water and spit it into the hole. But it didn't seem that the buzzard would be flushed that easily.

The boy who had spit the water was the first to notice Chun'gŭn; he ran off, with the other three boys following. They must have found another buzzard hole, because they all squatted some distance off, then went down to the stream.

It was then that the buzzard in the first hole emerged, beak and claws smeared with mud. Chun'gŭn grabbed it. The boys returned from the stream, mouths full of water, and squatted in a circle around the second hole. Repeating to himself "trespasser," Chun'gŭn walked past the boys, deposited the bird among them, and strode off to the streamside without a backward glance.

Down below the bank of the stream Kŭksŏ was watering his family's cow.

Chun'gŭn came to a stop in front of the animal. "She's chewed that grass right down to the stubble."

With a handful of mugwort stems, long-faced Kŭksŏ shooed flies from the animal's back.

"She knows where to graze. This is the only place she eats."

"You know, I used to come here to cut grass for fodder. And here you are, all grown up and strong as an ox. Remember back when it was just me against you and some other kids in a water fight and I won? Now it's the other way around—I wouldn't stand a chance against you even if I had a dozen guys on my side."

Kŭksŏ swatted half-heartedly at a gadfly on the cow's back.

"And then there's Myŏngju, she's all grown up too, she'd make a perfect wife...." Chun'gŭn realized that this was exactly what his parents had been telling him. Kŭksŏ probably had the same thought. Before he knew it he himself had swatted the gadfly; it fell to the ground. He stuck his blood-spotted palm in the stream.

Chun'gŭn kept his hand in the water while he tried to identify this bend in the stream among the various bends he had seen from the hillside. He had difficulty locating the place he frequented, so dense was the bluish-black growth on the hill.

Willow stick in hand, weighted down with frog legs so that it formed a U, Chun'gŭn was following the young man as he hunted frogs. His job was to skewer the frog legs. He made sure to avoid the remains discarded by the young man, the legless bodies with their innards showing.

The young man tore the legs from a frog he had just caught. "You have to rip the legs off as soon as you catch 'em—otherwise it gets real messy." So saying, he handed the still squirming legs to Chun'gŭn.

"Let's call it a day," said Chun'gŭn.

"Think there's enough for a meal? Naw, we need a few more." The young man resumed poking through the grass with his foot. He found a frog, hurled it to the ground, and stomped its head. Chun'gŭn's gaze was drawn again to the legs revealed by the young man's rolled-up pants. They were strange-looking, the thighs long but the shins very short. It was impossible to tell where the calves ended and the ankles started, for they were of the same thickness. One of those legs kicked the remains of the frog, its mouth agape, into the grass.

"Then let's take a break and cook one up," said Chun'gŭn.

"Yeah?" said the young man, the back of the hand that held the newest pair of frog legs wiping the sweat from his forehead. The legs touched his forehead, leaving a trace of blood, but the young man seemed oblivious and proceeded to gather grass to make a fire.

Chun'gŭn helped, taking care not to step on the frog's body, its viscera exposed where the back legs had been. The dry grass smelled not so much of grass as it did of earth, along with the scent of millet seeds after threshing.

Chun'gŭn had just reached out for another handful of grass when he recoiled. Crawling out of the grass was what remained of the frog, innards trailing behind it. Chun'gŭn kicked the crawling frog into the grass as hard as he could—how sordid the attachment to life could be! And with that thought he disposed of the other frog remains in the same way.

Beside the path the young man found a pair of sticks to enclose the fire, then touched a match to the grass within. Chun'gŭn placed the frog legs over the fire and they disappeared in a cloud of yellow smoke.

By and by the young man turned the frog legs.

"Smell good, don't they?"

Chun'gŭn watched the frog legs turn dark red and leak oil and then turned away, managing to suppress a wave of nausea.

"And they're tasty too, believe me. All right, I think they're ready—help yourself."

"I guess I don't really feel like it."

"What? You're the one who dragged me out here for this."

"Well, I used to really like frog legs when I was a kid."

The young man pulled one of the legs free of the willow stick and sampled it, ash and all.

"Sure you don't want some? Afraid they won't agree with you?"

"That too."

"Don't be squeamish—just pop it in. Me, I could practically digest a rock once it's in my belly."

Chun'gŭn took a well-cooked chunk and pushed it even farther into the flames.

"Hey, they don't taste good burned," said the young man. "There were so many frogs where I used to live, we kids went frog catching instead of fishing." He looked off toward the village. "Have to admit, the village looks pretty good from here with all those poplars." Then he exclaimed, "Darn, I almost forgot—my father-in-law's coming!" He rolled down his pants legs. "You know what my mother-in-law says about my legs? She says they're straight as sticks—she thinks I'm deformed! Well, heck, I can run as well as anybody. And you know what—she doesn't even realize her own daughter's deformed—she's got a growth to the right of her belly button that's as big as an egg! Heck—all I have to do is give it a tap and she says, 'Ow—I can't stand it!' So when I kicked her in the stomach that time, that's the spot I aimed for. Can you imagine how that must have hurt? She must have thought she was dying. Anyway—if that's not deformed, then what is? And my father-in-law's a blockhead; all he does is beg me to put up with her. Well, sorry I have to run off like this." And with that, he loped into the sorghum field and disappeared.

Myŏngju's head and the back of a bull came into view, moving through the millet field that bordered the sorghum field. Suddenly the bull jumped, its horns shooting skyward, and trotted away. Chun'gŭn set off, intending to drive the bull to the perimeter of the millet field. Behind him, Kŭksŏ came running from the corner of the sorghum field. Kŭksŏ passed him and Chun'gŭn followed, hoping to overtake the other man, but before he could catch up he collapsed. Presently Kŭksŏ ran past him going the other way, this time with Myŏngju. Chun'gŭn lay where he was, retching and spitting up bloody gobs of mucus. He noticed that the wild strawberries dangling from their stalks in front of him were more scarlet than his blood.

The cheeping of newly hatched chicks rose to a crescendo in the village.

Next to the cockscombs the balsams had lost their petals and were bursting with sun-ripened seeds.

Dogs lay prostrate in whatever shade they had managed to find. Chickens strutted in the shadows, but if the dogs so much as wagged their tails, the chickens fled, heads bobbing.

Chun'gŭn was sitting at the threshold to his room, cleaning the shade of the kerosene lamp.

In a shady corner of the yard his father was talking with Chaedong:

"In any event, we'll have to start plowing that land ourselves next year."

"Well, like I said, next year I can plant millet or I can plant sweet potatoes, and either way I can give you a share of the crop or I can pay you."

"Speaking of sharecropping, you should give us a share for this year."

"Well, I don't see as how I'll have much of a crop. I could kick myself not planting earlier in the year."

"Shows you how hard up we are when I'm thinking about having to plant the ancestral graveyard in order for us to get by."

"And I got nothing but sweet potatoes to get me through the winter."

"In any event, just so you know," Chun'gŭn's father said, emptying his pipe on the ground.

"And I don't even know if I got enough of *them*," said Chaedong. And then he departed, shaking his head vigorously and muttering, "Nothing doing!"

A balsam seed popped and fell onto another seed, which popped in its turn.

Chun'gŭn put the shade back on the lamp, took his walking stick, and set out after Chaedong.

As Chaedong's bent back disappeared beneath the poplar trees, a green frog croaked. The leaves moving in the breeze made a swishing sound like that of falling rain.

Chun'gŭn followed the bending path near the poplars and quickened his pace, catching up with Chaedong near the hills. "So, I guess the sweet potatoes are ready," he said.

Chaedong turned to Chun'gŭn, jaw quivering.

"Tell you what, let's dig them up tomorrow and divide them— what do you say?" Chun'gŭn wanted to laugh at his own joke, but his mouth merely twitched instead.

Not until they were close to his thatched hut did Chaedong say, just loud enough for Chun'gŭn to hear, "No way, not this year." And then he seemed to shake his head, but Chun'gŭn couldn't tell for sure because of the man's quivering chin.

Clouds flew by overhead, but unlike the wind they seemed to presage clearing rather than overcast skies.

Chun'gŭn's faint fever had returned.

His hand reached out in the dark like a feeler, located a match, and struck it. The flame was reflected in the shade of the kerosene lamp. A cricket hopped out from beneath the lamp. Chun'gŭn thought he could feel autumn through the cricket's unseen antennae.

A chill wind blew outside.

He recalled what Namsuk had said back in the city as she listened to the spring rain: "Are you really going home? I hope you'll come back before autumn." Sitting beside her, he had kept silent, listening to the rain. "The country air will be good for you, but I need you here with me." A strong gust of wind had followed, and she moved closer to him. "Why aren't you saying anything?"

All he had said was, "I'll have to make sure I don't tell my parents about the tuberculosis."

The sound of raindrops and wind grew distant.

"Aren't you going to ask where I've been?" Namsuk asked in an undertone.

"You're the healthy one—why should I be keeping tabs on you?"

"I went to a clinic," said Namsuk. "Remember that time you told me our generation should be the last one? Well, I'm on birth control now."

"I don't see why you have to do that to yourself."

After a time Namsuk said, "Remember, you have to come back by autumn. I won't ask you about home anymore."

While he was thinking these thoughts the matchstick in his fingertips burned out. When this finally registered he struck another match, but then he saw the perpendicular shadow it cast on the wall and the floor and he tossed it aside, rose, and left.

Chun'gŭn was making his way among the graves when in the faint light of the moon in the western sky he spied Kŭksŏ, coming down the spine of the hill. Chun'gŭn came to a stop. He could just make out Myŏngju at the far end of the sweet potato patch toward which the other man was heading.

The insects sounded louder in the silence.

Kŭksŏ approached Myŏngju, placed a hand on her shoulder, and turned her around. The empty basket in Myŏngju's hand fell to the ground and rolled off into the gathering gloom.

Myŏngju indicated the millet field before them. In the faint shade cast by the moon Chun'gŭn could see, where the millet field met the sweet potato patch, Chaedong's bent back with a fully loaded A-frame backrack turning out of sight.

Standing among the graves, Chun'gŭn rested his gaze on the tangled growth of the sweet potato patch, which he could only now make out, and on Myŏngju and Kŭksŏ side by side nearby. He took in the rain-dispelling breeze, a smile of satisfaction lighting up his face as if he had been presented with a scene of beauty.

Intermittent midday rain showers preceded Kŭksŏ's family's cow back to the village.

From the hollows in the hills the rainwater streamed down through grass and pebbles, collecting in puddles and making the moss growing among the pebbles jiggle like water bugs.

Chun'gŭn observed the reflection of his face in a puddle. White clouds filled the background of his image.

The young man joined him, hopping over the puddle. "Best view in the village as far as I'm concerned—better even than over there where we were looking down on the stream running through the fields."

"It's the season. And the fact that the leaves are still on the trees."

"For sure. You know, it looks lonesome when the leafy trees, the poplars and such, are all bare."

A solitary pheasant crept out from beneath some tiny pines at the foot of the hill, then dashed toward another pine some distance away. The young man hefted a rock, bent over, and approached gingerly. The pheasant emerged from beneath the pine and set out toward the hill. The young man followed, his stumpy legs disappearing from view.

Knock—the sound of the rock hitting a tree trunk.

The young man returned, wiping his sweaty brow with the back of his hand. "It shot into the pines and I couldn't find it. Makes me mad!"

"How come it didn't fly off?"

"Maybe it got crippled, or an animal took a bite out of it. Makes me mad!"

"You ought to be thankful you're healthy enough to run after a pheasant. Me, I'm spitting up blood."

"Don't tell me you're overdoing it again."

"Not so much that—it's just that I can't get to sleep at night."

"Once *I* lie down, I'm out."

"I worry about that, now that the nights are getting longer." So saying, Chun'gŭn reached out to snap off a wild chrysanthemum, but at the touch of his hand most of the petals fell off.

The young man kicked a stone lying at the foot of a pine. "What are these rocks doing at the bottom of every tree?" he said to himself.

"They're for trapping the caterpillars when they come down off the trees in late autumn," said Chun'gŭn. "I put some there myself once, when I was a kid. And when we came up here for wood in the winter and it got cold, I'd move the rocks and build a fire on top of the caterpillars. If the fire started to spread I'd put it out by beating on it with a branch, and then smother whatever was left. I'd end up scorching my hair and my eyebrows without realizing it. I can't believe that these same trees where I used to make fires on top of the caterpillars are so big now. A lot of them must have been cut down. I've never been as healthy as I was when I was putting rocks under these trees."

"This one would make a pretty decent post," said the young man as he passed a hand along the trunk.

"And so I thought I'd spend winter in this lonesome village looking at these nice evergreens."

Suddenly Myŏngju emerged from the shade, and just as quickly she hid herself behind a nearby pine. The two men saw her hand take hold of her beribboned braid and remove it from view.

The young man picked up a rock.

Realizing the young man was going to throw the rock at the tree that concealed Myŏngju, Chun'gŭn began half-heartedly to beat the tree next to it with his walking stick. To his surprise, the young man's rock hit the other tree, the impact louder than that of Chun'gŭn's walking stick, and shattered.

"Right on the mark," the young man muttered. He approached Chun'gŭn. "She'd do quite nicely, that one," he said, his long lips breaking into a grin.

"She must be out looking for grasshoppers to feed the baby."

"You know, I've always been open with you, but I just now realized why you want to be out here by yourself—you've got a good thing going." The young man produced a resounding laugh. .

"Don't get the wrong idea," said Chun'gŭn. "She's sweet on one of the local boys, Kŭksŏ."

"Me, on the other hand, I spill out everything. In recent days I've been going to the in-laws' to talk about the divorce, and when I have to spend the night, guess what—I sleep with my wife. The divorce is only a few days off."

With renewed interest Chun'gŭn observed this young man who had been studying law in Seoul—he was like a section of a worm, surviving even after being cut in two. With this thought, Chun'gŭn walked out to the grassy area beyond the pines.

"I guess I better not come out here anymore," said the young man with another boisterous laugh.

Chun'gŭn considered telling the young man that the day they had cooked the frog legs, Myŏngju's family's bull had gotten loose and when he and Kŭksŏ had gone after it, he had collapsed trying to catch up to Kŭksŏ and had vomited blood. But instead he said, "I'm glad you're open with me. And I won't hide anything, either. The fact is, I've been so hot for her I can't stand it. Those swarthy cheeks and big bosom—I want her to be mine. She's the only one I know who could produce a healthy baby for me. These days, as soon as it gets dark all I think of is running away with her someplace—not Seoul, but someplace far off."

The young man's eyes lit up in excitement.

For the first time in a long while Chun'gŭn was able to laugh aloud.

The barking of the village dogs close by sounded strangely muted as Chun'gŭn went out into the fields, the sun on his back.

The millet was almost ripe. Grasshoppers flitted everywhere amid the sorghum and above the raised paths that led through the fields.

The stream looked clearer and colder. A lone crab shell lay in the muck beneath the sweet flag. A carp stole up and pecked at it, eliciting only a few barely perceptible movements, after which the shell returned to its original position.

As Chun'gŭn was about to return home, the young man appeared, striding briskly toward him along the main path through the fields.

"Didn't see you in the hills, and wondered where you were. I guess it's better for you down here in the fields. They did a good job of stacking that hay."

"I figure it's gotten cooler up in the hills—that's why I'm down here."

A flock of sparrows settled onto a field where millet had already been harvested.

"Ah, yes," said the young man, "you wanted to be by yourself again." There followed his characteristic laugh.

The young man had assumed that a tryst with Myŏngju was the real reason for Chun'gŭn's desire to be alone in the hills, and now that Chun'gŭn realized this, the laugh that he would otherwise have shared with the young man came out as a grimace.

"And even if you didn't, I'll soon be leaving you alone," he said with a twinkle in his eye.

"So everything's settled?" Chun'gŭn asked, sensing that the young man was about to unburden himself again.

"It will be by the end of the day. The divorce is going through, but get this—she says she'll do anything to stay with the baby, even if it's just to nurse it. No way in hell will she do that. I never should have let her take care of the baby in the first place. She wants to be a wet nurse for it? No way!" And with that he clamped his mouth shut.

Chun'gŭn realized he had been wrong to speculate that the baby would help the troubled relationship between the young man and his wife, but strangely, this realization gave him a certain pleasure.

"It must be a relief to finally take care of this."

"Well, there's still a few things to do," said the young man, "so if you'll excuse me. Oh, and remember to take advantage of the sun—catch it from in front instead of turning your back to it." And then he was off.

"Thank you," said Chun'gŭn.

In no time the young man had disappeared behind the scarecrow that stood in the empty millet field, only to reappear briefly before going out of sight among the sorghum stalks.

The scarecrow's shoulders wore a blanket of shade—the result of the swarms of grasshoppers and flocks of sparrows on their way from the hills to the fields and from the fields to the village.

Chun'gŭn closed his eyes and let the sunlight gather on his chest. He felt as if the shadows of the grasshoppers and sparrows were layering themselves about him. He shook his head, imagining the shadows turning into white snowflakes and flying off on the wind. He imagined a blizzard. And when he imagined the snow weighing down on his shoulders, he opened his eyes.

Instead it was the lofty sky and the sunshine that he felt on his shoulders. He squatted where he was.

Before him was a pool of stagnant water. A dragonfly with torn wings hopped across the pool, dipping its tail in the water. As Chun'gŭn watched the resulting ripples spread out, he came to a decision: back in the city he would allow Namsuk to be her own woman.

Off in the distance stood other scarecrows in other millet fields.

ADVERBIAL AVENUE

"*Natto, natto-o.*" That's the tofu peddler hawking soybean relish. The sound of his voice and the call of his bugle are right outside, but the next moment they fade off into the distance. There's a narrow lane that angles sharply around one of the other houses, and that's where he must have gone. Sŭnggu once saw a crying child in this lane; another time he saw the same child tracing lines in the dirt for fun. Perhaps the child lived in that house.

Sŭnggu has to go downstairs to the kitchen if he wants to wash his face. And once downstairs, he has to pass the room where his landlady sits. The eyes in the mirror on the vanity case rarely miss him. She always sits in front of her vanity; it's as if she wants to befriend the mirror, lest it abandon her. The landlady's stumpy neck makes her long face seem even longer; neither neck nor face takes powder very well.

This is one of those situations where Sŭnggu has to be careful to give his landlady no cause to ask where he's from. He has the same worry when he's done washing his face and has to go back upstairs.

The room next to where the landlady sits is presumably where she keeps household items, but the door is always shut. Sŭnggu wonders if that's where the landlord is. He has seen him only once, the day he moved in—a man with eyes like slits.

He opens the window in his room. The shiny white layer of frost on the roof tiles is melting. Visible far off, down below the rooftops, is a storm drain. Light falling on the mouth of this drain makes it glitter, rather like a fish.

Sŭnggu lies down. The tatami feels moist and chilly. He is forever rehearsing what he'll do if the landlord emerges from his tightly shut room and comes upstairs to ask Sŭnggu where he's from. He's decided he'll say he's from Kyushu; he'll say he speaks the Kyushu dialect and that's why his speech sounds different. He tosses and turns, playing out this scene in his mind.

The beggar is sitting on the same park bench as yesterday, shivering like he was then. Sŭnggu sits down on the bench.

Diagonally to his left sit a young couple. The man swats idly with his walking stick at a branch over his head. The thick leaves are dust-covered but still green to the eye.

Extending past the park is a drainage ditch. Across this ditch is a dye shop; outside, fabrics flap in the wind like a swimmer's arms.

The man on the other bench rises, bats the leaves with his stick, and departs with the woman. Leaves tremble and fall.

The beggar rises and Sŭnggu follows him into the street.

The radios are heedless of Sŭnggu's movement. Back comes their sentimental song, just when he thinks it's fading away. Waves of humanity wash over him. Finally he loses the beggar. He feels as if his head and shoulders have been worn away and only his trunk moves forward. He sees another beggar, one with no arms or legs, rubbing his head against the pavement in supplication. The rooflines of lofty buildings fill the sky. *Those buildings had better prop up the clouds or else it will rain*, Sŭnggu tells himself.

Morning has come after a night of drizzle. Sŭnggu is lying on his tatami. Suddenly his back shakes, but he's not shivering from the chill. And it's not the wind shaking the wooden structure of the house. The shaking is coming from below the second floor, where he lies, and from below the main floor; it's coming from the ground. It's an earthquake, the first he's ever experienced. But instead of fear he feels a kind of pleasure.

Another tremor shakes Sŭnggu's back. The rice paper–paneled door rattles, then opens to reveal the landlady.

The landlady asks if he realizes it's an earthquake. Yes, he does, says Sŭnggu. The landlady's eyes open wide and she says that earthquakes this strong are rare, and that she's surprised at his calm response. To which Sŭnggu replies without thinking that there are no earthquakes in Korea, so he's never had occasion to be scared of one. It's a good thing there are no earthquakes in Korea, says the landlady, cocking her head in a coy manner; and it's good to know Sŭnggu isn't scared of them—but she didn't realize he was Korean. Sŭnggu asks if she would have believed him had he said he was from Kyushu, and the landlady says she thought all along he was from Kyushu because of his accent. And then she says she has a huge favor to ask. Her face falls, as if it is all she can do to break the news: she needs Sŭnggu's room for her younger brother, who is due to arrive from the countryside. Sŭnggu replies that he was thinking of moving anyway, so he will vacate immediately.

The landlady goes downstairs, then returns saying she is terribly sorry and that Sŭnggu can stay free of charge until he finds another room—say, ten days or so—and with that she returns to him the remainder of the month's rent. Sŭnggu says that she should keep the money that would cover the time he'll be there. The landlady shakes her long head no, saying she won't have a clean conscience unless she declines. Sŭnggu says he can't rest easy either unless he pays all that is due.

The landlady leaves the money on the tatami and scurries downstairs. Sŭnggu places the money at the side of the landing above the top step and goes out.

From the street he turns down an alley and there, directly in front of him, is the apartment house where Ung lives. The junipers flanking the building rise above the first story.

Ung occupies room 9 on the first floor. Sŭnggu pulls open the door, enters, and is greeted by the smiling face of a Western actress from the wall to his left. A wooden bed lies against the wall to the right; the window is also on that side of the room.

This two-story concrete building sits on a rise, and even from the first-floor windows you can see wave after monotonous wave of slanted roofs.

Ung taps his cigarette though there's no ash to be dislodged, then exclaims that he was leaving school a short time earlier and was thinking about having his shoes shined when he noticed that the shoe-shine boy was Chiun; wasn't it amazing what Chiun did to support himself in his studies!

Sŭnggu nods and his eyes come to rest on the pile of matchboxes on the windowsill. Collected from various drinking places, they're a bright assortment of colors.

Ung's head with its shiny smoothed-down hair, parted to the right, tilts back as he stretches and yawns.

Ung is so taken with the drinking places where he finds his matchboxes that night and day seem reversed for him. For all Sŭnggu
knows, it's now dawn for Ung and he's just risen. And if that's the
case, it won't be day for Ung till the sunlight has vanished from his
window. Sŭnggu has the impression that the lights will come on at
any moment in the low dwellings visible through the window. And
with that thought he leaves.

The door to the building opens whether you pull it or push it.

Where Sŭnggu lives the front door squeaks. For some strange reason
his chest is pounding. Carefully he climbs the stairs. But the more
carefully he places his feet on the old steps, the more they seem to
creak. Tomorrow he'll use the park for relieving himself and washing up. The pounding in his chest eases only as the number of remaining steps lessens.

The money is still there above the top step. He opens the door to
see a man; the man's head turns his way. He can't immediately place
the man, and merely observes him.

The man volunteers his name—Hunse. A face comes to mind—
the face of a classmate all through middle school, one who was good
at wasting the class's time by asking the teacher questions. Sŭnggu
superimposes that face on the face of the man who sits before him.
His first impression is that the man's cheekbones are too sharp. He
blurts out the first thing that comes to mind: he thought Hunse was
in Seoul.

Hunse doesn't respond to this. He takes in the room and mutters
that it's pretty big for a four-mat room.

The beggar is at the same bench, shivering. Sŭnggu goes to a drinking fountain behind where the beggar sits.

He takes a mouthful of water. Tilting his head back, he gargles.
He notices it's getting cloudier. He spits out the water on the street.
The water in the drainage ditch that runs past the park looks darker
than ever.

Sŭnggu sticks his hand under the water from the fountain and
keeps it there until it feels cold.

The beggar continues to shiver.

Sŭnggu washes his face and sits down beside the beggar. At this time of year the sun doesn't provide much warmth. He begins to shiver like the beggar.

Still shivering, Sŭnggu slides open the door to his room.

Hunse says he was just downstairs washing up; he chuckles. Sŭnggu thinks there must have been an incident with the landlady.

Hunse says he was coming out of the bathroom and shaking the water off his hands when he saw the landlady in her mirror. She got up and asked him to leave the bathroom as clean as he found it. Maybe she said that because he had blown his nose loudly while he was washing his face, he says with another chuckle.

Sŭnggu observes Hunse's bluish lips, then indicates the money at the top of the stairs and tells Hunse that the landlady returned part of his rent and said he could stay until he found another room, but he doesn't feel quite right about it.

Hunse's eyes open wide and he says he's never heard of such a kind landlady, but why should Sŭnggu feel compelled to move? Hunse goes on to say that he obtained his previous room by saying he was from Kyushu, paid no rent for four months, and still got enough money back to use as a deposit on other lodgings. From now on, he'll say he's from Manchuria. And then he asks if there's any good reason the landlady's money should just sit there. Apparently not: he goes out to the landing, gathers the money, and casually stuffs it in his pocket.

A fly makes lazy ovals in the air, alights on the wall, then drops to the floor.

Sŭnggu starts shivering again, but not just because he's cold.

It rains all afternoon, the rain sweeping sideways. Outside the window umbrellas seem to float on their sides, like the rain. The sky visible above the roofs is misty.

The steam rising from the cup looks like the misty sky. Sŭnggu holds the cup with both hands. It doesn't quite warm him all the way through. His shoulders feel weighted down by the rain that fell on them; they shake constantly.

Hunse asks how someone who can't tolerate weather this cold can survive a winter in an unheated tatami room. He crushes out his cigarette.

Sŭnggu begins to recite the contents of the menu posted on the wall: steamed rice with egg and chicken, steamed rice with pork cutlet, steamed rice with grilled eel, steamed rice with egg, curry rice. . . .

Without asking Sŭnggu's preference, Hunse orders two bowls of steamed rice with pork cutlet. And then he brings his face close to Sŭnggu's and says that when close friends from the ancestral home come here, they end up on their guard toward each other instead of getting along heart to heart.

Again Sŭnggu recites the menu: fried shrimp, steamed dumplings. . . . Hunse mutters that Chiun looks intelligent but acts dumb, and why does he have to shine shoes to get his university diploma? And then he asks Sŭnggu where he can find Ung. Sŭnggu is quick to respond that he doesn't know. And once again he shudders; he feels a chill different from the cold outside.

When Sŭnggu looks at the window he sees a frigid mosaic of rain streaks. If the wind comes up, it will really be cold. But the next moment the pane of glass is filled with dazzling sunshine and the streaks of rain disappear.

He wishes they would hurry up with the food.

Before they know it, the skies have cleared and the clouds are gone.

Hunse says he has something to do, and they go their separate ways. In the shade of the dwellings his body seems to take on different shapes as he walks away.

Sŭnggu tells himself that the rain heralds the approach of winter, but then he feels warmth on his back. It's a good day to go to the park and soak up the sun.

Perhaps the beggar is out begging; he's not in the park. Sŭnggu visits Chiun's place.

He calls Chiun's name but the doors are deaf to his calling. Chiun must have gone out to shine shoes.

Sŭnggu walks down Kanda, and with every step he takes, the book-laden shelves of the used-book stores fill him with apprehension.

The shoe-shine boys, spaced far apart from each other, work in the streets' vacant lots. There's Chiun, hunched up and absorbed in a book resting in his lap. Sŭnggu approaches. Chiun looks up and offers a hollow smile.

Has Hunse been there? Sŭnggu asks. Chiun startles, the book falling out of his lap. Did Hunse visit Sŭnggu too? Chiun asks. He says it was a mistake not to warn him about Hunse. He was suspicious when Hunse arrived a few days ago, he continues. Hunse made off with several of his books and hasn't returned. Chiun picks up his book, brushes it off, and says again that he made a mistake telling Hunse where Sŭnggu lived.

Sŭnggu remains silent.

Chiun urges him to go home, stay there, and keep an eye on his belongings.

Sŭnggu in his dirty shoes leaves the shoe-shine boy.

The mirror in the barbershop reflects more bodies than just the customers in the barber chairs. It reflects the face of a woman standing at the window.

Day leaves the barbershop window and night arrives.

Again the door squeaks when it opens. Sŭnggu's chest pounds. Again the steps creak as he goes upstairs. But this time, as the number of remaining steps decreases, his heart jumps all the more.

He slides open the rice-paper door. Hunse is not there.

He turns on the light. The cape that should be there on the wall is gone. As is the two-volume dictionary that should be there in the corner. But rather than regretting the loss of the dictionary and the cape—his only defenses against the oncoming cold—he is relieved to know that Hunse is gone.

Sŭnggu turns off the light and goes out. The streetlights are on tonight. Sŭnggu's shadow is in front of him. The next streetlight draws near. Now it is Sŭnggu who is in front of his shadow.

THE PLAYERS

Another clear day. On mornings like this it's good to be here in the small park, an enclave of cleanliness tucked away among the busy streets, no trash flying about.

Before he knows it he's yawning. With the yawn, moisture gathers in his eyes and the print of the newspaper in his lap grows blurry.

He returns to the missing-person notice. *Small but obvious wart between left ear and upper lip. Age nineteen. Average height. Western-style clothing. North Hamgyŏng accent. Dimple on right cheek when smiling.* He crumples the newspaper, tosses it on the ground—the park's first piece of litter that day—and leaves.

He examines the face of a passing woman. Wart between left ear and upper lip? Nope. She's somebody's middle-aged wife, and instead of a wart near her lip there's a red spot above her right nostril. Must have had several husbands.

He wonders how many men Suk had before him. There was the young man with the horse face, the champion speed skater. And before Horse Face there was Pretty Boy. Prettier, in fact, than Suk. And before Pretty Boy, High Pockets the piano player. Before the piano player he's not sure. So he himself was number four at least. He has no idea where she went after leaving him, or how many others she's left.

Before he realizes it his feet have brought him to Yongjae's studio.

Reclining on the platform, a nude model.

Yongjae is taking a break. "You're a little late," he says.

"Such a nice day I decided to catch some sun in the park."

The long hand of the model reaches for a pack of cigarettes. She lights up.

"She new?"

"Uh-huh."

"A dame a day."

Yongjae's head turns toward the model.

"I'll bet I finish this one."

"Is that a trumpet shell? Wasn't it a snail shell yesterday? And what happened to the winter landscape? Damned if I can keep up with you."

"I can't help it—I keep changing my mind about what I want to paint. And so the model has to change too. But I always use the old scene as background for the new one, so it's not a complete waste."

Against the dreary chrome yellow of the winter field crawls a snail whose crimson feelers are larger than its shell, and against the background of the crimson feelers a blue trumpet shell is taking shape. He looks in turn from the model to the part of the trumpet shell that's been sketched, and at that point the woman gets up, barely covering herself with a dressing gown. She doesn't look at the canvas.

Yongjae says in an undertone, so that only he can hear, "I think they're most attractive when they take off that last piece of clothing—you don't want them naked to begin with."

The model takes the coffeepot and disappears into the kitchen.

"What do you think? I got her from a friend. This time I'll finish for sure. But who knows? My painting has a way of wearing out the models."

"You mean *you* have a way of *bedding* the models. You ought to be thankful for what you've already had and make a donation to a poor guy like me."

"You mean you still haven't figured out where your wife went?"

"Change of plans—starting today I'm looking for a missing woman who comes with a reward. This woman has a wart between her upper lip and her left ear. Who knows, if she's nude maybe we'll find a wart near her left nipple. What do you think—would that get your creative juices flowing? And she has a dimple on her right cheek when she smiles. When I find her, how about if I bring her here instead of taking her back to her husband? Actually, though, a place like this might not be healthy for her."

"That doesn't sound like you."

The model returns with a steaming pot of coffee, coffee so strong it's probably not healthy.

Between sips Yongjae mutters, "So, you're going to ask me what else is new? Well, after Taeung split up with his wife, he fell and dislocated his leg. And Chohun, he's the luckiest of the bunch."

Off to lucky Chohun's place before the model has removed her dressing gown.

Chohun is by himself, a cigarette in his mouth, surrounded by a cloud of smoke, folding paper.

He takes a sheet of paper and begins folding it like Chohun's doing.

"What gave you this idea? It's amazing you still remember how to do it."

"Strange, isn't it? I don't know what gave me the idea, but I do know I started after Myŏngae went to work at the bar."

"Isn't it too early for her to be at work?"

"These days she always goes in early."

"Business must be good. Just don't let this one slip through your fingers. Even Yongjae says you're the luckiest guy of any of us."

"Luckiest, huh?" Chohun lights a fresh cigarette from the one still burning and produces a bitter smile. "Luckiest, my ass!" With a flick of his wrist Chohun launches the paper crane he's made and watches it turn upside down and fall to the floor.

"Sure you're lucky—look what you're smoking," he says, taking the pack of Kaida cigarettes.

"Not so fast. Look inside," says Chohun.

Instead of Kaidas the pack contains Hŭng'a and Midori cigarettes. He selects a Midori.

"Myŏngae brought those back from the bar. Isn't she sweet?"

He takes the paper boat that Chohun has just finished and sends it sliding.

"Can you guess what I do with those?" Chohun asks.

"You *do* something with them?"

With his pointed chin Chohun indicates a vase in the corner. The flowers in it are wilting. "It has something to do with flowers."

"I don't know—you got nothing better to do and you use the flowers to dye the paper or something?"

"Uh-uh. I float those little paper boats down the river." .

"You *do*?"

"Actually, Myŏngae does it with flowers. In the rain. I guess I got the idea from her."

Enveloped in smoke, Chohun starts another paper boat.

He rises, approaches the vase, and sticks his nose close.

"The next time you have a lucky-guy moment, how about floating my crane down the river too?"

And with that he leaves.

The most direct way to the street from Chohun's place is a narrow lane that's a quagmire rain or shine. The open space that borders it is just as muddy. From that space comes the sound of a gong and drum. He approaches.

A family—are they Manchurian? An aging couple; a boy, must be their firstborn son; a girl, their daughter; another son, can't be older than ten. Only a few onlookers, and among them moves the older son, juggling balls he produces from a worn bag. The balls are blue. The father bangs the gong, the mother beats the drum, the daughter beats a smaller drum, and the younger son plays a single-string fiddle. The older son produces more balls from his bag, along with an incongruous shriek for each.

He tries to anticipate the next shriek, but it always startles him. Is it because his stomach is empty?

On to the department store, which has a clean restaurant.

Up goes the elevator. The effect is of the first floor going down to the basement, and then the second floor to the first. The third floor arrives. A woman is sucked inside. She looks familiar. She smiles. A snaggletooth comes into sight.

"I know you," she says.

It's Taeung's former wife, Chŏmnan. She didn't used to have a beauty spot on her other cheek; maybe that's why he didn't recognize her at first.

The restaurant is on the fifth floor. They sit across from each other. Chŏmnan produces a block of chocolate from her handbag. He breaks off a piece and tries to guess what else is in the handbag.

Compact, lipstick, eyeliner, beauty-spot brush, and a mirror barely large enough to see one eye in. The mirror actually comes out and Chŏmnan proceeds to touch up her lipstick, keeping one eye on the mirror and observing him with the other eye as she speaks.

"So, Taeung's in the hospital with a dislocated leg. It must be difficult for him. I tell myself I'll go see him, but I just don't know where the time goes."

The next item in her handbag, he tells himself, will be the screenplay for that movie she's in.

"Did you finish the movie?"

"We finished shooting on location—that was ages ago. Now we're on set and we're behind schedule. What a bore. I'm thinking about going back to theater."

Their order arrives and Chŏmnan proves adept with knife and fork. When the apple is brought she halves it, halves again one of the halves, then peels and delicately eats these two quarters; she then eats the remaining half, skin and all. When the coffee arrives she nonchalantly chews a sugar cube, then drinks the coffee.

She certainly has a way with food. Where are the beauty spots going to show up next? On to the elevator, the beauty spot on her right cheek in view.

The effect now is of the fifth floor rising to the top level, and then the fourth floor rising to the fifth, the third to the fourth, and the second to the third. The first floor arrives.

"Are you going to the hospital?" Chŏmnan asks at the place where the street forks.

"Yes—part of the daily routine."

Chŏmnan marches into a flower shop. She emerges with a bouquet.

"I'd appreciate it if you could give these to Taeung. Please tell him I'm too busy to see him now."

Off to the hospital.

He doesn't like the twisting, noisy, disorderly street to the hospital, but he dislikes even more the hospital's long, dark corridor.

At the end of the corridor is Taeung's room. He enters to the usual greeting:

"Well, I was beginning to wonder if I was ever going to see you again. Have a seat."

With a grimace Taeung hoists himself to a sitting position, his injured leg stretched out.

"Aren't you going to hurt yourself moving around like that?"

"It's better than just lying here bored out of my mind. And it doesn't really hurt. But the bending and stretching exercises, that's a different story—they practically kill me. And I had another blackout today."

"*That* would have been something to see."

Until yesterday the next bed was occupied by a youth recovering from a tonsillectomy that was supposed to improve his vocal cords. Now a swarthy-faced boy lies there.

"Pop," the boy says, trembling all over.

An aging man sitting at the foot of the bed draws near.

"What is it, son?"

Both father and son speak with thick P'yŏngan accents.

"Don't go anywhere, huh?"

"I'm not going anywhere. Where would I go?"

The boy looks up at the gray ceiling.

"Let's go home."

"Good heavens, son." The man takes his walking stick in hand and rises. "Just relax, you're going to be all right."

"Look at him shake," he says to Taeung.

"His left side's paralyzed," Taeung says in an undertone.

The aging man looks in Taeung's direction, as if he knows what Taeung is saying. His eyes are set in a welter of wrinkled flesh.

"It's worse than yesterday," the aging man tells them.

"Is there any swelling?"

"No. All this time, been well over a year now, and never any swelling. One day, summer of last year, he went out to cut fodder, and that's when we noticed it, something wasn't right with him. He couldn't hold on to a bunch of grass to cut it, fingers just wouldn't work. . . . A few days later his fingers went back to normal. Then winter arrived, and guess what—his left hand got gimpy, the same hand. He was trying to braid a rope, couldn't even keep the straw in the palm of his hand. Whatever it was started at his fingertips, and by and by it got to his wrist. And then somehow or other it worked its way up to his elbow, and now it's down to his ankle—all on the left side."

At this point the man holds out the walking stick to the boy.

"Son, grab on, hard as you can."

The boy flexes a trembling elbow and reaches out, but now his fingers tremble all the more, and before he can touch the walking stick his arm falls limp.

"See? The boy used to be strong— worked like an ox. And to see him like this now. . . . We wondered if it was something in the grass, something poisonlike, or maybe a snake bite, so we tried a poison remedy and a snakebite cure, didn't work. We did the needles and the burning, no improvement. So finally we brought him here. And now he's shaking worse than yesterday."

As he says this the man rubs his nose with the back of his free hand, then rubs his eyes.

He can't find words to comfort the man, can only say, "He's listening, you know, so try not to worry so much—that just makes it worse for him."

After a brief pause Taeung speaks so that only he can hear: "That's the third time. The boy was admitted after you left yesterday, and the old man told me then, and this morning he told Mr. Throat over there."

Mr. Throat is a young man who entered into a suicide pact with a woman. They both drank lye, and when he came to, he had a tube coming out of his neck. The woman died, but even after learning this the man has never missed a feeding through his tube. At the moment he's pouring a bottle of milk into it.

"Imagine two of them kissing tube to tube—now *that* would be hygienic," he says, and then he gets up.

"You're not going already," Taeung fusses, as he always does.

"I've got something for you." He opens the paper wrapping of the bouquet.

"You got that for me?" Taeung exclaims.

"Easy now. It's from Chŏmnan."

"You saw Chŏmnan?" Taeung extends a large hand and takes the bouquet. "I'll bet she's prettier than ever. Probably too busy to come here so she sent the bouquet instead, right? Ladies-and-gentlemen etiquette, you know? I did the same thing a while back—sent her a wreath for the premiere of a movie her husband's the male lead in."

Taeung's laughter, so much like him before his injury, fills the sickroom and follows him down the corridor.

Off to the next stop on his daily routine—the movie theater.

He arrives at the theater—it's one that shows a lot of newsreels—just in time to see a film of a sumo match from Tsushima Island. Flesh collides with flesh. Pulling and pushing, the two opponents are evenly matched. Neither shows any sign of urgency; both look calm and composed. When the two bodies come together as one and he notices the referee circling quickly around the space they occupy, his tense anticipation changes to excitement as his interest shifts from the outcome of the match to the movements of the referee. But then unexpectedly one of the bodies sprawls to the mat, and the scene changes.

The screen is filled with the movement of antlike insects. But on closer inspection, isn't it a flock of raptors settling down on an island shore? The camera gradually brings the scene close up, until the raptorlike creatures become distinguishable as people. Disaster victims? No, refugees from northern China. Dishes or sacks in hand, they throng toward a place where food is being distributed. People pushing. Falling. Rolling. A melee.

In and out of the close-up pass the faces of the elderly, cross-hatched with wrinkles like the detail of a complicated map, and the twisted faces of children. He realizes that he is seeing over and over faces that resemble those of the Manchurian family in the muddy lane, playing the gong and drum. He looks for the faces of the aging man and the hemiplegic boy from the hospital, and when he finds himself looking for his own face on the screen, he scurries from the theater.

He's thirsty. On to a teahouse.

His first priority is a drink of water. He sprinkles the leftover liquid at the base of a potted palm.

Across the tearoom Chohun picks out a record. "Are you by your-self?" he says as he approaches.

"Yeah. When did you get here?"

"It's my first time out in a long while, but you know, it's even worse here. Let's go someplace else."

Out they go. The evenings are still a bit chilly. After making their way through several alleys, the last one long and gloomy, they enter a small bar.

Chohun finds a table, heaves a great shudder, and calls out to the barmaid: "Vodka!"

The vodka warms them from the inside.

Chohun downs three shots in quick succession; his face remains pale.

"Easy does it."

"Pleasy does it—we'll drink as much as we please. Myŏngae earns at a place like this, I spend at a place like this. Good plan, huh? Hey, Hanako! Hanako, right? We want good service, hear? You give us good service, we give you good business."

Hanako's smile creates fine wrinkles on the bridge of her promi-nent nose.

"What kind of service?"

"You know better than me, a little kiss here, a little . . ."

Chohun takes Hanako's extended hand in his, which has started to tremble, pulling her down close so that her full bosom bumps their table.

"All right," says Hanako, extricating her hand, and after another smile that wrinkles the bridge of her nose she gives Chohun a co-quettish scowl. "People are watching; maybe later."

"I'll close *my* eyes," he says.

This draws a cursory wink from Hanako, who then proceeds to the end of the bar where a man in Japanese clothing is licking a shot glass.

Chohun turns back to him. His eyes are bloodshot. "Better keep an eye on her. One of these days she'll be lying on her side, posing for Yongjae." He tosses down the rest of his drink. "I can see Myŏngae doing the same thing with some bum before long. That's how *I* met her, and I have a hunch it's only a matter of time before she hooks up with some other guy. It's not a problem as long as she brings home the cigarettes those bums leave behind. But the day will come when she gets all her cigarettes from one guy and doesn't want to bring them home. Next she'll be going out to the river and floating flowers with that guy, just like she and I used to do. I'm sure of it. It's not that I haven't thought about trying to salvage our relationship. It's just that I know things would work out if I could get her to quit working at the bar. But what do you think our living situation would be like if she stopped working at the bar? It would be over. So in order to save myself, my best bet is to dump Myŏngae before she dumps me and moves on to some other guy. If she left me I don't think I could bear it sober. I really envy you and Taeung. I envy you two to the point of resentment, the way you both took it in stride when the little woman left you. Every afternoon she goes to the bar, and every afternoon I decide to dump her. I decide to dump her as long as she's at the bar. When she comes home at night, I decide not to dump her; as long as she's with me I'm happy. The very next afternoon she goes to the bar and I decide to dump her all over again. And then I started paper folding. And when she comes home at night I tell myself once again that I'll offer to break up, but instead I smoke the cigarettes she's brought. The days are so long. I've started wondering which one of the guys with the cigarettes will end up marrying her instead of me. When she's at the bar and I'm at home I take her silk stockings and flatten out the wrinkles and I think of her body. And I imagine her pulling those stockings up higher than she has to, in front of some man. I couldn't stand it today; I had to get out. I had to see for myself Myŏngae pulling up her stockings higher than she has to, in front of some man. But before I knew it I was outside the city, away from where the bar is. I realized my legs were shaking, and then I saw where I was—I was standing at the edge of a cliff. And I had an illusion—I was a little pebble at the base of a large boulder. I made up my mind I was going to roll like a rock right off that cliff, but guess what—a rock near the tip of my foot went over first. I decided I'd roll myself over the edge after that rock came to rest. Well, it bounced off another rock and fetched up against *another* rock about halfway down. And then I sent a second rock over the edge. This one shattered against another rock before it got to the bottom. That's when I realized I could shatter against a rock and never reach the bottom—that scared me. So I came back into town. And once I was back I came up with a swell idea: use a place like this to blow what Myŏngae earns. I could kick myself—I should have thought of this sooner."

With a peculiar sparkle in his dreamy eyes, Chohun gulps down his new drink.

He can't offer any words of consolation to Chohun and doesn't feel like scolding him.

"So, a new routine for the man Yongjae calls Happy Guy," says Chohun.

"Well, I guess I need a new routine too. I'm looking for a missing person, and she comes with a reward. She must be pretty, judging from the description: a snaggletooth when she smiles, a wart to the left of her upper lip, double eyelids, long eyelashes. . . ."

"Sounds like your wife."

"Pretty sharp, aren't you? And the bridge of her nose sticks out like that one . . ."

Hanako approaches.

"You two look like you're having a grand old time. Bottoms up."

"Give us a smile, would you?" he says.

The same cursory smile as before, wrinkling the bridge of her nose.

"Okay, okay, I got it now. Dimple when she smiles, nineteen years old, and . . . Hanako—Hanako, where are you from?"

Hanako tries out several replies, each in a different accent. "Can you guess?"

"Wait a minute. You were in that newsreel, in Chinese clothes. You were in that crowd of refugees yelling and carrying on, trying to get a handful of rice."

"Listen to you!"

"When it comes to a fight, winning is the only thing."

Hanako turns away, and just then a huge man appears at the door. Hanako goes to greet him, the bridge of her nose crinkling.

"Where have you been hiding?" she says. "Did you find someone better?"

"Hanako, you're prettier than ever. Prettier by the day. What am I going to do with you?"

"There you go again. So, what can I bring you? Absinthe?"

The man flips back the tip of his felt hat. Taking the drink Hanako serves him, he finishes it in a few sips.

The man continues to proffer the empty glass and Hanako continues to fill it. Then, while the man is smoking, she approaches the two of them and pours more vodka.

"Down the hatch."

Chohun gulps his vodka and holds out the empty shot glass in his trembling hand. "Hanako, I bet you have more men here than you do hometowns." Slumping over the table, he adds, softly yet clearly, "And that man's one of them."

"There you go again."

The man bangs his empty glass on his table. "More!"

Hanako minces her way over.

"You look like you're feeling no pain."

"Feeling no pain?" the man barks. "When you don't listen to me? You say you'll see me but you just blow me off. Let's see what happens the next time you have a day off."

Hanako nods, her nose crinkling.

Chohun observes Hanako and shouts, "I want some of that absinthe too!"

The man looks Chohun up and down, then turns back to Hanako. "You better keep your word next time," he says, sticking out his chest. Hanako continues to nod. The man deposits a five-*wŏn* note on the table and leaves.

"Absinthe!"

"I think you're pushing your limit."

"I want absinthe!"

Hanako pours Chohun the drink and in no time it's gone. Chohun quickly fishes a few crumpled one-*wŏn* notes from his pocket and leaves them on the table. He rises, pushes open the door, and leaves.

He follows Chohun out, but Chohun is nowhere to be seen and the alley is draped in gloom. If Chohun were to go home now, he could see Myŏngae, forget everything, and turn into Happy Guy again. He treads the darkness and emerges from the alley, turns down another alley, and comes to a side alley, where he notices shadows. The shadows are moving. They're the shadows of people. He comes to a stop.

Two men are fighting. The smaller one falls, then rises, but before he can attack the larger man, that man's hand shoots out and knocks the smaller man back down. The larger man stands unyielding, waiting, it seems, for the smaller man to rise. The smaller man rises and the larger man knocks him down again. The fight with its fixed pattern is becoming monotonous when strangely enough, the rhythm of the smaller man's falling and rising quickens. At the same time, the larger man, instead of pressing the fight, begins to shrink back. And then the smaller man, as he's sent sprawling, grabs the foot of the larger man and clings to it. The larger man kicks free and retreats. Again the smaller man grabs the larger one's foot.

The curtain will fall on this peculiar fight with the smaller man sent flying so he can't grab the larger man's foot again. As he thinks this, he realizes that the larger man is the huge man from the bar. And the smaller man is Chohun. Before he can charge into the darkness of the alley, the larger man manages to free himself of the sprawled-out smaller man's hold on his foot. As the larger man runs past him in a flurry, his felt hat drops to the ground. From the direction of the smaller shadow comes a weird, bestial cry; it is Chohun laughing, and who knows when it will end?

TRUMPET SHELLS

White tongues of the dark sea's waves lap the sand. Seagulls fly off squawking into the breakers. Offshore, a squat island seems to be retreating an impossible distance into the gloom.

Curtains of darkness part to reveal the heavens' starry display, and at a point where sea, sky, and shore converge, a lighthouse lamp begins to wink on and off.

A young woman and a young man approach from the opposite end of the shore. Just when the incoming tide is about to wet the feet of the woman, she speaks.

"We're almost there."

The man casts a nervous look in the direction of the lighthouse. "Isn't it still kind of far off?" He comes to a stop and looks out toward where the horizon has been eroded by the dark sea.

"No, it's just past where the shore curves around."

"I like it right where we are—look at that ocean—shall we stop here?"

"But at night it's so nice to watch the ocean from where the lighthouse is. Besides, you promised."

The man remains where he is, looking out at the dark sea.

"All right, I'll go first. You can take your time."

The man's gaze follows the woman as she disappears into the gloom. "It's farther than it looks during daytime," he mutters.

Without warning, another young man appears. Taking a fistful of sand, he says, "How far could it be? Anyway, at night the best place is right where we're standing."

The first man peers through the darkness and inspects the other.

"Think about it: this sand is so hot during the day and now it's so cool—and tomorrow it'll be hot again."

The first man's gaze returns to the dark sea.

"Just like how the ocean is black at night and then so blue during the day."

The first man lights a cigarette.

"Could I please have a light?"

The first man obliges.

"The first time I met Wŏri," says the second man, "it was here at this blue-green ocean. There was so much seaweed swaying in the water—you could see it, the water was so clear. Wŏri liked to sit on a rock and watch the seaweed swaying in the water. She could sit there all day. And I liked to hide off in the distance and throw trumpet shells and things like that into the water where she was looking. As much as I used to do it, she'd still get startled and stand up—it never failed. But in no time she'd regain her composure and force a smile. Her smile was wavering just like that seaweed she was looking at."

He inhales deeply on his cigarette, then spews out smoke.

The first man continues to gaze out at the dark sea.

"When I saw the two of you just now, it brought back such memories—I was really happy then. Surprising Wŏri where she sat on her rock was happiness itself. And then one day, a day when sky and ocean were as clear as could be, I did the same thing I always did and tossed a trumpet shell from a distance, but I threw it toward her rock instead of into the water. Wŏri got up, as she always did. But she didn't act surprised. And guess what? Instead of me approaching her, *she* started walking toward *me*. Well, it wasn't Wŏri at all; it was someone else. I got all flustered. She came up to me and said, didn't I realize that I'd scare all the fish away if I threw rocks and such? I just stood there without saying anything—I didn't know what to do. Her cheeks were quite a bit fuller than Wŏri's. And she had unusually large eyes with dark pupils.

"And then one day I saw two women sitting side by side on the rock, looking into the water. I didn't throw trumpet shells anymore. And after that incident I wondered if I should stop going to the rock too. But there I was walking toward it. Both women were wearing the same outfit: a white jacket and a black skirt. And both had short hair tied with a ribbon. I went up behind them close enough to see the breeze moving the hair beneath their ears. And finally I looked at their reflections in the water. The faces were those of Wŏri and that woman from the time before. When they saw my reflection, that other woman was the first to turn her head. And then Wŏri rose lightly to her feet. And with a seaweed smile creasing that familiar look of surprise on her face, she introduced the other woman as her friend Ŭn'gyŏngi. Ŭn'gyŏngi broke into a toothy smile and said it was *so* interesting the way the fish jumped around. The finger she pointed toward the fish darting through the seaweed was just as smooth and clear as a fish scale. I'm sure that while Wŏri was looking at the seaweed Ŭn'gyŏngi was looking at the fish.

"The next day I began scaring the fish again. There was a stretch of days when Wŏri was in the city and was either late getting here or didn't show up at all. Ŭn'gyŏngi would arrive by herself and kid me about how sad I must be that Wŏri wasn't there. And I have to admit that while I was scaring away Ŭn'gyŏngi's fish, I did wish I was surprising Wŏri instead while she looked at the seaweed. You see, with Wŏri, when I threw the trumpet shells I'd then have to approach her before she would get up and flash that seaweed smile, but the days with Ŭn'gyŏngi, I would throw the shells and she would turn and look and then approach me first. Maybe it was Wŏri's doing, asking Ŭn'gyŏngi to come here by herself while she, Wŏri, avoided me. In fact, my relationship with Wŏri was strange in that we didn't talk much to each other. I tossed trumpet shells, she got up and looked surprised, but we never really talked. If anything, the clearer her seaweed smile became, the less we said. Granted, we didn't make much of an effort. But in spite of that we were happy as could be. Strangely, though, from the time Ŭn'gyŏngi appeared on the scene, our wordless times together began to feel awkward to Wŏri and me. Perhaps Wŏri realized this and avoided me because of it. In fact, I feared the awkwardness, so when I was with Wŏri I began to look forward to Ŭn'gyŏngi's presence. It was only when the three of us were together that Wŏri was bright and cheerful.

"One day we three were playing a phonograph in a pine grove on a hill overlooking the ocean. The cello sobbed, and before the piece was over Wŏri asked me to put on a waltz. And then she asked Ŭn'gyŏngi to dance, extending her hand cheerfully and saying she would lead. Ŭn'gyŏngi got right up, and there she was in Wŏri's arms. The ocean seemed to revolve about the waists of the two women. The waltz came to an end and Wŏri asked me to play it again. In the shade of the evergreens the waists of the two women revolved end-lessly in the ocean's embrace. Another day we went out on the ocean in a boat. Ŭn'gyŏngi was rowing. The boat approached the buoy where the water gets rough and just as Ŭn'gyŏngi began to bring the bow about, Wŏri snatched the oars from her. Out to sea she rowed. The water grew rougher. The sea pitched and Ŭn'gyŏngi watched the waves slap against the boat, and then she covered her eyes and lay down in the bottom of the boat. And there was Wŏri, her white face wearing that seaweed smile. I thought it would go away because of the swells, but it remained a while. And so the beach season passed. We were back in the city before the leaves of the oaks on that hill overlooking the ocean had turned yellow."

The first man flicks his cigarette butt into the sea.

"Back in the city Wŏri would visit me and bring cut flowers—cosmos and mums. Ŭn'gyŏngi was always with her. I made coffee for them. And then one day well into the fall Wŏri came by herself. She was wearing a light raincoat. I hadn't realized it, but outside it was drizzling. Out we went. We walked the streets in the misty drizzle, no words passing between us. We passed through the long, dark back alleys and walked all the way down a street with neon streetlights, which gave the effect of melted light on the pavement. Where the lights came to an end we turned right. The river is right there. I guess we wanted to see the autumn rain falling on the river. Some old boats, no longer seaworthy, lay overturned on the bank. The dark shadows of masts and the upside-down reflection of streetlights on the surface of the water rippled in the drizzle. Fine though it was, after a while it felt heavy on our shoulders. We turned back. Once more we were in the street with the neon lights. Our feet trod the neon stream on the pavement all the way to the end. Only the dark back alleys remained. Wŏri came to a stop. I did too. Wŏri slightly lowered her already bowed head, raised her coat collar, and walked a few steps down a side alley. She stopped, turned back, and approached me, and finally she spoke. What did I think of Ŭn'gyŏngi? she asked. Without thinking, I simply said I loved her. Even in the dark I could tell her face was trembling, and I saw her seaweed smile. And now it was I who walked off down the side street. I kept asking myself why I had lied, but unlike Wŏri, I didn't turn around and speak."

The first man kicks at the water lapping at his feet.

"And so winter set in. Wasn't that a lot of snow we had last winter? On one of those days when we had a large snowfall Ŭn'gyŏngi and I ended up getting married. And then one day when wet snow was falling Ŭn'gyŏngi went out, and she came back with Wŏri. I hadn't seen her after we parted on that rainy autumn night. The only news I'd had of her, by way of Ŭn'gyŏngi, was that she had married a doctor here in the city. Ŭn'gyŏngi disappeared into the kitchen to make coffee. Wŏri was wearing a gray skirt with red lines running across it. The skirt was wet from the snow and she kind of trailed it along as she walked to the window where we kept a vase of cineraria. She stood looking at the vase and murmured that flowers must have their own temperature, judging from the condensation where the plant touched the glass. And then she buried her face among the leaves and flowers. I observed her profile, noticed her face was thinner. There she was, her lips touching the blossoms and a single line of tears streaming down her cheek. Just then Ŭn'gyŏngi appeared carrying a tray with three coffee cups. The plant was quite fragrant, wasn't it, she said to Wŏri. Only then did Wŏri lift her head from the plant. It seemed she hadn't noticed her tears, because not until then did she dab at them with the back of her pale hand. Ŭn'gyŏngi wondered if one of the leaves had pricked her, with her face being so close to the plant. Wŏri's lips formed her unmistakable seaweed smile. Ŭn'gyŏngi put sugar cubes in the coffee and mused that after the cineraria had withered, it would still be a while before it was beach season again. In no time Wŏri had gone back out by herself into the wet snow.

"One day Ŭn'gyŏngi was playing a jazz record when she casually remarked that Wŏri had told her she had separated from her husband. When the record was over Ŭn'gyŏngi added that Wŏri had offered no particulars, but there was no doubt in her mind that the husband was infatuated with another woman and Wŏri must have asked for a separation. At any rate, she said, she couldn't leave Wŏri all alone now, and she adopted a grave expression I had never seen before. From then on she visited Wŏri occasionally. One day she came home and told me that the woman Wŏri's husband was infatuated with was a nurse he had employed. She then said that if there was any trouble involving me and another woman, she wouldn't feel jealous at all. When I said that must be because she didn't feel any affection toward me, she opened those big eyes with the black pupils even wider and produced a nervous laugh that I had never heard before. Then she flung open the curtain, and the warm rays of the early summer sun were practically enough to blind me.

"That blinding sunlight was coming through the window the next time Ŭn'gyŏngi brought Wŏri home. We turned on the record player. The sound issuing from the record was strangely lucid that day. Suddenly Ŭn'gyŏngi stood Wŏri up, drew her close, and asked her to dance. Wŏri dutifully rested her left hand on Ŭn'gyŏngi's shoulder. Compared with that time they danced in the pine grove on the hill overlooking the ocean, Ŭn'gyŏngi looked more ample, whereas Wŏri was drawn. The record came to an end. Ŭn'gyŏngi put another record on, and you can probably guess what it was—the waltz we had played that day. Ŭn'gyŏngi turned to me and said she'd make coffee, and asked me to dance with Wŏri in her place. And then she stepped lightly into the kitchen. I was at a loss, but I couldn't just stand there, so I approached Wŏri. I took her right hand in my left and placed my right hand on her waist. And that's when I felt it, a chill that went right through me. Before I could tell whether the chill came from her hand or her waist, the record ended. Ŭn'gyŏngi returned with the coffee. Wŏri picked up a sugar cube and I had the impression her hand was trembling, as if she had a fever or something. Ŭn'gyŏngi remarked that the coffee had come out a bit strong, but then she murmured that she didn't measure coffee as well as I used to do when I made coffee for them, and produced an innocent smile. Wŏri silently added cream to her coffee. Ŭn'gyŏngi spoke up again, saying that there were times when the aroma of strong, freshly brewed coffee was like the smell of the sunshine drying saltwater-moistened sand. All Wŏri did was stir her coffee. Ŭn'gyŏngi sipped her coffee and murmured that when the sun shone through the green curtains it reminded her of the ocean. Some color came to

Wŏri's face, and she wondered out loud about the seaweed and the little fish. Ŭn'gyŏngi said with a twinkle in her eye that they were probably doing just fine, and remarked that it was beach season now that the cineraria were long since gone. But there was no seaweed smile from Wŏri. I fiddled with the paring knife, poking at the apples. Wŏri left, walking off into the dazzling sunlight. Compared with the times she'd walked off into the wet snow, she looked thinner. The peonies in the garden had all withered. A longing for the ocean welled up inside me. And that's what brought me here."

The first man gives the second man a studied look through the darkness, then lights a fresh cigarette.

"I didn't realize mine was out," says the second man. "Can I use yours for a light?"

The first man obliges.

"As soon as I got here," says the second man, "I went to that rock. The one where Wŏri looked at the seaweed and Ŭn'gyŏngi watched the little fish. The seaweed and the little fish are still there, just like before. But unlike before, Wŏri and Ŭn'gyŏngi aren't sitting on the rock. The next day I went back to the rock. But I didn't throw a single trumpet shell. I sat by myself, looking down at my reflection in the water. And I realized it's just as easy now for Ŭn'gyŏngi to maintain our empty marriage as it was for me to lie when I was walking in the drizzle with Wŏri that night and she asked me what I thought of Ŭn'gyŏngi, and I said I loved her. And so to break this pattern of lies among us I made up my mind to meet Wŏri here."

The first man gives the second man a stricken look, and then his gaze drops to the incoming tide at his feet.

"But when it got dark, my daytime decision to arrange for Wŏri to meet me here faded away. All I did was walk this sandy beach, where on a night like this you can look out to sea but not make out the horizon. This sand that's lost the heat of the sun reminds me of how cool Wŏri's body temperature was. The following day, while I was sitting on the rock, I decided once more that I ought to have Wŏri meet me here. Today I was back, looking down at the seaweed and the little fish. And then it occurred to me that even if Wŏri did come, this time she could easily pretend she was looking at the fish and not the seaweed. I jumped down from the rock. And I threw one last trumpet shell."

At this point the second man tosses his cigarette into the water. " Say, do you hear a voice? Isn't that the woman you came with calling from over by the lighthouse?"

The first man looks toward the lighthouse. "It's the sound of the waves."

The second man scoops up sand with both hands. "All I'm going to do at night is walk this beach. This beach that's so like Wŏri's body. And over and over I'll feel this sand that's cold like Wŏri's body colder even than our flowers. The harder I grab this cold sand the faster it slips through my fingers."

The first man also grabs some sand, and proceeds to scatter it over the water.

"And I'll scatter this sand over the water too. Just now I had a feeling that I simply ought to go into the ocean. There's seaweed in that ocean. All I have to do is go into the ocean and that seaweed will wrap itself around me. Just like Wŏri's body. To go to sleep wrapped up in seaweed—what else could I ask for? And if the fish want to take a bite out of me when I'm decomposed, that's fine. All I have to do is jump into the ocean. And it would have to be a night like this, a night when there's no moon and the stars are faint. Simply turn my back on that lighthouse, go into the ocean, and let the seaweed wrap itself around me."

The first man looks out to sea again.

" I even thought of leaving my will on a sand dune. And even if Wŏri comes here, I won't be happy. The real Wŏri is in the ocean. If I get washed away by the wind and the tide before daybreak, it's fine."

The first man takes another handful of sand and scatters it over the water.

There is only the sound of the dark sea.

The first man walks off in the direction opposite the lighthouse, whence he came.

"Wait—isn't that the woman calling you?"

The first man comes to a stop. "It's the waves," he says, but with no indication that he has listened for a voice. He resumes walking.

White teeth gnaw at the dark sea's sandy edge.

A woman, walking quickly, appears out of the darkness from the direction of the lighthouse.

"Why didn't you follow me? It's so pleasant watching the ocean from the lighthouse."

The second man merely looks out to the dark sea.

"You know, at the lighthouse the smell of fish scales carries on the breeze more than the smell of seaweed." She approaches the second man and starts. "Who are you? Where did he go?"

The second man simply points toward the sea, in the direction the first man has gone.

"What?! He went in? Then he must be underwater. Save him!"

"He's down too deep."

"Won't you save him—please?"

"He's all wrapped up in seaweed."

The woman squats in a heap.

"I had something to tell him. Didn't he say anything?"

"I'll bet he left a note on that sand dune saying he used to be quite happy."

"Oh? Well, I don't believe it. It's a lie. And when I said it's nice at the lighthouse at night, I was lying too. I guess he wanted to find happiness on his own."

The woman buries her face in her hands and begins to sob, her shoulders heaving.

The lighthouse lamp continues to wink on and off. The horizon, the sky, and the sea are a seamless black. Without a word, the second man disappears over the sand dune and into the darkness.

SWINE

The chickens cluck furiously, beaks gaping, as they retreat from the straw mat where the millet has been hulled. Yongt'ae's mother is searching the grain for bugs. She flicks the bugs aside and the chickens flock to where they land, then disperse. Yongt'ae's mother shoos the chickens away and pours the grain onto a winnow.

Suddenly the chickens flock together, combs bristling, as a pig appears, snout to the ground. Interrupting her winnowing, Yongt'ae's mother drives the pig off with a stick.

As the pig runs past the bamboo fence that borders the vegetable patch, the bamboo casts vertical shadows along its back.

Yongt'ae's mother turns to see the chickens pecking at the millet in the winnow.

"Shoo, birds. . . . How come they don't feed that pig?" she grumbles.

"Did you feed the pig?" asks Ujŏm's mother. She and Ujŏm are out in the paddy. She's using a chipped wooden bowl to water the rice shoots.

"Uh-huh."

The rice shoots tremble as the muddy water splashes them. A sodden mole cricket grapples with one of the shoots, trying to climb it.

Ujŏm, when her mother isn't looking, throws a clod of dirt at the cricket.

Again her mother's voice: "Did you shut the pigpen tight?"

"Uh-huh."

The rice shoot droops under the weight of the mole cricket.

Ujŏm examines the cricket as it struggles to climb the shoot.

"Are you sure you fed the pig?" her mother asks. She straightens and proceeds to pummel the small of her back with her soiled hands, her shadow flickering on the surface of the muddy water in the irrigation pool.

Yongt'ae's mother moves the winnow under the eaves and continues to sift the millet for bugs. " Grain's never going to ripen," she mutters.

Yongt'ae is inside picking stray bits of reed from a reed mat. "We haven't had any rain, that's why." He goes to school in Seoul, and speaks in the Seoul dialect.

Grains of millet bounce above the back of Yongt'ae's mother's hand.

Yongt'ae's eyes follow the bouncing grains.

"All we get is the halo around the moon, and not the rain that's supposed to follow," he says.

His mother's hand sifts the grain more quickly.

"I wonder if your father found some water for the paddy."

Kŭnhu wipes his sweaty face with his sleeve. There's scarcely a breath of wind, not enough to ruffle the sleeve.

"Hey, Ujŏm, is our Yongt'ae still inside?" he shouts.

"Don't know," says Ujŏm, content with her mole cricket.

Ujŏm's mother shouts back, "Why don't you let him be? A boy needs his rest after all that studying."

"Rest? What for?"

" 'You can let an only son die, as long as the grain doesn't burn up.' Is that it?"

There's no breeze, but somehow wisps of cloud come together and float gently overhead. Before long they've vanished into the clear blue sky.

The water in the paddy is drying up. The yellowish-brown color of the rice shoots is getting darker.

Kŭnhu keeps digging into the irrigation ditch. The flow of water increases with each shovelful of dirt that's removed. Sunlight glints momentarily on the wet tip of the shovel. Herons skim the paddies, looking in vain for a place to light. The water level in the ditch drops as the water soaks into the dry ground.

Yongt'ae's mother is still picking through the millet, searching now for tiny cocoons, which she crushes between her fingers.

"That pig got loose again."

"Weren't Ujŏm's folks going to slaughter it and use the head for a rain ceremony?" says Yongt'ae.

"That's right."

"And the shaman's going to bring us rain?"

"Don't talk like that, child. She did last time."

Yongt'ae returns to his work with the reed mat.

"I tell you, that pig is a runt. They don't feed it right."

"The one they bought with the money they got for Ujŏm's elder sister?"

"That's right."

The pig works its snout beneath the bamboo fence and roots around in the vegetable patch. It finds a runner of baby squashes, uproots it, bites through the runner, and is startled by the resulting *snap*. The pig runs off, only to startle again, this time at the rocks in the path. It turns and runs in the opposite direction.

"Remember how they sent Ujŏm's sister off to her in-laws with just the clothes on her back, because they spent her bride price on the pig? Too bad for her, if you think about it. But she's a bit thickheaded, that one. She couldn't put up with all the children he had by his first wife, so she came back home. What an awful thing to do! I heard even a shaman got involved. But what can a person do if it's her fate to marry a widower?"

An insect bounces off the back of her hand and out of the winnow.

"Her in-laws live up in the hills, don't they?"

"Yes. Up there the millet and sorghum are still doing all right."

"Not their rice plants, though. I'll bet they're shriveled up."

"Now that you've got the sleep out of your eyes, go see how your father's doing. He was up all night trying to get some water to the paddy, but I'm afraid the sun has dried it out again."

With his weeding hoe Taegŏn digs a channel through the earthen barrier that Kŭnhu has built to dam the flow of water to the other paddies. Beside him Kŭnhu frantically shovels sod to re-block the flow.

Taegŏn scrapes furiously at the dam. "You're only looking after yourself—what about the rest of us?"

"What about *us*?" Kŭnhu says.

The back of Kŭnhu's shovel slants toward Taegŏn's shoulder, misses, and bounces off the ground. Off balance, Kŭnho tumbles, writhing, into the paddy.

Kŭnhu crawls back up to the elevated path through the paddies, blood oozing through the soil caked above his eyebrows. He claws at the mud, attempting to repair the dam.

The chickens gather beside the winnow.

Yongt'ae claps his hands to shoo the chickens away. Instead of scattering, they merely bob their elongated necks.

His mother works the winnow. Perspiration spreads through the clothing on her back.

"Does it get this hot in Seoul?"

"Even hotter."

His mother pours the winnowed millet into a wooden bowl.

"I hear in Seoul they've got all kinds of wild animals that people can go see. How can animals live in this heat?" She settles the grain in the bowl.

Yongt'ae scatters the bits of reeds in front of the chickens and rises. Instead of the chickens it's flies that swarm about the reed bits.

"I guess you don't need to go check on your father. He's probably all right."

Yongt'ae dons his straw hat.

His mother rises as well, bowl in hand.

"You're going after all?"

"You, child!" calls Ujŏm's mother, just as Ujŏm reaches out for a dragonfly resting on a withered mugwort stalk.

The dragonfly's head moves back and forth. Just as her shadow is about to cover the dragonfly, Ujŏm moves to the side.

"Where are you, you little mischief?"

The dragonfly flits away from Ujŏm's fingertips. It seems about to light where it was before, but then flies high into the air.

Ujŏm whirls around. "What's the matter?"

Her mother runs up to her, brandishing a fist. "What are you doing, you little bitch? You're supposed to be looking for the pig."

"Uh-huh."

Kŭnhu's mud-covered form appears in the distance.

"Ujŏm," he calls, "send Yongt'ae here."

"All right." Ujŏm's gaze drifts in the direction the dragonfly has flown.

"Grain's never going to ripen," mutters Yongt'ae's mother as she enters the kitchen.

The cloudless sky looks too far off for it to be evening already.

A bee falls to the ground. It's coated with pollen from the squash flowers.

Head to the ground, the pig makes its way through the vegetable patch. Its shadow, cross-hatched by the silhouette of the bamboo fence, is as long and thin as can be.

THE BROKEN REED

A single broken reed, one from the previous year, swayed above the new grass on a patch of undeveloped land. Swarms of mosquito larvae rose and settled in the black soil bordering a mud puddle. Maggots crawled out of the puddle to the thick, dark mud, then returned to the water.

A mangy dog with a bone in its mouth came slinking past the puddle and curled up next to a decaying log. After gnawing for a time on the already cleaned bone, the emaciated animal let it drop from its mouth, sniffed at the air, and rose. Completing a circuit of the surroundings, it returned to the bone.

A girl made a ball of mud and threw it at the dog as it licked the bone. The mud ball missed the dog, which hunched up and whimpered nonetheless.

The girl plopped herself down on her haunches and felt the boils on her calves, then drew her elbows in close to her sides and squirmed, as if the intermittent sunshine landing on her back tickled. A precocious smile played at the corners of her mouth.

The weather was as pleasant as could be.

The dog went toward the hut where the girl and her family lived, off to the side of the patch of undeveloped land. The girl's grandfather emerged from the hut and called to her:

"Sweetie, come check on your father."

But the girl remained squatting, her mouth still in a forced smile.

The girl's grandfather noticed the dog's bone underfoot. He found a large rock, placed the bone beneath it, and tamped down on the rock with his foot.

The dog disappeared behind the straw mat that draped the entrance to the hut.

Inside the hut the girl's father brought an opium-filled syringe to his yellowish-blue arm. His hand shook so much that the syringe kept slipping as he tried to penetrate the skin. Brownish mucus ran from his dark, flared nostrils and gathered on his lips. Finally managing to insert the needle, he gradually became still.

The dog licked the girl's father's face with its milk-colored tongue and went back outside.

The dog was beside the puddle licking its bone. Its tongue looked even milkier now.

The girl came walking past the decaying log, followed by a boy with a book bag strapped to his back.

"Can you tell what's in that dog's mouth?" she asked.

The boy looked from the dog to the girl and shook his head.

"It's a bone—a human bone!" With a satisfied smile the girl peered into the boy's fear-stricken face. "Once that dog eats a hundred skeletons it'll turn into a person. There are all kinds of bones here, you know. This place used to be full of graves. That puddle used to be a grave too. My grandfather was a grave keeper here. He still checks the graves every night. Pretty soon this place will be filled with big houses. Then there will be ghosts everywhere. The ghosts already put my mother under a spell and she ran off, and my father's possessed and he's going to die."

The heavens could no longer hold back the rain. The dog kept shaking the rain from its fur, losing its balance, and toppling over.

The rain was followed by a gloomy night. The dog continually whimpered.

The girl's grandfather looked off in the direction of the whimpering, then sat down on the log.

There was a wheezing sound beside the girl's grandfather. A woman from the streets had sat down at the end of the log. The woman's face and hands floated pale in the darkness, like a reflection on the surface of the puddle.

The girl's grandfather rose and walked toward the hut. From behind him the wheezing came to a stop. He looked back. From beside the log came a feeble gesture—a hand, perhaps. He went back toward the log.

The faint outline of the hand had disappeared, nor was the woman herself there. The girl's grandfather flinched, afraid of stumbling into a pine tree he knew was nearby, and came to a halt. Looking more closely, he spotted the pine, several steps in front of him.

From out of the gloom came the whimper of the dog.

Eyes closed, the girl's father trembled. The dog's tongue, darker now, licked his runny nose and his lips.

The dog left its bone beside the log and made a listless circuit of the surroundings.

Just as listlessly, the girl approached the dog. Her legs were still ridden with boils. Already the dog was yelping, tail between its legs.

The dog curled up beside the puddle and trembled. And as the dog trembled, the bone kept slipping from its mouth.

The girl brought another boy with a book bag strapped to his back. They sat down on the log.

"Can you tell what's in that dog's mouth?" she asked.

The boy shook his head.

"It's a human bone. Once that dog eats a hundred skeletons it'll turn into a person. There used to be graves all over here. You don't have to dig too deep to find a lot of skeletons. Want to try?"

The boy promptly shook his head.

The girl, smiling to herself, observed his face and said, "My grandfather checks on these graves at night. He used to be a grave keeper here. Soon this place will be full of big houses, and then there will be ghosts everywhere. They've already possessed my mother, and she ran off. They've possessed my father too, and he's going to die. When that happens, my grandfather will bury him and then that dog will dig up his bones."

The dog was no longer able to hold the bone in its mouth

On a day when clear weather had given way to more rain, the dog fell dead to the ground.

*   *   *

The rain was lighter that evening but still cold.

The girl's grandfather emerged from their hut with a shovel and set out toward the puddle.

A dark shape was moving near where the dog had died, and from the shape came a wheezing sound.

The girl's grandfather quickly approached. He thought he caught a glimpse of the street woman's milky face turned toward him, and then she ran off toward the street, the dead dog in her arms, and disappeared from view.

The grass on the patch of undeveloped land was higher now than the broken reed. The needles of the gnarled pine were greener.

The sun was stinging hot, and moss had reappeared on the decaying log, growing in crevices in the bark. Seductively green, the moss crawled with tiny red, threadlike insects.

Mosquito larvae once again thrived in the puddle. Maggots began to appear from the foul water. Cloudy or not, the sky was no longer reflected on the surface.

The bone hadn't been touched since the death of the mangy dog. The girl's grandfather finally noticed it, covered it with soil, and tamped the dirt down with his foot.

Fragments of earthenware dislodged by his foot shone blue in the sunlight.

The girl brought yet another boy with a book bag strapped to his back. Extending her boil-ridden leg, she said, "Here, squeeze as hard as you can, huh?"

The boy was slow to respond, and before his hand could reach her, the girl nonchalantly lay back on the ground where the dog had died, and squealed as if she were being tickled.

PASSING RAIN

There it was again, the whistling. Sŏp's hands continued with the task of knotting his tie. And now more whistling. He thought he would whistle back, but when he rounded his lips and blew, no sound came out. He realized instead that his tie was too tight.

Outside Sŏp found Yŏnhŭi relaxing her pursed lips, then pursing them again, this time in a pout.

"How can you make me wait like this?"

Finally Sŏp managed to whistle.

"Silly!"

Yŏnhŭi the canary, pouting, birdlike in her light-green jacket and in the way her long eyelashes flickered.

"I'm bored—it's rude to make a woman wait like this."

"Says who?"

Yŏnhŭi made the kind of face that a girl playing hide-and-seek makes at the one who's "it." This in fact was the game that Sŏp and Yŏnhŭi played, and almost always Sŏp was the one who was "it." But every time Sŏp was about to find Yŏnhŭi, she made new rules for "it" and managed to avoid him. Sŏp wondered if she would do the same thing today.

"I wish I could fly!" Yŏnhŭi blurted.

" So what's new?"

"I can't help it—that's what the river does to me. Even though we come here all the time. I really like it here."

Yŏnhŭi, as if floating on air, went to sit where the river was calm as it skimmed by. And Sŏp, as he always did, pitched rocks at their two images in the water; the reflections broke up. The water grew calm again and the gorgeous outline of Yŏnhŭi's mouth took shape. Today he could do it, he could draw her to him, he could embrace the Yŏnhŭi reflected in the water. And just like that, the game of hide-and-seek would be over. But before the reflection of Sŏp's hand in the water could touch Yŏnhŭi's shoulder, the cloud of cigarette smoke streaming from her mouth obscured her face. Sŏp turned toward the real Yŏnhŭi, who said,

"Your reflection looks so cheerful."

Back to her mouth went the lipstick-smeared cigarette.

Uneasy about this new game of hide-and-seek, Sŏp returned to their images reflected on the water. More and more lipstick smearing Yŏnhŭi's cigarette, more and more reflections broken by the rocks that Sŏp threw.

Yŏnhŭi tapped the cigarette with her thumb, knocking the ash off the end.

Sŏp thought of all the lipstick-smeared cigarettes that Yŏnhŭi would have given to all sorts of men. He thought of how she would put on new lipstick before the old had faded. And how she would take the cigarette right out of a man's mouth and give it a new smearing of lipstick and how the man would take it right back.

Sŏp, however, did not take Yŏnhŭi's lipstick-smeared cigarette. Instead he rose, produced his own pack of cigarettes, and mumbled to himself, "Don't women get more spiritual the more they break down physically? Don't they move on from a physical relationship to spiritual love?"

Yŏnhŭi heard this. She too rose.

"It's possible," she said, contriving a wide-eyed look, "but aren't you asking too much?"

"Maybe so."

"What about the all-for-love types? Kyŏl, for example?"

Kyŏl, who grew giddy just from passing beneath an acacia in full bloom. Whose acacia-leaf eyes shone like dew if she but laughed.

"You know, for Kyŏl the best thing would be to date by moonlight, or at least candlelight." Yŏnhŭi batted her eyes as she said this. "Did you know that Mae is modeling again?"

"Even though she still works every day at the bar?"

"Oh yes. And there's more: Kyŏl told her she thought that modeling was absolutely shameful. So Mae told *her* it's no different from pouring people drinks at a bar. You should have seen how red in the face Kyŏl got."

"Too bad you didn't get to see her cry. She's more cute when she cries than when she's embarrassed or laughing."

"There you go again. You're the only one I know who says things like that." Yŏnhŭi's cheeks puffed out in a smile and she brought her face close to his. "Are you going to take that teaching position at the girls school? You know, there's probably a lot of students like Kyŏl, crying and laughing."

"I decided not to."

"Whatever for? What are you going to tell Teacher Song'am, after he went to the trouble of letting you know about it?"

"Well, I'm not a hundred percent decided."

"But what's the reason?"

"Well, if you need a reason, it's my indigestion."

"Is it that serious? You're going to let a good opportunity pass you by, just like that?"

"I haven't made a final decision."

"So if you still want the job you have a chance." Yŏnhŭi thought for a moment, reached into her handbag, and took out three dice. "How about if we roll for it? I win and you take the job. You win and you can do as you please. Agreed?"

She came to a stop. As did Sŏp.

Yŏnhŭi bent forward and rolled the three dice on the ground: 2, 6, and 4. Sŏp shook the dice, then rolled: 1 (which in this game equaled a 6), 5, and 6.

"Darn," said Yŏnhŭi. She scooped up the dice and rolled again: 6, 3, and 5.

"You lose."

"Not so fast. I'm saving my best roll for last. Watch."

"Watch, botch."

Yŏnhŭi rolled: 1, 5, and 2.

"Had enough?"

"All right. So you're really not going to take it?"

"Didn't you say I could do what I want if I won?"

Yŏnhŭi tried one last roll; up came 5, 3, and 4. She gathered the dice and put them back in her bag.

"They just aren't rolling my way today. Yesterday with Taehyŏn they did a lot better."

"What did he promise you if you won?"

"A pair of socks."

"And what if you lost?"

"Take a guess."

And that was that day's game of hide-and-seek.

Sŏp remembered a drinking place with a barmaid who had said the very same thing: "Take a guess."

"Twenty-six."

"You're no gentleman," the barmaid said with a coquettish scowl.

"All right then, nineteen."

"Seriously, make an honest guess."

"All right. Show me your nipples and I'll tell you exactly."

"You must be drunk," she said, giving him a cuff on the shoulder.

"I bet you have two kids."

"Oh? Well if you can tell that, then I bet you have a sister in this line of work."

"Aha, how did you guess? Actually my mother, not my sister. I was born out of wedlock, and it could have been right here."

Wearily Yŏnhŭi transferred her bag to her other hand.

"You'll never guess if you think too hard."

"Okay, you were going to undo one snap of your dress for every roll you lost."

"Listen to you!"

"Well, what, then?"

"Give up? He was going to kiss me on my arm."

"That's original—what fine tastes you have, my lady."

Exchanges such as this scarcely drew a blush from Yŏnhŭi. Sŏp imagined Taehyŏn's short, bushy eyebrows and perpetually blood-shot eyes. His bluish-black lips. His sticky saliva marking her arm. Which might explain why Yŏnhŭi always wore long gloves outside, even when the sun was beating down.

The light at the crosswalk turned yellow. Yŏnhŭi dashed across the street, her sleek legs showing. The light turned red. Sŏp, partway across, had to retreat. From the far side Yŏnhŭi waved, then turned down an alley that branched off the street at a gentle angle. Her tight-fitting skirt was visible even at a far distance, its gray color same as that of the clouds that blanketed the sky, promising rain at any moment.

And rain it did that night.

Sŏp pulled the collar of his suit jacket close about his neck. The rain was fine as thread, but somehow it seemed to make the pavement come alive.

"Know what a child born out of wedlock means?" he mumbled to the streetlight as he trampled its streaming reflection.

Walking with his head down, he felt the weight of his rain-soaked jacket on his shoulders. Suddenly that weight grew heavier, throwing him off balance.

"It's me," said Mae, her arm around Sŏp's shoulders.

"What are you doing out this time of night?"

She rested her chin on his shoulder, and his nose detected the scent of her face powder and the reek of Western liquor, which reminded him of burning fat.

"Would you walk me home, please?"

"Don't tell me you just got out of work?"

"No, from work I went to another bar, and then another." Her hand slipped from his shoulder and she mumbled, "He can get as hot and bothered as he wants, that fraud of a painter, and I won't be tempted, no I won't."

Mae listed toward Sŏp, who supported her with his hand. Then she tilted her head back and opened her mouth. Every time she swallowed, a dark trail of liquid—rain or tears, it was impossible to tell—appeared beneath her moving chin.

"Isn't this romantic. Let's walk till dawn."

Mae's head drooped.

"We'd better dry off before too long."

They followed every twist and turn, the alleys growing darker and Mae heavier.

Arriving with Mae at her boardinghouse, Sŏp felt unbearably heavy even when relieved of her added weight, and once inside he plopped himself down.

Mae dropped to all fours, then collapsed against the wall. Above her was an unframed painting of her in the nude, from when she had modeled. In the painting she reclined lazily, her head in profile and cocked at a forty-five-degree angle. If she lifted her head a bit more where she lay now, her posture would be about the same as in the painting. Instead she squirmed, then smoothed back her hair, lifting her head higher than in the painting. And then she picked up the fishbowl beside her and drank from it. Agitated, the three goldfish did their best to settle at the bottom of the bowl.

As he listened to the rain Sŏp began to tremble all over. He found the tongs and stirred the brazier, searching in vain for a live coal.

Mae stopped drinking from the fishbowl and shuddered once, then took a stack of pictures from her vanity and tossed them to Sŏp.

"Here, use these."

The pictures were variously landscapes, nudes, and still-lifes. Sŏp tore them up and put them in the brazier. But his matches had gotten wet and the head of the match he struck crumbled without producing a spark.

Mae tossed a box of matches to him.

After Sŏp had started the pictures burning he said, "Could you talk to me about your mother?"

The face beneath the disheveled hair looked up.

"My mother?"

"Times like this, I feel like I can imagine my mother if I hear others talk about their mother."

Mae shuddered all over.

"You mean you never knew your mother? Well, mine was as fat as could be. When she got mad at me she grabbed me by the hair and shook me. When she was happy she used to hug my head, laughing and crying, until her tears got rubbed into my hair. Till it got as wet as it is now. And let's see . . . then she got to where she looked like she was wasting away. Listen to me, coming up on age forty, and here I am talking about my mother! Aren't I ridiculous?"

And then, while pretending to shade her eyes from the smoke issuing from the brazier, she wiped away her tears.

Sŏp, pretending to cough because of the smoke, went back out on the rainy streets.

He felt as if it would rain at any moment, but instead sunlight began to filter through the clouds and stream into the small alleys. Still, it was only a matter of time until he got caught in the rain.

Yŏnhŭi wouldn't be caught in the rain—she'd be in the beer hall by now, fixing her lipstick beneath an electric light. Taehyŏn would have been waiting; he would have arrived first. So even while she was with Sŏp her ultimate intent would have been to see Taehyŏn, and the sooner the better. The record would be playing that song about how sad it is to part at a rainy boat landing. No doubt Taehyŏn would be smoking one of Yŏnhŭi's lipstick-smeared cigarettes. And Yŏnhŭi would be planning her latest version of hide-and-seek with Sŏp. The dice would roll from her hands and from Taehyŏn's. The loser would be obligated to do something.

He turned down an alley and was back in the shadows.

Teacher Song'am's smallish dwelling looked all the more gloomy among the large homes that flanked the way.

Teacher Song'am was out on his veranda painting an iris. Sŏp could tell that the ink had been freshly prepared from the ink stick.

"How are your legs, sir?"

"Arthritic as ever," said Teacher Song'am as he polished the thick lenses of his glasses with hands that resembled bamboo. "I guess it's too much to ask for relief." That's what we get when we get old."

"I went to your exhibition, sir."

"You're too kind."

As Sŏp observed the collar of the traditional jacket worn by this man who was always at his ease, he felt again that his tie was too tight.

"And you, how's your indigestion?"

"It keeps getting worse. By the way, I've decided not to take that teaching position."

"Don't tell me." Squinting and blinking, Teacher Song'am methodically put his glasses back on.

"I don't think someone like me should be teaching the next generation of women."

"You're too modest."

"It's true. I just don't have the confidence. Well, I'll visit again, sir, if it's not an imposition."

And with that Sŏp withdrew from the gaze of the thick lenses.

Squatting to the side of the teacher's small yard, the girl who was his granddaughter, wearing a new school uniform, was transplanting four-o'clocks.

"Could I have one of those?"

The girl acknowledged Sŏp with a nod, then wrapped one of the flowers, dirt clods and all, in a sheet of newspaper and gave it to him.

"Thank you."

Outside the gate to his teacher's home Sŏp cupped the flower in his hands and brought it to his nose. It wasn't an iris, but he felt just then as if the ink lines of his teacher's iris were flowing into his eyes, and the odor of the ink stick wafting into his nose. He decided to leave the flower in the alley. He walked a short distance and looked back at the four-o'clock lying on the ground. Assuming someone picked it up, would that someone nurture it? From somewhere close by, the bugle call of a tofu peddler arced toward him before fading away. A student in her school uniform went past Sŏp, toward the four-o'clock. Would she take good care of it? Sŏp didn't wait to see if the girl would actually pick it up. Instead he turned down another alley and without realizing it began to whistle. It was the same tune Yŏnhŭi had been whistling.

He came to a stop outside Mae's boardinghouse room and whistled that tune. From inside the room came a short whistled response.

Mae, sporting a beret, was sitting next to her brazier, knife in hand, stabbing at the nude painting of herself that used to be on the wall. The part of the painting below the knees was already gone.

"How come you're doing that? Did you get a new one? In place of a modeling fee?"

"I'm not modeling anymore."

Mae tore off the section of the painting between the knees and the waist and then the section between the waist and the chest, and added them to the unlit brazier.

"Can you believe—he's been painting me all this time and then he comes out and says my chest doesn't have any bounce to it and I should turn around so he can paint me from the back. That really irked me. I asked him what he expected from a woman who's had two babies, and then I walked out."

Sŏp kept his eyes on the fishbowl beside her.

"Actually only one baby. And the painter is the father. It was a baby boy. After its hundredth day I abandoned it. I thought about giving it to someone—a gift from Mae—but I ended up leaving it in the park. I knew that someday I'd have had to tell him he was born out of wedlock. Back then the only feeling I had for him was resentment. That painting never, ever made me long for the past. Instead I felt resentful whenever I looked at it. But now that I'm no longer modeling, I feel a mother's love, I pray that my boy is doing well, wherever he is. Strange, isn't it? And that's why I decided to tear up the painting."

The hands tearing up the remainder of the painting were trembling visibly.

A bolt of lightning lit up the window; no thunder followed.

Mae adjusted her beret and rose to her feet.

"Looks like we're in for a shower."

"Why don't you put the fishbowl out in the rain?"

"No, the goldfish might die."

Mae took down her umbrella from the shelf.

The evening sky was like the umbrella, draping the streets with dark clouds.

"Would you tell Yŏnhŭi I'm not going to take that teaching job?"

Mae turned to him.

"It's not that I had other plans."

"So?"

"So, I just didn't feel like doing it."

The ropes that held down the wrinkled hot-air balloon looked like they would hold.

It seemed like the streetlights would never come on.

"You ought to take took care of your indigestion problem before you do anything else," said Mae. The lines on her face were distinct even in the twilight. "What's on your mind, anyway?"

"The fact that you're the mother of a child born out of wedlock."

"And?"

"Those fish you were afraid might die if they're left out in the rain."

"And?"

"A four-o'clock from Teacher Song'am's place that I left in the alley a little while ago, wondering if someone would pick it up and take it home."

"And maybe Yŏnhŭi too? She's a simple-hearted girl. Not a good match for someone like Taehyŏn."

"Neither of which is necessarily related to her being happy."

"Still, if you really loved her, you'd feel she was important enough to rescue."

"It's a fact that I love her, but she's free to find happiness on her own."

Sŏp came to a stop where the alley to Mae's bar branched off.

"I guess I'll be on my way."

"All right, then. Stop by again."

The passing rain beat a cold tattoo on the hand Sŏp raised in farewell.

THE OFFERING

The rooster was old, its neck bare and red. Only its tail and wing joints still bore feathers, but they lacked a healthy sheen. Its swarthy comb was shrunken and lifeless. The boy no longer beckoned it outside the gate, and so the rooster spent all its time in the yard, following the boy around on tottering legs and blunted feet. When the boy was away, the rooster was content to doze in the shade.

One day the boy and the rooster were resting in the shade. The boy ran his hand down the old rooster's neck and stroked the red flesh of its back, which was increasingly bare of feathers. The rooster had not been petted for some time and it responded with a shudder of its wings.

Just then the village headman happened along. That rooster ought to be slaughtered and eaten, he told the boy; and the sooner the better—otherwise it would turn into a snake. The boy jerked his hand away from the rooster's neck. Frowning, the headman said he reckoned the rooster couldn't crow any longer, and didn't its neck look just like the midsection of a snake? With that he walked off, hands clasped behind his back in gentlemanly fashion.

The boy took a long look at the rooster's neck and then gazed up toward the eaves, beneath which was a swallow's nest. A few days earlier, screeching from the swallows had brought the boy outside, where he saw a snake coiling its way up the pillar, the nest in its sights. The boy's father had hacked at the snake with a plowshare, killing it. Now the nest was silent, the grown-up swallows having flown off to gather food and only the yellow beaks of the baby birds showing.

The boy looked down again at the rooster's neck, thinking that it really did look like the midsection of a snake. No, he thought, shaking his head, he couldn't let this rooster-snake climb up to the swallows' nest. From the corner of the yard he fetched a length of straw rope, and then he beckoned the rooster. Responding to this rare opportunity, the rooster followed the boy outside on its tottering legs.

The boy and the rooster arrived at a reed field beyond the village. More than one villager had reported that a large snake lived there. And quite a few said they had seen the snake floating down the monsoon-swollen river laden with dark red silt before slithering into the reeds. On cloudy nights the grown-ups would tell the children it was the snake making the gurgling sound that could be heard from the direction of the field. And in late autumn where the reeds had been cut there would appear a large hole where the snake was supposed to live. It was believed that the snake would come out of its hole if a mixture of horse dung and water was poured down it, but the children had never seen the grown-ups actually do this. The boy was thinking the snake might have crawled out of its hole at the onset of spring and be coiled up somewhere in the reed field. He now entered the field with the rooster in tow, spreading the reeds apart with his hands.

The boy came to a stop at a place where the reeds had been broken off at their base. A red pigtail ribbon lay there. It belonged to the great-granddaughter of the village head. For some time she had been meeting the nephew of the village teacher there. The boy began to wind the length of rope about the rooster's neck.

At first the rooster seemed to sense that the boy was petting it again, and it responded with a shudder of its wings. But when the boy tightened the rope, the rooster flapped its wings once, then grew still. Leaving the dead rooster beside the ribbon, the boy plunged back out through the tangle of reeds.

Breathlessly the boy ran home. There he rubbed his face against the pillar beneath the swallows' nest and began to cry. He cried till the sun began its westward slant. When his parents returned from the fields and saw how pale his face was, their initial surprise turned to fear.

From that day on the boy kept to his bed. His parents tried various approaches, wanting to know if he was sick; the boy merely shook his head no. But he seemed easily startled, and he kept his face covered with his little palms and trembled. And sometimes he opened the door wide and gazed at the nest where the baby swallows were squawking as they were fed. The boy grew thinner from one day to the next.

The village head paid a visit. He asked what had become of the rooster, if they had slaughtered and eaten it, examining with his crusty eyes the corner of the yard. The boy's parents replied that they weren't sure, but the rooster hadn't been seen for several days now, and they turned reassuringly to the boy. He had seen this coming, said the headman; the old rooster had turned into a snake and exposed the boy to its poisonous vapor, and that was why the boy was sick in bed. In a fearful voice the boy's mother asked what was to be done, then declared that no good was to come from keeping an old rooster around. And concealing her face with the hem of her skirt, she began silently to weep. The boy's father muttered something to his wife about being carried away by superstition. But he too wore an uneasy frown.

The headman sent the boy's parents outside, then asked one of the boy's uncles to fetch him a branch from a peach tree. The headman lit his pipe, sucked on it forcefully, and began to blow smoke in the boy's face. The boy reacted by thrashing his head from side to side, eyes shut and coughing. The headman explained that the snake's poisonous vapor inside the boy could not tolerate the smoke, and he continued the treatment, following the boy's turning head. The boy began to gasp for breath and when it seemed he might faint, the headman stopped blowing smoke in his face and instead directed the uncle to whip the boy with the switch from the peach tree. When the boy began to squirm in response to the whipping, the headman explained that the poisonous vapor of the snake had been frightened into submission by the smoke but was now momentarily awakened.

In no time the boy's slender body was black and blue. Outside, the boy's parents flinched and shuddered at every blow they heard.

The village teacher overheard the onlookers saying that the village head was using tobacco smoke to release the snake vapor. He went inside where the boy lay and had the headman and uncle stand aside. The boy was panting, his eyes still closed. The teacher began to perform acupuncture on the boy's forehead and the furrow of his upper lip. By now the boy's mother had returned and was crouching

beside them. She dabbed with the hem of her skirt at the blood on
the boy's forehead and beneath his nose. When the boy opened his
eyes she seemed both happy and amazed, and once more began silently to weep. The boy's father had returned as well; he brought his
face close to the boy's and asked if the boy knew who he was. The
boy nodded, scanned the surrounding villagers, then lifted his gaze
to the swallows' nest beneath the eaves and asked in a feeble voice
when the baby swallows were going to start flying. The boy was raving, said his mother, and on and on she wept. The headman puffed
continuously on his acrid-smelling pipe. What was this silly business
with the needles supposed to prove? he muttered.

The boy continued to grow more emaciated by the day. His parents consulted this person and that and tried various medications,
but the boy's symptoms continued, the occasional startling behavior
and his covering his face with his hand and trembling.

One day when the five baby swallows were fully grown and were
poking their heads outside the nest awaiting food, and when the
boy's parents were out in the fields, the boy got out of bed and went
outside. Hobbling like the old rooster used to, he went out beyond
the village to the reed field. Tassels had begun to appear on the reeds.
Ignoring the lush reeds that scraped at his neck and the backs of his
hands, he arrived at the place where he had strangled and disposed
of the rooster. Only when he saw the old rooster with the straw rope
still about its neck did an expression of relief light up his wan face.
But he was too weakened to stand longer, and the next instant he
collapsed on the spot.

The rooster's breast and the area beneath its wings were crawling
with maggots. Blowflies lit on the boy's face before moving to the
decomposing rooster.

The boy's home was in an uproar. The villagers had gathered, but
none of them had seen the boy. The headman was among them, and
he declared that the boy had likely fallen into the pond on the other
side of the hill. This hill faced the reed field, and one had to cross it
to get to the pond. The thick layer of scum that grew on the water's
surface always bore a dark rust color. It was the consensus of the village grown-ups that buried in the muck at the bottom of the pond

was a mudfish that was turning into a dragon. The pond was always decidedly calm, except when a shower swept in, and then the drumming of the rain on the stolid lotus leaves was louder than it was on the leaves of the poplars across the hill in the village. On one such rainy day the body of a girl had been discovered floating in the pond, white belly exposed for all the world to see. This girl had left home a few days earlier to forage for greens and had not been seen since. The village head had had an explanation: the girl had been bewitched by the mudfish that was turning into a dragon. It was rumored about the village that on rainy nights the girl could be heard wailing as she did laundry at the edge of the pond. The ghost of the girl must be lonely and had no doubt lured the boy into the pond, declared the headman; the mudfish turning into a dragon had had nothing to do with it. Maybe so, the villagers responded, their heads nodding.

The village adults set out, each with a pole, the boy's father among them, and rushed to the pond. The boy's mother declared that she too would throw herself into the pond, and was barely restrained by her sister and the other housewives of the village. Whereupon the mother fell onto the shoulder of another woman and began to wail.

Just then the teacher arrived, and hearing that the villagers had rushed off for the pond, he asked how it was possible for the boy in his weakened state to have gone that far. Gathering those of the village youths who had stayed behind, he began to scour the village itself for the boy. One of the youths moved gradually out from the village and discovered in the reed field a trail of recently broken reeds. He made his way there and found the boy.

The boy's mother was the next to arrive. She took the boy in her arms and broke into sobs. The boy had opened his eyes, and his aunt asked if he knew where he was. The boy managed to nod, then turned his gaze to the decomposing rooster beside him.

By now the maggots swarming over the rooster were crawling about the faded pigtail ribbon that had belonged to the village head's great-granddaughter. Starting the day after the boy had strangled the rooster in the reed field, she and the teacher's nephew had moved their trysting place to the tile kiln beside the path that led over the hill to the pond. The teacher now took hold of the length of rope and the rooster's head came free at the neck where the rope had been knotted. Startled, the boy buried his face in his mother's bosom, trembling all over.

Back at the boy's home, the teacher stated his belief that the boy's illness was the result of the death of his pet rooster, compounded by the fact that he had strangled it in the reed field. The boy would get well if he were given another rooster. Presently the boy's maternal uncle set off past the tile kiln and around the pond to the local market and returned with a large speckled rooster in his arms. The rooster stretched out its neck and crowed. But the boy gave only a single look to the rooster with its red comb, before rolling over to gaze up at the swallows' nest beneath the eaves and ask when the baby swallows were going to be able to fly. The boy was raving again, said his mother. Taking the edge of her skirt in her mouth, she began her silent weeping.

All along, the village head sucked on his acrid-smelling pipe. What did that teacher fellow think he knew, talking the way he did? he muttered.

The boy continued to waste away, concealing his face behind his small hands when he was startled, and trembling all over. Meanwhile, on a night of dense fog, the village head's great-granddaughter and the teacher's nephew ran away together. The village head said he had never in his life been so humiliated, and what was so vexing was that she had run off with a no-good like the teacher's nephew. For some time he didn't appear outside his door. And then one day he made the rounds of the village, hands clasped behind his back, and let it be known that perhaps his great-granddaughter had done the right thing after all, for she had not forgotten to send her great-grandpa a set of winter clothes. No one, though, had actually seen the village head receive this new set of clothing.

Beyond the village the reeds blossomed white, and the day arrived when the five baby swallows took wing for the first time. A smile filled the boy's face as he looked out at the swallows. Seeing this, the boy's parents and aunt cried out that it was the boy's last smile, and they burst into tears.

THE GARDENER

It never failed. Once again he had placed the pork-blood sausage before his wife in her sickbed and once again she had closed her despairing eyes and begun to retch. He pitied her for having to retch at the mere sight of what she wanted to eat, but then again, wasn't it a good thing if foods that were bad for her peritonitis nauseated her before they touched her lips? As he looked down now at his wife retching and turning onto her side, he realized that the reason he had indiscriminately bought everything she wanted was that he knew in advance she would retch and couldn't eat them. When he asked himself if he did this out of reluctance to say no to someone who couldn't tell when her days might come to an end, he realized as well that the dizziness overcoming him these days whenever he was confronted with the prospect of his wife's death was making it impossible for him to linger at her bedside.

He went to the room he occupied, which was cooler, being farther from the firebox; he drew close his thick dictionary and lay down, using it as a pillow. When he had sufficiently composed himself he leafed through the travel guide beside him, thinking that he and his wife would take a trip somewhere once she was healthy enough to eat at least some of the foods she said she wanted. A quiet temple would be preferable, however attractive a hot springs or a seaside resort might be. The temple they had visited not long after they became acquainted seemed just fine. And then his eye came to rest on the arrival and departure times at a small train station he had never heard of. He had the illusion of boarding a train and traveling past a nameless expanse, and thought he would lay the travel guide aside, but at the same time he didn't want to lift a finger, and in the end he drifted out of wakefulness with the book resting on his chest.

Sleep was accompanied by the sensation of a weight on his chest different from the weight of the travel guide, and he was awakened by the maid's voice from beyond the paper-paneled door calling "Here, kitty, kitty." There on his chest lay a kitten. Startled, he pushed it off. The door slid open and the maid's hand grabbed the kitten by its midsection. He asked what the kitten was doing there and was told it had shown up a short time earlier from somewhere or other. The kitten's eyes left the hand that held it and shone now in his direction. Before he realized it he had met the kitten's gaze with a scowl.

The still-cold autumn wind gusted from time to time in their small yard. From the room where his wife lay ill came the voice of the maid exclaiming at how well the cat ate—"I'll bet you've never tried pork-blood sausage"—leading him to believe she was feeding sausage to the cat. He went outside to the pigeon cage and inspected the female, sitting on her eggs, and the male beside her. As he shut the door to the cage, he told himself he had to make sure to keep the door shut tight now that the cat was there.

His wife, it was clear, had developed a special attachment to these pigeons, which her family had given her as a possible diversion in her time of illness, and by now she could tell from the male's cooing whether the female was there beside him—a more plaintive cooing if not—and could even imitate the male's cooing in each case. And since her surgery she had grown sensitive in the extreme to direct sunlight. Even the reflection from surfaces such as the pigeons' wings was so strong that she kept the curtains lowered most of the time. But at night she kept the lights on, and the bulbs were of exceedingly high wattage.

Even now he could hear his wife in the next room, asking the maid to turn the lights down. The maid grumbled in response that she could do nothing, being as short as she was, and then she declared that the luck of the household would take a turn for the better now that the cat was here. Wasn't it supposed to be bad if animals appeared at a house? his wife asked. No, said the maid; it was bad if the family dog went off somewhere, but good if an animal joined a family. She proceeded to tell a story: in the house where she had worked before, there was a normal, healthy boy who had a puppy. One day the puppy disappeared, and then for some unknown reason the boy developed an illness that caused him to foam at the mouth every night. Ample medication was given, but the boy didn't improve. And then one day someone polishing his shoes happened to look under the shoe ledge and found the puppy's baked carcass inside one of the floor-heating flues. Once the puppy was removed, the boy miraculously recovered.

Hearing these words as he lay in his room, he feared they would irritate his wife, and this in turn displeased him. Suddenly his wife shouted in disgust, telling the maid to get the cat away from the bedpan. The thought that his wife had been needlessly upset because of the cat reignited his anger at the animal. He could hear the maid saying that the cat wasn't used to luxury, and so instead of finishing its rice and soup it had found something filthy to feed on.

The next morning he was preparing to take the thermometer to his wife in the next room when he noticed the kitten sticking its head through a hole in the rice-paper panel at the bottom of the sliding door. He hadn't realized the previous evening how absolutely filthy the kitten was. Its white fur was sprinkled with dark spots, and the white was so dirty it was almost as dark as the spots. He gave the kitten a fierce scowl but left it alone for the time being, head still poking through the hole in the door, and went into his wife's sickroom.

He inserted the thermometer in his wife's mouth and took her pulse. He had a bad feeling, and not for the first time. Her pulse felt faster than the previous day, but also weaker, and then his fingertips lost it altogether. He tried again, this time following the second hand on his wristwatch, but in doing so he lost count. The next time he finally succeeded; her pulse was over a hundred. Anxiously he removed the thermometer from her mouth. Ninety-six. He shook the thermometer. Then, on the chart he kept there, he jotted down her normal temperature as well as a pulse count quite a bit lower than what he had just measured.

Unknown to his wife, he kept a separate chart with accurate figures. Those figures suggested to him that it wouldn't be long before she would need a second surgery. But there seemed no way she could tolerate another operation, and with this thought in mind he turned toward his room, only to discover the kitten licking the mouth of an overturned milk bottle with its slender red tongue. He kicked the kitten, not that hard but enough to send it bumping up against the wall, and when the creature produced a short, sharp yowl he could scarcely convince himself that it was not his wife who had made the sound. The maid happened by and he scolded her, saying that if she intended to keep the kitten the least she could do was keep it clean. The maid responded that she had already bathed the kitten twice, and that once spring arrived, it would naturally shed, and its new coat of fur would be lovely.

The sunlight streaming down outside resembled the lovely fur of a cat.

One evening he was about to close the door to the pigeon cage when he noticed that only the female was there, sitting on its eggs; the male was nowhere to be seen. Wondering why it hadn't returned, he looked around outside but didn't see it. The male liked to perch between the curved roof tiles of the house next door and take in the last rays of the setting sun, but there was no trace of sunlight there now. He decided to look for the pigeon at his in-laws' home.

By the time he arrived there, the sun was down and it was difficult to tell one pigeon from another. His mother-in-law nevertheless peered into each of the cages, but it appeared that none of them contained his male. When she was finished she turned to him and asked about her daughter's condition. She was about the same, he answered, whereupon his mother-in-law said that she had been meaning to pay a visit but just hadn't gotten around to it yet. Knowing that his wife's brother had been leading a dissipated life of late, he allowed as how he didn't think there was much she could do by visiting just then. Before leaving he inspected the pigeons asleep outside the cage, but his Motley Fool (the name for a black-and-white-speckled pigeon) was not to be seen.

Nor was the male pigeon back in its cage when he returned home. As he peered through the gloom at the female sitting on the eggs, it cooed briefly in his direction. Finally he closed the door to the cage. He hoped his wife wouldn't learn of the male's disappearance. Or that the male would return to them first.

One day he noticed indications of constipation in his wife's stool and told himself the time had come for her next operation. Despite his uneasiness, he left to buy the beef liver she had said she wanted. When he returned, she was looking outside through the open curtains. Where had the male pigeon gone? Not wanting to agitate her, he replied nonchalantly that it was probably gathering food. She asked if the male had been there when he closed the door to the cage the previous evening; her face had an unaccustomed flush to it. He felt compelled to say yes. His wife said it was no good for the eggs if the male was gone; how could the female possibly do it all by herself? He shook his head vigorously in an attempt to allay her fears and replied that if it was the male that was by itself it would not sit on the eggs, but the female by itself would sit on the eggs until they hatched. Which was the best he could do to answer the question, since he didn't know for sure. His wife heaved a sigh of apparent relief, then said that in any event the male might be at her family's home, and she asked him to visit.

Off again he went to his in-laws' house, thinking optimistically that on his previous visit their pigeon may actually have been there, indistinguishable in the darkness, or that if it had gone elsewhere it might then have returned to his in-laws', preferring its previous home to their own.

But when he arrived he was surprised to see not a bird in sight on the roof, where normally pairs of pigeons would have been gathered. Had they all left to find food? But then his mother-in-law appeared, her face haggard, to say that her son was so dissolute these days he was eating a couple of pairs of pigeons a day as a drinking snack. So much for finding their pigeon, he told himself as he went to inspect a cage from which he could hear cooing. His mother-in-law explained that only one pair of pigeons remained, and she had prevailed with her son to spare them because they had just produced a young one, but for all she knew, he would end up taking them as well. A door slid open and the son's wife emerged from inside. When a child tried to follow, she pushed it back inside in annoyance and roughly slid the door shut. No doubt their pigeon had fallen into the hands of his brother-in-law, he thought as he left to the squalling of the child.

His wife was still waiting at the opened curtains when he returned. Uneasily she read his expression. He couldn't help silently shaking his head. His wife closed her tear-filled eyes. He was just about to return to his room, thankful that his wife hadn't inquired about her family, when she asked how her mother was; her eyes remained closed. She was in good health, he replied, and would shortly be paying them a visit. Perhaps her elder brother was vexing their mother less these days, she murmured. He called to mind the squalling of the child and the presence of the baby pigeon, and felt a chill along his spine. Yes, that appeared to be the case, he mumbled as if he were talking to himself.

From the next room he heard the maid enter his wife's sickroom. From the way she was calling the kitten, it sounded as if she intended to feed it the liver he had bought that day.

That evening he heard the maid enter his wife's sickroom, turn the light on, and say that the damned kitten had gone off somewhere. Where could it be? his wife asked; she had seen it only a little while ago licking the milk bottle. From his room he told them the kitten wasn't there either. To which his wife responded in a tone of concern that she was afraid it would starve if it went wandering, because it was still a kitten. The maid shot back that this kitten never missed an opportunity to feed itself, and there was no doubt in her mind that it would always be a stray. Then she lowered her voice and said that as long as the cat was gone she might as well say that in fact it was *not* a good thing for a cat to move into a house, so she had fed it the worst-smelling food she could to make it leave, and then it would have to fend for itself. His wife then asked, almost as an afterthought, if in that case the pigeon's leaving was a good thing or a bad thing. The maid replied in a louder than necessary voice that she didn't know, and then she laughed. His wife asked if the kitten had eaten the pigeon. Maybe so, said the maid, but even if it hadn't, it was a blessing that the kitten had left when there was still one pigeon remaining.

The thought of his brother-in-law capturing their pigeon, and the image of the lone pair of pigeons and their hatchling, rose in his mind, and in an effort to dismiss them he turned over onto his side. He hoped now that his brother-in-law hadn't taken the pigeon, and that instead the kitten had eaten it.

More frequently now, his wife opened the curtains during the day. She fell into the habit of gazing at length into the cage once occupied by the male pigeon. Her sunken cheeks and despairing eyes were paler now than when she had kept the curtains drawn, and if laundry happened to rustle in the breeze, she would startle and ask if the male pigeon had returned.

If his wife but heard the sound of a dish breaking in the kitchen, she would summon the maid in a voice loud enough to make him wonder where she mustered the strength, and have her fetch the broken pieces so she could try to put them back together. The maid would reply that the dish already had a crack in it when she had started to work there, and even gentle contact with the dishwashing basin was enough to break it. His wife would continue to fit the pieces back together and pass her hand over the design, saying there was no other dish quite like it in its flawlessness and its lovely pattern, and from the time the two of them had set up housekeeping at the foot of the mountain it had been a dish that was dear to her frugal heart, and that that period when they had first lived together, footloose in the hills, had been the happiest of her life, and her eyes would fill with tears, as if the future were as dark and gloomy as the reality of the broken dish that she would not allow to leave her hand.

He was tempted to scold the maid but realized that to do so would only chafe his wife's nerves all the more. Instead he suggested that once she was a little better they could go to the mountain to look at the flowers. But he sensed that this prospect no longer appealed to her. Picking up the vase at the head of her bedding as if to smell the flowers, she abruptly told the maid, who was standing off to the side, to move the vase farther away. It appeared his wife had declined to the extent that she could not even enjoy the scent of the tulips. But then she asked the maid to put some aspirin in the vase. The maid did so and then, as if she had forgotten about the dish she had just broken, she muttered that aspirin was for colds and maybe the flowers were withering because they too had caught a cold. With a smile that seemed more drawn than the desiccated petals of the tulips, his wife brought her weepy gaze to rest on the maid's broad back. This pained him, and he was preparing to go out when his wife reminded him of the seed they had gotten from last year's flowers and asked him to plant it on time this year, as he had the previous year.

In fact the season for flower seeding had arrived before he was aware of it.

Later that day, he went out to buy the chicken liver that his wife had said she wanted. Just outside the short, narrow alley to their home he caught sight of a boy who, upon seeing him, immediately hid his hands behind his back. Seeing that it was a pigeon the boy was attempting to conceal, he quickly approached. The boy retreated several steps and released the pigeon into the air.

A presentiment came over him, and he demanded that the boy produce their pigeon. The boy backed off another step, saying he didn't know anything. All he wanted to know was where their pigeon was, he told the boy. His large eyes blinking, the boy said he knew the family that had captured their pigeon. He himself had no doubt that the boy had taken it, just as he had taken this pigeon now, and he watched as the bird made a gradual ascending circle and headed south before descending and finally going out of sight among the roofs. He followed the boy toward the neighborhood to the south where the pigeon had disappeared.

They arrived at a house on whose thatched roof a pigeon perched, perhaps the one released by the boy, a dirty Typesetter (a white pigeon with dark spots on its head). Circling and cooing next to it was a dirty Blood Clot (a pigeon the color of red beans). Arrayed along a low wall in the yard were cages of pigeons. From among the cages emerged a huge man who looked down silently at the boy. The boy said, "Motley Fool," and indicated him. The man went to a cage, opened it, put in a hand, and drew out a pigeon by the head. Its feathers were dirty but it was clearly their male. The man demanded one *wŏn* for having fed the pigeon during this time. Taken aback, he nevertheless paid, thinking as he did so that each of the cages contained pigeons who had suffered the same fate as their male, which made the huge man before him appear all the more repellent. On his way home, this sentiment was transferred to the pigeon. Over and over his grip would tighten until the bird opened its beak.

Back at home his wife received the pigeon with an expression both happy and tearful. But when she attempted to bring it close to her cheek, the bird squirmed away. Relieving her of the pigeon, he brought it against her cheek. She remarked at how dirty its feathers were, then said to the pigeon that she was glad to see it safely returned and that it mustn't go off again.

He handed the pigeon to the maid beside him and began removing its wing feathers. Each plucked feather brought a look of surprise from his wife. Leaving half the feathers of its other wing intact, he released the pigeon outside. Tilting to the side whose wing had lost more feathers, it flew at an angle and barely made it inside the cage, where it commenced cooing. Suddenly the reality of what he had just done hit him, and when the maid declared that the pigeon wouldn't be flying off anywhere now, he shouted at her to dispose of the feathers. And when the maid had gathered the scattered feathers, he told her not to put them in the firebox but to get rid of them.

For a time his wife looked out at the pigeon cage, from which cooing could still be heard, before remarking that the male, left by itself while the female sat on the eggs, must have followed another pigeon off somewhere. And then she said to him that he was looking worn out from staying by the side of his sick wife, and urged him to go visit one of his favorite teahouses. And then she murmured, seemingly to herself, that she wouldn't feel bored or frightened if she were by herself.

For the first time in a long while he was at a teahouse, listening to a record and relaxing. His eyes came to rest on the package of chicken livers he had bought. The sight of the bloody paper wrapper gave him the incongruous thought that something had gone wrong with his wife's body, and hurriedly he left.

He realized that his wife's mention of not being bored or frightened if she were by herself indicated a presentiment of her own death. He grew dizzy at this thought. If the end came to his wife, then the moment would soon come when he would forget her, even if just for an instant. His legs trembled.

On the day they decided that a day or two later his wife would have another operation, he was turning over the earth in their flower garden. As he removed pebbles from the soil and broke up clods of dirt, the odor of earth moistened by winter snow and spring rain made his head swim. He squatted in a ball and without realizing it kept crushing the soil between his fingers, even though he had already broken up all the clods.

Only when the maid emerged with the bedpan from his wife's room did he straighten up. His wife had been given an enema, and as he inspected the stool with a branch from the previous autumn's chrysanthemums he made up his mind that she had to have the surgery the following day. He entered his wife's room hoping that this operation would proceed without complications.

To his surprise, his wife was sitting up and applying makeup. And she was wearing the pink traditional jacket she had worn back when they had lived such a healthy life at the foot of the mountain. She was too weak to hold the hand mirror up, so she rested it on her knee. She brought her face close and applied powder around her eyes, but the dark rings just wouldn't go away.

He observed his wife's meticulously combed but lusterless hair—the maid had no doubt done the combing. But why hadn't that infernal maid told him that his wife was sitting up? In spite of his anger, he merely asked his wife where she had put the seed from the previous year's flowers. A twinkle appeared in her despairing eyes as she remarked that she should be the one to plant the seed this year, but he should get seed from this year's flowers before the hard frosts of autumn and remember to plant it next year around the same time as now. Suddenly he had a bad feeling about the following day's operation. Too dizzy to stand there any longer, he disappeared outside.

The small flower bed with the turned-up dark red earth received a fair amount of sunlight, producing heat shimmers that made him even dizzier.

But he had to help bring his wife outside, and back indoors he went.

AUTUMN WITH PIANO

A man is kneeling on a packed trunk, trying to close it. The door opens and there stands a woman.

The man looks up.

—What's going on?

—Scared you, didn't I?

—Your color's not good.

The woman sits down at the piano.

—Did something happen? I thought we decided to meet at the station.

—Don't tell me you just finished packing. I was ready a long time ago.

—The train leaves at ten forty-four, so we've still got an hour or so.

—True, but we'll need twenty minutes to get to the station if we don't want to hurry.

—Why is your face so pale?

—Maybe because I was walking into the wind.

—Or because something's wrong with you.

—Kuhyŏn!

—Yes?

—Play the "Funeral March Sonata" for me.

—The "Funeral March Sonata"?

—Yes. Chopin.

—Why now?

—Because we're going away and I won't be able to hear you play it anymore. You know, the first time I heard you, that was the piece you played. And now that we're leaving for a new life I want to hear it again. It's still fresh in my mind, that spring evening when the skies had cleared after several days of carefree rain. My husband was all wrapped up in his law exams. I made him some coffee but he didn't pay any attention when I served it—just stuck his tired face up over the book he was leafing through. I added some sugar cubes, stirred, and set the coffee within close reach. He finally took a sip, but then his eyes went straight back to his book. He's never once said that it's too strong, too weak, or just right. And it makes no difference if I add cream—he doesn't say anything. And that's exactly what our marriage is like. We're not affectionate toward each other and we're not hateful toward each other. My husband never interferes in what I do. And he's not concerned about things like the color of my clothes. You might think that's a comfortable way to live, but I *so* wanted some excitement, even if it meant being hateful toward each other when we actually felt that way. And that day, I thought of pestering him to go to the pines out back or down to the river—it would have been relaxing for him—but I gave up. I'm sure he wouldn't have refused if I'd suggested it, but I don't think he'd have taken any pleasure from it. So I took the empty coffee cup, and then who should show up but Nan? She said, let's go to a concert. I didn't hesitate for a second. I was feeling down in the dumps, and at the prospect of being with cheerful Nan, well, I just followed her out, I didn't care if it was to a concert or what. On the way she told me it was a piano recital by her boyfriend. Your recital, Kuhyŏn. By the time we arrived, you were already playing. The "Funeral March Sonata." The place was full but we somehow managed to find seats, and from that point on I just listened to the piano. I couldn't have told you how well or how poorly you played—all I remembered was the rapture of the sound and my heart pounding as it hadn't pounded in ages. The soprano who came out later in the program had a plaintive presence, but I found her voice too cold and sharp. Nan was terribly sorry she couldn't sing that night—she had a cold, remember? That's Nan for you— I swear, she was born with charm. On our way home, she kept promising she'd get you to treat us on account of your successful performance. Every time she said this I thought, well, the next time I go to Nan's I'll probably see him there. Kind of a shocking thought, actually.

—You know, Chongsuk, when I first met you that time at Nan's, I had an illusion that you were one of the sculptures. And when Nan introduced you as the wife of a future lawyer, I was jealous of your husband even though I'd never seen him before. It was the first time I'd ever felt that way.

—And you know, when Nan mentioned the word "future," it seemed she was emphasizing it, and I had to remind myself that I was the wife of a future lawyer. The next moment I felt like laughing, but I managed to contain myself.

—The three of us played Catch the Joker that night, didn't we? And I got stuck with the joker, and that brought you and me closer together. So close I forgot you were someone's wife.

—And didn't that make us what we are today? Yes, Nan was the first one out of the game, and then the joker was passing between you and me. Perhaps our relationship would have turned out differently if I'd been stuck with it. Or if we had done as Nan suggested, and you had taken us out for coffee as a penalty when *you* got stuck with it. We had just walked out the door when I said, let's make him play the "Funeral March Sonata" for us instead, remember? You can't imagine how my chest was throbbing when I said that. And how thankful I was when Nan clapped her hands together and said, "Yes!" And so we came straight here. As soon as we arrived, Nan marched in as if she owned the place, opening the curtains, lifting the piano lid—wasn't she a whirlwind? She started playing and I told myself, here comes Massenet's "Elegy," but then she started fussing with the wrapping she'd had around her throat ever since the recital, because of her cold, and she never did sing it—instead she convinced you to play the "Funeral March Sonata." I was standing in the dark blue shadow of the piano, and strangely enough I began to feel jealous of Nan— though I didn't realize it at first. And then Nan looked back and forth between us and said that I was quite the alto back when we were in school. If I had still been a schoolgirl then, I would have scowled at Nan or gone up and pinched her, but this was different—my ears were burning and I couldn't even look at her. You were at the piano by then and I asked you to play the "Elegy" and not the "Funeral March Sonata." Why? Nan protested, and I said I simply had an urge to hear it. The truth was, I'd already decided that I would listen to you play the "Funeral March Sonata" when I was here by myself. And after that I started coming here without telling Nan.

—I was jealous myself, Chongsuk, and when you told me you had a young child, I felt jealous of her too for a time. Do you remember that summer day when we went up in the hills? That's when you told me. I was surprised, but eventually it passed— how could I be jealous of that girl who held a portion of your love? There was a boy, maybe nine or so, sitting at the foot of a pine tree right in front of where we were sitting; he was sketching a shade tree. Standing next to him was a girl who might have been his younger sister, licking an ice cream and gazing at the sketch. Of course it was the kind of sketch a child would do. The trunk was impossibly straight, there were only a few branches—as if someone had done a sloppy job of pruning it—and the leaves were overly detailed; and the bird perched on one of the branches was as big as the tree trunk. The boy stopped for a moment and looked at the girl, and the girl brought the ice cream up to the boy's chin. The boy stuck his tongue way out and took what was left of the ice cream into his mouth. As I watched this beautiful scene I began to feel happy, but then the face of your child, which I had never seen before, superimposed itself on the face of the girl, and that upset me for some reason. And then you said you were in the mood for ice cream yourself, and I tried to compose myself by running down that rather steep slope; I didn't realize how hot it was. When I returned with the ice cream the boy was drawing a likeness of his sister. And my, those eyes he drew were twice as big as the mouth! But there again, as I watched I also drew in my mind your child, with eyes that would be large like yours, but I took no pleasure from it. That was how much I wanted then to have you for myself.

—But as far as I was concerned, my relationship with my daughter was the same as my relationship with my husband. Maybe even worse. The girl still thinks the nanny who used to nurse her is her mother. Well, it *does* make sense. There was a time when I practically forgot I had actually given birth to her. I guess our nanny always reminded her that I was her mother, but she never called me that, not once. When I left home just now, I wanted to give her one last hug. But I didn't feel like a mother who was about to hug her own daughter; rather, I was going to hug a girl who happened to live in the same house. And guess what? The moment I put my arms out, she flinched and drew back, her eyes wide with surprise, and she shouted, "Mom, you're scary!" Before I knew it I'd pushed her away from me as hard as I could. Mom scaring her—the very idea! She tumbled to the floor and starting crying. That was the first time she ever referred to me as her mother—when she was scared of me—and as I looked down at her it occurred to me just how frightening my face must have been, and I shuddered all over. I told myself that maybe a woman who's a frightening mother and a frightening wife should be dead. But then I heard a voice inside me asking, are you so unhappy that you would kill yourself? Well, I didn't kill myself. And I didn't cry. I took one last look as I was leaving the house, and what do you think I saw? This girl whose eyes had been overflowing with tears had fallen asleep with the tears still wet on her face. I pulled up her quilt and tucked her in. And I tried to forget that I was dealing with my own daughter and just prayed she wouldn't grow up to be a frightening mother and a frightening wife. And I have no regrets about the first time you took my hand in yours. And I don't regret that time you threw your metronome at the mirror on the wall where my face was reflected—it must have been as frightening then as it was just now at home. Do you remember that time I asked you if maybe Nan was too wrapped up with the piano? Didn't you reply that you and Nan were so wrapped up with each other that you had almost forgotten that you were a man and she was a woman? Even though it was beyond me to understand such a relationship, your words by themselves gave me satisfaction. In truth, that was the happiest time.

—But it's from now on that we'll have *true* happiness. Isn't that why we're leaving? Everything in the past we have to bury. Even the small happinesses we had then. Plans for a new life await us now.

—Last night when we were walking those unfamiliar back streets and you decided we should go to a mountain village, my heart thrilled for the first time in ages. But hadn't we already made up our minds long ago? We were able to walk with assurance down those dark, windy streets—imagine. But then we left for a main street, and we heard that drum and bugle commotion and knew there must have been a circus nearby. We were drawn toward that sound and we came up to an old tent flapping in the wind, and outside it a cage with a monkey hunched up to keep warm, waiting for people to throw it peanuts or something. We weren't that excited, but somehow we ended up going inside. That was when the horse was jumping through the ring of fire. Next to the ring stood a girl dressed in red holding a long whip, and every time the horse was about to jump through the ring she cracked the whip, making it look as if she were whipping the horse. Close up we could see that the old horse was hobbling and the red color of the girl's clothes was faded. The drum and bugle played a sad song that used to be popular at one time. I was sorry we had gone in. The horse went off, hobbling even more. Another girl came out, lay down on her back, and began spinning a large vase with her feet. Whether it was upright or on its side, she moved the vase around as easily as if it were a ball. And then she stopped spinning the vase— maybe she wanted to rest her legs—and from the mouth of the vase, which I had thought was empty, there appeared a bony hand— remember? I felt myself tensing up. It was a younger girl, also dressed in faded red, and when she was all the way out of the vase she balanced one slender leg on the rim and spread out her arms. And that's when I got a shock, because that vase that the younger girl was standing on began to turn! Even though she was using her arms to keep her balance, she always looked like she was about to fall off as she switched feet along with the turning of the vase—I couldn't bear to look. The vase came to a stop again and this time the girl placed a hand on the rim and pushed herself up into a handstand. Her face was looking up in our direction, her arms were trembling, and just then I realized she was blind, and before I knew it I had stood up. As we left, you too looked like you were sorry that we weren't in the mood to be inside that circus tent. The young girl must have performed some other trick, because we could hear applause coming from the small crowd—the tent could have held twice as many people. All I felt was a chill down my back. Outside, the monkey was being led back in for the next act. The streetlights weren't on yet, and the wind was still blowing in the darkness. I wondered if because she was blind maybe the girl had less of a feel for how dangerous it was to be doing a handstand like that. The next moment I felt another chill all over. Encountering that blind girl gave me a bad feeling about our departure, and I couldn't bear to think about it.

—Then don't think about it. Once we've left you'll realize it was only a wild notion. Just forget everything. Think instead about our new life. Think about the ripened grain in the fields, the flowers in the hills, and the sky high above us.

—But Kuhyŏn, soon you'll be telling yourself that I'm someone else's wife and mother. And you'll no longer feel jealous of my daughter. You'll tell yourself that I'm someone else's frightening wife and mother. And you'll regret that you threw the metronome and broke the mirror. And I'll end up changed into a frightening woman. Maybe that will be the time for me to kill myself.

—You're awfully pale, Chongsuk. You didn't—

—It's the face of a frightening woman, isn't it?

—You didn't—

—No, I didn't. You needn't worry. I didn't take poison or anything like that. It's just that this frightening woman is exhausted. I want to sleep. So I took some sleeping pills, that's all. While I'm asleep, you decide what we'll do in the future. I was only joking when I talked just now about killing myself. Even if you feel like I'm a frightening woman, I'm not going to kill myself. I mean it. Even if you manage to close that trunk and you leave by yourself for some unknown place, I'm not going to kill myself. First I'd have to ask myself if I'm so happy or unhappy that I would actually do that. When I wake up I'll let my husband know everything. My husband passed the bar exam. But before he takes on the affairs of others, he'll take on his wife's affair. He won't have to lift a finger. Because he can judge it on the basis of simple moral principles. My husband will abandon his frightening wife and start a new living arrangement. And my daughter will forget her frightening mother. And that's as it should be. So while I'm asleep, you make the decisions. You can blame everything on the joker. What time is it?

—Ten ten.

—Then we still have time before the train leaves.

—What's going on? I can't figure you out.

—You can figure me out while I'm sleeping. So may I hear the "Funeral March Sonata" one last time?

—Get yourself together, will you?

—I'm sleepy. Come on, let me hear the "Funeral March Sonata."

With trembling hands the man begins to play. The woman interrupts him before he's half through.

—All right, good. Now let me hear about the new life that's awaiting us at the foot of the mountain. Quick, before I fall asleep.

—Everything's going to be all right. We'll have ourselves a little house in the village there. And in our little house you'll get the rice ready and I'll make the cooking fire. During the day we'll go up in the hills for flowers; we'll bet on who can collect the most. I'll always lose. And when the moon is out at night we'll follow our shadows through the fields. I'll tell you that the shadows of the sheaves of grain are goblins. I'll scare you over and over again telling you those shadows are goblins, and I'll take you in my arms to protect you.

—And the cold wind will blow.

—And I'll wrap you up in my cape.

—And the snow will fall. But if we can make it through the long tedious winter, spring will surely come.

—Yes, we can stay there till spring.

The woman lays her head gently on the keyboard. A dissonant chord sounds and then trails off. The man attempts to lift her. But the woman, her head on the keyboard, slowly shakes her head no and closes her eyes.

MANTIS

One by one the baby rabbits had disappeared, and that morning it seemed the last one was gone as well. Hyŏn could hear his landlady scolding the mother rabbit: maybe a praying mantis could devour its young or its mother, but no mammal, no matter how vicious, would ever gobble up four of its own babies. And then she asked herself out loud why she had ever told Hyŏn he could keep the mother rabbit there until the babies were grown. Hyŏn had bought the rabbit to use at the laboratory, and a few days ago it had spent an entire night pulling fur from its breast, making a nest, and giving birth. Now the landlady was cursing the rabbit. She was probably poking a stick into the hutch again, jabbing the rabbit in the side. Hyŏn then heard the little girl who lived there ask the landlady, whom she called Grandmother, whether eating its babies had made the rabbit's eyes red. "Damn peepers, those damn peepers," she kept saying. It sounded to Hyŏn as if the girl wanted to skewer the rabbit's eyes.

The girl never failed to call the landlady Grandmother while the young lady of the house was away; after the young lady returned she changed to Mother. Whenever Hyŏn asked this little girl her age, she would say "Six" and spread the five fingers of her hand before him.

The only one the girl always called Mother was her doll. She never carried the doll piggyback, as other little girls might have done. When playing house she would make food out of dirt and serve it in broken pieces of porcelain. Bringing the potsherds to the doll's mouth, she would say, "Eat, Mother." This too happened only when the young lady was out.

Whenever the young lady returned, an unfamiliar pair of men's shoes would appear on the narrow veranda outside her downstairs room. The shoes changed in color and size each time. When these unfamiliar shoes appeared, the lives of the little girl and the landlady also changed. The little girl's round face became prim and she would come upstairs, where Hyŏn lived. The landlady's face with all its tiny wrinkles would grow tense. And she would leave for the market in a flurry, basket hanging from her arm. She would still emerge from the smoky kitchen at dinnertime, wiping her eyes with the breast-tie of her *chŏgori*, but unlike other times, she could not cry out that her eyes were smarting. She would quietly finish washing the dishes, then go straight to Hyŏn's room, creeping up the stairs without making a sound. Only when the young lady's room became still did she tiptoe down the stairs with the girl and go to bed in the back room next to the kitchen.

When the landlady came upstairs on such occasions, she would sit silently for a while with her back to Hyŏn. Then she would turn to the glass fishbowl in the corner of the room as if seeing it for the first time. The girl would look at the fishbowl and the landlady for a moment, then start picking at her hangnails. With a look of amazement the landlady would observe how the swimming goldfish became huge or tiny according to its distance from the glass. She would then turn her eyes to the girl as if to draw her attention to the fishbowl. But the girl never looked back toward the bowl, although she would gaze upon it with great joy when the young lady was out.

When the young lady was away and the girl came upstairs to Hyŏn's room, the first thing she did was go to the fishbowl. The goldfish, which usually was swimming in one place slowly moving its fins, became skittish and started swimming back and forth. When it settled down again, the girl would catch a fly and place it on the surface of the water. The first time she did this, Hyŏn told her not to feed the goldfish such filthy things. The goldfish darted to the surface and nibbled at the twitching fly, descended, and returned to nibble again, but never swallowed it. The less the fly twitched, the less the fish would nibble at it. The nibbling finally stopped when the fly was dead. When the girl caught ants crawling next to the fishbowl and put them in the water, though, the goldfish would dart up and gulp them down. She would also go outside for ants to put in the bowl. The goldfish swallowed only the live, squirming ants, ignoring the dead ones.

The girl would tire of toying with the flies and ants before the fish would. Then she would entertain herself by dredging scales from the bottom of the fishbowl with a long, pointed stick. She would press one of the scales against the glass and pull it up little by little. But the scale would slip away before it reached the mouth of the bowl. When this happened, the girl would quickly reach into the water and pincer the sinking scale. She would glance at Hyŏn, and when he pretended not to see, she would swirl the water with her stick to set the other scales astir. Then she would pick them out in the same way. Having recovered all the scales, she would hurry outside to dry them in the sun.

Whenever Hyŏn went out to the well to change the murky water in the fishbowl, the girl would run to him and pick up the goldfish as it flopped in the empty bowl. As the fish struggled in her hand, she looked down with satisfaction at its shiny scales. After filling the bowl, Hyŏn would hold it close to the girl's hand. Only then would she put the fish back in.

There had once been a second goldfish. It had slipped from the girl's hand and fallen into the sewer drain as she was about to put it in the bowl. Just before Hyŏn could grab the fish, it disappeared down the sewer pipe, leaving a trail in the muddy water. The girl looked down at the scales remaining in her palm. Hyŏn was afraid she would burst into tears if he stood there any longer, so he hurried upstairs, all the while looking at the remaining goldfish, which was moving its fins and swimming spiritedly in the fresh clean water, as if unaware its mate had disappeared.

Once Hyŏn was out of sight upstairs, the girl became cheerful. She added the old scales she had collected to the new ones in her palm and arranged them all on the back of her hand. Next, she turned her hand toward the sun to make the scales sparkle. She repeated this movement again and again. Finally she stuck the scales to her cheeks, forehead, and nose and pretended to dart and swim like a goldfish, rounding her lips over and over and working her arms like fins. But the girl lost interest in this game too. So she found the cat and began scratching its face with her fingernails.

The young lady had a different way of playing with the cat. After returning from one of her sojourns she would take the cat in her arms, hold one forepaw, and caress her own cheek with it. The paw, claws retracted, would brush gently across her cheek. Closing her eyes, the young lady would stroke more forcefully. Red marks would gradually appear on her face, and a faint smile would rise on her lips, forming a dimple on her left cheek. The round outline of her face looked quite smooth from the front, but her profile was a different story altogether, revealing her sharp nose, mouth, and chin. The slight upward slant of her long eyelashes was charming when seen from the side, but from the front, the first thing Hyŏn noticed in her eyes was the fatigue that had settled there.

One day, after the owner of an unfamiliar pair of shoes had left, Hyŏn, on his way downstairs, made the chilling discovery that the dimple on the young lady's cheek was actually a deep scar. The young lady was standing outside her room, smiling, her arms extended toward the girl. Hyŏn was curious. This was the first time he had seen the young lady open her arms to the child. Perplexed, the girl stared up at the young lady's face. Then she looked back just in time to see the cat run out from behind her and jump into the young lady's arms. "Oh, my daughter," the young lady might have been murmuring to herself as she held the cat to her breast.

This black cat was the only one allowed to enter the young lady's room when a pair of men's shoes sat outside her door. The cat would nestle in her arms, crawl around her bosom, climb to her shoulders. And after attaching itself to the young lady, it would often lick the rims of her ears and her rouged cheeks. The young lady would then go into the kitchen, slice several pieces of raw meat, and place them on her palm in front of the cat. The cat would eat them, the blood staining the edges of its mouth like lipstick. Finally, it would stretch, yawn, and withdraw, leaving a couple of slices of meat uneaten. The young lady would then take the cat to the sunny part of the yard and give it a bath. The cat was used to this and merely blinked when the young lady lathered its fur with soap; it was more docile than the girl was when the landlady washed her hair. The cat was then carried to the young lady's room, where it played with the flowers.

The flowers were as various as the shoes of the men who visited. Only when a man left and the young lady went out could the little girl have the flowers of her choice. The girl would plant sprigs of these flowers around the sewer drain. There she left them until they all had withered.

Hyŏn then gave the girl a vase so she would have a place to put her flowers. At first she didn't know what to do with it, but finally she set it down and raced downstairs. She came back a little later with the sprigs she had planted near the drain and put them in the vase. All the flower petals were either torn or wilted. The torn petals must have been the work of the cat's claws and teeth. The girl changed the water in the vase as often as possible. If the cat tried to bat at the flowers, the girl grabbed it and threw it to the floor. But the sturdy cat would land on its feet and stand its ground, as if to prove it was a match for the girl. Then it would stretch and yawn, extending its middle and hunching its back.

The young lady's sojourns got longer and longer and the cat grew thin. When the girl threw the cat away from the flowers, it could barely land on its feet. Then it would climb onto the windowsill. One day the girl crept up behind the cat and tried to push it out the window to the ground below. But the cat managed to flatten itself against the sill and escape back inside, tipping over the vase. The vase broke at the neck, and the flowers, which were already withered away, fell out, their petals scattering. As Hyŏn gathered the petals floating in the water on the floor, the young lady's dimple-like scar kept appearing in his mind. He placed the petals and sprigs in the broken vase, then took it to a vacant lot at the corner of a nearby alley, where he threw it onto a pile of dung, dead rats, and broken dishes under a sign on the back wall of a house that read DON'T ANYBODY URINATE HERE.

As the cat wasted away, it sometimes came home from the vacant lot with a dead rat in its mouth. When that happened, the landlady cursed it and chased it with the stick she'd used to poke the mother rabbit. But not for its life would the cat part with the rat—it would climb up the outside of the chimney and hide on the roof. The landlady would rap the chimney with her stick and yell at the cat to let go of the rat and come down. Finally she would throw the stick aside and go into the kitchen. The cat would come down from the roof licking blood from its mouth and sun itself under the veranda.

Seeing this, the girl stole up to the cat and poked at its half-closed eyes with a stick, but the cat just batted the stick away. The girl then started clawing the cat's face, but the cat clawed the backs of her hands. The girl clawed more forcefully; then, when the cat was about to run away, she grabbed it around the middle and rolled it over on the ground. The cat got covered with dirt. The girl then tied a piece of colored fabric to the cat's tail. The cat chased its tail, trying to catch the fabric in its mouth. The girl went around in circles too. Soon, after tottering several times, she keeled over. The cat kept going. Exasperated, the girl got up and started turning in circles again, trying to outlast the cat. And again she plopped down, but this time she remained on the ground, dizzy, her upper body seeming to sway round and round. The cat kept turning in circles, trying to catch the colored fabric. The girl was clearly the loser in this game. A few minutes later she rose, picked up the landlady's stick, and hit the cat's belly as hard as she could. The cat rolled over with a howl and scurried away.

When the girl had nothing else to do, she could play with the mute boy who lived next door. The landlady called him an opium addict. The boy had come to live with some distant relatives after his opium-addicted parents died. Though mute, the boy could hear, and he would look down with shame when the landlady declared that the little bastard had turned his parents into addicts and destroyed them; it was rotten luck, but that's what happened when you had a boy whose nose turned up toward the sky. When the boy played with the girl, he undertook all the drudgery—kneading mud into the shape of food when they played house, putting the food in one of the larger, prettier-colored potsherds, and serving it to the girl and her doll. The girl never shared this food. Even so, the boy watched in satisfaction, with no sign of displeasure, as she kept touching the mud to the lips of the doll and saying, "Eat, Mother." But this sight had him drooling before he noticed it. When the boy's father had started taking opium, the mother nagged him, trying to get him to stop. The hounding ended when the father got her addicted as well. The two then had to compete for opium, and finally the father sold the mother away. But the mother secretly visited the boy and had him steal his father's opium. The boy was caught by his father and beaten again and again. In the end the father ripped out the boy's tongue to prevent him from communicating with his mother. Since then the boy had been unable to talk, and he drooled helplessly without realizing it. Whenever the girl saw him drool, she scowled and jumped up. "Dirty!" The boy understood, and sucked in the spittle. But the girl would disappear inside without looking back. At such times the boy also went home, never waiting for the girl to come back out.

After one such incident, the boy came to play with the girl, offering her a broken piece of porcelain he had smoothed. She accepted it as if it were her due. The boy then took a shiny blue potsherd from his shabby vest, placed it on a rock, and began smoothing its edges. It was a piece of the vase Hyŏn had thrown away in the empty lot. Whenever the boy struck one of the sharp edges with a stone, bits of porcelain flew up. The girl stood far enough away to avoid them. The boy kept smoothing, and didn't seem to mind when the chips flew in his face or down his neck and inside his sleeves. Suddenly he lifted his left hand, the one holding the potsherd. He had struck his thumb by mistake, and immediately blood had begun to well up from the cut. In no time it stained the piece of porcelain. The girl retreated a step and wrinkled her nose at this awful sight. But the boy flicked his hand back and forth a couple of times and went back to smoothing the potsherd. The bits of porcelain flew faster than before. Finally he was done. He polished the smoothed potsherd on his threadbare pants and handed it to the girl. The girl received it as if this were only proper, and added it to her other potsherds.

Sensing that the girl was getting bored, the boy took two clamshells from his vest. After fitting the shells together, he began rubbing the hinged side against a crock of soy sauce to make holes to blow through. The rubbing produced a ringing screech. The girl covered her ears, withdrew farther than before, and watched the boy. The landlady came out of the kitchen, wiping her hands on her skirt, and yelled that the damned addict ought to be grateful he was allowed to play with the girl, but instead he had the nerve to make that terrible racket. But before the landlady could make the boy stop, the girl snapped at her to go away. The boy kept rubbing the shells. The landlady went back to the kitchen, mumbling to herself that the handicapped didn't have an ounce of kindness. Finally the boy stopped rubbing, his hands worn out. But he had made holes in the shells. He started to bring the place with the holes to his mouth, but then he noticed that he was drooling again. His face crinkling in alarm, he offered the girl the shells. "Dirty!" The girl spat, then took them. Showing no desire to blow into them, she threw the shells under the soy-crock terrace, breaking them to pieces.

After a few moments the boy ran out through the gate. The girl picked up some of the prettier and more shapely pieces of shell as if nothing had happened, and added them to her pieces of porcelain. She had started playing house with her doll when the boy returned, panting. He took a handful of sawdust from his vest pocket and held it in front of the girl. He had gotten it from where the sawyers worked at the corner of the empty lot. Squatting and emptying his vest pockets on the ground, he buried one of his hands in the saw- dust and began patting it with the other firmly and evenly. Then he carefully withdrew his hand from the sawdust. Instead of forming a cave, however, the sawdust crumbled. Again the boy buried his hand in the sawdust and patted it, and again the sawdust crumbled. Impa- tient, the girl scattered the sawdust with a sweep of her hand. The sawdust flew into the boy's face. A smile of enjoyment rose at the cor- ners of the girl's lips, and she sprinkled the boy's face with a handful of the sawdust. The boy didn't move, merely closed his eyes. The girl sprinkled his face with another handful of sawdust. This time the boy recoiled as if surprised. Her interest heightened, the girl now sprinkled the sawdust with both hands. The boy flinched again. The girl raked the sawdust together again and again with both hands and showered the boy with it; by now she was giggling. The louder she giggled, the more forcefully the boy ducked. Eventually the girl lost interest in this game and her laughter died out. The boy got up with a sudden look of satisfaction and dashed out the gate without looking at the girl. That was the last time he came to play with her.

On his way home from the laboratory Hyŏn sometimes saw the boy playing near the two elderly sawyers in the empty lot. A sign reading IF YOU'RE NOT A DOG, DON'T URINATE HERE was now posted beside the sign reading DON'T ANYBODY URINATE HERE. The two men worked their saw lengthwise down a large log that was propped up at one end, dusting the hair of the boy and the lower man. The boy heaped sawdust into a mound. A keen scent of wood rose from it. The log, the bent back of the elderly man standing on it, and the saw being pulled and pushed—all were in dull silhouette against the glow gathering in the evening sky. The sawdust was like falling snow. Whenever he saw them Hyŏn thought that real snow whiter than the sawdust would surely begin to fall before the men finished sawing all the dark logs piled in the corner of the lot.

Hyŏn returned from the laboratory and sprawled in exhaustion across the floor of his room. The late-summer evenings were darkening more and more quickly. Suddenly he could smell the rats he had been handling at the lab. Surely the smell was coming from his hands. Hyŏn raised his head and looked at his hands, but it was already too dark to distinguish them. The walls and ceiling seemed to press in on him. The corners of the walls and ceiling were not square but round. He could not sense which way he was lying. Sometimes he had awakened, his heart quickening, to find he wasn't lying where he thought: the window that should have been above his head was at his feet, things that should have been on his right were to his left. But today he hadn't even fallen asleep before he sprang up in alarm, thinking that the blur of the window was in the wrong place.

"Damned cat! That damned cat!"

The thumping of the landlady's feet on the stairway followed her voice into Hyŏn's room. Hyŏn turned on the light. The stairs he had thought to be at his feet were at his head. He opened the door. The cat came in with something in its mouth, the landlady in pursuit with the stick she had used to poke the mother rabbit that morning. It was a dead baby rabbit. The landlady's wrinkled face twitched, and she tried to grab the cat, saying she hadn't realized the damned thing was eating all the little rabbits. The cat easily eluded her.

The girl ran into the room and grabbed the cat by the middle; the animal tried to squirm free. When she yanked at the dead rabbit, the

cat arched its back, hissing spitefully through clenched jaws, hate filling its eyes. Hyŏn grabbed at the rabbit, and part of it tore free. The
girl went down the stairs clutching the cat in her arms. "I'd better
kill that damned cat," muttered the landlady. "All it's good for is
bringing dead rats into the house and eating up baby rabbits." Hyŏn
went down the stairs holding what was left of the rabbit. In the
darkness outside he could barely see the girl hurl the cat to the
ground. The cat howled and disappeared beside the rabbit hutch.
Hyŏn went to the hutch and showed the remains of the baby rabbit
to the mother. The hutch was quiet, as if the mother rabbit, like the
goldfish that had lost its mate, was unaware. Hyŏn had to kick the
hutch to make his point, and only then was he able to startle the rabbit. He decided to take it to the lab the next day.

Hyŏn took the rabbit remains to the open sewer beside the street
leading to the park. The farther his eyes traveled down the ditch, the
darker it appeared. The smell was repulsive. Hyŏn dropped the remains into the ditch. There was a soft plop and the ditch became
still again, filling the air with its stench. The goldfish the girl had
dropped down the drain at his boardinghouse would've been dead
and rotten before coming this far, he told himself. While gazing into
the dark sewer, he had a recurring illusion that it was flowing upstream. He walked on toward the park.

At the park Hyŏn went to a broadleaf tree and stretched out his
hand. The dewy leaves infused him with their damp coolness. Hyŏn
withdrew his hand, but then stretched out both hands and rubbed
them with the leaves. He went to a bench and sat. The clouds had
not parted for even an instant. With the moon cloaked, the sky
was as black as the ditch. The shadows in this part of the park
were darker because the few lights along the paths were screened by
trees.

Hyŏn left the park and went to a well-lit market. In one of the
stalls near the entrance sat an elderly woman surrounded by brightly
colored toys. She sent a toy tank wheeling about, knocking down
other toys. Then she sent a self-righting doll rolling down a slide.
When the doll reached the bottom the tank knocked it over. The
doll rolled away and then righted itself.

Hyŏn returned to the park. A boy and a girl were sitting on the bench he had occupied. They were laughing in a shrill, affected manner. Hyŏn turned away. His hands still felt sticky, as if bloody and exuding a smell. He returned to the broadleaf tree. This time he picked some leaves, rubbed them between his palms, and wiped the backs of his hands and each of his fingers. Their grassy smell was stronger than the bloody stink. Then he noticed a different smell, not blood or grass—the scent of cheap face powder. He lit a cigarette. No one was there. He was about to reach up to the leaves again when something whitish appeared right in front of him. He stepped back in surprise. A woman was next to him. She laughed nervously and asked for a light. But her outstretched hand snatched the cigarette from his mouth before he could hand it to her. The area around her nose, which looked reddish in the glow from the cigarette, was discolored with a mark that her thick facial powder could not conceal. The tips of their cigarettes fell away from each other, and the woman's face disappeared in a cloud of smoke. The woman held Hyŏn's cigarette out to him in the darkness. Hyŏn reached for it. She brushed his hand aside. Her hand that held his cigarette probed for his mouth. Hyŏn stuck out his lips, only to find that the woman was trying to pass him the lighted end of the cigarette. He slapped the cigarette from her hand and strode away. Behind him, the woman giggled.

Hyŏn found his way out of the park. Just before the sewer ditch he took a shortcut down an alley next to a small shop, and in no time he was home. He went upstairs to his room and found the cat inside, licking the floor—probably some blood had dripped from the baby rabbit. The cat noticed Hyŏn and lifted its vigilant eyes toward him, but the next moment its red tongue was diligently licking the floor again. Hyŏn decided he would give the cat to the woman he had just seen at the park. He approached the cat, petted it briefly, then grabbed it. The cat licked its mouth, unconcerned, twitched its ears this way and that, and started licking the backs of Hyŏn's hands— still that smell. Hyŏn tied a small towel around the cat's eyes. The cat struggled a moment, then licked Hyŏn's hands some more.

Hyŏn held the cat to his chest and stole from the house. This time he took the long way to the park, following the sewer. Moonlight suddenly appeared as he walked along the ditch. Hyŏn tucked his jacket tightly around the cat. Now it was dark again. Hyŏn entered the park and went straight to the foot of the broadleaf tree. The leaves, damper and cooler than before, brushed against his ears, chilling them. Hyŏn placed the cat under his arm and struck a match, but the flame touched a moist leaf and went out. He struck another match, but there was only the blackish gleam of the leaves; no one was there. Hyŏn lit a cigarette and went to the bench where the boy and the girl had been laughing. He sat down. The market had closed, and it was dark there now. Hyŏn spied something shadowy moving back and forth in the gloom in front of him. Wondering if this was an illusion, he looked carefully and discovered two dogs mating. Locked end to end, they were taking turns trying to move forward. The moon reappeared. The thin dog nearer Hyŏn, its eyeballs and long, drooping tongue glistening, pulled the other dog a couple of steps forward. The other immediately pulled the first dog back those few steps. This action was repeated over and over under the moonlight.

Clouds covered the moon again and Hyŏn got up, but there was a weight on his shoulder. It was a drunken woman—whether the same woman, he couldn't tell. Hyŏn tried to move aside, but the woman wrapped her arm roughly about his neck and brought her lips close to him; they reeked of liquor. "Bet you thought no one knew. You're abandoning a baby. Yes, you are." Instead of explaining, Hyŏn gripped the cat more securely and tried to avoid the woman. But she kept after him, asking whether the baby was a boy or a girl. Hyŏn heaved the woman aside. She staggered and then squatted in a heap. "This is the best time of year to abandon a baby," she said. She herself had given birth to twins, a boy and a girl, and gotten rid of them here. The woman broke into hollow laughter. Hyŏn escaped before the moon came out again.

He reached the edge of the park, and it occurred to him that giving the cat to the woman with the cigarette might be tantamount to returning it to the young lady in his boardinghouse. The cat would be better off as a stray, he thought. He decided to set it loose in the park. He removed the towel from the cat's eyes and flung the animal into the darkness as hard as he could. Then he ran from the park.

When he got to a street that had some lights, he took a good look behind. The cat wasn't following him. Hyŏn took the shortcut home rather than the route next to the sewer. He wondered what would happen when the young lady returned to find the cat gone.

But when he got up to his room, Hyŏn found the cat lapping the water in the fishbowl. He turned off the light. Moonlight filtered through the window. The cat kept on drinking. Hyŏn approached the cat as if to pet it, then grabbed it around the belly. But as he picked it up, the cat's forepaws hooked the fishbowl and it toppled over. In the moonlight the goldfish looked like a single huge fish scale flopping in the spilled water. Hyŏn seized the cat by the neck. It had eaten up all the baby rabbits; now it would be the goldfish. The cat licked the hands clutching its neck. Hyŏn gripped harder. *Die!* The cat clawed at Hyŏn's hands, its eyes burning blue in the moonlight. Hyŏn squeezed the cat's throat harder and harder. *Die! Die!* He finally let the cat go when he saw sparks in its eyes. The cat fell to the floor, and after clawing at the air, it bolted up and slinked out the door, which had been left open a crack.

The goldfish had stopped moving. Hyŏn returned it to the bit of water remaining in the fishbowl and took the bowl outside to the pump. Its white belly listing to the side, the fish lay motionless in the water, which was too shallow to cover its back. Hyŏn ran fresh water into the bowl and was about to turn around when he spotted something at the dark opening of the drain. Something was moving among the flower stems the girl had planted there. Hyŏn gently parted the stems, whose petals had already fallen, and picked up a small fish. Could it have come up from the sewer through this pipe? Did it mean there were fish living in the sewer? And if there were, how could this one have gotten all the way here? He quickly rinsed the fish, placed it in the bowl, and took it upstairs.

Hyŏn turned on the light and examined the fish from the sewer pipe. In the place where its eyes should have been there were faint hollows like festering sores. Blind and dark all over, the small fish wriggled about. Time and again it collided with the goldfish, which had barely been able to right itself and was moving its fins anxiously. The goldfish's reaction was to wiggle briefly. Indifferent to the blind fish, it came to rest, finning vigorously. The blind fish got more jumpy, butting the sides of the bowl and almost leaping out of the water. Suddenly it turned on its side; soon it had stopped finning. The goldfish now began to swim about animatedly, as if completely recovered. The blind fish rocked slightly in the churning water, its tail resting on the surface.

Hyon picked up the blind fish. Its belly had already begun to swell. He went to the window and threw the fish out. It continued to shine like a muddy scale as it fell in the moonlight. The cat dashed over from the rabbit hutch, took the fish in its mouth, and ran back under the hutch.

The day Hyŏn took the mother rabbit back to the laboratory, he passed the empty lot on his way home and saw the sign reading IF YOU'RE NOT A DOG, DON'T URINATE HERE. Next to it, DOGS' TOILET had been written on the wall. Decomposed rats, dung, and broken dishes were scattered every which way. He got to the place where the sawyers worked. Today the boy was sitting apart, his back to Hyŏn. Probably making a mound of sawdust, Hyŏn thought. But then as he passed behind him he caught a glimpse of what the boy was doing. Hyŏn stopped in surprise. Wasn't that a baby rabbit? The boy was about to serve the rabbit some sawdust in an attractive, smoothed potsherd. But the rabbit didn't budge. It was dead. Had the boy taken the baby rabbits one by one after losing the girl as a playmate? Had he been playing with them like this? Hyŏn was about to leave before the boy noticed him, when suddenly the cat appeared and just as quickly was gone, the dead baby rabbit in its mouth. With a guttural shout the boy set off in pursuit. Hyŏn joined the chase, following the boy into the evening shadows.

CUSTOM

"Now what are you doing with those?"

He was on his way outside again when my wife took the scissors from him.

Was that all she could do, snatch the scissors from the boy? It gave the impression that she was dull-witted. She tossed the scissors aside, but the three-year-old went after them again as if this were the most natural thing in the world.

My wife pushed the boy aside: "You little nuisance, what's a boy doing playing with scissors?"

Unfazed, he found his ball in the far corner of the room and headed outside with it.

"Play inside, you," said my wife. Then she stuck her knitting needle in the bun of her hair and mumbled to herself, "It's about time you pooped," and she led the boy to the chamber pot.

By now the boy was more than able to answer nature's call by himself, but my wife treated him as if he were younger. Granted, that's the way my own mother treated me—and still does.

The boy strained for a time but produced nothing.

"Remember, if you do it in your pants, I'll spank you," my wife said.

The boy didn't seem concerned and began to play with the ball.

I produced two coppers from my pocket and tossed them in front of the boy. "Son, I want you to go outside and play."

The boy looked more surprised than my wife. This had never happened before, and he looked back and forth from my wife to the money.

"Tell him to pick it up!" I said.

"Yes, pick it up," said my wife.

"I'll give you some more in a bit. Now go out and play."

This surprised the boy again, and the ball rolled out of his hand.

A piece of sorghum stalk had come to rest in the room across the courtyard. The boy had probably been playing with sorghum stalks.

Hand trembling, Father flicked the piece of stalk aside. His hand continued to tremble as he placed it on his knee.

"And where have you been gadding about?"

Finding fault is Father's job, and at home he has to do it whenever he can.

"Why don't you stay put and sweep the yard or something if you don't have anything else to do?"

I observed the fingers of Father's left hand, which continued to tremble even after he had rested it on his knee. Father's frowning face turned toward Mother.

"I keep telling you you're spoiling him and still you give him money."

My mother's large frame was slumped over as she sat. Her moist eyes looked up, then lowered. For some reason I didn't understand, Mother was scared of Father.

And then Father muttered to himself, "I've never seen an only son who cares so little about family matters." He sighed.

Along with his fault-finding Father had, not too long before, started feeling sorry for himself. The wrinkles in his face seemed always to have been there, but now they were deeper.

I didn't feel like letting Father feel sorry for himself, and said, "Educating your children and planting grain are two different things."

Usually Father would respond to such words by shouting "Unfilial son!" But not this time. I was displeased, though, by the absence of that response, so I said, "We don't always reap what we sow."

Father would certainly have been within his rights to take his wooden pillow to the head of a son who made such untoward comments.

Mother's face blanched in fear. "Now, child." She was pleading with me to desist.

Still I carried on: "No matter how Father tries to get me to harvest the crop, it won't work. I've no mind to work in the fields and paddies."

But Father wasn't shouting today and he wasn't throwing the wooden pillow. Just the fingers of his left hand trembled.

Mother's face, cocked at me, changed color as she grew more fearful. Her cheekbones were more prominent, and from the side her face looked older.

Mother's reddish eyes tended to pool with tears if she peered at something too long. That's why she was forever dabbing at her eyes.

Mother pinched the end of the thread and tried to stick it through the eye of the needle. She missed. She moistened the end of the thread, twisted it between her fingers, and tried again. It was as if she were waiting for me to help her thread the needle. But I kept to myself.

Mother brought the end of the thread to the eye of the faintly glinting needle, then gave up. "Here, you do it."

I held the needle against the lighter background of the rice-paper door panel, threaded it, and returned it to her.

"You've been good at threading needles since you were young. You probably started doing it around the age Changson is now," Mother said while she knotted the end of the thread. And then: "Is something worrying you?" She turned her tired eyes my way.

I shook my head, noticing as I did so that numerous fine wrinkles had appeared in Mother's eyelids. I found myself wondering which of them, Mother or Father, would pass away first. Maybe Father, and it wouldn't take much.

As Mother began her stitching she said, "Is it because you don't like your wife?"

"Why do you say that?"

"Well, the fact is, there's something about the color of her face. . . . And she's not much to look at, is she? Too bad she couldn't change her looks with yours—you've had a very pretty face ever since you were a child. But it wouldn't do to abandon her, no it wouldn't. And it won't do to mistreat a wife who's produced a child. I've never seen a family that got on well when the wife was mistreated, no I haven't."

"You know I don't earn enough to feed one woman properly, let alone two. What's more, a healthy wife has her own kind of beauty."

Those words must have reminded Mother of the time Father kept a concubine, because she turned up the hem of her skirt and dabbed at her eyes.

A spider was descending from the corner of the ceiling. I grew dizzy looking at it.

One day I was watching the spider weave its web on the ceiling.

"Did you know," I asked my wife, "that a spider will devour its mother? And supposedly if you eat a lot of roasted spiders you won't feel dizzy and you'll put on weight."

My wife kept her head lowered instead of answering. Her hair was especially dark and also thick. Long, drooping tresses of hair were probably the fashion when she was a girl.

After a while she replied, head still bowed, "I don't know anything— I'm ignorant."

"Your hair looks darker these days. How about if I eat some spiders and see if I can get strong like you?"

Her thick earlobes flushed. Suddenly I noticed that the hair in her bun had been trimmed.

"Why do you make your hair so ugly when you cut it?" I couldn't help saying.

She hung her head even lower.

The spider that had been weaving its web scuttled into hiding in the corner of the ceiling. A single thin strand of web was left to dangle in the air.

"You better not let me see you do that to your hair again!"

Before I knew it my wife was weeping, her shoulders heaving.

Wasn't Mother going to cry too, as she usually did at times like this? I asked myself.

"For heaven's sake—I can't even open my mouth without somebody starting to cry. I feel stifled, staying home all the time," I said, as Father did on such occasions, and then I left.

The street is so long. I feel dizzy. Before my tired eyes balloons fly dizzily. Their surface is moist and I can see rainbows all over them.

The rainbows twist and fly along with the balloons. One rainbow collides with another and both dissolve. Balloons, popped and un-popped. I paw the air in front of me, but from the place where the balloons pop, all sorts of new balloons float into the air. Balloons, balloons, balloons—when enough of them fly into the air, the rainbows dissolve. Like foam spit by fish. Foam, foam, foam, rainbows, rainbows, balls, balls. . . . I'm thirsty.

There must be a teahouse around here. Water. Ah, that's better. A young man tells me that life is like collecting streamside pebbles at sunset. I leave him like I would leave a pebble, and emerge from the teahouse.

Outside a house-front shop a squirrel is scampering on a wheel inside a cage. The wheel makes a circle. The circles keep accumulating. Circles, circles, circles. . . . Finally only one circle remains. That's why the scampering squirrel is now a stationary squirrel. I want to lie down. Home we go.

I was lying down.

"Who is better-looking, Grandfather or Grandmother?" my wife asked our boy.

"Grandfather," the boy drawled. No doubt this was the first lesson in cunning that my own mother had given me.

"Grandmother or Mother?"

With his chin the boy indicated my wife: "Mommy."

Her earlobes flushed.

The boy answered after his own fashion, no matter what she tried to teach him, so she couldn't help being embarrassed.

My wife glared at the boy and asked again: "Who?"

"Grandmother," the boy drawled.

Often my wife followed by questioning the boy about herself and myself. The boy would go along with her and answer, as instructed, that it was I who was better-looking.

But this time I sat up and asked first: "Who's better-looking, Daddy or Mommy?"

The boy remained still, then gazed at my wife.

"Me?" I asked.

He began to cry, this boy who normally didn't cry even when my wife snatched the scissors from him and pushed him away.

"And who's better looking, Daddy or Baby? It's Baby—this much."

I spread my arms wide. But there was only emptiness to embrace.

The room across the courtyard was littered with crumbs from the cookie our boy had eaten.

Mother, sitting by herself, picked up the crumbs and ate them, then said, "It's looking like rain—don't tell me the rainy season is here already."

"Maybe so."

"The wheat must have ripened by now."

It was a cloudy day, but the mention of ears of wheat made me feel nostalgic for the first time in a while.

"Do you realize what a stir you caused that night you got so sick gobbling wheat off the stalks?"

She looked in my direction for a time, then with the back of her hand wiped the tears squirting from her eyes. "You got scared within an inch of your life, and then the next night you went right back out and did it again. I was terribly worried."

"Did I used to wander the fields back then?"

"Yes, and you didn't come back till dark. I worried *so* much. By the way, your father wants you to go down to the countryside and take care of the harvest. I wonder how you're ever going to last even a few days in the country—there isn't much variety in the food, and the insects have always feasted on you. I'm afraid you won't be able to tolerate it. But whatever your father tells you, just keep quiet and don't talk back. I'll do the talking. Before we die, you need to learn something about managing a family. We're not going to live forever, you know."

"There you go again, talking about dying."

"When you grow old like us, that's all you think about—except for the grandchildren."

I found the beginning of a line that our boy had probably drawn on the wall, and wondered if, when he was older, he'd have the same conversation with his mother that I was having now with mine. That wouldn't do, I decided, and in my imagination I forcefully shook my head no.

My wife was in the family room unraveling a skein of thread that our boy appeared to have tangled up. Beside her the boy was by himself, playing with his ball.

I looked down at him and said to my wife, "If I go down to the countryside to help with the harvest and come back with my face all sunburned, all I'll have to do is look at him and he'll start crying."

The boy looked in my direction; he seemed to have forgotten his ball.

Before I knew it, there was my wife bringing the ties of her jacket to her eyes again.

The thing that aggravated me was not so much her crying at the drop of a hat as it was the dirtiness of those jacket ties.

Head lowered, she blurted, "If you want me to go live somewhere else, I will."

"Stop touching your eyes with those dirty things."

She immediately let go of the ties.

"But even if I did, part of me will always be here."

"So I should leave? And how would I survive?" So saying, I laughed for the first time in a long while.

My wife's shoulders heaved, but she wept silently.

I tilted back the mirror on the dressing table beside her. A portion of the ceiling filled the mirror. I tilted the mirror forward and my wife appeared.

My wife in the mirror spoke to herself: "The one I feel sorry for is the boy." And she proceeded to weep more sorrowfully than the situation demanded.

The boy was cutting up a scrap of cloth with the scissors as if oblivious to it all.

Mother probably said the same thing to yours truly every time Father went to visit his concubine.

I'll see if I can feel sorry for myself, I thought. But then I considered both the self that wanted to feel sorry for himself and the self that was being felt sorry for. Which was my real self?

And with Father feeling sorry for himself and not fault-finding these days, which was my real father?

His latest refrain went something like this: "As long as I'm alive you'll never be able to do as you want, because I worked too hard for what I've earned to turn it over to you now," followed immediately by something like, "Which is not to say I'll be living that much longer."

The fingers of his left hand trembled more now, as if to express the long suffering he had experienced in making a success of himself.

Beside him, hunched over and worrying as always, Mother said, "When we're dead you can do things your own way. I'm sure you'll have your own thoughts about raising Changson."

Father merely swallowed. His neck looked so slender.

Once again I played with the notion of which of them would pass on first. But when my thoughts reached the point that upon their passing, the responsibility for our family life would rest with me, I felt a stinging in my chest.

Father and Mother mustn't pass away, they mustn't.

"Changson, fetch me that broom," said Mother to our boy, who was playing with his ball.

I picked up the broom beside me and held it out in front of the boy. Mother stretched out her hand for it. I ignored her and offered the broom to the boy.

He hesitated before accepting it, then with an effort, as if it was too heavy for him, he passed it on to Mother.

Father and Mother mustn't pass away, they mustn't.

Father was feeling sorry for himself. "I had gravestones made for us, seeing as how you wouldn't have a mind to do it yourself," he murmured.

Who else but yours truly, though, would be the one to have the dates of their passing carved on those gravestones?

In the end, I couldn't let Father get away with thinking about death and feeling sorry for himself. So like him I murmured, loud enough for him to hear, "I'll probably end up losing the land, family burial ground and all—I don't even know what's ours anymore."

The Dog of Crossover Village

BOOZE

When the Nakamura distillery in Sŏsŏng-ni was taken over, Chunho
was chosen to manage it. In terms of age and work experience he was
a logical choice. For one thing, the distillery was the only place he
had ever worked, starting there in his mid-twenties running errands
and now as a head clerk who had passed the milestone age of forty.
And this is spite of an education consisting solely of the Chinese
character primer he had memorized back at the old-time village
school. And so his rise from errand boy to head clerk he had accomplished entirely on his own; his native intelligence enabled him to
assimilate what he saw and heard, but much of his success was also
due to his characteristic persistence. The result was that Chunho
knew the distillery business inside and out—if you ever wondered
how a distillery worked, he would be the one to ask.

Add to this the fact that Chunho had made every effort to prevent Nakamura from looting the distillery after the August 15, 1945
Liberation. Chunho had by then taken up residence with his family
in the night watchman's room at the distillery, so he could keep an
eye on the buildings day and night.

Nakamura's primary facility was a large grain warehouse in
Chinnamp'o, and that was where the boss could generally be found.
He was there on Liberation Day, and in the following days he and his
men made several attempts to drive off with a truckload of *soju* from
the distillery. But Chunho was always there to stop them, the first
line of defense. Danger lurked everywhere, what with disarmament
not yet accomplished and people more often than not in a vicious
frame of mind. And yet Chunho refused to negotiate with Nakamura and his men. "From now on, everything's ours!" This declaration by Kŏnsŏp, a clerk who worked with Chunho, filled Chunho
with heartfelt emotion.

Nakamura and his men gave up on the *soju* and tried to drive off
with the trucks alone, but once again Chunho was there to stop them.
At one point a Japanese approached Chunho on behalf of Nakamura,
subtly nudged him out of sight, and placed in his hand a roll of

hundred-*wŏn* notes. Chunho, already surprised at being approached, grew bug-eyed at the sight of the money; he took the roll and threw it in the man's face, the notes scattering to the ground. There were no further overtures from Nakamura.

Because he had proved so passionate and tenacious in his stewardship of the distillery, and with the time nigh for the appropriation of Japanese businesses, it was only natural that Chunho was chosen by his co-workers to be the new manager. His first order of business was to register the distillery, renamed the Yugyŏng Distillery, with the authorities. The same day, he prepared to move from the night watchman's room to the manager's residence. It was unusual to have lived with one's family in the same rented room for fifteen years or so, as Chunho had, the kitchen never failing to take in water during the summer monsoons, but his circumstances had been difficult and the rent was cheap. But unavoidably, the house in which they had rented this room had been torn down that spring—it was among a cluster of dwellings that had to be thinned out amid fears of an Allied firebombing—and in searching for another room he found not only that rents were exorbitant but also that no one would let a room to a family with so many children (five of them— Chunho had started a family somewhat later than others). He felt as frustrated as the proverbial mute who can't express his feelings to a beautiful woman and he began to recite to himself, *If you want to live inside the city walls of Pyongyang you can't have offspring; otherwise you're out of luck.* Finally he had decided to move his family into the night watchman's room at the distillery, after first throwing together a makeshift kitchen next to it. He was fortunate to have found a rent-free place to live, but it couldn't be considered permanent, so it made sense for him to take advantage of the opportunity to move into the residence of the former distillery manager.

The day before Chunho was to move, a rumor arrived that Nakamura, under cover of night, had loaded a truck with his most valuable household possessions and had fled Chinnamp'o for Seoul. The same day, Chunho and three other employees went to the manager's residence to ask the current occupants to vacate and to prepare for his family's arrival the following day. The house was on the eastern fringe of Namsan in Pyongyang and had a south-facing view.

At first glance the home appeared somewhat weathered, but it was well designed, with a U-shaped structure and an outer wall plastered with cement. It had seen four occupants, whom Chunho had visited to pay the customary New Year's greetings, but all that this involved was leaving his business card at the front gate; he had never seen the living spaces of the home. A week or so before Liberation the former manager had suddenly died of a heart ailment and Chunho had gone to offer condolences, but he had been received in a visitor's room off the entrance, where he had kneeled on the tatami floor to pay his respects before departing. So he knew little about the layout of the interior. Before, this hadn't really been an issue, because there had been something forbidding about this house. But now, as it came into view in its not-so-cramped alley, Chunho felt the peace of mind of a homeowner, and this gave him a sense of satisfaction.

Chunho's only reaction when they arrived was that the house looked somehow vacant. He wondered if this was because only women had lived there after the passing of the manager: the man's widow, who was in her early fifties; her daughter-in-law (her son had been drafted into the Imperial Army); and their maid. Or had the three women fled with Nakamura to Seoul? And the front door, which would open to the tinkling of a bell, was locked. Chunho ventured a hello, to which a woman's voice responded from a distance, almost as if from another house. There followed the even more distant sound of footsteps coming down a hallway, and finally the door opened.

Instead of the maid it was the aging widow who appeared. The woman probably hadn't seen Chunho more than two or three times, but she seemed to recognize him, even though he was wearing Western rather than Japanese clothing. More surprising, she proceeded to kneel before them—a courtesy not even the maid had extended to him—and bow repeatedly. The woman's skin had a familiar metallic bluish cast and exhibited the loss of elasticity characteristic of those entering old age, but she looked thinner since her husband's passing, and her skin was darker and coarser. Chunho explained the purpose of his visit, then left the woman where she was and entered the reception room.

Thinking they should wipe out every last vestige of the Japanese presence, in accordance with Kŏnsŏp's "Everything's ours!" Chunho called out "Comrades!" and proceeded to remove all the scrolls and framed pictures from the walls. Some of the scrolls were carefully taken down and rolled up, others were pulled down so forcefully that they ripped across the middle. "It's all right—do what you want with that Japanese crap," was all Chunho said.

The tatami mats were still serviceable. With houses, once you set your hand to renovating them the expenses never stopped, and with that thought in mind Chunho looked into the next room and saw that the mats there were also in good condition. As he was thinking that there ought to be a room with the traditional heated floor, and hoping that such a room wouldn't need repairs, he looked up and a paulownia wardrobe caught his eye. *Let's get this Japanese stuff out of sight.*

Chunho was about to return to the woman, but there she was right behind him, her face a mixture of surprise, sorrow, and fear. Was she so attached to the house and its furnishings? He asked where the storage room was. The woman indicated a far corner of the house and said she would show Chunho the way. "Comrades!" Chunho called out, and he instructed the others to remove the wardrobe to the storage room.

The next room was small and had a wooden floor. The paper-paneled door had been slid open and sunlight flooded the inside. Chunho's eye was drawn to a potted plum tree resting on a table. It was the same kind of miniature plum tree that had occupied the table in the manager's office at the distillery. Rumor had it that the manager, who himself had had the emaciated, desiccated appearance of this little plum, was more fond of plum trees than any other flowering tree. Now that Chunho thought about it, this might have had something to do with the fact that the owner himself, Nakamura, was even more enamored of plum trees. According to what Chunho had heard, the manager had come to know Nakamura while working at a bank in Chinnamp'o; until then he had never been that fond of plum trees, but upon learning that Nakamura liked them immensely he had read books on the subject and had proceeded to cultivate a miniature plum tree, and at some point in his dealings with Nakamura had presented the tree to him and had then obtained the position of manager at the distillery. But according to another report, the manager had always been fond of plum trees. Plum tree enthusiasts had formed an association and held an exhibition in Chinnamp'o, and it was there the manager and Nakamura had been introduced. At the time, through his position at the bank, the manager had frequent business dealings with Nakamura and the two men became close. The manager had once visited Nakamura at his home, at which time he noticed a stand with a miniature plum tree with two blossoms and commented that when there were two plum blossoms a third one would ruin the mood, and in this way he ingratiated himself to Nakamura, who thought likewise, and in the end it had been an offer from Nakamura and not a request from the manager that brought the latter to the distillery.

Chunho took this plum tree and left for the storage room, intending to dispose of it just as he had the plum tree in the manager's office at the distillery. The storage room was where the woman had indicated, at the end of one of the wings of the U-shaped house.

Opposite the storage room was another reception room, this one a Western-style space that was filled just then with dazzling sunlight. One of the men was removing a picture from the wall. The other two were about to leave for the storage room with another miniature plum and a potted white chrysanthemum. Chunho asked the man with the chrysanthemum to leave it.

The chairs, sofa, and carpet looked the worse for wear, but still had some use left in them. The woman was standing to the side. She had managed to compress her large frame into a deferential, hunched-over posture but gave no indication that she would leave the men to themselves. Seeing how attached she was to her furnishings, Chunho advised the woman that she need concern herself no longer with the house. The woman responded with a deep bow, as if in agreement, and said that as long as she had to give up the house and furnishings, she was happy that they were going to Chunho.

In replying to the woman, Chunho again relied on something Kŏnsŏp had said: as far as the assets of the Japanese in Korea were concerned, originally they had all belonged to Koreans—what had the Japanese brought from Japan?—and since they had arrived empty-handed, wasn't it enough that they had lived well in Korea? What did they have to be dissatisfied about? They ought to be thankful that they had survived safe and sound. Luckily for them, there were Koreans living in Japan who needed to return home, so the Koreans in Korea had to exercise forbearance with the Japanese. Why, the very fact that Koreans couldn't raise a hand against the Japanese even after Liberation showed just how much the Japanese had stripped Korea during thirty-six years of colonial rule. While saying this to the woman, Chunho realized yet again that there was something to what the young clerk Kŏnsŏp had said. He then told the woman that it wouldn't do to complain about having to give up the house and the furnishings and such—why should they feel dissatisfied, anyway? The woman once again bowed deeply and said that she and her family had come to the same conclusion, and as she had just said, she was happy to know that the house was passing on to Chunho. Still, Chunho could see in her face that the woman had yet to give up her attachment to living there.

Along the corridor that led to the toilet was an open door that revealed a large room in which there sat a young woman who looked to be not yet thirty. She started as they entered, and her bowed head sank lower. This must be the wife of the manager's only son, who had left to fight in the war. The room was layered with tatami mats, and the various household items indicated it was being used as the family room. Among the furnishings was a new paulownia wardrobe, probably the wife's.

Here too Chunho instructed the others to carry off to the storage room whatever they found. While the men were removing the room's contents the young woman seemed frozen for eternity, head bowed. The widow for her part asked Chunho over and over again what if he simply left the things where they were for his family to use, since she and her family no longer needed them. Chunho replied that he and his family had lived without such items till now, and so he had no interest in them. Chunho's gaze wandered off to the side, and when the widow saw where he was looking she cried out in surprise. Only then did the young woman look up, and when the widow nodded toward the wall she rose in alarm.

There on the wall were two photographs, mounted side by side. One was of the deceased manager, the other of a young man clad in uniform and cap, presumably his son. The photograph of the manager seemed to be recent, and it showed a man with an unyielding personality. Chunho had never seen the son in real life, but could tell from his photograph that he resembled his mother more than his father; the cheekbones stood out in his wide face, and his broad shoulders suggested a strong build. It occurred to Chunho as he observed the photos that if the son were to return from the battlefield he would probably live to an older age than his father. The two women seemed apprehensive lest Chunho call out "Comrades!" and have the photos removed, and so they scrambled onto chairs and did it themselves, clearly agitated at the prospect of these photos passing into the hands of others. Chunho wondered what the fussy and supercilious manager would have done if he'd been there at that moment, and in spite of himself he broke out laughing. The two women were startled.

Next to this room and toward the entrance to the house was a room with a floor heated in the traditional manner. The lamination on the floor was several years old but usable. And a good thing it was: the room was too small for a family of seven, but as long as they could move their household items into the family room next door they could squeeze into this room just for sleeping. On the far side of this room was a tatami room that appeared to be the maid's. But by the looks of things she had left already; she was nowhere to be seen.

Chunho stepped down to the inner courtyard. And there, as always with a house of this scale, were not only rocks and various trees but also a small, cozy man-made pond. At the far end of the yard a side gate opened onto the street, and in front of that gate was a bomb shelter that was supposed to have been excavated by workers from the distillery. Between the shelter and the gate stood a pair of stone figures facing each other. *Have to get rid of that Japanese crap!* Chunho called out to the two women for an ax.

Presently the widow scurried out from the back yard with the tool. Chunho began to roll up the sleeves of his suit jacket. But they were too narrow. At least he didn't have to worry about a necktie; if he had been wearing a tie, his suit would have looked even more awkward on him than it already did. Chunho gave up on the jacket sleeves and took the ax from the woman. He was small of stature, but he tensed his body, his protruding eyes bugging out even more, and with a swing of the ax he cleft the head from the first stone fig-ure. It rolled into the bomb shelter.

Next he lopped the head clean off the facing figure. This head did not roll into the bomb shelter. The other men had appeared from the house in the meantime, and with his foot one of them sent the sec-ond head rolling into the shelter. "They dug themselves a grave for the stone men," he said, and they all laughed. The woman flinched, seemingly startled more by the laughter than by the crack of ax against stone. Chunho next took the ax to a stone lantern near the pond; a chip from the shade fell to the ground.

The others went down to the basement, beneath the reception room, and returned a short time later to report that there were three barrels of *soju*. The men sounded disappointed—they had thought there was more. They all smelled of alcohol, and Chunho wondered if they had tapped the barrel with a hose and each taken several mouthfuls. A drink would be nice, he told himself, but he had to keep up appearances, so of necessity he desisted.

By way of explanation the woman said to Chunho that when her husband had passed away she had brought the barrels of *soju* home to use during the mourning rituals, and the times being what they were, had simply kept them there. But Chunho knew that when the man-ager had died, only one barrel had been taken to his home. There was no doubt in his mind that the manager had previously brought home liquor under the pretext of using it for a gift, but in fact had been bartering it.

The woman told Chunho they had a bathroom—would he like to see it? She seemed intent on softening his mood. *I've had enough fussing with this Japanese woman*, thought Chunho. And so instead he left, after telling the woman that he would move in the following day and to be sure the house was vacated, and, again following Kŏnsŏp's words, that individual ownership was a thing of the past and she shouldn't touch a single item in the house.

The next day, when Chunho and his family arrived at the house in a truck from the distillery containing more people than belongings, the widow was still there. Was it too early in the morning to have moved his family? But as he looked about the house, the young wife was nowhere to be seen. The widow tagged along behind Chunho and in a low voice pleaded with him, saying she had sent her daughter-in-law off to her relatives and asking if Chunho would allow her to remain there herself for the time being. Chunho assumed the woman was reluctant to impose on her relatives and asked why at a time like this the Japanese were concerned about saving face, and was she going to make a fuss about this, and why hadn't she simply gone with her daughter-in-law to stay with her relatives? In fact she had done precisely that, the woman replied, but upon arriving at the relatives' home she had found it full of refugees recently returned from Manchuria, so the house, spacious though it was, couldn't possibly accommodate another person, and even though it was unreasonable she had arranged for her daughter-in-law to stay there while she herself returned here, and that before long the Japanese would be gathering to evacuate, and until that time, wouldn't it be possible for her to stay here?

Chunho looked for a moment into the woman's tired, dark eyes. The whites and the pupils seemed to have blended together. Then, without telling the woman yes or no, he began moving his family's belongings inside. The woman seemed to interpret Chunho's lack of a response as a yes, and when Chunho's wife arrived to inspect the kitchen, the woman received her in the large tatami room with an air of satisfaction, as if to say that for a Japanese kitchen it wasn't that cramped and would serve their needs, and then proceeded to help her arrange their meager belongings. Not so long ago Chunho would have been ashamed to have his meager household belongings exposed to view in the presence of this Japanese woman, or to allow his children to run riot from room to room and down the halls as if they owned the world, but now he did not feel this way in the least.

And so the woman ended up remaining with Chunho and his family. Chunho asked himself why he hadn't expressly told the woman yes or no. Was it because Koreans had always felt sympathy for those who had fallen into a wretched state, even if they were enemies? Chunho himself felt such sympathy and in spite of himself was unable to suppress it.

Starting the following day, the woman took it upon herself to rise at daybreak and go about cleaning the house—a routine that seemed to derive in equal measures from her lingering attachment to her home, impossible to sever, an obligation she felt to be doing her share if she was to remain there, and her habitual practice all along. First light brought with it the sound of the dusting stick. Most days Chunho, who rose quite early, would still be in bed.

Every evening, tipsy with drink from the barrels of *soju* in the basement, Chunho had a nice warm bath and fell asleep in the guest room, only to be awakened from a sound sleep at daybreak by the *slap-slap* of the dusting stick. He would grouse to himself that the stick was driving out whatever good fortune might be poised to enter the house, and that all the dust that was being scattered would simply resettle. Annoyed, Chunho wished he had told the woman to leave in the first place.

As one day led to another, though, and as Chunho lay in bed at daybreak listening to the *slap-slap* of the dusting stick, he came to realize that the hard life he had led during his forty years had not been fruitless and that from now on he would be able to live more comfortably, and after considering this he would fall back into a languid sleep, as if the exhaustion that had accumulated till then had all at once been whisked away. Not only did he grow used to the *slap-slap* but eventually he needed to hear it before he could rest assured that all was clean and tidy in his home. His children had the run of the large house, and there was little that his wife by herself could do to clean up after them. Instead it was the widow who was forever occupied with this task. Lacking children of her own who needed constant supervision, she couldn't stand even a hint of squalor, and perhaps that was why she swept and cleaned as she did. There was no harm in having kept this woman, thought Chunho; indeed it was fortunate that she was here. If not for her, there would have been no one to heat his bathwater to just the right temperature, not too hot and not too cold.

On one such day a peculiar feeling came over Chunho: wherever he looked in the various rooms of the house, it felt like something was missing. Was it the absence of the furnishings, which had been removed from their proper places through no fault of their own? Well, of course it was. And they probably weren't what Kŏnsŏp had in mind when he had talked about getting rid of all things Japanese. In any event, it wouldn't do for a high-class house to be so bare. Time to rescue the furnishings from storage and put them back where they belonged.

In the Western-style room Chunho re-hung the pictures, restoring the brightness you would expect in such a room. Next came the miniature plum tree. And among the widow's furnishings, all those that were pleasing to the eye or would come in handy were brought out of storage as well. When the paulownia wardrobe was returned to the room next to the guest room, that room once again became properly inviting. Among the framed pictures and scrolls that had been taken down, he re-hung the undamaged ones. The table in the south-facing room with the wooden floor once again bore its potted plum tree. Next he had to reattach the heads to the stone figures in the yard. No self-respecting garden lacked stone figures, stone lanterns, and such. So out Chunho went to retrieve the heads of the stone figures and replace them on the bodies. The stones were considerably heavier than they looked. Next he recovered the chip from the stone lantern. He'd have to cement it back on to the shade.

Chunho sat himself down at the table with the miniature plum in the Western room. He was pleased with himself—except for a nagging thought that something was still missing. *Yes! A picture of myself, big as the previous manager's, right here on this wall.* He readied himself for a visit to the photography studio, brushing his Western suit till it was cleaner than ever before. It was a spring-and-autumn suit he had bought more than ten years earlier at a ready-to-wear shop—just the thing, said the shop owner: fabric thick as rawhide, a dark-gray color that would never show dirt, wearable not only in spring and autumn but also in winter and summer—but as Chunho was to find out, it was actually much more of a winter suit and not really meant for summer use. What's more, he had rarely worn the jacket, which felt a bit tight; while it was in storage at the bottom of his wardrobe both it and Chunho remained the same size, but for some reason as he was trying it on now the sleeves felt narrower and the length of the jacket seemed shorter, but the pants were just as long and baggy on his short frame as they had ever been, with the result that the top and bottom of this suit just did not go together. He looked even more awkward when he knotted his tie. Even so, he could still wear a self-satisfied look as he stepped outside, though no amount of brushing could have remedied the mismatch of the garments.

When Chunho returned that night, his face wore an ugly scowl, he smelled of liquor, and he was spluttering and shouting: "Those bastards will rue the day!" After having his photo taken, instead of going to the distillery he had visited the Office of Private Commerce and Industry to check on the status of his application to take over management of the distillery.

The clerk at this office had leafed through a sheaf of papers in an obliging manner, cocked his head meaningfully, then looked over the rims of his tortoiseshell glasses and reported to Chunho that two applications had been received. Chunho's heart sank but he managed not to show it. It couldn't be, he said to the man, there must have been a mix-up; could he check again to make sure? The man, peering at the sheaf of papers, said there was no mistake. What happens now? Chunho had asked, and the man had looked through the papers again and in his obliging way had asked Chunho his name. Chunho told him, and the man nodded knowingly and looked at him again over the tops of his glasses. Chunho asked who the other applicant might be, but the man merely produced a vacant, bovine smile, as if to say that this was privileged information. Which led

Chunho to chide himself for having asked— the thing to do in a situation like this was back off for the time being.

Chunho's mind got busy, and after leaving the office he estimated when the man with the glasses would finish work for the day, waited, and proceeded to intercept him as if they were encountering each other by chance. The sun was going down, observed Chunho, and it was time for a drink. So saying, he led the man to a quiet place and a two-man drinking party commenced. The man in glasses soon was showing signs of tipsiness; he kept saying how good the liquor tasted. You could hardly call that stuff liquor, Chunho commented; next time he'd treat the man to some honest-to-goodness liquor. Chunho decided the time was right. Organizing his thoughts, he said, "Sir," and after a pause to let this polite salutation sink in, he asked who the other person was who had applied to take over the distillery he himself was now managing, trying to sound as nonchalant as possible, as if this question had just occurred to him. The man produced his bovine smile and asked what difference it made—Chunho was the heir apparent, so there was nothing to worry about. No, he wasn't worrying, Chunho said, smiling in his turn, as etiquette would demand.

By then Chunho had determined that this thirty-two-year-old man with the glasses was a drinker like himself, the kind who gets drunk fast but then shows no signs of further intoxication, and there the man was now, sitting quietly, peering over the rims of his glasses at Chunho as he nursed his drink. It wouldn't do to inquire further, to show how hot and bothered he was, and so Chunho decided to speak no more about the distillery. Instead he urged more liquor upon the man, consistent with what he had told him on the way there—that sundown had put him in mind of a drink and he had wanted some company.

But Chunho had scarcely parted with the man when he found himself thinking that even though this obliging, sincere-looking person had told him not to worry, that didn't necessarily mean he wouldn't say the very same thing to the other party. The man had made a point of not identifying the other applicant, which suggested to Chunho that those two were on good terms. At the very least, that clerk sure was clever when it came to the art of etiquette. *Just goes to show that a guy who's sincere and obliging on the outside can be a snake on the inside!*

So then—who was this other person who had put in an application? Well, whoever he was, he'd better watch out. Chunho was not about to let himself get swallowed up by someone else—*no way!* What a wretched state it was, with Koreans trying to swallow each other up. "You better watch out!" he practically screamed, as if the other person were actually there, lurking in the darkness. And that night, after the alcohol had worn off, Chunho kept waking up and had difficulty getting back to sleep.

The following day Chunho told Kŏnsŏp as soon as he arrived at the office that someone else had applied to take over the distillery. Anyone who was loyal to the distillery should have been shocked at this news, but not Kŏnsŏp. Instead he told Chunho that he had been waiting for him since the previous day, when he had gone to the union and heard that it had been decided that the takeover of the distillery would be handled not by the Ministry of Commerce but by the Ministry of Finance, and that if the union became responsible then the purchase price would be divided into annual payments, whereas if a private party took charge then a one-time lump-sum payment would be required. While acknowledging to himself the importance of what Kŏnsŏp had said, Chunho pressed on: What would become of their distillery, then? Kŏnsŏp replied that as he had said, there were just the two possibilities: the distillery would be entrusted to the union, or it would pass into private ownership. Well, what would happen if the union took it over? asked Chunho. "It's the right thing to do," Kŏnsŏp stated. "Our future lies with the union." What Chunho had meant by his question, though, was what would happen with his application to take control of the distillery.

But Kŏnsŏp seemed unmindful of such matters. Chunho felt compelled to try to obtain further particulars from Kŏnsŏp but ultimately thought better of it. Not because Kŏnsŏp was unconcerned; rather, it had suddenly occurred to Chunho that just as a second party had applied to the Office of Private Commerce and Industry to take over the distillery, Kŏnsŏp through his recently assumed status as contact person with the union might be campaigning to represent the distillery once it came under the control of the union. Clearly he must be. You couldn't survive at that time without deceiving others. Just look at Four-Eyes in the Office of Private Commerce and Industry: even though takeovers and such were no longer the responsibility of that office, he had lied to the end in telling Chunho not to worry about the distillery. (In all fairness to the clerk, he had learned only the previous morning of the second party's application.)

It was all becoming clear to Chunho. That rascal Kŏnsŏp's pretense of right conduct and his "Comrades" blather had been a ploy to convince others that what he was saying made sense. Chunho saw now that the big words that rascal used—words that the illiterate couldn't understand—had all been parroted from the newspaper. And to think that he himself had thought nothing but the best of the guy till now! Talk about getting stabbed in the back!

Now that he thought about it, you didn't often see someone as grasping as Kŏnsŏp. Didn't he look like a greedy sort, with those big fat blue lips and that drooping chin? And what's more, from the very day he had started working at the distillery as a clerk—and he had come highly recommended!—he had never revealed himself to others. People like that were *wicked*! From now on, Chunho told himself, he would have to be very careful with that rascal. And not just careful: if Chunho found out that Kŏnsŏp was up to no good in other ways, he'd have to do something about it. He would see the end of this. But since he had no specific proof for his suspicions, it was necessary to bide his time. Meanwhile his own priority was to find the capital he would need to run the distillery.

When he returned home that evening, his head spinning with such thoughts, his wife greeted him with the news that for some time she had suspected the widow of secretly removing her possessions from the house, and she appeared to have done so again that day. The widow had been going to the market every few days, presumably out of gratitude and to show that she could feed herself, but it seemed she used those opportunities to smuggle her belongings out. At that very moment, his wife reported, she was in the storage room rummaging around for something. As if Chunho wasn't already out of sorts! Flaring

in anger, he stomped off toward the storage room and sure enough
the widow was just then emerging with a bundle she could barely
manage. What did she have there? Chunho demanded. An electric
heater, the widow replied. And before Chunho could question her
further she said that she had visited her daughter-in-law that day to
find her ill and lying on an unheated tatami floor, and that she felt the
least she could do was take her the heater.

In an angry voice Chunho said they knew she had been sneaking
things out like this, and that even if her daughter-in-law was sick,
there must be at least one room in that house with a heated floor, and
that's where the daughter-in-law should be, and he imagined that
whoever occupied that room with the heated floor might be expected to have sympathy for a fellow Japanese, and what's more, if he
and his wife had a distinguished visitor they would need the heater,
and with that he told the widow to speak no more and to put the
heater in the Western-style room. "And if you do that again, you
won't be forgiven," he scolded her as she set off. Without realizing it,
he was scolding her as a household head would scold a servant while
forgiving her for a mistake. And the widow for her part, as a maid
would have, came to a halt and bowed deeply at the waist, as if to say
she wouldn't do it again.

Not until he saw the woman emerge from the Western-style
room did Chunho turn to leave, but just then he saw his two youngest children scampering toward him from the far end of the hall.
For the first time in his life he shouted at the two little ones to be
quiet. "What's going to happen if you kids screw around like this
and end up breaking a window or something? I don't want to see a
single paper panel ripped. If we have a distinguished guest, I want
him to think we deserve to live in a grand house like this. What will
such a guest think if you kids are running wild?" As the children retreated, chastened, Chunho shouted once more: "Make a racket like
that again and you can count on a whipping." Yes, indeed, he told
himself, he had better make a whip.

All of this had put Chunho in a drinking mood. Retrieving the
empty bottle next to the head of his bedding in the guest room, he
went out to the yard.

In the past he would have wanted to offer the liquor in the basement to all the other employees, but he no longer felt this was necessary. Instead he would save it for future use. His gaze traveled to the stone lantern and the stone figures and he realized he'd forgotten to get the cement to repair them. That proved how busy he'd been, he lamented to himself. *The least a man can do after a hard day's work is have himself a drink in the evening!*

He filled his bottle in the basement, went to the quiet guest room, had his wife bring kimchi, and poured himself a drink in an empty rice bowl. In the past Chunho had been second to none in his capacity, albeit for drinks to which he was treated by others, but now, owing perhaps to his regular usage, half a bottle was sufficient to get him good and drunk. And today, drinking from a larger vessel than usual, he felt the alcohol even more quickly. Holding his not quite half-finished bottle, he launched into another silent tirade: *Just you guys wait!*

So, Kŏnsŏp, you figure you're going to move in on me, huh? You little shit! So worked up about the distillery you forgot your job and only have eyes for my position? That's why Koreans are in such a mess! And where do you get off calling me "Comrade" when I'm ten years older than you? Okay, when all of this started I trusted everyone and called them "Comrade" myself, but I can't believe a bloody whelp like you calls me that. And that's just for starters! Now all the riffraff in the distillery call me "Comrade"—every plug-ugly one of them! . . . No matter what, I have to dig up a source of money and get the wherewithal. There must be somebody. . . . Yes! P'ilbae—he's made a pile with his clothing factory. Why didn't I think of that? He's my hometown friend, for heaven's sake! Should I go see him now? No, it's too important, I need to be sober.. Tomorrow morning, then. All right, I'm set! One more drink!

He poured himself a full bowl, delighting in the *glug glug glug* of the liquid, then drank it straight off and went to bed. But again, once the liquor had worn off he awakened and just couldn't get back to sleep.

The next morning Chunho gave his suit another brushing, knotted his tie, and set off to visit P'ilbae before going to the distillery. Along the way he considered: before, when he had wanted to barter his allotment of liquor from the distillery for rice or fabric he had thought of P'ilbae, but the thing was, the closer you are to someone the more difficult it is to work the exchange to your advantage, so he had given up on the idea. How thankful he was that he had never worked an exchange with P'ilbae, so there had never been occasion for the two of them to develop a bad impression of each other.

It turned out that P'ilbae the clothing manufacturer was shrewd enough not to barter with anyone he knew. In the course of their conversation that morning this shrewd clothing king in his forties told Chunho that as a matter of principle he would never try his hand at a line of business other than the one he was comfortable with—clothing manufacture—and so Chunho had to deliver a lengthy, detailed explanation just to get a response of "I'll consider it" from his counterpart. He started by telling P'ilbae how Nakamura had arrived in Korea with empty pockets, had done clerical work for a liquor wholesaler, and then with an investment from a hometown friend had established a small distillery. Now, seven or eight years later, look how big it had grown, and Chunho knew this for a fact because all along he had been working there; and Nakamura's mill at Chinnamp'o had been established with proceeds from the distillery. That distillery was now to be taken over and probably at a very good price, and if he, Chunho, were given control of it there was no doubt in his mind that he could repay any investment within two or three years—"Mark my word." In any event, Chunho considered it a success to have extracted an "I'll consider it" from P'ilbae, and after telling him he would return that evening, he left.

As soon as he arrived at the distillery he told Kŏnsŏp that he had found a backer. Kŏnsŏp responded with a frosty stare (or so it seemed to Chunho) and said that these days there were a lot of guys entering into a position of responsibility in the factories and companies who seemed to think of themselves as if they were a company president back in the colonial period, and when such people then got financing in addition, their thinking got even more grandiose. And that was why the distillery employees should entrust their distillery to the union.

Chunho realized that Kŏnsŏp was including Chunho among those who fancied themselves old-time company presidents. *That's all I need to know!* Clearly Kŏnsŏp was going to use the power of the union and connive to make himself the distillery representative. It was obvious from the icy look in his eyes.

If Kŏnsŏp was going to campaign to become the distillery representative, Chunho told himself, he couldn't sit back and do nothing, so he said to Kŏnsŏp, "As long as we have a reliable source of capital, why do we have to fall back on the union?" To which Kŏnsŏp replied that in any case there were other issues to discuss, and that they should call a general meeting of the employees the following day and talk about the matter. *That no-good must have formed a gang with those stupid employees, and I bet he's trying to work the situation to his advantage. But once the funding starts flowing in it'll be a piece of cake to win those employees over. Plus, almost all of them started working here before Kŏnsŏp, and it's to my advantage that they've worked longer with me than they have with him.*

The day was waning when one of the employees approached Chunho and asked for a word with him outside. What the man had to say was this: he and his family had no place to stay and were having a hard time of it, and could they occupy one of the rooms at Chunho's home? Chunho recognized the man as one of those who had helped clear the house the day before Chunho and his family had moved in. "As you know," Chunho told the man, "it's a big house, but all the rooms are tatami rooms, and it really isn't set up for two families." To which the man replied that in that case he could remove the mats from one of the rooms and put in the traditional floor-heating system.

Chunho thought of the night-duty room at the distillery and told the man to move his family there. The man responded that not only was that room also a tatami room but that in order to live there for the winter he would have to put even more labor and expense into fixing it up than had been needed for the house Chunho occupied, and he implored Chunho to allow his family just a small corner of the house. Chunho wondered why the man couldn't move into the night-duty room—after all, Chunho and his entire family had managed to live there, untidy as it was. Besides, if he let out a room, the image of grandeur he associated with the house would be ruined, and quite frankly he had gotten to like the privacy of the guest room he occupied. No, it just wouldn't work. And so he cut the man off, saying he simply couldn't let out a room in his house. The man was clearly displeased. He would be on Kŏnsŏp's side, Chunho told himself.

And now that he thought about it, Chunho had sensed, starting the previous day, a change in the employees' attitude toward him. He could imagine the complaints whenever two or three of them got together: if they'd known that the distillery would be in limbo for so long, they would have found other work; so-and-so in his neighborhood was making such-and-such a day cutting firewood, and so-and-so was earning such-and-such carrying loads on his backrack; they really shouldn't complain because their jobs at the distillery didn't require them to get their hands dirty, but then, if things went on this way, even their lice would starve and their children would have so little to eat they wouldn't even poop; and that's why they'd proposed divvying up the barrels of liquor, but no one had listened and now they couldn't even go near those barrels, and what a fine situation that was—Chunho could imagine all the grumbling.

All of these complaints were for his benefit, Chunho told himself. But as for the disposition of the store of alcohol remaining in the distillery, when Kŏnsŏp had said that this wasn't a matter for them to decide, Chunho had gone along with him and agreed, and if this turned out to be a mistake, it wouldn't be just Chunho's mistake. He felt, though, that the resentment over that issue was being aimed at him. (In fact, the employees' complaints were more for Kŏnsŏp's ears than for Chunho's, because Kŏnsŏp was frequently consulting with the union and the employees felt that if he told the union about their situation, it might work out that they could do as they wished with the liquor that was currently in storage.)

But Chunho wasn't worried. The employees could resent him all they wanted for now, but once he'd secured his capital, they would all fall in line behind him!

Early that evening Chunho set out for P'ilbae's home with three liter bottles of *soju*. P'ilbae, it turned out, didn't drink much, and it was he who kept offering liquor to Chunho. Chunho felt compelled by etiquette not to drink much himself. In the end, P'ilbae stopped short of giving Chunho a clear go-ahead. Whether he wouldn't commit himself to an unfamiliar line of business or was reluctant at such a chaotic time to let the whole world see him investing such a large sum of money, Chunho wasn't sure. It was all he could do to get P'ilbae to request that he provide an itemized list of the brewery facilities and a rough figure representing the required investment, but to achieve this he had had to address P'ilbae as "Big Brother" out of etiquette, even though P'ilbae was only a year older and the two of them had grown up together not standing on such ceremony, and he also had to repeat the story of Nakamura arriving in Korea penniless and becoming a success, and say that by now he, Chunho, could run the distillery with his eyes closed—this business was as safe as a duck in water. Chunho did feel anxious at the lack of a clear go-ahead from P'ilbae, but to keep after him could easily lead to a breach of etiquette, so with this thought he took his leave, telling P'ilbae he would look him up again in a few days.

Outside it was getting dark. Chunho felt unpleasantly tipsy, and his head was drooping. On his way home, from the docks at the Taedong River past a police station and skirting the plaza, he worried about what would happen if his dealings with P'ilbae went sour; reminded himself that something important like this would not come easily, but for today anyway, to have gotten the answer he had from P'ilbae, who had always been an astute businessman, meant that something was working. In this way he comforted himself.

As Chunho was thinking these thoughts, someone collided with him and he flinched and came to a stop. Before him stood a middle-aged woman. A wicker basket of radishes she had been carrying on her head had fallen, the radishes scattering. As the woman retrieved them she kept looking behind her. Chunho turned to see what she was looking at and started. A man, he must have been a policeman, pistol upraised, was walking backwards with measured steps. Half a dozen paces away a dozen men were walking toward him, their hands up. Chunho had never seen anything like it. Although the men were simply following the policeman's orders, it looked almost as if their steps were synchronized with his. The man with the gun kept a close watch, and with every backward step he took, the dozen men went one step forward. Chunho was reminded of a nursery school teacher instructing her children in a simple dance movement. It was a frightening and yet perfectly harmonious tableau, one that continued until all of the men had been reeled into the lower level of the police station.

As soon as the last man had been swallowed up, Chunho thought he could hear some of the onlookers asking what was going on, followed by voices saying that Jap conspiracy groups were being nabbed. But to Chunho, who had felt out of sorts since leaving P'ilbae's house, there was something pleasing about the fact that a dozen men had been led away single-handedly. It was amazing how compliant they had been!

Back home, Chunho didn't know what to do about his mixed feelings: on the one hand there was this pleasant sensation, and on the other the unpleasant question of who would manage the distillery. And so it was back to the *soju*, this time with supper, Chunho first filling a beer bottle from the downstairs cask. After a time the Japanese woman informed him that his bath was ready. Which made Chunho realize he'd skipped his bath the past several days. He would have himself a bath and for once a good night's sleep. *But before I do, one more nip!*

In the event, Chunho drank until the bottle was less than half full, which was enough to get him drunk. His lingering concerns about the management of the distillery dissipated, leaving him only with a relaxed sensation. After picking at his meal, he lost interest in a bath and fell into a comfortable sleep.

Again that night, once the liquor had begun to wear off, Chunho awakened, and when the new dawn found him still awake, he had to drink a large bowl of *soju* to get back to sleep, but even then his rest was disordered by all sorts of dreams. At first he was in his bath at home, but then it wasn't his bath but rather one of the vats at the distillery. *Well, then, might as well drink to my heart's content.* And as he drank, he swam around, dove beneath the surface, and drank his fill. And when he could drink no more, he wanted to climb out of the tank, but he couldn't—there was nothing to grab on to. Now he was in a fix! He looked up, and who should he see looking down at him but that son of a bitch Kŏnsŏp. Down he looked with those cold eyes.

And there next to Kŏnsŏp—the man who had asked Chunho for a room in his house. That son of a bitch too looked down on Chunho, and he was just as upset as when Chunho had told him he couldn't rent him a room. And it wasn't just those two; all the other employees had surrounded the vat and were looking down at Chunho. And not one helping hand from the lot of them. *Fine! I'll get out under my own power—just watch!* But he couldn't manage. He was all played out. But he wasn't about to ask those sons of bitches for help. *I've got my dignity!* He struggled desperately but in vain, until the effort finally brought him awake. He was covered with a cold sweat.

Chunho was late to work as a result. When he arrived, there was Kŏnsŏp telling him not to forget the meeting that evening. Chunho felt compelled to say once more that he had obtained a reliable source of capital, to which Kŏnsŏp, looking him in the eye with his cold stare (or so it felt to Chunho), said in his haughtiest tone (this too as perceived by Chunho), "Well, I realize we have to discuss these issues this evening, but I can tell you now that since we employees can't put together the funding to manage the business, it's better to allow the union to operate the distillery than to use the capital of a single individual."

The union—*it's always the* union! thought Chunho. *Arrogant son of a bitch—he's got some nerve talking the way he does—it's probably for the benefit of the employees, and you can bet they have their ears to the door listening. If this is something that an individual can handle, then why make things complicated by handing the distillery over to the union?* He couldn't figure it out. In any event, he would say something at the meeting that evening. That day Chunho prepared the itemized list of the distillery facilities to show P'ilbae, and when he had finished he felt heavy all over, short as he'd been on sleep the past few days.

The meeting was scheduled for six, and Chunho went home for an early dinner. But once he was there his thoughts turned to drink instead of food. His initial thought was to drink only a little, but then he had a change of heart and decided he would drink his fill and then at the meeting spill out all he had to say, and he proceeded to drink a beer bottle full of *soju*. Before he knew it, it was dark enough to turn on the lights. He had already taken off his suit jacket, which felt confining.

By now they were all at the distillery, waiting for him. Sure, but that son of a bitch Kŏnsŏp had probably already stood up and was talking about the liquor in storage at the distillery; or maybe he was proposing that there was something they could do right then, and that was to divvy up the liquor in Chunho's basement; or maybe he was revisiting the management issue and explaining that it was better to let the union take over operations, but using big words and phrases too difficult for the ignorant employees to understand. The employees probably thought that son of a bitch Kŏnsŏp was a great guy; they probably thought that everything he said was right. *He even pulled the wool over my eyes.* An image of Kŏnsŏp and his big mouth rose in Chunho's mind. *So, you sons of bitches are going to leave out the man who spent the last twenty years at the distillery, you figure you'll have your meeting before I get there?*

Before he knew it he was shouting, "It's a conspiracy!" Just like the Japanese conspiracy he had seen the previous evening. His bulging eyes, bloodshot from drink and lack of sleep, bulged out even more, producing a strange gleam, and before he knew it he was on his feet. But he had no pistol. *Must be a knife around somewhere.*

Chunho went out to the kitchen. His wife was in the next room, the room with the heated floor. She opened the small serving door to the kitchen and asked if Chunho wanted his supper. Chunho offered the excuse that he was thirsty and was looking for water, and would eat after he returned from his meeting. And then, to get his wife to shut the serving door, he actually drank some water. Once he started drinking he realized he really was thirsty and gulped several mouthfuls, but the moment his wife shut the serving door he quickly located a kitchen knife, pocketed it, and left. *Sons of bitches, wait till you get a taste of this!*

The streets were dark. It was full autumn, and a chill wind penetrated the dusk. The wind cooled his face and chest—his jacket was unbuttoned—but Chunho grew more unsteady on his feet nonetheless, owing to the alcohol and his lack of sleep. Even more unsteady was his mind.

As he stumbled along he kept shouting, "You sons of bitches, you scheming sons of bitches, wait till you get a taste of this!" Passersby laughed and said, "Yeah, let's hear it for Liberation!" but Chunho paid them no heed. "You sons of bitches, if you aren't a bunch of scheming sons of bitches then what are you? Look at me, I spent my entire youth at this distillery—and somebody else is gonna be the rep? Listen to me, you sons of bitches—who was the man who threw that pile of hundred-*wŏn* notes, it was five or six thousand *wŏn*, easy— who was the man who threw it all up in the air when they tried to bribe him? Who's the man who's going to give you sons of bitches a living in the future? And you're going to cut me out? You sons of bitches deserve to die!" He passed the jail from the previous evening; it was shrouded in darkness. "Yeah, I'm gonna stick all of you scheming sons of bitches right here in this jail—yes I will—just you wait."

The light was on in the night-duty room of the Yugyŏng Distillery in Sŏsŏng-ni. "You sons of bitches deserve to die!" And with that Chunho half stumbled, half ran to the door, yanked it open, and entered. "Hands up!" he shouted, producing his knife. "Hands up, you sons of bitches, and don't move an inch—hands up!"

The employees recoiled. Kŏnsŏp rose. "Hands up!" Chunho barked, his hoarse voice even louder. He advanced toward Kŏnsŏp, but his wobbly legs got tangled and he pitched forward on his face. The employees swarmed around Chunho. His mouth and nose bleeding, he produced a low moan from deep within. The hand holding the knife quivered. Without a word Kŏnsŏp removed the knife and tossed it into the corner.

Chunho opened his teary eyes halfway, looked up, and tried to lift himself, but then his eyes closed shut and his face sank back onto the tatami mat.

October 1945

THE TOAD

One man's death is another man's cold. This was Hyŏnse's thought as he walked toward the South Gate.

The old saying fit the events of that morning. When the girl had died, the young daughter of fellow refugees, her worm-infested body swollen all over, Hyŏnse's first response was not to try to console the young couple squatting on either side of her and stifling their tears. Instead he was irritated by his wife with her sad face and her whimpering and by his daughter, who was the same age as the dead girl, asking, "Why doesn't she wake up?" and he scowled at them both. Here he was, about to leave to try to raise some money, and all of this was a bad omen. Even when he got around to comforting the young couple, telling them to bear up because the matter was out of their hands, his only thought was that instead of lingering there he ought to out be selling his suit at the South Gate markets so he could buy his family some edibles.

It hadn't been like this when they had returned from North China a month earlier on the boat. Three children had died on the voyage. All three had recently been weaned, all three had developed severe diarrhea, and a day or two before the boat arrived at Pusan they were dead. Right up until they died they had produced foul-smelling, watery diarrhea. Disgusting as that had been, no one on the boat had wished the children to be dead and gone. When the liquid and powder remedies provided by the medical aides didn't work, a stranger came forward with what he claimed to be a wonder drug for diarrhea, and this was fed to the children as well. It had no effect either. Although the corpses were not contagious, they couldn't remain on board with the days growing hot and humid, so the only option was to consign them to the sea. There wasn't much they could do, said the parents, but they would regret for the rest of their lives not being able to bury the bones of their children in their native land. All who witnessed this burial at sea felt heavy of heart, as if they themselves had been bereaved. For the first time they felt with fervor, each of them, that they were all brothers and sisters of the same homeland.

For Hyŏnse this fervor had cooled before he knew it. Actually he did know it: he knew it from the moment he realized that his homeland would not provide him and his family a livelihood. And as he walked along now he could tell who was in the same predicament: there, that man walking by—and that one—and that one there. . . . *Heck!* He told himself to think instead about selling his suit at the South Gate markets and buying some potatoes at the East Gate markets. The South Gate markets were supposed to offer the best price for whatever you were selling; it was there that he would sell his suit for as much money as it would bring. And the East Gate markets were supposed to offer whatever you were looking for at the best price; it was there that he would buy some cheap potatoes. Then he could put something into his stomach. With that thought came a little voice from somewhere inside him saying, *I've got to survive. Yes, I do,* he told himself, and he tightened his grip on the suit he was carrying.

He looked up to see the South Gate. Its protruding eaves, top to bottom, were blurry. Not because of tears in his eyes or haze in the air, but because he had skipped breakfast that morning. As he observed the South Gate with his blurred vision he had the illusion that he had returned not to his homeland but instead to Manchuria or North China. He recalled eaves like that on the houses in those places. Maybe all the people he saw now were people he had seen in those alien lands. And maybe that meant that he himself was now in a foreign land.

Lost in these thoughts, he noticed a fleshy face passing before him. That face belonged to someone he knew, someone from before he had left his homeland. Who exactly was it? And then a face came to mind, that of a chum from primary school. And if it was a childhood chum, then he really was back in his homeland and the man must be a fellow countryman. He turned and saw that the man was continuing on his way. Now what was his name? He had a nickname—was it Fatso? Bulldog?

He had just arrived at the entrance to the South Gate markets when he felt a tap on his shoulder.

"Hyŏnse—is that you?"

Hyŏnse turned in surprise and there before him was the homeland face he had just seen, only now it was smiling. A shout escaped him.

"It's me, Tugap," said the face.

"Yeah!"

It was then that the man's nickname occurred to him—not Fatso or Bulldog but Toad, because his given name, Tugap, was similar to *tukkŏbi*, toad, and because his mouth resembled that of a toad.

"Didn't recognize me, did you? When you passed me by I said to myself, 'I ought to know his name,' but it took me a moment to recollect it. What do you say we have ourselves a hot drink?"

Without waiting for an answer, Tugap started back the way he had come. Hyŏnse followed.

Hyŏnse kept falling behind and Tugap kept looking back and remarking, "How long's it been, anyway? Must be twenty years. We're a couple of old men now! But you know, if you stay alive long enough, you're bound to run into somebody like this."

At a tearoom in the Chin'gogae area they sat down across from each other at a table.

"How long has it been?" asked Tugap. "I'm so glad we ran into each other."

So saying, he produced a handkerchief and mopped his sweaty face, then proceeded to fan himself vigorously with a folding fan decorated with the yin-yang trigrams. Smiling, he acknowledged with a glance the men seated here and there around them.

A serving girl approached.

"What do you want?" he asked Hyŏnse.

"Anything's fine."

"One tea," Tugap said, and with a practiced air he made for the girl a number one with the index finger of the hand holding the fan. "I had mine a little while ago," he told Hyŏnse.

A glass of milk would be nice, thought Hyŏnse, something to take the edge off his hunger.

Compared with Hyŏnse's poverty-stricken self and the worn-out clothes he wore for construction work, Tugap wore a serge suit that, although faded from white to yellow, was well pressed and sleek. But the first thing you noticed about him was his shiny oiled hair. If you were looking for flaws in his appearance, there was only his toadlike mouth—if you could call that a flaw.

The tea arrived and when Hyŏnse had taken a sip, Tugap leaned toward him and said, "How long has it been, really? You went to North China, right? I was stuck in P'yeyang until Liberation and then I came here. I tell you what, let's leave it right there. Even supposing we hashed over all of that, what's the use? We should think about the future instead, time's a-wasting and all that.... So where are you living now?"

Every time Tugap opened his mouth, Hyŏnse detected an unmistakable smell—grilled beef and garlic, washed down with *soju*, last night's dinner.

"In a house where a Western missionary used to live—supposedly it's where the Kyŏngshin School used to be."

"That's what I thought," said Tugap. "I hear there's a whole lot of refugees in that missionary's house. Well, perfect! I tell you what—I'm going to get you a room. And I want you to know, a vacant room here in the capital is like pie in the sky. Yessir, it's a good thing we ran into each other. And even better that I didn't just walk on by.... We have to help each other out; nobody's going to do it for us. Now, this room, see, we need to put on a little act—and it's a pretty simple role, really."

In fact Tugap had had a scheme in mind before coming across Hyŏnse, but he spoke as if he were letting Hyŏnse in on a clever idea he had just come up with. He paused to allow Hyŏnse to catch his meaning.

"This room I'm talking about is in a house at the top of the hill in Samch'ŏng-dong. And here's the point of our little act: actually there's no vacant room at the moment, so what we're going to do is get all the renters to leave and then we give the rooms to other people. You're probably wondering how in heck it's possible to get renters to leave in this day and age—well, what we do is, we pretend someone is going to buy the house. And because someone's buying the house, all the renters have to move out. You get what I'm talking about? Then we have the house all to ourselves and you move into one of the rooms. That's all there is to it. So all you have to do is be the person who's buying the house. There's just one thing you have to be careful about: you don't ever tell anyone about this little act you're putting on."

Again Tugap paused, looking across at Hyŏnse as if to say, *Well, how about it?*

"And you're probably wondering, why go to the trouble of putting on an act to get the current renters to leave? Here's why. The man who owns the house is a trader; he's got his hands on a solid chunk of money and plans to be buying and selling on a large scale before too long, and he needs one of the rented rooms, the one that's beside the gate, for storage. But you can't ask one renter to leave and not the others, and no amount of talking is going to get them all to go—it's been tried. These Seoul people are tough nuts to crack, in case you didn't know. So we have to do our little act—it's the only way. The owner of the house was the first person I knew in Seoul and we thought that maybe I could play the main role, but the problem is, I'm in and out of the house so often the renters and I know one another's faces. So that won't work. And I was trying to find someone to fill the bill when I ran into you, and it's a good thing I did. I'll bet you've had a hard time finding a room, so you're just the man I'm looking for. You get yourself a room, the owner gets rid of the renters, and there you have it—two birds with one stone."

So saying—and Hyŏnse realized that Tugap was speaking almost like a native of Seoul—Tugap produced his toadlike grin as if to say, *Make sense?*

Hyŏnse was not so inclined. His immediate concern was not a room to live in—there were no worries there—but his empty stomach. He was anxious to get to the South Gate markets to sell his suit, and then to the East Gate markets to buy the potatoes, and then to take them back to his family and steam them. . . .

"So what do you think?"

"I'll think it over," said Hyŏnse without actually considering what he was saying.

"You'll think it over? Sounds like you don't have a worry in the world about where you're going to live. Maybe you're feeling sorry for the people who have to leave, maybe taking their place doesn't sit right with you—well, don't waste your sympathies. Like the fellow says, put out your own fire first and then think of the other guy. Those renters have survived in Seoul till now—they'll manage. See what I'm saying? You don't want to miss this opportunity. Today, or tomorrow morning at the latest, you're going to see a realtor in Samch'ŏng-dong and tell him you want to buy a house—that's all there is to it. You see, the owner has already put the house up for sale with this realtor."

Tugap wrote directions to the realtor's office and the house on a piece of paper, gave it to Hyŏnse, and said, "Listen to what I'm telling you and forget the think-it-over. I'll see you here tomorrow around one."

After they parted Hyŏnse sold his suit at the South Gate markets, bought the potatoes at the East Gate markets and put them in a sack, and started back to where his wife and children were. He was so hungry he couldn't help walking slouched over; he didn't even have the energy to wipe the sweat that was streaming from his forehead into his eyes and his mouth. Now it was the perspiration that was blurring his vision. All he could think of was steaming those damned potatoes and taking big bites out of them . . . blowing on them first if they were too hot . . . that light, powdery texture . . . but wait, just potatoes? . . . No, there had to be some cabbage-leaf soup to slurp, and he shouldn't eat the potatoes too fast. . . . These thoughts had him drooling and swallowing the rest of the way home.

Back home everyone was in bed. Except for those who had been picked for day labor for road construction or street cleaning, everybody spent the morning in bed. By eating breakfast as late as possible they attempted to stretch two meals a day into three, or even one meal a day into two. Those with children prepared a mixture of potatoes and rice when the little ones' pestering became too much, but were unable to resist eating along with them, and then would go back to bed for fear of digesting their meal too quickly. The young couple who had just lost their child had gone back to bed too, almost as if it were their turn to be invalids.

From here and there Hyŏnse heard the voices of the ill; it sounded as though they were talking in their sleep. From their wretched appearance you would think their condition was serious. The ground floor of this Western-style house had been opened up and all the partitions removed, and with all the people lying there it resembled a public clinic.

Hyŏnse likewise went back to bed after appeasing his children with a meal of steamed potatoes and cabbage-leaf soup. He lay still but was sweating profusely. This was unusual. He decided it was because he had taken hot food on an empty stomach. And the really hot days of summer were still to come. Hyŏnse hoped they would go by fast. Then again, they could complain all they wanted about the heat, and before they knew it they'd be complaining all they wanted about the cold. But for refugees, hot summer was better than cold winter, no two ways about it. Just in terms of a place to live, you could spend the summer on a nice cool wooden floor like this, or practically anywhere for that matter.

But in winter? Forget winter, the problem was right here and now. Elder Kim upstairs had been pressuring them at every opportunity to vacate. Elder Kim with his rimless glasses, paunch swelling out to the sides, Bible in its leather cover always in hand. He was a very dignified man. He had arrived, with the title House Manager, only a few days after Hyŏnse and his family. Two days later, in the morning, the elder had come downstairs, hand resting gracefully on his leather-bound Bible, and declared, "Brothers and sisters, you who have no place to live, I have much sympathy for you, but though I know not why, from my first night here, sound sleep has eluded me, I dream fitful dreams on account of you, my brothers and sisters, and I know not what to do. Brothers and sisters, sympathize with me in your turn and vacate this house, vacate it with all due haste. You shall not spend winter in this house, and I beseech you to sympathize with me and vacate with all due haste." He was a very dignified man, from his carriage to his manner of speaking and the tone of his voice, a voice that brooked no opposition.

Instinctively Hyŏnse glanced about at the refugees spread out on the floor, in front of him and in back. An image came to mind, stark

and clear, of each of these refugees bundling up belongings and setting out for who knew where. If this scene became reality, then no
matter how intimidating Elder Kim's words, Hyŏnse would speak
out on behalf of the refugees, even at the risk of danger to himself.
Please be patient just a little while longer, he would say. And Elder Kim
would most likely say, *Brothers and sisters, have sympathy for this old man.
Have sympathy for this old man who is the same blood as you, this old man who cannot sleep on account of you, my brothers and sisters.* Elder Kim had an unusually prominent adam's apple. It made him resemble someone—who
was it? Yes—just like Tugap's mouth resembled that of a toad, Elder
Kim with his rimless glasses and his paunch swelling out to the sides
was the very image of a toad. The strange thing was, his resemblance
to a toad somehow made Elder Kim seem even more dignified. By
now Hyŏnse felt incapable of speaking up by himself after all, and
instead he gazed around at his fellow refugees, intending to ask their
support. But all he saw was an empty interior—all had packed their
belongings and disappeared. Nothing for Hyŏnse to do but beg as he
had never begged before: *They have all left, we are the only ones here, please be
patient just a little while longer, my wife will have a baby within the month and we
can't live out on the streets.* But all Elder Kim said, his voice as dignified
as always, was, *Have sympathy for me, brother, have sympathy for this old man.*
And below his prominent adam's apple, his toad belly was getting
larger and larger. If it kept growing it would fill the entire ground
floor of this Western-style house.

Hyŏnse bolted up to a sitting position. Perspiration had soaked
his shirt. Someone was moaning. He had to leave.

Once outside, Hyŏnse set out for Samch'ŏng-dong. The realtor's
office was just where Tugap had said it would be—on the left, not
far past the entrance to Samch'ŏng-dong, marked by a gate bearing
a worn piece of fabric reading REALTOR. Hyŏnse opened the gate,
and there on the veranda sat an elderly man, clean-shaven and not
bewhiskered like other men his age, his head jerking down and then
back up as he tried to keep from nodding off. The man straightened
at the sound of his visitor and acknowledged Hyŏnse.

"Would there be a house for sale in this area?" Hyŏnse asked almost before he realized it.

"Certainly." Donning a pair of spectacles, the man regarded Hyŏnse. "A very fine house is available. It has nice spacious rooms; would you care to see it?" And with that he led the way outside.

Hyŏnse followed the elderly broker up a street bordered on the right by a stream. The streamside was dotted with housewives doing their laundry in the clear water. *A perfect place to do the wash* was his first impression.

They turned away from the stream and went up an alley. Where the alley came to an end they turned right into another alley, and there, higher still, sat a house on an outcropping. Below was the stream, and into it rushed a cataract.

The elderly broker, seeing Hyŏnse's eyes travel from the stream to the pine grove facing them, said, "Well? People were meant to live here, don't you think? You know that Samch'ŏng means 'three-clean,' right? Clean hills and clean water make clean people . . . it's such a nice place to live." The man observed Hyŏnse, gauging the effect of his words.

Hyŏnse was feeling the uphill trudge, and his only thought was that the house they were to visit had better appear before too long.

Finally they arrived at a gate that was a couple of houses before the very end of the alley. The realtor went inside, but Hyŏnse could not bring himself to follow just then. Only when the realtor called him did Hyŏnse step through the gate.

Fortunately the owner of the dwelling did not present himself. There was only a woman at the soy-crock terrace, one of the tenants perhaps, glancing at Hyŏnse; she seemed to be sizing him up. He couldn't let on that he was play-acting, so he gathered his hands behind his back as a gentleman would do and proceeded to look about. The house must have been built some time ago, and for a building of that age, the quality of the wood left something to be desired. Because of the construction work he had done, these were the first things Hyŏnse tended to notice in a house.

The realtor gave Hyŏnse a detailed tour, pointing out the lived-in rooms, the kitchen, and the toilet. As the man's words buzzed about Hyŏnse's ears, he couldn't help wishing that he and his family could move in then and there, and thinking he'd gladly take the room across the veranda or even settle for the room next to the gate.

The realtor then took Hyŏnse out back, and there he found a yard, albeit a cramped one, with a small gate that opened onto a steep path. They followed the path down to a spring. The water came up from beneath a large rock and could be scooped with a gourd dipper.

A girl was there fetching water and the elderly realtor borrowed her dipper, scooped, and tasted. "That's good water!" So saying, he offered the dipper to a thirsty Hyŏnse, who took several gulps. As soon as the dipper had left Hyŏnse's lips the realtor asked, "Not bad, eh? This isn't just any old spring—it never runs dry even in a bad drought. People come a long ways to drink this water. Compared with a spring like this, tap water—god, how can they call it tap water when more days than not nothing comes out!"

By now the realtor must have worked up a thirst himself, for he scooped water and gulped it noisily. "That's goooood! Just as fresh now as the first time I tasted it." The old man was growing more exclamatory by the minute.

Back up the path they went, through the back gate, and around the house, emerging into the alley.

"This here is a temple." The realtor paused at a place Hyŏnse re-membered having seen on the way to the house, and indicated a build-ing with multicolored eaves. "Perfect spot for it. Wonderful location. Behind it you can imagine the hills spreading out like a folding screen. Clear spring water. You could look the rest of your life and never find such a blessed spot."

As the elderly realtor looked up to scan the surroundings, a bald spot the size of a small dish on the crown of his head came into view. Hyŏnse noticed beads of perspiration there. The realtor didn't have an easy time of it, Hyŏnse told himself, having to make a living by his gift of gab.

"How much are they asking back there?" said Hyŏnse in an effort to get moving.

The realtor set out again. "That's the thing—it comes with a good price too. They're asking eleven thousand a *k'an*, and these days you can't buy a decent house downtown for less than fifteen thousand." And then he gave Hyŏnse a backward look as if to say, *You probably knew that already, since you're in the market for a house.* "But I'll see if I can get you that house for ten thousand a *k'an*."

"Are you saying the difference between this house and one downtown is only five thousand?" asked Hyŏnse. "You'd have to walk miles to catch the streetcar from here—people with money won't want to do that. Besides, the house needs some work."

"And that's why I said I'd get it for you for ten thousand a *k'an*. If it was a new house, it wouldn't be worth any less than houses downtown. You've got clean air, clean water; why, you wouldn't believe how many people have bought houses here. If you figure on buying, then do it—don't lose out to someone else. So, at ten thousand a *k'an* the price would be a hundred and twenty thousand *wŏn*."

Hyŏnse realized he had to say something to keep the act going. "Well, if it was a hundred thousand I might consider it."

"I'm afraid there's no chance of that." The realtor arrived at his house and came to a stop. "In any event, let's take care of the earnest money. Once that's done, the seller will negotiate in good faith."

"Let me give it some thought," said Hyŏnse, to give the impression that he was done for the day.

Whereupon the realtor seemed to realize that he should back off for the time being, and changed the subject. "Say, where are you headed? If you're going in the direction of Chongno I can show you a shortcut. Follow me if you will." And off he went.

When they reached the street that led to Anguk-dong the realtor said, "Let's take care of the earnest money tomorrow at the latest. Then we can get down to business and find out how much that house is really worth."

It was obvious to Hyŏnse that the realtor had offered to show him this shortcut in order to repeat those words.

By the time Hyŏnse walked into the tearoom in Chin'gogae where he was supposed to meet Tugap, he was a sweaty mess. It was as if all the liquid he had taken in as spring water had passed out of him as perspiration. Tugap had yet to arrive, though the appointed hour of one o'clock had passed.

The serving girl came to take his order.

This time Hyŏnse was ready. "Milk."

He drank it down but it was hardly satisfying. When some time later Tugap had still not arrived, Hyŏnse got to thinking: that toad-faced asshole was scheming; Tugap had played him for a fool, hadn't he? And if that was the case then he'd just wasted fifteen *wŏn* on a glass of milk that hadn't begun to fill his stomach. Fifteen *wŏn*— that would buy a small sack of potatoes. And a small sack of potatoes would be enough for his entire family to live on for a day. These thoughts occupied him for a time, and finally there was Tugap, flinging open the door and swaggering in, shoulders pumping up and down.

After Tugap had greeted some of the other customers, his toad-like mouth forming a beaming smile, he came to Hyŏnse. "Must be fixing to rain—it's damn humid." And with that he removed his suit jacket and hung it on his chair, then mopped his neck and forehead with his handkerchief.

"I was just at the house."

That's good, thought Hyŏnse. Now he wouldn't have to repeat details that Tugap must know by now.

Tugap produced the familiar folding fan and heaved a sigh as he fanned himself. His breath reeked of grilled beef, garlic, and *soju*. Hyŏnse found himself thinking that the woods behind that house wouldn't be a bad place to have a hunk of meat and a bottle of *soju*, and he wondered if perhaps Tugap had been there the previous day drinking with the owner.

"Let's get you a drink," said Tugap. "I already had some, just before I came here."

"I had a glass of milk while I was waiting for you."

"All right, then." Tugap reached inside his suit jacket and came out with a check, which he placed before Hyŏnse. "That there's your earnest money."

Hyŏnse picked up the check. It was for ten thousand *wŏn*.

"I tell you, these Seoul people don't miss a thing," said Tugap. "See that line there? That means that even if you happen to lose this check, all you have to do is call the bank and they'll take care of it."

Not just people in Seoul but probably anybody would take that kind of precaution when dealing with a lot of money, Hyŏnse told himself. And so what Tugap really meant was not that Seoul people "don't miss a thing"; rather, he wanted Hyŏnse to know that he shouldn't get any notions about that check. Actually, if the check were Tugap's and not the homeowner's, how much money could Tugap be expected to trust Hyŏnse with? A few hundred *wŏn*? Forget it. Maybe twenty or thirty at the most.

"So, no later than tomorrow you go there and sign the purchase agreement. Now here's what you have to remember. You have to make sure there's a clause in the agreement that says the house has to be *completely* vacated before you pay the balance of the money. And you have to say it's a joint purchase by you and some fellow refugees and you need all the rooms. For the move-out date, make it as soon as possible—say that as of now, you don't have anyplace to live. In return you pretend you'll pay the asking price. In any event, you don't let anyone suspect you're putting on an act. So tomorrow, after you sign the purchase agreement come back here. I drop in around one o'clock, every day. And of course I'll go to the house beforehand to make sure the purchase agreement's been signed. And then on the day you pay the balance, we'll meet here at ten in the morning."

The following day Hyŏnse went back to Samch'ŏng-dong. But instead of going to the realtor's he went straight up to the house. He had to show the renters that he was taking another look at the house and get them thinking about moving if he ended up signing a purchase agreement that day.

Hyŏnse entered the yard as the realtor had done the previous day, and announced he was there to look at the house. A door slid open and a girl who must have been about ten told Hyŏnse that the grown-ups had gone out. This was fortunate, as Hyŏnse was not looking forward to meeting the owner. It seemed the renters were also gone, leaving only this girl at the house. Hyŏnse had seen a relief station on his way up and thought that perhaps the grown-ups were part of the long line waiting there for food rations.

Thinking that all his huffing and puffing had been in vain, Hyŏnse was about to leave when the door to the room across the veranda slid open and the head of an elderly woman poked out. She seemed to have been sick in bed, for her hair was disheveled. Her long neck was serpentine.

"I came to look at the house."

"I see."

"I was looking at it yesterday and I noticed it's kind of run-down." Hyŏnse was so tired from the uphill walk that he sat down unbidden at the edge of the veranda in front of the opened door. He spoke so that the girl couldn't hear him: "Are there any places where the floor has settled?"

"We haven't noticed any water in the flues, if that's what you mean. You sound like you're from the north."

"Yes, from P'yeyang, originally," said Hyŏnse, using the dialect word for Pyongyang. "We were refugees in North China, and now we're back here. There are several of us who don't have a place to live and we thought we'd go in on a house together." He said this almost before he realized it.

"I seeeee." The old woman nodded, head bobbing on her elongated neck, and then she too lowered her voice lest the girl hear: "The floor hasn't sunk, but the room's a mess. During the monsoons last year the rainwater didn't all drain—there were puddles inside— you can imagine."

It seemed the old woman was letting Hyŏnse in on a secret, but it also appeared she was saying this in hope that the sale would not go through and she and her family would not have to move.

But a structural defect in the house was no concern of his, Hyŏnse thought on his way back home.

It was very humid and Hyŏnse felt rain in the air in addition to the heat. Having to walk to the house and back didn't help matters. It wasn't really that much of an uphill walk, but he could see how it would be difficult for someone who didn't get three square meals a day.

He arrived at the realtor's hoping only that the owner of the house would hurry up and return home. He found the elderly realtor sitting on his veranda.

"Come on in. It looks like you've been up there already—that didn't take long."

So, the realtor must have seen him passing by on his way up to the house.

"The thing is, there's been a lot of damage from the monsoons. The rainwater pours right in." This was the issue that Hyŏnse was most curious about.

"Who says? Was it old Snake Neck?"

Didn't take long for him to figure that out, thought Hyŏnse. *Amazing how people's minds tend to work in similar ways.*

"Old Snake Neck knows she has to move if the house is sold. She's pulling a fast one on you so you won't buy. You believe everything you hear and you'll end up without a house. Shilly-shally around and someone else will buy it right from under your nose."

"Still, you need to mention those defects so we can get the owner to lower the price. Anyway, I'm going to trust you with the earnest money. You see, we P'yeyang people are up front about things."

Hyŏnse took out the check. The realtor accepted it, took one look, then pocketed it as if Hyŏnse might ask for it back.

"Now we're in business."

"All right, now, about the move-out date for the renters, do your best to make it soon. Because it's not just me, there's a group of us, and at the moment we don't have a place to live."

"I understand. I'll go see the owner when he's home." The realtor rose to his feet.

"I don't think he's home," said Hyŏnse.

"I saw him heading home just before you arrived," said the realtor, and with that he hurried out the gate and was gone.

That meant he himself must have crossed paths with the owner, thought Hyŏnse, but he couldn't recall having encountered anyone on his way here. But the next moment he was telling himself he had in fact come across several people. He couldn't figure it out. In any event, now that the owner was back home, everything would be fine. *Darn, it's sticky,* Hyŏnse thought, *what we need is a good old downpour to cool things off.* He sat for a time, drifting between sleep and wakefulness, then heard the realtor returning.

"Wasn't easy, I'll tell you." The realtor heaved a sigh before displaying for Hyŏnse a purchase agreement and a receipt for the earnest money.

"He said he wouldn't budge from a hundred twenty, not one copper, no sir. I told him it's hard to get anywhere from there, there's no running water, everything under the sun, and finally I got him down to a hundred fifteen, but he told me it would cost me my commission. You can lead a horse to water but you can't make him drink—well, I made that horse drink, barely. As far as vacating goes, the usual thing is to give the tenants a month's notice, but I said I'd see to it that they get themselves another room, so we settled on the end of the month. Not to brag or anything, but without me this wouldn't have happened. So you should think about coming up with a nice little commission."

The realtor was perspiring freely. Was it that difficult for him to have to ask for a commission?

Rain finally arrived. The dry spell had lasted so long it was as if the people were as parched as the landscape, and even after a few days the steady rain hadn't worn out its welcome.

Hyŏnse and his family were happy to see it. The other refugees had also been looking forward to the first soaking rain and the refreshment it would offer. So when they saw nursing babies blowing out through their mouth the way nursing babies do, they would say to each other, "Look at the little darlings, it's amazing, they knew it was going to rain, but enough's enough and now they should make it stop," and they would laugh and laugh. But then a week went by and still it continued to rain. Normally the monsoons didn't arrive until a month later, and by now the adults who had been predicting the rains were about to stop no longer laughed at the babies blowing out through their mouths, took no pleasure from talking about them, and instead did nothing but lie pathetically in bed. For the women the only refuge was the kitchen, where they gathered once or twice a day to prepare meals and to vent their pent-up emotions.

Those who ventured out returned with the alarming news that Map'o was under water, P'yŏngt'aek was under water, and this was going to be the worst monsoon season in 40 years, with more rain expected. More astounding still were the reports that not even 500 *wŏn* could buy a sack of rice—there was no rice to buy—and that to buy enough potatoes to feed a family of four for two days running you'd have to pay 80 *wŏn*.

As Hyŏnse lay in bed he would tell himself the war was supposed to be over, but for him and his family it was still going full tilt. The news that Map'o was flooded and P'yŏngt'aek was under water sounded to him as if those places had fallen to the enemy. And that's why they were refugees—refugees in a place that didn't seem like their homeland.

The refugees who had found work on road construction crews and as street sweepers, and the children who would normally be playing outside in the daytime, were now indoors out of the rain, thronging the large room of the refugee house and making it feel cramped. Now and then Hyŏnse heard the moans of the sick. The lot of them presented a graphic tableau of ill refugees.

Hyŏnse braved the rain to visit the man, a native of Seoul, who had been a neighbor in Beijing and had returned to Korea on the same boat as Hyŏnse and his family—the man he had earlier approached about finding construction work. The man's only response was for Hyŏnse to try and wait a little longer.

One day Hyŏnse's wife, large with child, complained of itchiness and began to scratch repeatedly at her elbow. She must have shown the affected elbow to someone because she now reported that it was poison ivy, that people didn't die from scabies but they died from poison ivy, and it would be her good fortune if a worthless thing like her could drop dead on the spot. Hyŏnse found this unsettling. Recalling that you were supposed to treat poison ivy by washing it with water that had been used for boiling a black hen, he figured it would be a good idea to buy a chicken, which he could then feed to his family. But he couldn't afford a chicken and so he decided on the next best thing—to apply egg white to the affected area. Braving the rain, he brought back an egg, which his wife cracked before transferring the white to a small bowl. From the way she applied the egg white back and forth over her elbow it seemed she wasn't so eager to die after all. Their little daughter pestered her mother to steam the yolk. Looking in turn at his wife and his little girl, Hyŏnse told himself that people don't die from things like poison ivy; they only die from starvation.

The moaning of the ill increased by the day, and among the moans would be voices saying that this damned rainy season was going to kill off every last one of the refugees. And when the sound of the rain softened, Elder Kim could often be heard upstairs singing hymns. His voice when he sang was by far the clearest and most resonant voice to be heard. Ever since the monsoons had started, Elder Kim had refrained from asking the refugees to vacate, but it seemed only a matter of time before he started up again.

As if Hyŏnse didn't have enough worries already, he found himself wondering if the other house was taking in rainwater, as old Snake Neck had said it would. With two days left until the move-out deadline Hyŏnse grew anxious about whether the tenants would all vacate, and he took advantage of a lull in the rain to visit the realtor.

As before, he found the elderly broker sitting on his veranda, looking up at the sky with a watchful eye. "Come on in," he said in delight. "I was hoping you might drop by today. You know, those tenants—I just got back from seeing off the ones in the room beside the gate. But old Snake Neck in the room across the veranda is making a stink. The day after tomorrow is the deadline for moving out, right? Well, I told them it was today. To speed up the process, you know? So the room beside the gate's empty. But old Snake Neck is going to put up a fuss right to the end. Her grandson and his family live with her, and the grandson is the reasonable one—he realizes as long as the house has been sold and the new owner wants all the rooms, it makes sense us asking him to vacate. So he and I went out and got him a room in Hwa-dong, the other side of the hill there, but the old woman flat out said no, she wasn't leaving. I think I can understand why she's being so ornery—there was a time when the owner wanted to raise the rent, so he told a lie, said he had sold the house, and then he asked her and the other tenants to leave. So this time she's not having any of it. The way she talks, I suspect she'd move out easily enough if you gave her some money, but don't worry, sir, you just leave it all to me—everything will work out. Just remember that commission, sir.

All right, let's you and I go up there now and get this over and done with."

And out the realtor went.

As Hyŏnse followed, he recalled what Tugap had said about not letting anyone suspect that he was performing a little act. Now that the realtor was asking the tenants to leave, Hyŏnse finally began to understand that his little act was saving the owner from having to pay the tenants to move out.

As the realtor led the way up the gradual slope to the house, he kept saying, "We're not going to give any sign that we're going to ease up on them. In a matter like this, once you drag things out an extra day or two it becomes endless."

They arrived at the house to find the veranda filled with what appeared to be the belongings of the owner. So, the owner must be part of the act, thought Hyŏnse. The man was certainly being careful to avoid giving it away.

Outside the room across the veranda stood a young man gazing up at the sky. This must be old Snake Neck's grandson.

The realtor approached the young man. "Now think about it— today is the deadline for moving out, and here we have the buyer of the house. So let's do what's right for both sides."

The realtor seemed to be expecting an argument, but all the young man did was turn toward him in acknowledgment; he said nothing. But then the door to the room slid open and old Snake Neck's head appeared, her hair white as a scallion root and tangled as a scouring pad, her neck stretched out longer than ever.

"I don't care if it's the man in the moon who's asking us to leave!" she shrieked. "We're not leaving!"

This was evidently meant for Hyŏnse and not just the realtor.

"We're not leaving! Where's a sick person supposed to move to in the middle of the rainy season? We may not have a home of our own, but we're still human—just because someone wants to kick us out doesn't mean we're going along with it!"

Sure enough, the old woman was bringing into play the lies of the owner when he had wanted to raise the rent. And now that the house was actually being sold, she intended to give the owner a hard time and demand moving expenses, as the realtor had warned Hyŏnse. At this point the owner might have been expected to appear, but there was no sign of movement in the main room, his living quarters.

The realtor had prepared for this, and he turned to the young man and spoke loudly enough for the old woman to hear: "Like I said, the purchase has been completed and the house has a new owner." The point being that the old woman could resist all she wanted, but she was mistaken if she thought she was going to get some money from the previous owner.

This brought worse shrieking from old Snake Neck: "I don't care whose house it is, we're not going!"

"I'm sorry to be meeting you like this," said the young man to Hyŏnse, "but could you give us a day or two? With my grandmother the way she is, I'd like to calm her down, and if you can give us a day or two I promise we'll vacate." His words were practically a plea.

Hyŏnse, thinking that sympathy would be dangerous at this juncture, said, "You have your situation, but consider our situation too: my family and two other refugee families have been living on the streets waiting to move in."

The young man seemed to realize there was nothing more he could do. Going inside their room, he spoke, evidently to his wife: "Get our things together; I'm going to take Grandmother before the rain starts up again." Whereupon he reemerged, his back turned to old Snake Neck so that she could ride him piggyback.

But instead old Snake Neck began beating on the young man's back with her bony fists. "Cussed boy, go if you want; I'll die before I leave. Taking your sick old grandma to a place without a heated floor, you want to kill me? Then kill me where I am, kill me now!"

Finally the young man hoisted his grandmother to his back and rose, absorbing the blows. He said something more to his wife, but it couldn't be heard, not so much because of old Snake Neck's fuss as she continued to beat him, but because his voice was choked up and muffled. As he stepped down to the yard Hyŏnse could see that his eyes had reddened.

By now old Snake Neck seemed too tired to beat her grandson; her shoulders heaved as she tried to catch her breath, but she continued to shriek: "I hope all of you are struck by lightning and drop dead; I hope the rains wash this damn house away!"

Hyŏnse stood mutely as this scene unfolded.

As old Snake Neck's grandson approached the main gate, she buried her face in his back, seemingly exhausted, then cried out one last time: "Wash away this damn house! Drop dead, all of you! I want to die! Take me to the public graves, you wretched people, and bury me! Bury me!"

Head bowed, the young man silently went out through the gate and was seen no more.

Hyŏnse couldn't erase this scene from his mind. At the same time, his thoughts turned elsewhere. The fact was, the young man and his family had a place to go. What would have become of Hyŏnse had he not encountered Tugap?

Blinding shafts of sunlight fell between lingering layers of clouds. Summer was here to stay and the sun's rays were strong and hot. This was the day to pay the balance of the purchase price, and Hyŏnse was on his way to the tearoom to meet Tugap. The sun had been out for a while, and with every shaft of light his legs felt wobbly. It was as if the sunlight had a life of its own, and when the rays hit the backs of his knees he felt he had to struggle to stay upright, and that made his legs feel shaky.

And when his legs felt shaky, he wished he could get rid of the light bundle he was carrying. But the next moment he would grip the bundle as if it were a lifeline. Inside the wrapping cloth was another suit he had to sell, along with a sack for the potatoes he would then buy. After today, of the suits he had brought back from North China—which were pretty much the sum of his assets—only one would be left. It made him feel sick inside.

This suit had to fetch a better price, he told himself. And he had to find the cheapest potatoes, which were so absurdly expensive this monsoon season. The thing was, the same marketplace sold the same potatoes for wildly differing prices. Difficult as it was, he had to make the rounds of all the markets in order to find the best price.

Before long he would see freshly boiled potatoes steaming before his eyes. Believe it or not, someone else had said he was sick of potatoes, but Hyŏnse thought, wouldn't it be nice to eat them until his stomach bulged, blowing on a nice hot one to cool it off? No matter how warm the day, potatoes had to be steaming hot. Oh boy, if he could stuff himself just once, blowing on those nice hot ones to cool them off.

Once again sunlight broke through the clouds and once again Hyŏnse's legs felt wobbly. He looked like someone just discharged from the hospital, or else on his way there—complete with a bundle of belongings.

The tearoom was practically empty—the hour was still early—but Tugap was there, wearing a dress shirt, holding up the fan to signal him. Hyŏnse joined Tugap, who then ordered milk for him.

With his other hand Tugap rubbed his forehead and the back of his neck, from which he had already mopped perspiration. "Here's the balance," he said, retrieving two bank drafts from inside the suit jacket slung over his chair, "and the commission." He indicated a bank draft for 1,000 *wŏn*; the other draft was for 95,000 *wŏn*. Like the bank draft for the earnest money, both drafts had a line drawn across them.

Hyŏnse pocketed the drafts. "Is a thousand going to be enough? The broker is talking like he expects a healthy commission."

"The old man's being unreasonable. The owner said he gave him a proper commission the day he made up the purchase agreement, and then the night before last the old man was pestering the owner to give him some money for helping the renters move out. So the owner had to cough up another hundred *wŏn*. And the people who actually found a room for the renters, you don't think they offered their services for free, do you? He's like a leech, and he's going to stick to us for all he can get. You get soft with people like that and there's no end to it. You got to tell him flat out, no. What did the old man do for us? Tell me."

Did that mean the realtor had lied to him when he said he hadn't received a commission from the owner? Hyŏnse asked himself.

The milk soon arrived and when Hyŏnse had finished it Tugap said, "Want to go over there now?" Hyŏnse picked up his bundle and rose, whereupon Tugap added, "I'll wait here. I have to meet someone."

In spite of the glass of milk Hyŏnse felt the same as before, legs wobbly every time the sun came out.

Hyŏnse reached the realtor's home in Samch'ŏng-dong to find the old man nodding off on his veranda, reed fan in hand. At the sound of Hyŏnse's arrival the realtor opened his eyes.

"Huh—oh, it's you. . . . Why don't you have a seat and I'll go fetch the owner."

That wouldn't be necessary, Hyŏnse said, thinking their little act was over now. He gave the larger bank draft to the realtor.

As he sat fanning himself while waiting for the realtor to return, Hyŏnse felt his mind go hazy. His eyes closed and he began to nod off.

"You must be all worn out" was the next thing he heard, and it brought him wide awake. "You should have laid yourself down and used the wooden pillow." Hyŏnse realized he hadn't heard the realtor return.

The realtor handed Hyŏnse a receipt, then picked up his fan and, seating himself a respectful distance from Hyŏnse while he cooled off, began fanning himself and Hyŏnse in turn.

"The owner has already made a copy of his seal imprint, so he's ready to transfer title anytime you want. Oh, and he told me he'd arranged with you to occupy the house for a few more days—is that correct?"

Hyŏnse nodded, knowing he had no choice in the matter. "That's fine." And with that he rose. He had already walked out the gate when he heard the realtor's voice.

"Uh, sir," he called out in an awkward tone. "I hope you won't mind my bringing this up, but the fact is, we've run out of grain and I need to go out and buy myself some rice."

Only then did Hyŏnse remember the commission. "Well, I guess I still haven't woken up yet." So saying, he reached into his pocket.

"Sorry about this, but like I said, we've just run out of grain." The realtor accepted the bank draft from Hyŏnse and examined the amount. Instantly his face hardened. "Don't do this to me, sir—you need to give this some more thought."

"Can't we leave it at that?"

"You know as well as I do, sir, that you just got a swell deal on that house. Just yesterday a house out back there sold for fif-teen-thou-sand a *k'an*. Compared with that, you got your house practically for free! It's your good luck, sir, but I had to work every trick in the book to get a cheap price for you—think about it. And you'll remember me mentioning that I make the sale and what do I get from the owner? Not one copper! And that's not all—I know you're war refugees, so I worked it out for you and your family to move in early, which means getting the renters to move out—I've gone to all this trouble. You were with me, sir, so you know how cantankerous that old woman was. Can you imagine how many times a day I had to put up with her pestering? I feel like I've been to hell and back, I tell you! I'm not bragging when I say that if it wasn't for me, those renters never would have left. But I got them to leave, and I did it so you and your family could move in early—and you know that. I want you to take all this into account, sir."

He wasn't denying that the realtor must have had difficulty re-moving the renters, thought Hyŏnse, but if Tugap was correct, then hadn't the realtor received not only a commission from the owner but also a fee for helping the renters move out? Yes or no, Hyŏnse wished only for this business to be ended.

"We are refugees, after all."

"So you say. . . . But that's beside the point. Compared with a man like you, sir, *we're* the refugees. I have a lot of mouths to feed—fourteen to be exact. Here I am an old man and the only breadwinner—my son was helping out a little, but darned if he isn't sick in bed now. And on top of that, the day before yesterday his wife had a baby. So as long as I'm healthy I've got to see that the sick ones get their gruel and the new mom gets her seaweed soup, don't I? Think about it, sir, and don't do me wrong."

By now the elderly realtor was a sodden, perspiring mess; his eyes were bloodshot.

Shouldn't I be buying the fixings for seaweed soup for my *wife?* Hyŏnse felt an urge to come clean with the elderly realtor about the house pur-chase. But the next moment he realized it wasn't the right time, and more important, he didn't have the energy. Hyŏnse started to walk off, but the realtor called to him, his tone urgent.

"Wait, sir, I'll tell you what, let's just talk about the commission. Usually it's one percent, so if you're giving me a thousand *wŏn*, that would mean the purchase price is a hundred thousand—but it's more than that. You can do this," said the realtor, gesturing as if to return the bank draft to Hyŏnse.

Hyŏnse recalled Tugap's characterization of the realtor as a leech and his admonition that sometimes you simply had to say no. But the more important consideration now was that he didn't have the energy to stand there and keep talking, so he walked off.

The realtor must have thought that if he returned the bank draft, Hyŏnse would take it and walk away. And so he bowed over and over and pleaded, "Please consider it some more, sir, and do the right thing. Take care, now."

The clouds had lifted noticeably. Now it wasn't just Hyŏnse's tottering legs making him feel off balance; in addition, everything looked hazy to the eye. It helped a little if he squinted, but when he did this, a sandy, stinging sensation came to his already sunken eyes and tears welled up.

One man's death is another man's cold. No longer did Hyŏnse recall this proverb. His only thought was that he had to drop by the tearoom and give Tugap the receipt for the balance of the purchase price, sell the suit at the South Gate markets and buy the potatoes at the East Gate markets, and hurry back to his family. The street seemed neverending. Which made his legs feel all the weaker and heavier. His bundle felt ever so bulky. What if someone gave him a sack of potatoes that he could barely sling over his shoulder? Well, he would carry it home if it killed him. This thought took the starch out of him.

By the time he entered the tearoom at Chin'gogae his vision was so dark and hazy he couldn't tell what was what. Hyŏnse could only vaguely make out Tugap, seated across from someone else, raising the familiar fan in greeting, before he plopped himself down in the first available chair. Tugap came over to him.

"Damn hot, isn't it? God job!" Tugap fanned Hyŏnse with the yin-yang fan, then turned toward the serving counter and barked out, "Two ice coffees!"

Hyŏnse was desperate to slake his thirst, whether with milk or something else. As soon as the ice coffee arrived, he gulped the entire drink.

"You look really hot—why don't you finish mine too?" said Tugap as he pushed his coffee toward Hyŏnse. "You brought the receipt?"

Hyŏnse realized he had forgotten to hand it to Tugap. *Why am I so forgetful today?* Once again he felt how exhausted he was, physically and mentally. He quickly finished Tugap's coffee, and was thinking that before he left he should tell Tugap it would be good if he and his family could move the following day.

"By the way, I'm kind of sorry to say this," began Tugap.

A chill came over Hyŏnse.

"But the thing is, something's come up and the owner needs all the rooms."

Hyŏnse felt his heart drop.

Tugap produced a wad of ten-*wŏn* bills from his back pocket and set it on the table in front of Hyŏnse. "This is the owner's way of saying he's sorry. It's really too bad. I try to do something nice and instead I cause you resentment." He gave Hyŏnse a deliberate look. "I can't believe it—at first he tried to get away with a measly five hundred. I had to yell at him—'Do you think my friend put on that stupid clown act just for this? Five hundred *wŏn* might seem like a lot to you, but my friend, even though he's a war refugee, would rather get by on his own than take a measly handout like this.' And so he came up with another five hundred. I tell you, these Seoul skinflints. . . ."

Tugap sounded and looked indignant. Hyŏnse for his part felt something square in the middle of his chest, a vicious anger, but directed at no one in particular, like a viper rearing its head.

"Even though money's lost its value these days, a thousand *wŏn* is nothing to sneeze at. And I'll see what I can do about a room for you—once I roll up my sleeves and get to work, no problem. I'll make it my responsibility. Whatever you do, don't be upset over that house—it's probably just as well. It's too far from downtown, and besides, the money the owner brings in nowadays, any food supplies he wants he can have delivered—you wouldn't want to live in the same house with someone like that. So I'm going to find you a nice room."

Hyŏnse now realized that the target of his vicious anger was none other than Tugap. The old-fashioned P'yŏngan Province way would be to punch this guy in his prominent nose. But that impulse was only the anger of a dying little snake.

Tugap leaned toward Hyŏnse, held out the wad of bills, and fanned them, saying, "There's a lot of fake number-two series ten-*wŏn* bills going around, but you won't find a single number-two series in here." His toadlike mouth reeked of grilled beef, *soju*, and garlic.

Hyŏnse could no longer stand the smell; he had to get away. And before he knew it he was out the door, money in hand, the distant ring of Tugap's voice saying they should be sure to get together and Hyŏnse knew where to find him.

Just like a toad, a warty toad that crawled out from under a rock. . . . People don't die from scabies, right? They die from poison ivy. . . . Was it the egg white? Or maybe it wasn't poison ivy in the first place. Whatever the reason, his wife had gotten better. But what was he going to tell her about the house? . . . *That toad, that warty toad, the only difference between that guy and a toad is that it's beef, soju, and garlic that go into his yap, not flies. . . . It's not right that a man with an empty stomach should have to put up with the stink that comes out of that damn toad mouth.*

There flashed through his mind the thread of a folktale he had heard from the elders when he was a boy. There was a girl with a pet toad, and one day a serpent appeared, intending to take the girl away. The toad breathed its poisonous vapor at the serpent, which fell from the ceiling and died. But in the process the toad died as well— its poisonous vapor was that powerful. And so it wasn't surprising that the toad's breath had chased him out of the tearoom. It could easily have killed him, tiny little snake that he was, and barely hanging on to life. . . . *And that sick old Snake Neck lady too. I wonder what happened to them. Poor old Snake Neck. . . .*

Hyŏnse was struck by an image of Tugap stretched out comfortably in the room once occupied by sick old Snake Neck. The toad in the folktale had lived in the kitchen. . . . Hyŏnse imagined Tugap with his toad mouth staring down in his direction and breathing out that peculiar stink that a hungry person like Hyŏnse couldn't endure. *Puff puff.*

Before he knew it, Hyŏnse's field of vision grew dark, even though the skies above had cleared. He was overcome with a dizziness he had never experienced before, even the time he had stood high on the roof of a building. He felt a numbness in his ears, but a voice managed to penetrate. *Please, vacate this house, my brothers and sisters, now that the rainy season has passed. Have sympathy for this old man who is the same blood as you, this old man whose dreams are troubled, who cannot sleep at night on account of you, my brothers and sisters; have sympathy for me and vacate this house with all due haste.* A toad with a leather-bound Bible in hand, speaking in a dignified tone that brooked no opposition. Hyŏnse felt like collapsing. He closed his eyes tight and clenched the wad of money and his bundle, as if by doing so he could keep himself upright. And from square in the middle of his chest he heard a cry: *I have to stay alive! I have to stay alive!*

July 1946

HOUSE

The rumors swept Sŏdanggol overnight: Maktong's father had gone to the upper village to buy an ox and had gotten mixed up in gambling again. And this time he had sold his family's home, their old, run-down thatched-roof house. It surprised no one that the buyer was said to be the new landlord, Chŏn P'ilsu. One of the local elders, Song Saengwŏn, said he had seen Maktong's father come back home the previous evening—that's when he must have sold off the house. All the villagers who heard this assumed that Maktong's father had sold cheap—if you were a buyer, would you offer a fair price to someone who was desperate to get back to the gambling table? And they assumed that even the proceeds from the house had ultimately been blown. After all, Maktong's father's opponent, a gambler from other parts, was said to know every trick in the book. But according to a second rumor, Maktong's father was cleaning out this man using the money from the house sale. At the same time, it was reported that at Maktong's family's home, when the grandfather heard that his son had sold the house he had lamented, "We're wiped out," pounding the ground in frustration, and had said that if he caught sight of his son he would cut his throat with the sickle, whose blade he had sharpened to a fine edge.

True to the rumors in Sŏdanggol, Maktong's father had indeed used all the money for the ox to gamble, had lost that money, and had proceeded to sell off the family's house plot along with the vegetable plot. And the buyer, the man newly arrived in the village, who the previous April had purchased Min Ch'angho's paddy and dry fields together, was Chŏn P'ilsu. But in one particular the rumors were wrong: although the land had in fact changed hands, the dilapidated house had not. And contrary to the villagers' supposition, the purchase price was fair, consistent with the current market. In this respect Chŏn's sense of propriety was different from that of the average person.

Chŏn P'ilsu had been different from the day he arrived in Sŏdanggol to purchase Min Ch'angho's house and his paddy and dry fields, at a time when news of the land reform in the northern sector of the peninsula was making the rounds. More than others, Chŏn had long harbored a passion for owning farmland. Witnessing from an early age the hardships and hunger of his father and grandfather slaving away on their measly tenant plot, he had always kept in mind the thought that someday, somehow, he would have himself a healthy amount of farmland. He had operated a small secondhand shop in Seoul, but with Liberation in August 1945 he had skillfully brokered items belonging to the Japanese, and his thoughts had immediately returned to land. With farmland he could expect over time to receive 30 percent of the crop from his tenants, and even if land reform were to come about here in the south, it wouldn't be like the land reform in the north, which involved confiscation without compensation. And so he decided he would buy farmland at rock-bottom prices. At this time he happened to hear from a broker about the plots belonging to Min and his family. Chŏn had only recently gone down to the countryside from Seoul to look into the land situation. There in Sŏ-danggol he had met Song Saengwŏn, who had told him that Min and his family had been run out of town shortly after Liberation and had moved to Seoul, and that Min had declared he would never again come face to face with the ignorant, ingrate farmers who had driven him off. *Here we go*, Chŏn had said to himself. A disadvantaged seller would sell, and he could buy, for a rock-bottom price. And in succeeding to the position of a landlord who had been run out of town, he could win the hearts of the local people just by doing a little bit of good. *Buy*, Chŏn told himself. *Drive down the price and buy.*

In this way Chŏn had acquired Min's land for a rock-bottom price. And from the day he settled in Sŏdanggol, he had continued to amaze the villagers he met by the way he conducted himself with them. When he had come earlier to investigate the farmland situation, he had first visited Song Saengwŏn and had addressed him most appropriately with great respect, even asking Song not to speak deferentially to him. And with the villagers in general, if his counterpart was even slightly older he would confer the old-time title of Saengwŏn and treat the person very respectfully. This could not but surprise the villagers, because Min, the former landlord, by contrast, had talked down to all of them, with one exception—Maktong's grandfather, who unlike the other villagers was not completely dependent on Min. And even to him, Min's reluctant attempts at polite speech came across as mumbling.

Chŏn had devoted considerable thought to these matters. Among the multitude of reasons the previous landlord, Min, had been run out of the village, the most important would have been that he had made no attempt to mix with the villagers. Wasn't there something to be learned from this, even though not all the previous landlords had been run out of the village? So the first thing for Chŏn to do was get comfortable with the villagers, and the best means to this end, he decided, was alcohol. Chŏn himself was not a heavy drinker, but starting with Song Saengwŏn, and afterward as the occasion arose, he treated the village elders to drinks.

The efficacy of this policy soon became apparent. Shortly after Liberation the young men of the village, together with a group of young strangers from the town nearby, had vandalized the house in which Min was living, leaving it in ruins. But when the time came for Chŏn to move in and he had to restore the house, the only people he ended up having to pay for their labor were Big Nose the carpenter and a plasterer. The others, tenant farmers, all volunteered their labor for the various tasks.

Chŏn himself turned out to help with the repairs. On one such day his eyes came to rest on the house where Maktong's family lived. It was an old thatched-roof dwelling whose left side was leaning precariously forward. If it were to collapse, the rock wall that helped retain the rainwater in back of Chŏn's house would be breached. This wall and Maktong's family's house were practically touching. Chŏn had had a feeling about that house when he'd first arrived to check out farmland: the day he settled in this area, he would have to buy that thatched-roof house and the land it sat on. His intention was not simply to expand the landholdings in back of his house. Rather, by adding that other lot, and its spacious vegetable patch, to his own, he would have himself a nice square plot of some five hundred *p'yŏng* to cultivate. He would put the land and the vegetable plot of that thatched-roof house to use. Fruit trees could be planted there, and next to them subsistence crops. And when the trees were fully grown, the yield in fruit would fetch a nice income. Besides, even if land reform went into effect in the future, the land that you yourself cultivated would remain yours, so the best policy for a man like him, who couldn't do much in the way of labor-intensive farming, was to make the fruit trees behind his house his own, which he could do by tending to them regularly. So when the opportunity came to buy that house and its land, he would act upon it, he told himself.

Min had also been interested in purchasing this land. Min's motive, though, was that the land in back of his house was too small and he needed more space. So he had sent a few elderly sharecroppers to visit Maktong's grandfather, and then he had torn down his old house, intending to replace it with a modern one complete with slanted eaves attached to the rafters. This was five or six years ago, and by that time he was sending his messengers to Maktong's grandfather practically every day, but they were sent back empty-handed. And then the previous year, Maktong's grandfather, who had farmed his own land until then, had begun sharecropping Min's dry fields, but he remained attached to the land on which his own house sat and to his vegetable patch, and he declared he would be dead and buried before he would let anybody buy them. What was Min to do about this pig-headed old man, the one person he had failed to get in his clutches? Well, for starters, the new house he had built was a massive tile-roof structure, and there it sat, right alongside Maktong's family's house, looming over and dwarfing it, as if to say, *Try this on for size; how much longer do you think you can hold out?*

Chŏn had a plan for buying Maktong's family's land, but his method was altogether different from Min's. When it came to buying land, Chŏn would not rush into a deal, whether through intermediaries or otherwise; it was best, he thought, to wait for the right opportunity. And with Maktong's family's land, he never once hinted to others of his intentions, even when he was treating them to drinks. He had decided to wait until the time was right, and he believed that that time would ultimately arrive. And it did, unexpectedly soon, when Maktong's father appeared before him in person to offer the precious land.

Chŏn had been unaware till then that Maktong's father gambled. And in fact Maktong's father had given up gambling more than a year earlier—it didn't seem that long ago—and by now his habit was no longer a topic of conversation among the villagers. What Maktong's father had to say when he showed up at Chŏn's door he said matter-of-factly: an ox was for sale in the upper village, and he was a bit shy of the money he needed to buy it—would Chŏn advance him some money if he put up his land as security?

Chŏn was well aware that this was not the time of year to be ar-ranging mortgages or lending money, but he also realized that if he really wanted that land, he couldn't very well come right out and suggest that Maktong's father sell it to him. So he merely said that he had no money to lend. Maktong's father grew anxious when he heard this. But then he remembered how Min had tried to buy his family's land—maybe this new landlord would be similarly inclined. And so it was Maktong's father who broached the issue: "Then why don't you buy our land?" The bait was set. Chŏn feigned reluctance, saying that if Maktong's father really intended to buy the ox, then it so hap-pened that he did have some money he'd been planning to use to buy an ox cart (for working the two plots of well-irrigated paddy he had begun cultivating that year); maybe he could use that money. As for a price, Chŏn decided not to try to negotiate and instead went along with Maktong's father's proposal of ten *wŏn* per *p'yŏng*. That way there would be no bad aftertaste, as there would if he were to per-suade Maktong's father to lower the price. He considered asking Maktong's father to include their run-down house in the deal, but ultimately thought better of it. Not only did he have no use for the house in the first place, he had no need to buy with the intention of demolishing it because it would probably collapse within the year anyway and then Maktong's family would most likely have to rebuild it. And judging from the timber in the corner of their yard, the fam-ily knew they would soon have to rebuild, and when that time came, he would provide them a house site elsewhere. And if by chance there were no suitable site, then perhaps the farming shack built by the previous landlord in the lower village, which Chŏn now owned, could be sold to them cheaply.

But when at the same moment Maktong's father realized he was finally going to unload his family's land, the image of his father's frightfully angry face came to mind, and he closed his eyes in an attempt to block it out. *I have to win a jackpot with this stake. Then I'll get the family land back, and just like in the old days we'll have enough land to work on our own—that's all I'm hoping for.* Maktong's father was sure that with this stake he would win, so he quickly proposed that if he could not buy the ox, then the very next day he would return the money and Chŏn should give him back the land. Chŏn willingly agreed. From now on, he would have to bend a little in his dealings with the villagers, just as he was doing now. It would be to his future advantage to do so. And this is how Maktong's family's land changed hands. The rumor that the buyer had no good reason to offer a fair price, because Maktong's father was desperate to sell, was inaccurate.

It was understandable that the two different rumors had arisen about Maktong's father: that he had gambled away all the money he had raised from selling the land, and that he had made a clean sweep at the gambling table. In fact, early on he lost almost all of his stake. But then he won several hands in a row and was comfortably ahead. As always, though, he didn't know when to stop, and he began to lose again. Generally speaking, when a man's family is ruined because of his gambling, it's because the man doesn't know when to stop—it all depends on that. When your pockets are empty you have the illusion that if only you have a stake you can empty your opponents' pockets, and you'll do anything to get that stake; after you've won a good sum of money you feel you're going to clean up, and in the end you can't stop yourself—and although this demonstrates how greedy people can be and how strong the lure of gambling is, Maktong's father was especially vulnerable, and incapable of seizing an opportunity to quit. In comparison, Kaptŭk's father, a villager nicknamed Slit Eyes because his eyes were narrow like a crow tit's, was quick-witted and knew when to stop. When Slit Eyes's losses reached a certain amount he would withdraw for a while and look on, saying he was waiting for his lucky streak to arrive. The way he put it, if you got agitated after losing money, you were as good as done. After a time he would notice that the luck had run from one man to another, and at that point he would join in again. And when after winning a certain amount he started to lose again, he would leave, saying he had to use the bathroom. When it came to luck, he would tell you, it went to one man for a while and then to another man, so when you had won for a while and then began to lose, it was a sign that the luck had begun to move to another player, and the best policy was to withdraw. Slit Eyes would take his earnings home, then head back to the gambling table with his original stake. In this way he became an uncommonly skillful gambler, one who could support his family on his earnings.

Slit Eyes's feel for gambling was something Maktong's father had always lacked. Such was the situation when Maktong's father took on the card player from out of town. True to the one rumor, he lost almost all his money. But then he won for a time, then he began to lose again, and his fortunes proceeded to go back and forth, but after his initial reverse he was never far from breaking even. The following day passed, the day when Maktong's father was to have returned the money to Chŏn and reclaimed his land. But by then Maktong's father's only thoughts were of the next hand; the gambling bout was still going on. Slit Eyes for his part was keeping tabs, joining in and then dropping out, playing for a while and then withdrawing, and when he had sufficient winnings he made sure they stayed in his pocket. At first Maktong's father didn't like it that Slit Eyes was playing—he thought it was bad luck—but Slit Eyes kept to his routine, and as Maktong's father became ever more consumed with the play of the cards, he ceased to pay attention to what Slit Eyes was up to.

When Maktong's father gambled he was like a man possessed. The end of a gambling bout would leave him with his face drawn, his body languid, as if he had just recovered from a high fever. And he would drink, as if alcohol were a kind of medication. Once, after one of these bouts, Maktong's father had had his fill of drink and proceeded to cut off the tip of his right thumb with a fodder chopper. To a gambler the right thumb is the most important digit. At the critical moment in a hand, when each plays his final card, it's the thumb that keeps that card from showing. And if that card doesn't win the hand, the gambler inevitably curses the thumb, as if it were

responsible for the outcome. It was this offending thumb that Maktong's father had mutilated. This had happened sometime before
Liberation, when a rumor had reached the upper village that two
young men from other parts were throwing their money around in the
local gambling den. This was all Maktong's father needed to hear,
and off he went. Sure enough, the two men, who appeared to be in
their early twenties, had a seemingly endless supply of cash. For a
while Maktong's father was winning, but when the following day
dawned he had lost his entire stake. Maktong's father hurried home,
saw that his father was out, stole one of his beehives, and returned to
the upper village to sell it. But the proceeds were soon gone. He returned home again, intending to sell one of the two remaining hives.
If he were ever caught sneaking off with one of the beehives to which
his father was so devoted, there would be instant calamity, but Maktong's father was no longer mindful of that possibility. Fortunately,
this time too his father was out. He was leaving with the beehive
when his seven-year-old daughter Chŏmsun opened the door from
the family room and looked out, only to close the door the next
moment.

By the time Maktong's father returned to the upper village the
two young gamblers, who, it turned out, had come from the city of
Taejŏn, had disappeared. But instead of taking the beehive back home,
he sold it and drank with the proceeds. Some five days later, when he
was finally about to return home, another rumor arrived in the upper
village: the two young men from Taejŏn were notorious crooks, gambling cheats. Finally, Maktong's father realized he had been taken.
He who had been gambling practically since he was old enough to
count—a period of more than twenty years—had been cheated by two
guys still wet behind the ears. Why hadn't he caught them cheating?
He would have wrung their necks on the spot! But gradually his anger
was displaced by a feeling of shame—he had been disgraced. *Damned if
I'll ever touch a card again!* The next moment he had rushed outside and
chopped off his thumb. And from then on he wouldn't go near a gambling table. The villagers said that now that Maktong's father was
approaching age forty, the age of wisdom, he seemed finally to be
acting like a man should act. Among them Song Saengwŏn praised

Maktong's father, telling the story of another gambler who had cut off his thumb, saying he would never again touch the cards, but before the wound had healed this man was gambling again, and complaining he had cut off his thumb in vain because now he couldn't use it and all he had gotten out of it was pain. In truth Maktong's grandfather would not have seen fit to entrust his son with money to buy an ox if his son had seemed less than fully cured of his gambling fever. But it did appear that he was one hundred percent cured.

And so it was most peculiar how Maktong's father had become involved in this latest gambling bout. He had gone to the upper village, and when he located the man who was selling the ox, the man told him he had just sold it to another man from Sŏdanggol, who was going to slaughter it for meat; this other man would be coming back for the ox, and Maktong's father should talk with him then. Maktong's father decided to wait inside the gambling den for the man to return, but to his misfortune he saw that a round of gambling was under way, a high-stakes game involving the man from out of town. Before he knew it, he had joined in. When the buyer of the ox returned and told Maktong's father that he was willing to sell it, his words had fallen on deaf ears.

The news about Maktong's father's gambling woes came from the ox-slaughtering man, and the news about the sale of his family's land came from Chŏn P'ilsu. As soon as Chŏn came to the unexpected realization that Maktong's father was a gambler, he told himself he had made a mistake. Maktong's father was old enough to know better, so Chŏn had entered into business with him directly—and to think someone like that was a gambler! He had to be careful and not act rashly. The first thing to do was inform Maktong's grandfather that he had bought the land. But rather than tell him directly, he decided it was preferable to spread the news and give the grandfather time to get wind of it, and not visit him until he sensed the old man's anger had cooled. It would be unpleasant if the first thing he did was visit this stubborn old man and be confronted with a denial.

Just as Chŏn had thought, Maktong's grandfather did not take well to the news. "We're ruined! You son of a bitch, you deserve to have your throat cut!" He bellowed like a rutting bull, the roars sounding as if at any moment they would bring down the decrepit house. And this was how the rumor started that he was sharpening his sickle to a fine edge to cut his son's throat. But in truth it was his own throat he felt like cutting. His son had gone and sold their *land*—it was wishful thinking to hope the family could recover. What remained to them was two plots alone: a tiny paddy that depended on rainwater and drank it up like a sand field, and a rocky dry field. And if that were not bad enough, the previous year his family had felt compelled to begin sharecropping Min Ch'angho's dry fields. Even so, Maktong's grandfather had never lost hope that they would somehow be able to get back on their feet again. Now, even that hope had gone up in smoke.

There was no denying that Maktong's father was to blame for his family's having to resort to sharecropping the previous year; until then they had been proud, self-sufficient farmers. But their situation also resulted in part from a decision the grandfather had made three years earlier. To pay off a debt, he'd had to hand over to Min Ch'angho a spring-fed paddy. As if this weren't regrettable enough, he had then sold Min a fertile dry field, and that proved to be a big mistake. Maktong's grandfather had had it in the back of his mind to use the proceeds from that sale to buy a hilly plot three times as big as the dry field, and then to reclaim that plot and develop it into a productive dry field. Because of all their mouths to feed, the family needed at least that much land to provide them with an adequate supply of grain each year. Maktong's grandfather considered: there's no land that's productive right from the start; it all depends on how you cultivate it. That fertile dry field he had sold wasn't fertile from the very beginning—it was made fertile by his father, who, winter or summer, went about the village at dawn before anyone else had risen, gathering dog manure to spread on it. This was not an easy task, but then again, he had never seen anything in this world come without effort. Best of all, reclaimed land was exempt from the Japanese grain tax for three years. But as it turned out, developing that hilly plot required several times more labor and effort than he had anticipated. In addition to the grandfather and father, Maktong's mother and even Maktong and Chŏmsun had to help with uprooting the trees and digging out the rocks.

But in spite of all their labor, when tilling season arrived they still hadn't cleared the plot of all the roots and rocks, and since they didn't have access to a plow, they planted their barley crop with shovel and hoe. You couldn't expect much of a yield in such circumstances, not even enough for seed to plant the following year—though it might have been different had they had enough manure for fertilizer. Since there was no grain tax on reclaimed land, they had initially thought they should fertilize the hilly plot, but if their original dry field didn't produce and they ended up without enough grain to pay the tax, they would have to supplement it with the yield from the reclaimed land. So whether they fertilized the one plot or the other, the total yield minus the grain tax would be the same. And so the fertilizer ended up going to the original plot, which offered somewhat more assurance of a good yield. As Maktong's grandfather sowed the barley, he wished and wished he could apply just one sack of that chemical fertilizer they called ammonium nitrate. But that was not something his family could even hope to have. Nothing to do but keep trying to enrich that reclaimed land.

At tilling time the following year, though, they again didn't have enough manure to go around, and most of it went to the original plot. If there was anything better about that year's yield, it was the seed grain they had left over to plant the next year. But this was cold comfort when the Japanese colonial administration proceeded to institute a grain tax on reclaimed land. This measure was apparently necessitated by the administration's desperate need for the county's grain.

But Maktong's grandfather continued to believe that his reclaimed land, unlike others' land, would be somehow exempt—until the officials began to press him for payment. He was told that no matter what, he was responsible for paying his grain tax, the amount of which he had already been notified. In that case, he responded to the officials, they could come and watch at harvest time, and he would give them the entire yield from his reclaimed land. The township superintendent then went into a long spiel about how the grain tax was not meant to deprive the farmer of all his grain; rather, what was left after the family stockpiled enough for its own consumption was offered to the nation. And finally he took Maktong's grandfather by the shoulders and shook him, asking how he could let his no-good son gamble and yet be unaware of his duty to supply the nation with grain. Maktong's grandfather made up his mind that he wouldn't give up a single grain more than what he harvested from the reclaimed land, and if that meant being beaten to death, then so be it. Actually it would be better if his old self were beaten to death, he thought, because if he had to supplement the grain tax on the reclaimed land with grain from the original fields, his entire family would starve. *Go ahead, let them beat me to death.* But his son and daughter-in-law couldn't countenance this prospect, and in the end they paid the shortfall from the harvest from the original field.

They couldn't afford to continue working the reclaimed land. He had to sell it, Maktong's grandfather told himself. *Next year's grain tax will ruin us—I've got to sell.* The problem was, who would want to buy it? This was the situation when Min Ch'angho appeared with an offer to buy the hilly plot for the same price Maktong's family had paid for it. Maktong's grandfather challenged Min, asking if all the labor they'd put into developing the land shouldn't be reflected in the purchase price. Min responded by asking if the loss of all the trees they had cut down to use shouldn't be considered as well. The way things were going, he added, the grain tax would be so bad that even if that worthless piece of land were offered for free, no one would take it. Maktong's grandfather realized Min was right. There was no other way but to sell it for the price they had paid. His family needed that money to subsist on.

But now there was another worry: which field would they cultivate the following year? And so his family had to begin sharecropping a portion of Min's land. And in that case, thought Maktong's grandfather, they might as well work the fertile plot they had sold Min some years back. And so he visited Min and proposed as much. *Well, well,* Min told himself, *the old man is finally under my thumb. I've been telling him all along to sell me his house and land, but the stubborn old goat never listens.* And then, to see how much he could push the old man, he said that if his family really wanted to sharecrop, then they'd have to do it on the reclaimed land they had sold him. Maktong's grandfather was in a fix. If they were to work that land, he told Min, they would need a couple of bags of ammonium nitrate. There he was again, up to his tricks, thought Min, but for the sake of the field he reluctantly agreed. He knew that under the old man's care, that land would develop into a nice field.

Spring came and when Maktong's grandfather applied ammonium nitrate to the reclaimed land, he imagined that he was sprinkling not fertilizer but what they called granulated sugar—he had seen it at the market some time ago. And as far as the land was concerned, perhaps this powder he was sprinkling was as good as sugar. But just as sugar isn't as good as honey, the ammonium nitrate wasn't as good as fertilizer made from ash. *So finally this year this piece of land is getting a taste of sugar.* As if oblivious to the sad fact that the land he now stood upon no longer belonged to him, he felt gratified that the land was enjoying this sugar he was sprinkling on it.

From the time the seeds began to sprout, the reclaimed land produced as well as the original fields. He weeded, he removed rocks, he trimmed the grass along the raised path through the field, and he lamented over and over, "We can't even get a handful of this for our own." There was nothing he could do about it, but he remained regretful nevertheless. At the same time, he was happy to see the grain ripening before his eyes. *At least we ought to be able to get some gruel out of it....* In the meantime the day of Liberation, August 15, arrived. To Maktong's family, as to other farming families, Liberation held out the expectation that the grain tax would disappear—as if the grain tax by itself were the cause of their scarcity of clothing and insufficiency of food.

Even after Liberation, Maktong's grandfather ate only enough to stop his stomach from growling, and he made money by selling grain. At the same time, his honeybees were multiplying and he was able to sell one of the hives. And he scraped every last spoonful of the honey that came from the buckwheat blossoms and sold that as well. Once again it was truly a fine world to be alive in. The family would have to get back on their feet again. And now that his son had made a clean break from his compulsive gambling, what more could he want? For farmers there was nothing besides farming. He even laid in a supply of timber for fixing the house. He scraped together the money he had tucked away from the sale of the reclaimed land along with the coppers he was able to squirrel away, and decided to buy the ox that he had had his heart set on for ten long years. This was the money that Maktong's father had lost at the gambling table—after which he had sold the house and the land. So you could understand the grandfather's reaction: "We're all ruined! That son of a bitch deserves to have his throat cut!"—though it was his own throat he felt like cutting first.

But Maktong's grandfather didn't have time to kill himself even if he'd really wanted to. His immediate priority was to do something about those weeds in the rainwater paddy—everywhere it was open to view, all you saw was weeds. The first thing he had to do was go out to the paddy.

One day Chŏn P'ilsu went out to check on the sluice gates of his paddies and saw Maktong's grandfather off in the distance. *Looks like he's simmered down*, he thought. He waited until Maktong's grandfather had gone home for lunch and paid him a visit.

Maktong's grandfather had just stepped outside, intending to go back out to the fields. Maktong had come down with malaria, and the old man had decided to dig up some granny flower roots, which were supposed to be good medicine, and send them home with Chŏmsun, who was in tow.

After greeting the old man, Chŏn said, "I'm afraid I've made a huge mistake. I never dreamed that Maktong's father frequented those places. No one in his right mind would have done what I did knowing that. I just now found out. Please, sir, don't think ill of me. I will cancel my agreement with him right now."

"Why should I think ill of you? It's all because that no-good son of mine is in a damnable state of mind. I'm right thankful for your offer, but where am I going to get the money?"

Thinking he had done well to show his generosity in offering to cancel the agreement, Chŏn said, "People are saying I bought very cheaply, your house included, but the house was never part of the bargain, only the land, and I paid ten *wŏn* a *p'yŏng.*" By saying this he wanted Maktong's grandfather to think that even if the money for the land had disappeared by now, he had paid a reasonable price for it. "Well, the price isn't the point—if I had known what kind of man Maktong's father is, I wouldn't have bought at any price," he added by way of reiterating that Maktong's grandfather should not think ill of him.

The damnable person in this affair was sure enough his own damned son, Maktong's grandfather thought. Near the pass behind the village he began digging for granny flower roots, but he couldn't seem to get this thought out of his mind, and only when Chŏmsun took his arm and said, "Grandfather, what are you doing?" did he realize that he was digging up plants other than granny flowers.

After he had dug up two granny flower roots they went down to the stream, where Maktong's grandfather washed them as clean as he would have washed a gutted fish. And then, as if he had just begun to feel the hot sun, he left the roots spread out on some grass where they wouldn't get dirty, took off his clothes, and waded into the water. It would be good to take a dip before going back to work in the paddy.

The water level didn't come up to a man's navel, so he had to crouch down in order to get in up to his neck. After giving his face a good splashing of water, he finally seemed more composed and he turned to Chŏmsun: "Come on in."

The girl obliged.

"Come here," he said in the gentle voice of a grandfather.

But Chŏmsun had no mind to venture deeper than where the water went up to her knees.

Her grandfather came to her and swept her up in his arms. She clung fast to his neck. Even before the water reached her waist, she cried out and tried to squirm upward.

"My goodness, you're falling, you're falling," her grandfather said as he lowered her into the stream. White whiskers trailing in the water, he produced a broad smile that revealed a mouth with no front teeth. Where in that wrinkled, leaden, dead-looking face had that smile come from?

But after he had washed Chŏmsun's face, emerged from the water, and dressed, the smile disappeared before you knew it, and there again was his wrinkled, leaden, dead-looking face. Placing the two granny flower roots in Chŏmsun's hand, he said, "Give these to your mom," in a tone that was no longer gentle.

Straightaway he set out for the lower village, where his family's paddy was located, plodding like an ox and weighed down by the thought that he should hurry up and do his weeding while the ground was still wet, and that if Maktong weren't sick in bed, his mom could be there to lend a helping hand, and that the damnable person in this whole affair was his own damned son.

The two granny flower roots were placed in Maktong's ears. The roots were potent enough that they first needed wrapping in a scrap of cloth, but after a night of this treatment the insides of the boy's ears were swollen and puffy and no one could tell if the roots were having an effect on the malaria. From daylight the next day Maktong began to shiver uncontrollably, and then his entire body was on fire. This was clearly a case of diurnal malaria.

Eleven-year-old Maktong was by himself in the family room, lying on his back. His mother had joined the others in the fields. Chŏmsun was in the front courtyard playing house beneath a blazing sun.

The fever-ridden boy kicked away his ragged quilt. A swarm of flies buzzed about his blackened mouth and his nose, but Maktong kept his eyes closed and didn't move. The only sign of life was the rapid heaving of his chest. All was still, both inside and outside the wide-open door. Now and then Chŏmsun would mutter to herself, but her voice didn't carry into the room. A rooster crowed, the sound as long and lazy as this midsummer day, as if to say there was life in the world outside. But the crowing was slower and more feeble than the beating of Maktong's heart. When it faded, there was only dead silence.

Suddenly Chŏmsun rushed inside. "Brother, Brother, come look, look!"

Maktong didn't move.

"Brother, look there! The bees, the bees!"

Finally Maktong opened his bloodshot eyes and stared at Chŏmsun, unable to make out her words because of the granny flower roots in his ears.

"Look there!" Chŏmsun blubbered, pointing toward the beehives. "The bees!"

Maktong sprang to his feet. He saw that the bees were on the move, a basket-sized swarm that was one moment rounded and the next moment elongated, already high up and moving off into the western sky. *Oh my god!* Before he knew it he was running off after the swarm. He remembered his grandfather saying a few days earlier that there were too many bees and he needed to move some of them—now he could see why. If he didn't get those bees where they first lighted, they would be gone forever. A couple of years earlier something similar had happened, the bees swarming out on their own because they hadn't been divided up and given more space. The bees had lighted at the pass behind their house, where some villagers gathering wood had spotted them. But by the time Maktong and his father and grandfather had run there to retrieve them, the swarm had taken off, and for as long as they chased it the bees didn't light again and finally were lost. This time he had to get them when they lighted. *Oh my god!* Beneath the blazing sun he ran after the bees on shaky legs, calling out to them. Chŏmsun didn't know what else to do and ran, whimpering, after her brother.

The swarm came to rest in a willow tree outside the entrance to the village. Maktong ordered Chŏmsun to stay there and ran off toward home. He reappeared shortly, coming around the village drinking house, a net on a pole resting on his shoulder and inside it a clump of wax from the beehive. He went to the base of the willow and, before he had stopped panting, began crawling up it. Before he could reach the first branch he slid helplessly back down. He had to catch his breath and he did so clutching the tree, a cheek resting against it, his eyes closed.

At the cost of repeated stings, he finally managed to get the swarm, with the queen bee in the middle, to settle around the clump of wax inside the net, and then he returned home, where he collapsed on the floor of the family room. A feverish moaning escaped his lips.

Beside him, inside the net covered by the ragged quilt, the bees buzzed as if to keep Maktong company until the adults returned.

The following morning when Maktong's grandfather left for the fields he looked back at the house seemingly for the first time in days. It was leaning more than ever. Someone seeing it for the first time might have been reluctant to venture near, thinking it was about to collapse. Because the family had more important things to do at that time, their only recourse was to temporarily shore up the leaning area with wood.

They called Big Nose the carpenter, and as he was selecting some of the timbers obtained by the family for the repairs, he saw Chŏn P'ilsu rounding the corner of the rock wall out front. He looked as if he had been keeping an eye on the house and waiting for this moment to visit.

After the customary greetings Chŏn spoke to Maktong's grandfather: "Goodness sakes, this is going to need more than a couple of timbers. I've been meaning to mention this, but I wasn't sure what you'd think and so I kept quiet. . . . You know that farming shack down in the lower village? What would you think about moving there? It doesn't have doors, but we could hang these good doors there and move you in right away."

Maktong's grandfather couldn't help but feel thankful. Big Nose the carpenter said, "That's a good idea. Then I can fix the house up right." And so the family began preparing immediately for their move.

It so happened that Slit Eyes was home just then depositing his winnings and learned of the move, and he reported this to Maktong's father when he returned to the gambling den. For a time Maktong's father simply stared at his cards as if he hadn't heard; then he flung the cards down and rose.

On his way to Sŏdanggol Maktong's father kept thinking he was forgetting something. He wondered if it was because he had left in the middle of a winning streak. He kept asking himself what he had forgotten and finally realized he hadn't bought that ox. But that other man, the one who had bought the ox, had probably slaughtered it by now. Oh well, he could always buy an ox later. First he had to get the land back. But the agreed-upon date had passed—what if Chŏn refused? *I'll beg. I'll beg him if it kills me.* But what if he still refused? What if he flat-out refused? A dismal feeling came over him.

He crested the pass and looked down to see that his family seemed mostly to have left already. There was only his father off to the side of the yard, near the beehive.

Maktong's father went straight down to Chŏn's house. As soon as Chŏn saw him he noticed his face was frightfully distorted and wondered if he would soon be hearing some outrageous story about the loss of a gambling stake.

Inside, Maktong's father produced a wad of money from his pocket and slid it toward Chŏn.

"I want my land back."

Chŏn slowly counted the money, kept only the amount that covered the land sale, and said, "This is all I need." And with that he returned the rest of the money and the sales contract to Maktong's father.

Maktong's father left, dazed by this unexpected display of generosity and vowing never again to sell the family land, no matter how desperate he might be. A good portion of daylight remained and he told himself he would wait until dark to go home. In the meantime, how about a drink at the village drinking house? On his way there he encountered some villagers on their way home with beef they had purchased. He had thought that Chungbok, the middle of the three Dog Days, had already passed; he realized now that it was the very next day. He decided he ought to buy a few pounds of meat for his family. He went to see the slaughterer, who lived in Magpie Hollow, and there he learned that the meat was from the ox the man had purchased in the upper village and had slaughtered that very day.

Maktong's father bought a couple of pounds of beef, and returning to Sŏdanggol, he found an idle boy and sent him home with it before continuing on to the village drinking house. Red dragonflies flew low in the sky, as if they had sensed an oncoming rain shower. Maktong's father had just finished his second bowl of *makkŏlli* when Song Saengwŏn passed by outside on his way home from the fields.

Catching sight of Maktong's father, Song came inside, saying, "Is that you?" and half hoping Maktong's father would feel inclined to buy him a bowl of *makkŏlli*. Maktong's father did just that. Song drank the bowl in a few gulps, then licked his lips clean.

"I heard you won big," he said with an insinuating look at his counterpart, thinking it would be nice to have another bowl of *makkŏlli*.

"Not really." Maktong's father displayed the sales contract for the land.

"So you got it back." Seeing this, Song told himself, *Maybe there's hope for this guy after all.* "Well done.... So he just gave it to you? Didn't make a stink?"

"Yes, just like that. No argument."

"Good for him. That Chŏn P'ilsu is some kind of man. So, all's well that ends well."

It was the perfect occasion for Maktong's father to be treating, thought Song, and with that he had the barmaid refill his bowl.

Song was about to drink from his newly filled bowl when the interior grew dark and from a distance came the sound of raindrops. The next instant they felt a gust of moisture-laden air, and then the rain came pouring down. Bowl still raised halfway to his mouth, Song said, "A good soaking downpour—" What came next might have been "would be nice" or "is just what we need," but whatever he said was lost in the clamor of the rain shower.

Song finished his second bowl as quickly as the first, and as he was licking his lips and his mustache the shower abruptly ceased. There followed crimson twilight that was uncommonly bright, and then dusk began to settle. Song had not had supper, and the two bowls of *makkŏlli* on an empty stomach did the job. To Maktong's father, who had silently been drinking his *makkŏlli*, he said, "Well done, I mean it—but I'm not so sure you can quit. I guess we'll see. And you cut off your thumb as a reminder, but..." Even though he was tipsy, Song realized he shouldn't talk that way, especially since he was being treated, so he added, "Still, I say well done—I mean it. Getting back the land you sold.... You know, you ought to build yourself a new house. Well done—really.... Well, we'll see what happens...." Song had meant to say something pleasing to Maktong's father, but decided that in his tipsy condition the words might come out wrong again, so he rose. "Well, I ought to get going." And out he went.

So, he thinks I can't stop? And I'll end up selling off the land again? Damned old man, I ought to rip out that yap of yours. . . . Well, it was true that he'd gambled in secret from the time he could count, and when caught by his father he'd been beaten with a pine bough until the side branches broke off, and still he hadn't stopped, and even now. . . . But this time was different. *I'll quit if it kills me!* But as Song Saengwŏn had said—*No, no way!*—but—*No, no way!*

When Maktong's father emerged from the drinking house it was pitch dark. There was no moon.

The following morning the body of Maktong's father was discovered beneath the ruins of the house. He was embracing one of the pillars on the side of the house that had been leaning—evidently he had pushed it, causing the house to collapse on top of him. But the villagers couldn't decide if he had been trying to kill himself or if in his drunken state he had been trying to take down the house but couldn't escape once it gave way. The collapse of the house had knocked out part of Chŏn P'ilsu's back wall. Maktong's grandfather, afraid the bees wouldn't find their way back to the hives because of the evening rain shower and the onset of darkness, had decided when the family moved to leave the hives behind until the following evening. He had now buried those hives, but the bees continued to crawl out and fly away. It was as if they were departing the body of Maktong's father.

That night a vigil was held in the farming shack and Chŏn arrived with a crock of *makkŏlli*. He sat with the village elders as they offered each other drinks, then turned to Maktong's grandfather, who was sitting next to the boy. Whether it was the granny flower roots or the shock of the events of the past two days, Maktong had recovered from his bout with malaria, though he was still drawn. To Maktong's grandfather Chŏn said that until their new house was built they could continue to live in the hut; he asked only that they repair his back wall.

The circle of villagers nodded in spite of themselves, acknowledging the compassion of this man Chŏn. Song Saengwŏn, observing the gathering, was as moved as anyone by Chŏn's benevolence, but it suddenly occurred to him that the more compassionate such a man became, the more likely it was that Maktong's family would eventually come under his thumb. But when it was his turn to be offered a drink, he put such thoughts aside. *Let's have that drink!* And he proceeded to gulp his bowl of *makkŏlli* with a flourish.

The day after the burial of his son, Maktong's grandfather took his family to Chŏn's house and they set about repairing the wall. No one spoke. A solitary bee circled the ruins of the shed and flew off overhead while Maktong and his family went to work. Perhaps it had lost its way, or maybe it was flying by instinct to its former home.

No one seemed to notice the bee except Maktong. No sooner did his drawn face look up than his field of vision was blocked by a gigantic tile-roof house. But the next moment his gaze had streamed over the roofline of the house and out to the skies beyond.

August 1946

BULLS

Pau just couldn't put his mind at ease. Surely something was going to happen to his father tonight. Pau was with the other boys twining sack-rope in Sshidol's family's work shed. He stopped his work and went outside, pretending he had to pee.

It was dark out, no stars in the sky. He remembered his father asking his mother that morning what day it was by the lunar calendar. It was the twenty-sixth day of the month, said his mother. And then Father had muttered to himself, "So the moon won't be out till later in the evening." And tonight, not only was it dark, it was cloudy too.

Around dinnertime his father had smoked several bowls of tobacco in his long pipe, and suddenly he had blurted to Mother, "Are you sure it's the twenty-sixth?" His face wore a serious expression. To be sure, it wasn't the first time Pau had seen him with that look. Just a few days ago his usually dignified father had come inside and said in an angry voice to no one in particular, "The world has gone to hell—we're always getting cheated," with that same serious expression.

At times like this his father's face seemed especially old. The wrinkles on his forehead were deeper and more numerous. Maybe they were a little more numerous and got a little deeper each time his face wore that expression.

But his father's face today told him somehow that something was going to happen before the night was over. Pau recalled what his father had said the day before yesterday when the rumor had arisen about the farmers being taken off somewhere in connection with the grain tax: "Even worms will squirm if you step on them." He thought he could tell what it was that would happen that night. As he hurried back home, the image of that fearsome rifle barrel rose in his mind. His heart wouldn't stop pounding.

He arrived home and sure enough, there in the dark of the courtyard were a group of village men. *So there—I knew something was going to happen.* His heart started pounding again. A fireflylike kerosene lantern glowed behind every patchwork paper-paneled door and window, but the light wasn't enough for Pau to make out who the men were. Or to count how many there were. At least ten, he estimated.

He thought back to last autumn, when his grandmother had passed on. The villagers had gathered in the courtyard then too, and Pau had heard the buzz of voices. But those voices weren't hushed and careful like the ones he heard now. Granted, what was going to happen tonight was more serious than his grandmother's death. He had wailed along with his mother then. Even little Ŏnnyŏn, who was too young to understand, had wailed with them. He had always felt a thrill at the buzz of the villagers when they gathered at his house. But not tonight.

That guy over there flicking away the cigarette he'd smoked down to his fingertips—that was Kŏbuk's big brother, he was sure of it. And he was just as sure that the squatting man who had intercepted that butt so he could add the tobacco to his pipe was Kaettong's father. He saw the glowing butt in the pipe bowl rise to the level of Kaettong's father's mouth, glow red, then fade, and then it began to float in his direction. He looked closer and saw that the group had broken up and were coming his way. *Can't let them know I'm here.* He scurried off toward the ash shed. And now he really did have to pee. When he was finished, and even after the villagers had scattered, he remained where he was for a short time so that anyone who came along and saw him would think he was peeing. As he did, another memory came back to him, triggered by the earlier memory of his grandmother's passing: as soon as they had put her in the coffin, he had taken her pillow and hid it in the rafters of this shed. The pillow of this grandmother who had been so terribly fond of him was somehow so unsettling that he didn't dare go near the ash shed at night. He'd been scared by something that now seemed completely harmless. He was too old for that—thirteen already. His father had told him that when he was Pau's age—actually, when he was fourteen—he was already wrestling in the championship matches. Still, thinking about that pillow he'd hidden, Pau had to admit that being by himself here in this shed at night was not pleasant. His feet took him quickly toward the house. *No, I wasn't scared*, he told himself; *I just want to hurry up and see what my father's doing.*

The courtyard was empty now. Pau heard only the heavy breathing of the bull from the cow shed. In the family room he came across his father, who was putting on his overpants. He was about to go somewhere, Pau was sure of it. His mother had put little Ŏnnyŏn to sleep and was sitting near the kerosene lamp, mending clothing. She didn't look up when Pau arrived, merely asked why he wasn't twining rope with the other boys. Pau lied, saying he had come back home for more rice stalks. He went to the cooler part of the heated floor, where some sheaves of rice stalks were stacked in a corner, and rummaged among them.

His father left. His mother didn't say anything. *Why is she asking me about the rope and not asking Father where he's going?* Maybe his father had told her before Pau got home. *But there she is, looking like nothing's wrong.*

He thought back to the winter before Liberation, when the grain tax was collected, when his father had caught that awful beating from the Jap constable and been taken off to jail in Ch'ungju—well, his mother had been doing her mending then too, every night, all by herself. She looked like she had eased her concerns about Father being taken away, and would stay awake in case he happened to be released from jail that night, to welcome him home.

Back then Pau would awaken several times during the night, and he would always see his mother sitting there just like that.

But tonight he had to catch up with his father and see what was going on. With half an armful of rice stalks under his arm, he slid open the door and stepped out. He thought his father was already outside the brushwood gate, but in the faint light filtering through the open door behind him he saw his father take the supporting stick from his A-frame backrack where it rested beneath the eaves and head toward the gate. From behind he looked like a very old man.

Ever since that terrible beating the winter before Liberation, his father had had trouble with his back. When he was in the prime of his youth, his strength and his wrestling prowess were known throughout the neighboring villages. Even at the age of forty, he would from time to time challenge the strongest of the village youths to a bout, his

face breaking into a dignified smile; then he'd grab hold of his opponent around the waist and before the smile had faded would lift
the young man and throw him to the ground.

But after that beating it was all he could do simply to walk. It was
really frightening, that beating. The Japanese constable had come
riding along on his horse, urging the villagers to pay their grain tax,
his mustache giving him the appearance of decency itself. And then
out of the blue, as if to make an example of Pau's father in front of
the other villagers, he had grabbed him by the collar and said, "You
bastard, you'd rather wrestle than pay your grain tax, eh? Why don't
you and I have a go?" And with a scream he went at Pau's father, who
was standing there wordlessly, and using some technique called judo
threw him all over the frozen ground. And as his father lay on the
ground, blood gushing from his mouth and nose, the constable worked
himself up some more and stomped on his back with the heels of his
riding boots. When it was over, his father couldn't get up on his own.
All the onlookers could do was shudder. And then the constable took
his father away to Ch'ungju. Pau was transfixed; he couldn't even
follow as far as the entrance to the village. His father disappeared
around the corner of Sshidol's family's house, and not until a short
time later did Pau burst into tears. *What a fool I was! All I did was tremble
and watch!*

Tonight he wasn't going to stay home and do nothing. He had to
be with his father. He placed the rice stalks in his own small backrack, next to his father's, then took his supporting stick and out the
brushwood gate he went.

Even in the dark he could make out his father in the distance. He
followed along, maintaining enough of an interval between them to
keep out of sight. His father passed through the lower village and
beyond the last of the dwellings. Once outside the village it was half
a mile to the bank of a stream, and just before that stream bank,
where the road narrowed, there stood an ancient zelkova tree. Pau
saw his father walk toward that tree; he seemed to be stopping there.
Pau likewise came to a stop. He saw that his father was not alone;
several others were gathered there. He could hear their muffled

voices. Each of these others, like his father, carried what looked like a backrack stick.

Pau wondered if the villagers gathered beneath the zelkova were there for a different reason—were they after a thief? Several days ago someone had supposedly made off with beans from Ojaeng's family's bean field, and then the same thing with Kaettong's family last night. Quite a few families had run out of grain, even barley, and were starving, and there were frequent cases of people taking for themselves newly ripened grain, regardless of whose land it was.

So maybe the villagers gathered there were lying low in hopes of catching a thief, and the reason his father asked his mother what day it was by the lunar calendar was that on a moonless night it was easy to hide and catch a thief in the act. But then the villagers left the zelkova and went down to the stream. Maybe they wanted to keep watch over the far side of the stream. *I'm going to follow him anyway.* He went beneath the zelkova and looked toward the stream. In the darkness he heard Ojaeng telling the others that they didn't have to wade the stream—he would carry each of them across on his back. Ojaeng with the stubby neck, short waist, and solid, stocky build—he was very strong. Pau remembered how the villagers had joked about him. When Ojaeng was born his father had swaddled him in a grain basket and hung it on the wall, because that was supposed to make a baby grow fast, but this newborn wiggled so much that the nail holding the basket came out and the basket fell. Luckily the baby landed right side up, but his bottom hit so hard that his neck and his waist were compressed—and thus the grown-up Ojaeng's stubby neck and short waist.

When he was sure no one remained on this side of the stream, Pau ventured down to the water. Quickly he took off his shoes and rolled up his pants legs, and then he crossed the stream. The water chilled his toes and calves. On the far side of the stream he dried his feet on the grass, put his shoes back on, and without rolling down his pants legs, set out after his father and the villagers. They were some distance beyond Kŏbuk's family's tobacco plot before Pau spotted them. None of them spoke; there was only the sound of their footsteps. It wasn't like a group of people moving forward; instead, the way each man silently followed the one in front of him, they looked just like a line of cows walking this dark road. No, a line of bulls.

Pau thought back to the year before last when he had gone to Ch'ungju with his father to buy a bull calf. They had returned at night on this very same road. The sun was setting when they crested Masŭmak Pass, and by the time they reached the Han River it had dropped below the horizon. The calf had balked at the ferry landing and the boatman and Pau had to pull on its nose ring while his father pushed its rump before they managed to get it on board. By the time they reached the three-way fork that led to Hŭinbawi Hollow, it was dark and Pau was frightened. But unlike tonight, stars had dotted the sky and there was a crescent moon, so it wasn't pitch black. Pau had tried to comfort himself with something he had heard from the grown-ups—if you had a bull with you, you didn't get scared, no matter how rough the surroundings. Well, the animal he and his father were taking home was a calf, but it was a bull calf, and with that thought he had tried to put his fears to rest. But then Pau had remembered a story he'd heard from the grown-ups, something that had actually happened a few years earlier. One evening a young man went outside around dinnertime to graze the family's bull. When sometime later the bull came back by itself, its horns bloody, his family panicked, certain the bull had gored the young man. But then the young man reappeared, and he didn't have a scratch on him. He had been grazing the bull, he explained, when without warning it startled, knocking him over. He thought he was going to be trampled. But once he had managed to gather his wits, what should he see but a tiger? The tiger seemed to be toying with the bull, leaping back and forth over its back. And every time the tiger leaped, the bull turned to avoid it. (Here the young man explained to Pau that actually the bull wasn't trying to avoid the tiger; instead it was trying to meet the tiger head-on so it could charge.) Anyway, he hadn't been trampled. The bull somehow managed to gore the tiger and then ran off. The young man saw that the tiger was dead, its belly ripped open. (Here again the man telling the story added that it's the nature of a bull when it finally hooks its adversary to keep goring it, flipping it up into the air like a shuttlecock, until finally its innards spill out, and then it gives up.) This story had made Pau wish that their bull calf was a little more grown up. And then there were the stories about tigers attacking people while they slept or people walking country roads, and supposedly the tiger always snatched the middle person because it thought that person was the most fearful. And yet Pau hated walking in front of the calf or behind his father, so he stayed between them, and by the time they got home he had been kicked by the calf more times than he could count.

But at least back then he had the bull calf and he was with his father. Tonight he was by himself, separated from his father. If only he had the bull—it was full grown now—he wouldn't have a worry in the world. *On the other hand, you're two years older now, right? Don't tell me you're scared of a dark road. Besides, you've got the stick. And all you have to do is shout and those bulls from the village will come running.* But he had never been able to erase such fears from his mind, and now he walked faster so as to shorten the distance between himself and the villagers.

But if the villagers intended to catch whoever was stealing the grain, shouldn't they be hiding somewhere nearby? They were almost past the croplands; if they went much farther they'd be at the three-way junction to Hŭinbawi Hollow. And then it occurred to Pau that maybe they weren't trying to catch a thief after all. Maybe they were going to fight the people from Hŭinbawi Hollow.

Almost every year fights broke out over water during irrigating season. They were murderous brawls in which teeth were knocked out and skulls split open. Behind each side was a powerful landowning family urging the fighters to get the water first and worry later. This year the son of the Hŭinbawi Hollow landowner had supposedly gotten himself a high government position in Seoul, after which his father had ordered the villagers to irrigate only his paddies. Some time previous, the oldest grandson of Old Kim Long Pipe, the landowner in the village where Pau's family lived, had likewise obtained a high government position in Seoul, and once he was established, Old Kim launched an attack on the other landowner, calling him an ungrateful wretch and warning him to watch out. And so, thought Pau, maybe the men from his village were going to fight the men from Hŭinbawi Hollow tonight.

Wait a minute. Didn't some men from each village get together and decide not to fight anymore?

And sure enough, the villagers had reached the three-way junction and were not taking the road to Hŭinbawi Hollow. Instead they turned down the road to Ch'ungju. *So there.* As he had reckoned in the first place, his father and the villagers were on their way to Ch'ungju.

That fearsome rifle came to mind. Pau could see it whipping down in the darkness, cracking Ch'unbo across the shoulder blades. He hadn't paid his barley and wheat tax. Ch'unbo hadn't flinched under the first blow. Ch'unbo, face pale from long years of malnourishment, who shouldered the burden of so many mouths to feed. That fearsome rifle struck again. This time Ch'unbo would go down. His shoulders would be injured, just like Pau's father's back. The man with the rifle struck the unresisting Ch'unbo's shoulders yet again, and finally he went down. There was a glint in Ch'unbo's eyes. It came from tears. And then Ch'unbo began to shudder all over. He looked like he was wiggling. This wiggling spread to all the villagers looking on, and to Pau among them. But that was the end of it. Ch'unbo, like Pau's father before him, could not get up on his own, and was led off to Ch'ungju. And it did turn out that Ch'unbo's shoulders were never right again. Just like Pau's father's back.

The villagers arrived at the Han River. They seemed to have already spoken with the boatman at the landing, and were crowding onto the boat. Should he wait for the next boat? Or take this one? If he took this boat they would know right off that he'd been following them. If he took the next boat he'd fall too far behind them, and he wasn't sure of the route where the road went up from the other side of the river—that would really be a problem.

He decided to take the first boat. Even if he was discovered, the villagers wouldn't have the heart to send him back home by himself. *And I wouldn't go back even if they did.* But once he was on the boat, no one recognized him. Then again, he wasn't able to tell who was who either. No one spoke, or even smoked. The only sound in the darkness was the creaking of the oars. Pau listened to the creaking. He remembered thinking, when he was on this boat before, that if they went down the river for three or four days they'd get to that place called Seoul—wouldn't it be fun to go there sometime? But no such thoughts came to mind now. His mind was occupied by the creak of the oars and a feeling that the river was so much wider now than before.

On the other side the villagers started walking silently up the hill, still resembling a procession of bulls. Pau followed at a safe distance.

They were getting closer to Ch'ungju, and once again that fearsome rifle came to mind. Pau's heart was racing. He thought back to the news two days ago about all the farmers who had been taken into custody. Young as he was, he realized he could not pretend to himself that this was simply someone else's concern and not his. Now he knew. He knew why his father and the other villagers were going to Ch'ungju—"Even worms will squirm if you step on them." From now on, he would be there for his father.

Oh no! Yet again the image of that fearsome rifle loomed in his mind, only this time the bodies of his father and the others were sprawled out beneath it. There was a glint in their eyes, the glint of tears. All of them were squirming, just like worms will do if you step on them. They were crying out, all of them: *If you keep this up, we'll starve! We're not asking to get rid of the grain tax, we just want it to be fair! Why do you let people fill up their sacks in the granary and sell on the sly in Japan or god knows where else? Why do you let them do that? Why do you harass the needy night and day—what will you get out of them? If things don't change, we'll starve!*

All these outcries Pau had heard from the villagers. And every time, he couldn't help thinking back to when he and his father had gone to Ch'ungju in autumn two years ago to buy the bull calf. They had to borrow money first, and that was when Pau had seen all the sacks of rice stacked to the ceiling of Old Kim Long Pipe's storehouse. And the ink-black iron padlock bigger than a man's fist.

Again they came to mind, the storeroom filled with sacks of rice and the padlock on the door. That padlock wasn't about to open. And that led to the image of something whipping down. But not to break open the padlock; rather to break the back of his squirming father. Pau imagined his father's back giving out, his father collapsing on the spot. *Now I'll have to carry Father. I can do it. That time Father's back gave out in the middle of the harvest, I carried him home on my own back, didn't I—even though I had to stop for a rest three times along the way.*

The sky couldn't have been darker; not a star was to be seen. When his father had muttered to himself that morning about the moon not being out until later in the evening, Pau didn't know if his father was hoping for a moon or for no moon, but for Pau on a night like this, even a waning moon would have been welcome. And if not the moon, then even a sprinkling of stars. And just then there appeared far ahead a cluster of stars. *Wow, they're beautiful!* But the next moment he realized they were the lights of Ch'ungju. This was the first time he had seen Ch'ungju at night. Before he knew it he had arrived at Masŭmak Pass, comfortably warmed from the effort of following the villagers uphill. There at the high point of the pass the breeze, absent till then, swept past his ears and down his back. Pau didn't mind.

The next instant he was telling himself he had to be ready, and his hand tightened on the backrack stick. But what was this? Instead of heading straight down into Ch'ungju the villagers were making their way up the left-hand slopes of Nam Mountain. He couldn't understand it, but he climbed after them nevertheless. And then it seemed they had staked out an area and squatted. Pau squatted too, still keeping his distance. As ever, no one was speaking.

Pau heard someone cough, and then cough again. It sounded like Kŏbuk's big brother. He could tell that Kŏbuk's brother was standing, not squatting, and that he wasn't coughing in Pau's direction but in the opposite direction instead.

And then from out of the darkness in the opposite direction came a similar cough, followed by the sound of movement. Who? Pau's heart began pounding. And then someone, it looked like Kŏbuk's brother, was moving straight toward the oncoming person. Pau heard whispers. Much to his relief, the two whispering voices were not arguing. And then he noticed that they were not the only ones on Nam Mountain. He could now see many other people as well, villagers like them, also squatting. Pau felt safer.

And it was better now that he could see light coming from the streets of Ch'ungju. It was almost like having starlight. That place off to the left, where a lot of light was concentrated, had to be the train station. Pau heard no whistle—when would the next train be coming? Wouldn't it be fun to take a train to Seoul sometime? And now he was imagining a bus coming into Ch'ungju by way of the main street in front of the train station, a bus from Seoul, raising a cloud of dust as it rattled along and then coming to a stop, and passengers getting off, quite a few of them. How could so many people fit into that little thing? Now it was the bus he wanted to ride, rattling and shaking, to Seoul.

Hmm, where is the bus station anyway? His eyes scanned the lighted streets of Ch'ungju. There? Or there? He remembered it being across the alley and a couple houses down from where Old Kim Long Pipe lived, and then his eyes came to rest on an area that was brighter than anywhere else—*maybe there*. And popping up once again in his mind's eye was that magnificent house of Kim's that he and his father had visited the year before last, when they had come to Ch'ungju to buy the bull calf.

As soon as his father had entered the stately gate that time, he had bowed from the waist toward a sliding door to the right. Was that where the old man was sitting? He too, as his father had taught him, bowed deeply in that direction. But all that Pau perceived as he bowed and straightened was the play of light on the glass-paneled door; he didn't notice the nose, which the villagers said (but never in Old Man Kim's presence) resembled the gall bladder of a slaughtered animal, nor did he notice the pipe with the large bowl that never left Old Man Kim's hand. Then again he shouldn't stare through the glass, and so he directed his gaze to the palm-sized patch on the back of his father's traditional going-out jacket, which his father had changed into before leaving on their outing. And then from the other side of the door came a booming voice calling for Kwidong, the errand boy, a voice loud enough to startle Pau and to rattle the glass panes.

From the middle gate there emerged a boy even smaller than Pau who took the wicker basket wrapped in cloth that his father had brought and went back inside. Both their presence and their gift must have been clearly visible to Old Kim Long Pipe behind his sliding glass door.

Telling Pau to wait, his father removed his shoes and carefully brushed off the soles of his socks. Pau went toward the middle gate, where the errand boy had just disappeared. He heard the sliding door open and close. His father would be meeting now with Old Man Kim. Once he had the loan, he could buy that calf he'd had his eye on.

The middle gate opened and Kwidong handed Pau the empty basket. Visible through the open gate was an array of glass-paneled doors to the inner quarters. What a magnificent sight it was! *So that's why the villagers talk themselves silly about this house.*

"Are there lots of persimmons where you live?" asked Kwidong.

He must have seen the persimmons they had brought. And he talked funny.

Pau nodded.

"There's lots where I live too." Kwidong was about to say more when a woman's voice called him back in.

Kwidong soon reappeared with a small meal table set with two bowls of soup-and-rice. He carried the table to the sliding glass door, which opened to reveal Pau's father. Instead of receiving the table where he was, his father came out to take it. From inside came Old Man Kim's voice asking both of them to eat inside. "We're fine out here," said Pau's father, who then joined Pau and set the table on the ground.

Pau sat down opposite his father and began to eat. It was honest-to-goodness rice. Even before the grain tax came along, it was all you could do to get a bowl of rice not mixed with other grain, and after the grain tax, forget it! And even though there was no meat on their table, the broth was definitely meat broth. As soon as this food was in his mouth, it went straight down. They probably ate like this every day—judging from the fact that the meal had been brought out right away. Boy, was it good!

His father transferred a spoonful of his rice to Pau's bowl. Kwidong stood outside the middle gate, watching. Pau felt ashamed of himself. "I don't want it," he said to his father. But instead of returning the rice to his father's bowl, he ate it himself. Next his father found a morsel of meat in his soup and added it to Pau's bowl. "I said I don't want it"—louder this time.

As soon as they had finished, Kwidong took the table inside and Pau's father returned to the master's quarters. *I wish Father would hurry up and get that loan so we can buy the calf and go home.*

Suddenly he heard a loud tapping sound—it must have been Old Man Kim's pipe bowl in the ashtray. Pau had been told that the old man liked to bang things around when his dander was up. Maybe the loan hadn't worked out.

The middle gate opened again and out came Kwidong. He approached Pau and said, "How old are you?"

"Eleven."

"Eleven? I'm ten."

Kwidong gestured with his chin toward the master's quarters. "So that's your father. Good for you." He still talked funny.

"You don't have a father?"

"Why shouldn't I? He's with my family. In Mungaeng." By which he meant Mungyŏng. "Ever heard of Mungaeng?"

Pau shook his head.

"Kyŏngsang Province. That's where we—"

The rest was lost as the same woman's voice called Kwidong, who hurried back in.

Pau wondered why Kwidong wasn't at home with his mother and father. He peered through a gap in the gate and saw, off to the side of the yard, Kwidong emerging from the storehouse, a sack of something or other slung over his shoulder. Just before Kwidong closed the door Pau's eyes were drawn to the sacks of grain stacked inside the storehouse with its padlock bigger than a grown-up's fist. He quickly turned away, as if he had witnessed something shameful.

Presently Kwidong reappeared, his face suffused with a smile that revealed dimples in both cheeks.

This time Pau spoke first: "So what do you do here?"

"Grandpop here asked my father to send him a boy to run errands—and that's me. Our family works his land, see? And me being here is a big help to my family because now they have one less mouth to feed. There's nine of us—but that doesn't include my two big sisters, who got married off. . . ."

"Don't you get homesick?"

"Sure I do. More for my mom than my father. When I left to come here she followed me out to the main road—she couldn't stop crying. I eat better here, but I still wish I was home. But my father told me not to think about home and just take care of myself here. . . . We got persimmon trees out in back of our house, and the persimmons are bigger than the ones you brought. We pick them in the fall—"

Yet again the woman's voice called Kwidong, and again Kwidong left off in mid-sentence, the smile gone from his face.

It looked to Pau as if Kwidong would keep thinking of home in spite of his father's instructions. When he came out again Pau would ask when he was going home to all those big persimmons. He wished Kwidong would hurry up and come out.

And then out he came. But this time he scurried past Pau, saying he would see him after he ran an errand, and disappeared through the main gate.

A short time later the glass door slid open and his father emerged. His face looked careworn. *Maybe he didn't get the loan.* Behind him came Old Kim Long Pipe's raspy voice: "Look here, I just gave you a three-percent loan, that's practically free money, so why the long face?" *I guess he got the loan after all.* But why did his father look so down in the dumps?

His father approached him, picked up the empty wicker basket and the wrapping cloth, and used the corner of the cloth to rub off a reddish-orange stain on the tip of his right thumb. Pau didn't realize that his father had just used that thumb to seal the loan agreement.

His father led Pau back to the sliding door and performed a bow, as he had done when they arrived. Pau did likewise. Again he was aware only of the gleam of the glass panels; he couldn't see Old Kim Long Pipe, but knew the man was there on the other side.

Outside the main gate, his father gazed at the sun setting in the west, his face still careworn. "The market's probably shut down, but let's hurry there anyway."

But it bothered Pau to have to leave without saying good-bye to Kwidong. When Kwidong got back from his errand maybe he'd look around wondering where Pau went. As he and his father emerged from the alley he kept looking back, but Kwidong never came into sight....

Pau wondered now if Kwidong was still there at Old Kim Long Pipe's house, where all the lights were coming from. His father had since paid several visits to the old man, and upon his return Pau would ask if Kwidong was still there, but his father never had a definite answer. It looked like the grown-ups didn't pay attention to things like that.

From the darkness he heard Ojaeng's muted voice: "How long till ten o'clock?" It sounded as if he were talking to himself. "Isn't it about that time?" That was Ch'unbo's trembling voice, muted like Ojaeng's. *So, something's going to happen at ten o'clock.* Again the voices fell silent.

Ch'ik ch'ik—flint striking on rock. And then an urgent shushing sound, telling whoever it was to stop. *I guess you're not supposed to light a cigarette.*

The back of his neck and from his waist down felt cold. His body, sweaty from the uphill walk, had cooled off, and the chill was working its way in. The pants legs he'd rolled up before crossing the stream had come partway down; Pau pulled them the rest of the way down over his ankles. Then he put down his backrack stick and wrapped his arms around himself.

That's when it happened. All the lights in the Ch'ungju streets went out. The next moment all the villagers stood up, as if they'd been waiting for this signal. Before Pau knew it he was standing too, backrack stick in hand. He thought he heard Kŏbuk's big brother say something and then move out in front, and then the villagers began to flock downhill, like riled-up bulls. Bulls from his own village and the other villages descending toward the streets of Ch'ungju, the bulls that Kŏbuk's big brother had been whispering to, the bulls just beyond them, the bulls hidden all over Nam Mountain, those bulls just like the bulls from his own village.

So surprised was Pau that for a moment he couldn't move his trembling body. *You idiot, you idiot, you've come all this way and look at you now....* Finally his hand tightened around the backrack stick and he began to chase after the grown-ups. He kept stumbling and falling. *Got to catch up.* But instead he gradually fell farther behind and eventually he lost sight of the grown-ups altogether. And still he ran.

It was virtually black in the direction of Ch'ungju, now that the streetlights were off. There were other lights, flitting through the darkness this way and that, coming in and out of sight. Pau realized they were coming from cars, but the cars were making a strange noise. His heart kept racing.

He heard a popping sound and straightened in spite of himself. *It's that horrible rifle!* And then people crying out. He imagined his father among those people, sprawling onto the ground. *Oh my god, oh my god. Why couldn't you catch up with the grown-ups? You idiot, you idiot!*

Flames shot up through the darkness. He felt as if those flames were flaring up inside him. The outcries from the people were sounding inside him as well, his father's voice distinct among them. And then he realized that the voices were coming from where the flames were rising. He ran toward those flames. It didn't seem that far.

Breathing heavily, he came out onto a street. The fire was farther off than it looked. Voices in the dark asked where the fire was. And then from nearby came gunshots. And once again a confusion of outcries. He imagined, there in front of him, a formation of those fearsome rifles, stopping him. *Go anyway, you've got to go!*

He arrived at what looked to be a main street. The clamor was louder. He saw people running recklessly in the dark. The next moment, as Pau ran breathlessly along, the street fell silent.

A strange noise cut through the air and a large light sped past. In the light Pau could see running figures, and then in a split-second their shadows enlarging, shrinking, and enlarging again, before disappearing. He spied an alley to the right—maybe a shortcut to where the fire was—and turned down it.

Just inside the alley he bumped into something and the next thing he knew he was huddled on the ground. He heard a cry of pain and saw a man with a bulging straw sack. There was a dull pain in Pau's head, he was out of breath, and he couldn't get up. But he was glad to see that the man hadn't been knocked down. "Are you fucking blind?" snapped the man. Off he went. Finally Pau got to his feet.

He had taken only a few steps when he saw someone else coming. He couldn't see clearly in the dark, only that the person was carrying something heavy and that the effort was costing him dearly. *Make sure you don't bump into him.* He quickly dodged the man. *Wait a minute!* The house that the man had come out of, a house in a dead-end alley—it was Old Kim Long Pipe's house. *How did I end up here?* He'd never expected this. He went closer, saw that the main gate and the middle gate were both wide open, and slipped inside. There in the yard, peering toward the storehouse, was a man holding a candle. Pau was sure it was Old Kim Long Pipe—though he had actually seen him only twice, and from a distance, when the man had come to their village.

"Hurry up, there, hurry! . . . I can't believe those sons of bitches set fire to the police station."

It was Old Kim Long Pipe's voice all right, but not the intimidating voice Pau remembered. It was stifled, urgent. As always Old Kim had his pipe, the pipe that never left his right hand. When he gestured with it now, the candlelight glinted off the metal bowl. The candle flame was fluttering. *Why is it doing that? There's no breeze.* The glass-paneled door, so magnificent before, was merely a dark background that reflected the flickering candlelight.

The candle rose up head high, then was lowered; up and down, up and down it went, as Old Kim Long Pipe tried to see inside the storehouse. The candlelight shone on the drooping bridge of his nose.

"Come on, boys, hurry it up!" His voice was louder now.

From out of the dark storehouse came a man hefting a straw sack of grain. He walked past Old Kim in Pau's direction. And then someone else emerged from the darkness, approached Old Kim, and took shape in the candlelight—an elderly woman.

"Dear, what's the use—"

The woman's fragile voice was silenced by Old Kim's angry bark: Be quiet! What do you women know, always getting in the way!"

The old woman disappeared helplessly back into the dark.

Suddenly the candle in Old Kim Long Pipe's trembling hand went out. *Did the wind do that?*

"Kwidong—bring me some matches! They ought to kill 'em off—what did they have to cut the electricity for?"

Kwidong's still here! Pau's heart jumped for joy. *Kwidong—here I am—I just plain forgot you were here.*

A match was struck, and there in the light of the match was Kwidong. Pau barely managed to keep from calling out to him.

Kwidong was noticeably bigger, and maybe because it was night, he looked different, especially his face, which was more coarse. Pau wondered if he still had those dimples.

Kwidong lit the candle but the flame immediately died.

"What's the matter, can't you light a candle?"

It wasn't his fault, thought Pau.

Kwidong struck another match, and this time he managed to light the candle, in spite of Old Kim Long Pipe's trembling hand.

The next moment Old Kim was shouting into the dark: "Come on, be quick there! Hurry up!"

Kwidong disappeared into the gloom of the storehouse. Once again Pau felt an urge to call out his name, but managed to contain himself. Another man with a sack of grain came out past Pau.

The cries from outside sounded closer. *Shouldn't I try to keep all that grain from being sneaked away?* He momentarily forgot about trying to find his father, and his sweaty hand clutched the backrack stick more tightly.

And then the men who had carried off the sacks of rice scuttled back in out of the dark, hurrying one after another past Pau, still toting their loads. Old Kim Long Pipe's candle came close to reveal the first man, who said in a panting voice, "We're in big trouble—they just raided Chief Yi's home." Without waiting for a response, he staggered toward the storehouse and disappeared inside.

"They went to the chief's?"

As Old Kim said this, the sleeves of his traditional jacket trembled. The candlelight kept glinting off the bowl of his ever-so-large pipe. Old Kim seemed not to know what to do with the candle he held.

An idea seemed finally to have come to him—he brought the candle close to his mouth and blew. Pau caught one last glimpse of his drooping nose before it and the candlelight disappeared, and then the trembling hand and the ever-so-large pipe were no more.

December 1946

TO SMOKE A CIGARETTE

It was a habit developed over the ten long years he had been a junior clerk at the courthouse, and by now a daily routine: every morning when he rose, he took from the shelf his bag of leaf tobacco and a page of newspaper, rolled a cigarette, and had himself a smoke.

And so that morning he slipped out of bed, picked out his clothes and put them on, and with a shiver retrieved his Puyong tobacco and a sheet of newspaper from the shelf. He began to tear off a strip—it was the same newspaper he had used the previous day—but his hand came to a stop. There on the page he had been tearing was the headline CHRONIC STOWAWAY PROBLEM, along with the subheading MOST ARE STREET WOMEN, followed by the article itself. Judging from the small headline, it was a low-priority item.

Several months earlier, each of the dailies had carried a lengthy report on the plight of Koreans who had gone to Japan during the colonial period, had returned to what they considered their homeland, but within a year had felt compelled to go back to Japan as stowaways in order to make a living. It was a story that had left readers choked up. Since then, similar articles had appeared from time to time, so that by now the account had been relegated to the city pages, and readers, himself included, were hardened to it.

The reason his eyes had come to rest on this article was the MOST ARE STREET WOMEN subheading. The phrase "street women" reminded him of that woman he had seen the previous evening at the bar in Ta-dong.

This brief article related how on January 5 a boatload of stowaways bound for Japan had been intercepted off the coast of Ulsan by the Coast Guard. Almost all were Koreans who had lived in Japan, and of these the majority were street women. To stem the increasing tide, the authorities were subjecting the stowaways to summary trials. He wondered if the woman he had seen the previous evening was one such woman. *I'll bet she was.* As if to seal this verdict, he finished tearing the strip from the newspaper page and rolled his cigarette.

Returning the tobacco and the newspaper page to the shelf, he made his way around the head of his son, who was curled up asleep on the warmer part of the heated floor, then slid open the door to the kitchen. This was the signal for his wife to take an ember from the cookstove and light his cigarette. The next moment all was forgotten. All except the thought of that first deep drag.

He returned to where he had been sitting. As the cigarette paper, that is to say the newspaper article, burned, the image of the woman in the bar the previous evening flickered across his mind: her lack of a coat; her tight-fitting, faded red sweater; the long, slender neck; and the way she slurped her soup and rice, which told him she was starving.

The episode at the bar had resulted from his chance encounter with Teacher Suam in front of Tŏksu Palace after his deliverance from the daily routine at the courthouse. As he was walking home, head hunched down because of the cold, someone took his arm. He looked up, and there was Teacher Suam. At first he couldn't help feeling a prickling sense of guilt at not seeing to the favor that the teacher had asked of him. This guilty feeling, combined with the fact that Teacher Suam's face was noticeably more haggard than when he had last seen him several days earlier, produced a twofold weight that hung heavy on his heart.

Pulled down over Teacher Suam's forehead was a shabby felt hat he had never seen before. Beneath it were lusterless eyes tearing from the cold. Teacher Suam's drawn face with his breath freezing on his untrimmed white mustache was that of a sick man. Was Teacher Suam ill? he asked. The answer was an unconvincing "No." Blinking twice and releasing a couple of tears, Teacher Suam explained that he had been on his way to the courthouse when he tried to take a shortcut and ended up lost, and he had been wandering around ever since. "I almost missed you," said Teacher Suam. He tried to smile, but wrinkles appeared instead.

Again he reproached himself for not doing what Teacher Suam had asked of him, and after he had confessed to his failure, Teacher Suam said, "I'm sure you're terribly busy," in a tone of voice that told him the teacher actually believed he was busy. The realization that Teacher Suam was not simply providing him an extenuating circumstance or making small talk overwhelmed him with shame.

Teacher Suam suggested going someplace nearby where they could sit for a moment. He offered his home, and when Teacher Suam responded, "Next time" he realized that even if he took the teacher home, there wasn't much he could offer on short notice. And so, thinking he would treat Teacher Suam to a nice hot meal of rice and soup, he set out across the streetcar tracks in the direction of Ta-dong.

Along the way, his departed father came to mind, the youthful face of a man in his thirties. A face in a photograph. His father and Teacher Suam had been as close as brothers. The two families had lived next to each other in the ancestral home in Masan, and his father and Teacher Suam had gone to the village academy together. Teacher Suam had always been praised for his talent at reciting the classics, whereas Father had been a mischief maker, never any good at his studies, scolded or whipped almost daily. He still remembered these stories, which he would hear at home when Father and Teacher Suam were drinking together. The two of them had continued to be close as adults, after Teacher Suam became headmaster at the village academy and Father went into business. Father, never good at studies, proved in business to be a man of unusual talent and resourcefulness, and was able to provide a comfortable living for a family that until then had never had enough. In contrast, Teacher Suam, as a headmaster, was indescribably destitute. And so Father provided him with endless assistance. When he became headmaster, Teacher Suam moved into a room attached to the school, while Father within a few years had moved his family to the pier district, some distance away. Thereafter, without exception on every holiday and festival day throughout the year, Father sent Teacher Suam grain and meat as well as a variety of delicacies prepared at home. He remembered being sent on these errands. And then the day came when Teacher Suam had to leave. A new wave of education had washed ashore at Masan, and Teacher Suam's only option was to look for a village school up in the mountains. His father made a proposal: "Since you and your wife don't have children yet, why don't you move into our guest room and you can teach our boy classical Chinese?" Teacher Suam replied that if it were a few years earlier he would have gratefully accepted, but in the new order of things, subjects like classical Chinese weren't of any use in the big cities, so the boy should be educated in the new learning. So saying, Teacher Suam left for a mountain village. Thereafter, letters of greeting arrived frequently, Teacher Suam's calligraphy redolent of the scent of ink. Perpetually busy, Father was always saying he should send a reply, but he sensed that Father never got around to it.

And then, beginning in the spring of his third year of primary school, Father began spending days at a time at home—something without precedent in his working life—until finally he was bedridden. In no time a rumor arose that he had failed in some sort of business. What he didn't realize until he was grown up was that the business was grain speculation. The illness hadn't seemed serious, but Father ate practically nothing and wasted away by the day, and in early autumn he passed on. It was a stunning development. How he had cried, along with his mother. His little brother wasn't yet old enough to feel sorrow. He remembered it to this day, remembered how his mother would weep whenever she saw him, and how he had tried to avoid her by staying at school until evening instead of going straight home after dismissal.

One day about a month after his father had passed away, he returned home as usual in the evening and was startled to hear from the guest room the sound of a man weeping. He went into the family room and found his mother crying as well. Sometime later he learned that the man weeping in the guest room was Teacher Suam. He had never known a grown man to cry like that. Teacher Suam had made it a point to pay them a visit on each of the first two anniversaries of his father's death—which required inquiries on Teacher Suam's part because they had moved. Some two months after Father's funeral, Mother had sold their house and they had taken a smaller one. The former house had been their only asset, but you can't make a living just from owning a house. And then a year later they moved to a house that was smaller still. Most of the furniture they sold off.

Mother then got to thinking that since there were only the three of them they could get by with just one room, and that by minimizing their belongings she could give both boys an education. And so he was able to go to Seoul for middle school. But the family fortunes were such that he alone finished middle school, and even that was barely affordable. They had long since sold their tiny house and were renting a room, and there remained no piece of furniture that could fetch a price. In spite of the income from Mother's various labors, his middle-school fees would have been beyond her reach if not for the sale of the house and furniture—indeed, it had already been a year since his little brother had had to drop out of primary school in the middle of the school year. Things got so bad they had to skimp on meals. Fortunately his grades had been good enough for him to secure temporary employment at the courthouse, but it was not a job that would support a family of three in Seoul. So Mother decided to move with his younger brother to a village not far from Masan and farm—there was no other choice. She was still there, past the age of sixty, farming with his younger brother. Now as then, the fact that his own middle school education had cost his brother a grade school education, combined with his inability to provide a comfortable living for his mother, who had spent half her life in hardship, caused him bitterness and regret. After three years of temporary employment he was able to pass the examination that qualified him for the lowest level of the government bureaucracy, and over the course of the following ten years, working as a junior clerk, he had taken a wife, fathered a child, and settled into his present rut. His seemingly endless life as a junior clerk had continued after Liberation to the present day.

And then ten days earlier at the courthouse, he'd been told he had a visitor. He went out to the hall and found an elderly man, who asked, "Is that you, Mr. Kim?" Yes, he replied, whereupon the man said he was Suam and took his hand in his. Teacher Suam? He was so surprised he just stood there, his hand in that grasp. The old man's hands were rough and knotted. At that moment he felt as if he understood all that Teacher Suam had undergone in the thirty years since he had seen him last. It was a good thing they were both alive to meet again, said Teacher Suam, tears filling his eyes, while for his part he realized that he would never have recognized the old man if they had passed each other on the street. After saying he had known about his job at the courthouse, Teacher Suam asked about his family—how many children did he have, and how were his mother and his brother doing? He asked when Teacher Suam had arrived from the countryside. Not very long ago, replied the teacher. And actually he had come to ask a favor. He had had a son late in life and wanted to send the boy to middle school, but couldn't think of a way to pay the school fees and wondered if an old man such as himself might be able to find work here at the courthouse—scribal work was something he could manage. The father had always helped him when he was alive, and now here he was in the same situation with the son. "I know you're busy and I've bothered you enough for one day, but I'd like to drop by again in a few days." And with that Teacher Suam released his hand. He walked Teacher Suam out to the main gate, but not until the teacher had disappeared around the corner did he realize it was almost lunchtime and that he was being less than gracious in not inviting him home for a meal. Wanting quickly to see to Teacher Suam's request, he went to the courthouse registry. But the registry head was away, so he returned to his desk, planning to go back the following day. But when that day came, he put it off another day, and so on, so that when Teacher Suam next visited, he still had not been back to the registry. He explained that he had to go through several more levels before he would have an answer. Teacher Suam said he was sorry for bothering him when he must be busy, and turned to go. It happened to be near the end of the work day, and he suggested that they go to his house, but Teacher Suam said he would visit on a subsequent occasion, and with that he left. And so today had been the third time Teacher Suam had come to see him.

But he still couldn't give Teacher Suam a definite answer. He had in fact met once in the meantime with the registry head, who had said he might consider a scribe who was licensed but that otherwise there not much hope. And then the head had said, "Don't you know this by now?" It wasn't that he didn't know; rather, he was hoping the head would approach his superior, but when he broached this issue the head said, "You've been here a lot longer than I have—wouldn't it be better if you spoke to him directly?" And with that the head had skillfully washed his hands of the matter. His only option now was to speak with the superior, something he had been putting off. He had a hunch that somehow it wouldn't work out even if he did speak with the superior, and this prevented him from acting. But lately an honest-to-goodness cold snap had set in and his concerns about fuel and food for his family took precedence over all else. Under the circumstances, was he wrong to have neglected Teacher Suam's request?

Maybe not, but then he had not done right by Teacher Suam either. *My efforts have been lacking. Father would not have acted like I have. If only he were alive!* But all that was left of Father was the coat he used to wear. He himself had managed to get by until now with that coat. It was so faded, and the fabric so worn, that it was difficult to tell just what color it had originally been. He raised the collar of that coat against the wind, as if this had just now occurred to him. Genuinely sorry that Teacher Suam had had to venture out on this cold day, he turned to look at the old man, and when his eyes traveled to the worn-out felt hat pushed low on his head, he was struck by the thought that perhaps he had just picked it up at a second-hand shop. He doubted Teacher Suam had owned that hat for as long as it had taken to become so shabby. The sun-darkened, careworn face beneath the lowered brim told him this, as did the rough, knotty hands stuck in the pockets of his traditional overcoat. Besides, Teacher Suam hadn't been wearing that hat the previous two times—doubtless he had bought it used. Quite a few times he had seen the ragpickers who exchanged taffy for second-hand items collecting such hats. But even hats such as these were probably useful in cold weather. And the weather, after all, couldn't have cared less as he and Teacher Suam walked along the darkening streets.

Happiness in the form of toasty warmth welcomed them into the bar in Ta-dong. This warmth was due not to a blazing stove but instead to a charcoal brazier rigged on top of an oil drum and used for grilling snacks and warming drinks, and to the body heat radiating from the customers already there to those coming in out of the cold.

On the bare earth floor near the oil drum three long tables were laid out, each with a long bench on either side. It was spacious for a bar, and already a party were drinking at the middle table. After he and Teacher Suam were settled across from each other at the far table, he asked Teacher Suam what he would like for a meal. Teacher Suam suggested they first warm themselves up with some *yakchu*. He obliged, asking the boy grilling ribs over the charcoal to bring them half a kettle.

When the warmed *yakchu* arrived, he poured Teacher Suam a drink while asking if his son had been admitted to school, then said he would pour his own drink. But Teacher Suam insisted on taking the kettle and filling his glass for him, before replying that he had sent his son to night school, but he had no idea how he was going to pay the fees; the boy wanted to earn his own school fees and had found a job delivering newspapers, but that barely put a dent in the amount due; so saying, he heaved a sigh. Teacher Suam said no more, but that much was enough to tell him that apart from the problem of the school fees Teacher Suam needed scribal work or something similar if he and his family were to live another day. In the presence of Teacher Suam, this man with dimming eyes, whose hands were accustomed to holding a writing brush but had in the meantime performed all kinds of rough work, and who now wanted to work with the brush again, he upbraided himself yet again that he had let the teacher down. He had sat like a bump on a log instead of visiting the registry head's superior—and just because of a hunch that it wouldn't work. He ought to be ashamed of himself. He would see the superior face to face no matter what. And if that didn't work he would go back to the registry head and pester him to let Teacher Suam work as an assistant to the court scribe. The registry head wouldn't try to weasel out this time. With that in mind he asked Teacher Suam to come see him two days later. And then he changed his mind and said he felt sorry for Teacher Suam having to be out and about in this cold weather and asked where he was living, offering to go see him instead. Not to worry, Teacher Suam responded—he would pay the visit.

Meanwhile, the young bunch at the next table were feeling no pain and jabbering away loudly. Something or other about hunting.

The first two drinks had begun to warm him, and he was tearing some strips of dried pollack for snacking when the door opened and in walked a woman. A woman in Western clothing, wearing a red sweater and a lot of makeup. Not a woman from a respectable family. His first thought was that you don't see many women in a bar like this, especially a woman by herself, and he wondered if she had come to the wrong place. The young bunch at the next table must have had the same thought, because their conversation came to a stop and they turned their gazes to the woman.

The woman nonchalantly took a seat at the far end of the near table, her back to them, and began to rub some feeling into her frozen hands. The barmaid came out from behind the serving counter and asked, "The usual?" The woman responded with a faint nod. And that's when it occurred to him. Maybe she was one of the women who worked at the Ch'unhyang Pavilion, just outside the alley to the bar. On their way here, at the corner of the alley, they had noticed women of the same sort as this one, accompanied by men of a different skin color, coming and going from that building, a dance hall with a sign reading FOREIGNERS ONLY. Yes, that had to be it. She worked there and was a regular customer here. And she must have been starving, the way she slurped her bowl of beef-and-rice soup and the way her long, thin neck moved.

He too was hungry by the time they finished their half kettle of *yakchu*. After checking with Teacher Suam, he ordered each of them a bowl of cod soup.

Seemingly for the woman's benefit, one of the young men at the next table, speaking with a Hamgyŏng Province accent, steered the conversation about hunting in a more lurid direction. Tigers are fiercest in mating season, he began, and in lunar January, in the middle of the night when the moon is bright as day, you'll hear them roar like nothing you've ever heard before, and from miles away. Dogs want to slink away and hide, and they scratch and whimper at your door; even big horses shudder.

The cod soup arrived and he was about to take a spoonful when he noticed that the young man had both hands in the air, one of them still holding a grilled rib, and was shaking his imposing frame, apparently mimicking a scared horse. Which prompted one of the others to say, "That's not what a horse does, it's what *this* does," and he pointed to his crotch and his drink-reddened face broke into a leer.

He ate, and when he next looked up from his bowl the woman seemed to have finished her meal and was wiping her mouth with a handkerchief. Suddenly the leering man shot out of his seat, approached the woman, took a pack of Lucky Strikes from his overcoat, and offered her one. The woman momentarily considered the man, then silently accepted the cigarette. The man produced a lighter and lit it for her, winking at his buddies as if to say, "What do you think of that!" Then the young man noticed that he and Teacher Suam were watching, and with a sheepish expression he drew near and placed two cigarettes on the table in front of them.

When the young man had returned to his table, the man across from him produced an insinuating smile and said, "Women sure have it good these days. They get to do anything that strikes their fancy. Want to go for a ride in a car? No problem. They have fun with the big-noses and when they're done for the night they've got chocolate, gum, canned food, you name it. They got the world in the palm of their hand, yeah."

The woman rose. After paying she turned to leave, her expression as nonchalant as when she had arrived, showing no hint of anger or disgust toward the young men. The only noticeable difference was that the meal had brought color to her face in the short time she had been here. As soon as she went out the door the young men erupted in boisterous laughter. That woman was "really something." Teacher Suam paid them no mind and drank the rest of his broth. He finished his bowl as well.

It was the first time in a long while that he had indulged in a tasty meal. In this satisfied state he watched as another party rushed in out of the cold, and then he and Teacher Suam rose. He reached into his pocket intending to pay, but Teacher Suam was immediately at his side, grabbing his arm. "Absolutely not." And before he knew it, Teacher Suam had produced his wallet. The bills he took from it had been folded several times over, probably tucked away for emergency use. The use of such funds to pay for a meal made him wonder if the teacher was treating him because of the favor he had asked—in other words, out of a sense of reciprocity. If so, then he understood. Wasn't this very same idea of reciprocity involved in his hunch that even if he spoke with the registry head's superior about Teacher Suam things might not work out? And hadn't it occurred to him that things might not work out because Teacher Suam lacked adequate "reciprocity funds"? And his own inability all these years to advance beyond junior clerk—wasn't that because he had failed to take the proper reciprocal steps? But no, no, he couldn't allow his relationship with Teacher Suam to be like that. He shouldn't even consider it. *Teacher Suam produced that money thinking he had no better way to spend it than on me, and he's treating me as if I'm his own son or his nephew.* As if to reinforce this thought, he lit his Lucky Strike from the brazier and offered it to Teacher Suam, who had paid for the meal and was ready to leave. In turn Teacher Suam offered him his Lucky Strike. He politely declined several times, as was customary in the presence of an elder, but finally relented, accepting a light from the teacher.

The short winter day had come to a close, and as they walked out of the dark alley he felt the drinks and the hot meal of soup and rice—so rare in his recent experience—mitigate the cold, to the point that his ears registered the sound of music. *Yes, from there.* As he turned his attention to the Ch'unhyang Pavilion, something flew through the air and dropped with a *thunk* onto the frozen ground half a dozen paces in front of them—an empty tin can. Immediately from both sides of the street shadowy figures, three or four of them, rushed toward it. The next moment they had dispersed whence they came. There was another *thunk* as another tin can landed on the frozen ground. He realized that this one had been thrown from a second-floor window in the Ch'unhyang Pavilion. Again the dark figures rushed out, and again they dispersed. A closer look revealed that each of the figures was clutching a can and licking it.

A sound and an image surfaced in his mind—a long, drawn-out whistle, announcing the arrival of the passenger train from Seoul, and then the thin legs of boys running, each wanting to be the first to meet the train. Among those legs were his own. It was cherry blossom season, and the passengers had come to New Masan to view the flowers. It was a long passenger train, unlike the local trains, which had only a few passenger cars at the rear. The whistle was not the shrill screech of the local but a long, drawn-out *tweee* that was more pleasing to the ear. Every day during cherry blossom season the children from Old Masan eagerly awaited that *tweee*. Once it sounded, they scampered up to the tracks, knowing that the passengers on this train were going to drop something through the windows for them: numerous wooden lunchboxes, a gift, as it were, from the people of Seoul. The children fought over those lunchboxes, and each child who got one would scour the inside for any stray grains of rice.

Wooden lunchboxes and tin cans. Cherry blossom season and the dead of winter. Boys barely in their early teens and shadowy figures who looked to be adults.

In front of the Ch'unhyang Pavilion he and Teacher Suam went their separate ways, Teacher Suam saying he would visit in two days' time. The music seemed to lead him off into the distance. It was a poignant image, the more poignant for the gay music. *Tomorrow I'll take care of him for sure.*

When he could no longer make out Teacher Suam he turned away. He remembered his cigarette and drew on it. It was still burning. That was the good thing about Western cigarettes. The wind was sharp. With that realization everything faded into nothingness, including Teacher Suam's request. He raised the collar of his worn-out overcoat against the cold. His only thought was that he needed to get home.

And now he told himself that if he hadn't seen that woman the previous evening, his eyes wouldn't have been drawn to the CHRONIC STOWAWAY PROBLEM article in that piece of newspaper he'd used to roll his cigarette, and if he hadn't noticed the article he wouldn't have recalled the woman. He took one last drag on his cigarette and blew the smoke out. If the woman from last night was like the women in the article, what guarantee was there that she wouldn't try to go back to Japan as a stowaway? Or wouldn't be caught and subjected to a summary trial and sentenced?

He could hear the judge asking, *What is your name?* And the defendant answering, *I was born Kim So-and-so, before Liberation I went by the name Hanako, and since Liberation I've been called Anna. What is your age? Twenty-five. Your place of residence? I was born in Masan, before Liberation I lived in Japan, and since Liberation I've been in Seoul. Your occupation? Before Liberation a waitress, since Liberation a dancer. You returned after Liberation? That's correct. If the reason you returned home was that you missed your homeland, then why did you attempt to stow away?* No answer. *Are you aware that stowing away is a crime? Yes. If you knew it was a crime, then why did you do it?* Again, no answer—as if to say, "I think you can answer those questions yourself." *I've heard many reports of disasters involving stowaways; how can a frail woman in the dead of winter think of doing such a thing?* The defendant is silent, but her nonchalant expression indicates that she long ago dispensed with any thoughts of the past or future.

The mention of stowaway disasters reminded him of a book he had read in middle school containing a story about a slave ship. The slaves were blacks from Africa, some three hundred of them. Even now he recalled vividly that the slaves had not been treated humanely; they had been crammed into a hold where the headroom was less than thirty inches. Slaves kept suffocating, slaves kept falling ill. Those who appeared hopelessly ill were thrown overboard. There was no one to look after them. And there was no one to look after the women stowaways either.

The verdict: *Be grateful that there are laws to protect the defendant! It is my duty, though, to carry out the sentence according to the dictates of the law. I hereby fine you the amount of one thousand five hundred wŏn. I have no money. In that case I remand you to the workhouse, where you shall serve a sentence of thirty days.*

He crushed out his cigarette, which had burned down to his fingertips, and muttered mechanically, "It's never going to end."

The next moment he shivered and everything faded away—the woman, her sentencing, the newspaper article—everything except the worry foremost in his mind: how would he and his family get through the rest of the winter?

January 1947

MY FATHER

I've heard various stories about the March 1 Independence Movement; some of them more than once, from my father. But when I finally considered jotting something down about them, I thought I should refresh my memory, and with that in mind I decided to pay him a visit. On my way to the Samch'ŏng-dong home I tried to recall this story and that one, stories I had heard him tell. . . .

The first story that came to mind took place when my father was twenty-seven. One early-winter day he and An Sehwan went to what was then known as Pyongyang Catholic Hospital to visit Namgang Yi Sŭnghun. Teacher Namgang was not ill but had had himself admitted on the basis of a nonexistent malady so he would have a place to meet privately with his comrades. Teacher Namgang had asked An to find a few young men who would commit themselves to the independence movement, and Father was one of them. At the time he was teaching the upper grades of Sungdŏk School. The task given him by Teacher Namgang for March 1 was to distribute the Korean flag and copies of the Declaration of Independence to the throngs of people who would come to Pyongyang for the March 3 funeral for King Kojong. He then was to lead these people in cheers of "*Mansei!*" (It had been decided that in Pyongyang the funeral ceremony would take place on the athletic field at Sungdŏk School.)

The first thing Father did was select activist students from the upper grades and station them at various places downtown to distribute the declaration and the flag. He told them not to hesitate, if detained by the police, to say that they were acting on the instructions of a teacher named Hwang, and he added that the tolling of the bell at Changdatchae Chapel would be their signal to begin. This plan proved successful. At Sungdŏk School, meanwhile, other selected students each took responsibility for a row of people, and the distribution was so well coordinated it took place virtually in the blink of an eye. Then the Declaration of Independence was read aloud, after which everyone began shouting "*Mansei!*" at the top of his lungs. Plainclothes police were present but didn't dare lift a hand. The assembly then split up into several groups who went downtown by various routes. By then downtown had erupted in a sea of "*Mansei!*" cheers. But the following day Father found himself in jail. When I first heard this story about Father I was in middle school, and I was quite moved—probably more so at that age—by the scene I imagined of the students on March 1 hearing the tolling of the bell and bravely running down this street and that, each holding close to his chest the Korean flag and a copy of the Declaration of Independence.

These two men, Teacher Namgang and An Sehwan, I had seen in person. Teacher Namgang passed away when I was in middle school, year four I think it was. His will made it known that he wanted his cremated remains to rest in the specimen room of the school he had established, Osan Middle School—but even a request such as this was met with rejection from the Japanese administration, and that made our young student hearts boil over in anger. I saw Teacher Namgang during the one term I studied at Osan Middle School as a first-year student. At that time, even though he had been succeeded as principal, he came to school without fail every other day. Small of stature, with white hair and beard, he always wore traditional attire. He also had sideburns, about an inch long. You might almost say he was pretty. Quite a few times I wondered that a man's appearance could become so graceful as he aged.

And Teacher Namgang had a way of making what he said genuinely interesting. Now and then he would use assembly period to say that he intended to establish a two-year college at Osan, a place for young men and women, and what a thrill that gave us.

But when this gentle teacher got angry, it was unbelievable. Once, during a school intergrade sports competition, the teacher in charge of scoring mistakenly placed the fifth graders higher than the fourth graders in the final standings. The students at this school were already notorious for boycotting classes, and everybody was talking about how this incident would lead to a boycott as well. It was a situation in which none of the teachers dared open his mouth. And then Teacher Namgang appeared. He gathered the students and launched right into them: "You rascals, if you intend to boycott, it has to be for an important reason—a boycott over a scoring mistake is just plain stupid!" This wasn't so much a scolding by a teacher to his students as it was grandfatherly or fatherly advice. The students could no more have oppose their teacher than they could have their father or grandfather—and this was not the first such instance.

As for An Sehwan, I can remember the rare occasions he visited our home when I was in my first two years of middle school. I'm pretty sure he had visited us before. But by the time I had started middle school he was not always in his right mind—the outcome of the various tortures he'd suffered in jail. Summer and winter alike, he went around in the same auburn-colored coat. That coat is clearer in my memory than his face—though it's equally clear to me that in spite of the damage to his psyche, his face was neither wicked-looking nor frightening. The coat was worn out, as you might expect. When he arrived at our home he simply came inside rather than asking first if the master was in. He liked pickled garlic, and whenever he appeared, my mother always served him this dish. He was a man of few words. As soon as Father saw him he would inquire after his family, and would receive in reply a simple "They're getting along." I don't believe I ever saw him initiate a conversation. His home was in Sun'an. When his mind was reasonably clear he would go home, but when he was not himself he would leave, and at those times it was always our house to which he came. He would enter and seat himself without a word, accept the meal tray that Mother prepared for him, and then disappear as silently as he had arrived. I can't recall when it was that he passed on. I would have to ask Father in more detail about this gentleman.

But as you might suspect, the stories that really interested me during my boyhood were the ones about my father's imprisonment. I was forever hearing bits and pieces of these stories. And whenever I heard them, something invariably came to mind—the straw hat, or rather the half of it that remained, that occupied a shelf in our dark, cramped storage room until I was in third or fourth grade.

That hat was woven during the year and a half Father spent in Sŏdaemun Prison in Seoul. The stories also involved Pak In-gwan, a minister who, like Father, was imprisoned after the March 1 movement (and who I believe might still be living in a locality called Kiyang). One story was that Father's job in prison was to weave those hats, and upon his release he was given five *wŏn* that he had earned in this way. Of that amount, he gave two *wŏn* to a fellow prisoner released the same day, for travel expenses, and by the time he arrived in Pyongyang only seventy *chŏn* was left. Another story concerned the prisoners who glued cigarette packets together. They used the glue sparingly and then ate what was left over. And then there was the story about how pairs of men shared the same bedding, which scarcely covered both, and when in winter they were awakened by the cold, each man would try to cover the other before himself. And the story of how Father and Pastor Pak had such a bad case of scabies that no amount of itching would help, and when they squeezed out the discharge from the bumps, they would help each other with the hard-to-reach places, and the cell was so cold that the squeezed-out discharge practically froze.

Sharing the cell with Father and Pastor Pak were two other ideological prisoners, both young men. One had been apprehended in a village in the southern provinces for reasons related to the March 1 uprising, and the other, also working in the independence movement, was based in Manchuria and had been captured there. The southerner was the youngest of the four, from a farming village, and the calluses on his palms were hard as nails. He must have had the toughest skin, because he alone didn't develop scabies and he held up best under the beatings by the guards. The young man from Manchuria frequently sang a song about An Chunggǔn, the martyr executed at Yǒsun Prison, and he taught it to the other three. Although they initially sang the song to themselves, it wasn't long before they warmed up to it and sang it in a loud chorus, after which they were summoned one by one by the guards and each given a terrific beating. My father still remembers that song:

Bright moon shining on lone mountain,
Cuckoo crying in the deep of night
Till throat bleeds dry and moonlight wanes.
Tell me, cuckoo, are you the soul

Of he who is ever mindful
Of his native land?

When I arrived, Father put aside the newspaper he was reading, asked me how the grandchildren were doing, then removed his reading glasses. Mother was ill, lying on the warmer part of the heated floor, a moistened towel wrapped around her forehead. She looked up as I entered. "You aren't feeling well?" I asked her. She said she was fine and expressed her concern about my family and me, asking if the children were well and how they were getting along.

Father said in an undertone that Mother was having her dizzy spells again; it had been several days now. Practically every year when winter set in she was susceptible to the cold drafts. There was no mystery about this recurring ailment, for she was almost sixty and in recent days had been up in the hills behind Samch'ŏng-dong gathering the leaves and branches used to heat the room. But never did she complain that her hardships had come about because I had brought her to Seoul to live.

What a fine son I had turned out to be, so enamored of Seoul that I had uprooted my parents from the ancestral home and dragged them here, and now look at me! For their part, Father and Mother made sure that this fine child of theirs understood that when times were difficult it was even more important to do the right thing.

And here this fine child was proposing to turn out some fine writing. So I began to question Father: "Can you tell me why Teacher An was tortured more than Teacher Namgang, until it broke him brutally?"

Father readily responded: "Mainly it had to do with him representing a group of people and making a statement of their views to the Japanese government."

"Did the mental problems start after he got out of prison? Or while he was there?"

"While he was there. And that's what got him paroled."

Father had once told me that the March 1 movement had to do with President Wilson's Doctrine of Self-Determination of Nations, but the larger issue was Koreans' increasing resentment under

Japanese military rule, and in this light it seems obvious that Teacher An's breakdown resulted from his torture as an ideological criminal by the police, who were instrumental in that rule. Because Father had been forced to witness Teacher An's torture, I thought I would try to get a more detailed account from him, but before I could ask, Father spoke up.

"You know, a couple of days ago," he began in his P'yŏngan-accented speech, putting his glasses back on and staring off into space, "I went downtown, and on my way home, in Anguk-dong, I saw someone coming my way. I've never been one to examine everybody I see when I'm out and about, but this person was examining *me*. He passed by, and then someone called out to me, and I turned to see a country fellow in a fur cap pulled low over his face, wearing a coat that had seen better days. I wondered who he might be, and he asked me if my family name was Hwang and said he was Kim So-and-so, and perhaps I remembered him? I couldn't place him, and I told him so. Well, what do you know? He said he was Kim So-and-so who was in Sŏdaemun Prison with me in 1919 because of the independence movement, and didn't I recognize him? And that's when it hit me—he was the young fellow from down south, the one who was the youngest of us four. I took his hand, and when I saw all the calluses I knew it was him, sure enough. And after a close-up look at the dark face with all the lines beneath the fur cap, I could see, clear as day, the way he looked back then. . . . There was a place to eat right close by, so we went inside and caught up on everything. He got around to telling me that the reason he was in Seoul was the UN trusteeship matter. Said that where he was in the country it was hard to get a good grip on the issue—he didn't know whether he should be for it or against it. So first he would get it clear in his mind, and then he'd go and educate the folks back home. One thing was for sure, he said—Jap-style military rule should never again be allowed on our land. Lately he kept coming back to thoughts about the March 1 movement, and it got to the point where he felt he had to come to Seoul. And once he was here, it was only natural that memories of our prison experience had come to mind along with all the rest. So when he saw me on the street he knew right away who I was. . . . He's got plenty of white around the ears. But there's such a nice glow to that wrinkled, sun-darkened face of his, and then the way he talks and thinks, it makes him look so young, and him looking young made me feel younger myself."

The way my father told this story made me forget for the moment what I was going to ask him. As I observed him, hair half white and half dark, I felt as if he too was the kind of man who aged gracefully.

February 1947

THE DOG OF CROSSOVER VILLAGE

Strike out in any direction, and you had a narrow pass to cross over. Except for the long, winding valley to the south, mountains were all around, and whatever your destination, a mountain pass awaited you. And so the settlement had come to be called Crossover Village.

There was a time, from early one spring to late in the fall, when quite a few people bound for the Jiantao region of Manchuria passed through Crossover Village. Those arriving by the pass from the south inevitably stopped to rest their tired legs at the well in front of the shacks beneath the mountains to the west.

These were not what you would call small families. There was the occasional young couple—man and wife, most likely—but it was mostly large families who filed through the narrow pass from the south. The younger people toted cloth bundles from which tattered clothing poked out, while the old folks limped along trying to keep the youngsters in hand. The women carried babies on their backs and loads on their heads.

Reaching the well, the travelers would first stop in the shade of the weeping willow and wet their throats. All would take turns drinking, again they would drink, and then water would be given to the children, restive by now, and to the young ones not yet weaned. The mothers seemed to prefer feeding their babes water to giving suck with breasts that no longer produced much milk.

Next they would splash the cold water over their chafed and blistered feet, again taking several turns. When the adults had finished, the children drew water by themselves, all they wished, and splashed it over their feet. And when it was time to leave, these travelers would shuffle along as before, disappearing over the pass to the north.

Some groups arrived near dusk. They too stopped beneath the mountains to the west, passing the night at the decrepit mill there. Once settled, the women would untie the gourd each carried from her waist and go begging for a meal. Their destination: the two houses with the tile roofs at the foot of the mountain directly to the east. Usually the children would tag along, and if a grain of cooked rice were to fall from the gourds, it would be gobbled up at once. The women would remind the children that the grown-ups also needed to fill their stomachs. Still, by the time they returned from the houses with the tile roofs, some of the gourds would be nearly empty. The next day, these wanderers would set out in the gloom sometime before daybreak and stream north, ever north, and out of sight.

One spring, a dog appeared in Crossover Village at the mill beneath the western mountains, next to where Kannan's family lived. There it began licking the underside of the winnow, which was thick and gray with dust—the mill had lain idle for what seemed the longest time. The dog, which looked ravenous, was a bitch of medium size. Her coat must have once been a lovely white, but was now a dirty ocher yellow. Her belly, pinched in toward the hindquarters, pumped in and out with every breath. From her appearance you would think she had walked a long distance to get there. And a close look would show where a leash of some sort had been tied around her neck.

Which suggested she had come from far away. For when people bound for Jiantao passed through, you would see now and then a dog led by a rope around its neck. The owners of this white dog might very well have been such wayfarers. Among their modest household items they undoubtedly had sold those they couldn't take a long distance, in order to raise more cash for the journey. But in leaving home with their meager possessions they had probably allowed this dog to tag along like any member of the family—perhaps one of the children had badgered them. And on their way here to P'yŏngan from Chŏlla, Kyŏngsang, or some other region, when they had run out of conveniently transported foods such as chaffy rice cake, they would beg food or go without, until finally they had nothing to feed the dog. Perhaps the best they could think of then was to leave the animal tied up beside the road, hoping someone would take her home. And so it may have been that this white dog, howling for her master, had managed to struggle free and had drifted into Crossover Village searching for him.

Then again, wayfarers bound for the P'yŏngan region might have sold the dog before arriving at Crossover Village, realizing they couldn't take her all the way to their destination. Or perhaps in thanks for a meal they had given her to a family. In any case, the dog may have been unable to forget her master and may have set off after him, making her way to the village.

Finally, if you looked carefully you might have noticed that the ocher color of her coat was somehow different from the ocher of the P'yŏngan soil.

Now, finding nothing but dust beneath the winnow, the dog moved to the millstone and nuzzled it all over, the limp in one of her hind legs suggesting just how far she had walked to get to Crossover Village. She lapped and lapped, but the millstone too wore only a layer of gray dust. Still, she licked for some time before giving up. Then she began nosing around the rest of this mill, where her master, bound for P'yŏngan, might have spent a night of troubled dreams, worrying about the wretched lot of his family and about the dog they had abandoned beside the road.

This white dog left the mill and slipped through the gate of millet stalks in front of Kannan's house next door. The family's yellow dog, lying prone in the yard at the foot of the veranda, looked up and rose to confront this stranger. Fearing a bite, the white dog tucked her tail between her legs and against her shrunken belly and limped away. She passed a cluster of humble shacks, and beyond them a vegetable patch, hobbling along even after realizing that Yellow had given up the chase. After the patch were some hardscrabble plots, and beyond them a ditch that showed only gravel in times of drought but now held an occasional pool of water. Whitey lapped up some of the water.

Directly opposite the ditch was a rise. Tucked against the top and set a short distance apart were the tile-roof houses of the two brothers who were headmen of Crossover Village. Between the houses sat a mill used solely by the two families.

Into this mill limped Whitey. Here, at least, chaff was mixed with the dust. Around the winnow she went, licking industriously. Her shriveled belly pumped faster.

After a time, the elder headman's large black dog caught sight of Whitey from a distance and dashed over. It stopped at the door to the mill and growled, teeth bared, glossy fur bristling. Whitey, yelping as if a chunk had been taken from her hide, tucked her tail between her legs but kept licking. Blackie, perhaps deciding Whitey was no match for him, stole up and began sniffing her all over. Aha, a bitch! Blackie let down his guard and began wagging his tail. In the presence of the other dog Whitey quivered in fear. But she never stopped licking.

After licking beneath the winnow and the grindstone, Whitey visited each house's privy, then returned beneath the winnow and settled down on her stomach. She began blinking drowsily. The blinking became more frequent, and finally the eyes closed altogether. Blackie, sitting a short distance away, kept watch.

That evening a woman's voice could be heard calling the dog from the elder headman's house. Blackie ran for home. Whitey returned to where she'd been earlier and resumed licking. But then, as if on a hunch, she set out for the headman's house.

Sure enough, from outside the gate she could see the open door to the kitchen, and just beyond it a basin where Blackie was slurping up his dinner. Instinctively Whitey stuck her tail between her legs and approached, trembling. But before she could get near the basin, Blackie bared his teeth and growled, fur bristling. Whitey stopped, stared at the basin, and hunched down to wait.

Before long Blackie was licking his snout with various contortions of his long, drooping tongue. Then he withdrew. Whitey rose immediately. Still quivering, she went to the basin and stuck her snout right in. Fortunately, some rice was left at the bottom, as well as a few grains stuck to the sides. She attacked the basin, quivering more and more violently. She licked and licked, and when nothing was left she slunk past Blackie, who had kept to himself, and out the gate.

A dog with black and white spots—the younger headman's dog—blocked the path to the mill. Again Whitey cringed instinctively. The spotted dog sniffed Whitey all over. This time it was Whitey who perked up; she smelled something. The other dog's snout was still moist from his dinner, and Whitey began licking it.

Annoyed, Spotty struck out for home. But Whitey was right behind. Spotty went through the gate and sat down in the middle of the yard. Whitey went directly to the basin outside the kitchen door.

This basin also held rice, some on the bottom and quite a few grains on the sides. Whitey busied herself licking, and when the basin was clean she returned to the mill and her place beneath the winnow.

It began to rain in the middle of the night, and the next day was gray and sodden. From daybreak Whitey was in and out through the dog holes beneath the walls of the headmen's houses. She walked better than the day before, but still with a limp. Her first few visits she found only rainwater in the basins. When food finally appeared, she had to wait until the master's dog had eaten its fill and withdrawn. And so she licked up what the two dogs had left, and after a stop at the outhouses she returned to the mill and lay down beneath the winnow. Around noontime she crawled outside, licked up some rainwater, and went back to her resting place.

That evening the rain finally stopped. Whitey had already made the rounds of the two houses with the tile roofs, finding food in the basins. Spotty seemed to have lost his appetite; he had left a fair amount of food.

The next day was clear and fair, springlike. Again Whitey found food by making the rounds of the two houses, starting at dawn. Her limp was almost gone. She returned to the mill, found a sunny spot, and lay down to bask in the warmth.

Late that morning Whitey heard someone approach, a farmhand who worked for the two headmen coming to hull rice. He thumped down a bundle of rice stalks and went back the way he had come. As he was leaving, Kannan's grandmother arrived with a hand winnow. With her was Kannan's mother, who carried on her head a mat to collect the hulled rice. Although Kannan's grandfather no longer did farm work for the headmen, his wife and daughter continued to set aside their own duties when necessary to attend to the various chores they had always handled for the brothers.

While Kannan's mother was sweeping the grindstone, the farmhand returned with an ox and another bundle of rice stalks. The farmhand untied the bundle, and the first thing Whitey noticed was a savory smell—more food. She drew near. But the farmhand wasn't having any of this and kicked her in the ribs.

"Mangy bitch—can't you see we're busy?"

It wasn't a very strong kick, but the farmhand's leg was firm and stout, and Whitey tumbled to the side with a yelp. Back she went to her resting place nearby to soak up the sun.

When the hulling of the first batch of stalks was almost finished, the younger headman appeared. He was a stumpy fellow, solidly built, hair closely cropped. His color was good, and though he was approaching forty, he certainly didn't look his age.

"Better be dry enough to hull," he said in a firm voice—to no one in particular, it seemed, because he didn't wait for an answer. "Just make sure you don't crush it."

Kannan's grandmother, guiding the ox from the rear as it turned the grindstone, picked up a handful of hulled rice and examined it closely, seemed to find it properly hulled, then returned it without comment to the mat.

As the headman turned to leave, he noticed Whitey.

"Whose dog is this?"

Before the others could turn and look, he had kicked Whitey square in the ribs. Whitey scurried outside, yelping. At a little distance she turned around, as if reluctant to leave the mill. The farmhand and the two women were once again absorbed in their work—ownership of the dog was none of their affair. But the headman was staring in her direction, and when he bent over as if to pick up a rock, Whitey fled with all her remaining strength. She started down the gentle hill, and sure enough a rock flew by, landing at her side.

She crossed the ditch, where water had pooled from the previous day's rain, and kept running through the hardscrabble plots worked by Kim Sŏndal and others. At least she wasn't limping anymore, and under the circumstances this was fortunate.

At the mill next to Kannan's family's house at the foot of the mountains to the west, she lay down beneath the winnow, which still wore a coat of dust but nothing else. Some time later she set out again for the headmen's mill. Reaching the gentle rise, she stopped and gazed toward the mill. The younger brother was nowhere to be seen, so she continued on. But the sight of the vicious-looking farmhand turning the winnow brought her to a halt, and after inspecting the scene she retraced her steps to the mill next to Kannan's family's house.

As the day began to wane, Kannan's mother and grandmother came into view along the millet-stalk fence of the house across the way. Before entering their own house, they looked into the mill. Whitey rose apprehensively, but the women paid no attention to her and disappeared inside their house.

In no time Whitey was back at the headmen's mill. It had been swept, but there remained a generous layer of rice husks on the posts and other timbers. Whitey started beneath the winnow and licked everything clean.

Early that evening, as Whitey stood inside the gate to the elder headman's house gazing at the basin while Blackie finished his meal, a door slid open and the headman emerged. Like his brother, he was a stumpy man with closely cropped hair, his complexion was good, and he looked much younger than his age. At a glance you might have wondered if the brothers were twins. And in fact people meeting them for the first time often confused them.

Stepping down to the yard, he discovered Whitey intent on the basin and realized he'd never seen this dog before.

"Damn mutt!" he shouted, stamping his feet. His tone was firm like his brother's.

Startled, Whitey wriggled through the dog hole and fled.

Just as the headman emerged from his gate in pursuit, his brother appeared, making an after-dinner visit. Spotting Whitey, he realized she was the dog he had chased from the mill that morning. She was now being driven off by his brother, and it occurred to him that this damned mutt no one had ever seen before might be mad.

"Mad dog! Grab it!" he shouted in the same firm tone.

The older brother followed suit, also struck by the thought that this unfamiliar mutt with the pinched belly, this damned mongrel running off with its tail between its legs, might indeed be mad: "Mad dog! Catch the damn thing!"

He flew inside his gate, emerged with a good-sized stick, and set off after Whitey, shouting over and over, "Mad dog! Grab it!"

By the time the brothers reached the bottom of the gentle slope, Whitey was cutting through the hardscrabble plots. Kim Sŏndal, still working his plot, heard the brothers shouting. He looked around and spotted the dog.

"That damn mutt must be the mad dog."

He ran after Whitey, shovel in hand.

The headmen stopped at the plots, their energy flagging. "Mad dog! Catch it!" they kept shouting in turn.

It was as if through their shouts they were ordering Kim Sŏndal to step up his efforts to catch the mad dog and beat it with his shovel, as if by the sound of their voices they were calling on the people living at the foot of the western mountains to arm themselves, burst forth from their homes, and slaughter the mad dog. They continued shouting until Whitey had disappeared among the shacks beneath those mountains, until they could no longer see Kim running in his distinctive way, trunk bent back instead of forward.

After the brothers had stopped bellowing, an eerie silence descended upon the evening. And then from the foot of the mountains to the west rose a commotion that carried so clearly you might have felt you could reach out and grab it. A short time later a thin mist began to rise, and out of it Kim returned, at the head of several villagers. No mad dog had been caught. Kim passed the vegetable patch, but before he had reached the hardscrabble plots the younger brother called out.

"What happened?!"

It was such a loud shout, spreading throughout the village in the still of the evening, that he thought maybe he'd overdone it.

Frustrated by the lack of a response, his brother took up the cry.

"Well, what happened!?" he shouted just as loudly.

"We lost it. Damn mutt ran like the devil. It's up in the hills somewhere."

Kim's voice seemed to come not only from the depths of his body but also from far in the distance. How was such magic possible? Ah, through the silence of early evening in this mountain valley.

"You mean it ran so fast it got away from you?" sneered the older brother. "I'll bet you gave up. You were scared—scared of a worthless mutt. . . ."

Kim could joke with the best, but this time he strode off silently into the mist and retrieved his hoe and shovel from the plot he'd been working. It was as if he were admitting to what the headman had said.

It was still a bit early in the year for people to be gathering outside in their yards, but nightfall found a few of the neighbors squatting in the corner of Ch'ason's family's yard. They discussed farming: Was there enough to eat until the first barley crop was harvested? And then someone brought up the mad dog.

Kim Sŏndal spoke up at once. Just the night before last, he'd gone to South Village to borrow an ox—hadn't come back through the pass till late. Just then he'd heard a dog howl somewhere off in the distance. Weird, it was—scared the hell out of him. Sounded like the dog was sick, or like someone was dragging it at the end of a rope. But if someone was dragging a dog along, you wouldn't expect the howling to come from the same spot each time—that was the weird thing. Now that he thought about it, it was probably the mad dog.

All Kim had to do was open his trap and out came a fanciful story that was sure to bring laughter. So he had long been known, not only in the village but also in the surrounding area, as a latter-day Pongi Kim Sŏndal, after the famous jokester of old. For this reason the listeners couldn't be sure how much of his story was fancy and how much was true.

In between puffs on his pipe, Ch'ason's father sent a stream of saliva flying. The part about the dog being dragged by the neck while the sound seemed to come from the same place was calling something to mind. Maybe, he offered, the dog belonged to one of the P'yŏngan-bound travelers who had passed through the village a few days earlier. Perhaps it had been tied to a tree and left behind and had gone mad. That would explain why it was in the village now. Animals, you had to remember, go mad after several days without food. In fact, Ch'ason's father continued, he was quite certain that the dog Kim Sŏndal had heard was such a dog—howling while trying to break free of the rope about its neck.

Kannan's grandfather, while admitting to himself that this was plausible, recalled something his wife had told him a short time before—that the dog she'd seen that morning at the village heads' mill, and again on her way home at the mill in their own neighborhood, didn't look rabid. In any case, he now declared, you couldn't tell if a dog was mad unless you looked at it up close. But mad or not, the dog would soon be back—that much was clear. Ch'ason's father agreed, adding that everyone had better be careful.

Whitey, under cover of darkness, had already come down from the hills and trotted through the hardscrabble plots toward the headmen's houses. You would have seen her moving cautiously, in spite of the darkness.

At the top of the gentle slope, she paused to inspect first the mill and then the two houses with the tile roofs. And then, with the greatest of care, she approached the older brother's house.

Through the dog hole she went. Blackie acknowledged her without growling, as if she were now familiar to him. Whitey went straight to the food basin and began to lap.

In the younger brother's yard, Spotty accepted Whitey in similar fashion. There too Whitey went straight to the basin and lapped up what was left.

Then she was off to the brothers' mill, where she licked the places she had covered that afternoon, and the rest of the mill as well. But she evidently had no intention of sleeping there, and set off toward the foot of the mountains to the west.

The next morning Kannan's grandfather, who was known for rising early, emerged from the millet-stalk gate of his house and discovered Whitey prone beneath the winnow in the mill nearby. He returned home, fetched the supporting stick for his A-frame backrack, and reappeared at the mill, hiding the weapon behind his back. It might be mad, but a blow with the stick would kill it.

Whitey rose, startled by the sound of someone approaching. Instinctively, she tucked her tail between her legs.

Not a good sign, the old man thought. He stood motionless, glaring at Whitey, tightening his grip on the stick. *Still,* he told himself, *I don't see it drooling or foaming at the mouth. If it's rabid, it can't be that serious.* He looked at her eyes. *If it's rabid, those eyes ought to be bloodshot, or have a bluish tinge—but not this dog.* All the old man saw in those eyes were crust and fear.

Whitey looked right back, wondering if this man meant to hurt her. Kannan's grandfather looked dangerous because of his tall, robust build and the salty beard covering his swarthy face. His glaring eyes were also crusted, with crow's-feet. As she looked at those eyes, Whitey sensed this wasn't someone who intended to harm her, and her tail between her legs lifted ever so slightly.

It wasn't rabid after all, the old man decided. At least not yet. He relaxed his grip on the stick, and it came into view. Startled, Whitey slinked past him and fled.

Yellow, outside in his master's yard, chased Whitey. A thought flashed across the old man's mind: What if the dog *was* rabid and bit Yellow? He called his dog. But by then Yellow had caught up to Whitey and was blocking her path. Whitey seemed ready to tuck her tail even tighter between her legs, but then Yellow, recognizing her scent, touched his nose to hers. Whitey nuzzled right back and her tail began to lift. No, Kannan's grandfather told himself again, the dog wasn't rabid.

That day Whitey went up the gentle slope to the mountain behind the headmen's houses, almost like waiting for the two brothers to leave, you might think.

After breakfast the headmen walked to a ravine below the village where they were having a dry field regraded. The steep upper portion of the field, owned by the older brother and worked by Ch'ason's family, was being leveled; the deep lower portion, owned by the younger brother and worked by Kannan's family, was being filled in. The two portions were to be combined into a rice paddy that could be properly irrigated. Since the spring thaw, virtually every member of the two families had been turning out for this reclamation project.

Some time after the brothers had left to oversee the work, Whitey cautiously ventured down to feed at the basins. Then she went to the mill for the new layer of dust and chaff. Finally she visited the brothers' outhouses, before retracing her path uphill and settling beneath a tree. There she lay prone while the day wore on into evening, and when night had fallen she went back down to the houses with the tile roofs and on to the mill beneath the mountains to the west. She didn't forget, either, to lap up some of the water in the ditch near the vegetable patch.

Every morning when Kannan's grandfather emerged from the gate of millet stalks in front of his house, he would see Whitey leave the mill and walk along the path through the hardscrabble plots. It was as if she had decided to be the earliest to rise.

One night Whitey was licking the food basin at the older headman's house. The man came outside and tiptoed to the granary, where he got a stick. He stole up behind the dog. Whitey was not unaware of his movements, but her hunger kept her at the basin. Finally, with the man close behind her, she whirled about and scampered toward the front gate. At that instant the man saw a strange blue gleam that seemed to be coming from her eyes. It struck him that the dog really was mad, but for some reason he couldn't shout this news.

Whitey stole through the dog hole beside the gate, and finally the headman shouted, "Mad dog! Catch the damn thing!" and gave chase. He realized that the dog was skipping off in the darkness toward the mountain behind his house. On he ran, shouting, "Mad dog! Catch the damn thing!" But he wouldn't get within striking distance. Instead, he grew more and more afraid of a close encounter with Whitey, and his shouts became louder and more fierce. Whitey disappeared up the mountainside. After several more shouts, the headman turned toward home. As his brother and their families ran toward him, he remembered how he had chided Kim Sŏndal for being afraid to get near a "harmless" mad dog. If only he had broken the damned dog's back in his yard once and for all, he scolded himself; he could have caught the dog if he'd tried, but he'd been afraid to get close. His temper flared. "What took you so long!" he barked at the people thronging toward him.

The next morning, before leaving to supervise the reclamation project, the older headman paid a visit to those who lived at the foot of the mountains to the west. There he told everyone he met that the dog was surely mad. He had seen a blue gleam in its eyes the previous evening. The dog had attacked him and he'd barely managed to beat it off with a stick. Anyone who caught sight of it ought to kill it on the spot; otherwise the villagers would have hell to pay. The headman's shouts had carried clearly the previous evening, and the villagers knew the mad dog had reappeared. If the dog had actually attacked someone, blue gleam and all, then it must be crazy for sure. Ill at ease, they made up their minds—they'd take care of that dog, you bet.

For her part, Whitey seemed even more cautious. She remained out of sight of the villagers beneath the western mountains, not to mention the two headmen and their families.

One night Kannan's grandmother, using the outhouse, rushed back inside saying she'd just seen the mad dog with the blue gleam in its eyes. When Whitey had been called mad and driven from the village, the dog had not seemed mad to her. But now that she'd seen that blue gleam, there was no doubt in her mind—the dog was mad.

Kannan's grandfather, though, argued that dogs were no different from people: you could see a gleam in their eyes if they went hungry or got their dander up. Why should this dog be any different? No need to be so frightened just because it was on the loose. But suddenly the old man realized something: the dog had come to the outhouse to feed on his valuable supply of nightsoil. That was the last straw. He headed for the outhouse, hefting the supporting stick for his backrack. Sure enough, near the pit for the feces he saw a blue flash. "Damn mutt!" he shouted, giving one of the outhouse posts a crack with his stick. The blue gleam whirled away, and the dog, a white blur, escaped through the millet-stalk fence.

From then on, no glimpse was to be had of Whitey. Summer arrived, and with it the rains—just in time for transplanting rice seedlings into the paddy newly graded by the two headmen and their tenants. Then one day a rumor spread through the village: as Kim Sŏndal was having a smoke while weeding his plot, he saw a fleeting movement among the trees on the mountainside behind the houses with the tile roofs. Looking carefully, he had seen it was the mad dog. But it wasn't alone, it had other dogs in tow—Blackie, the older headman's dog; Spotty, the younger brother's dog; and with them still another dog he hadn't seen clearly enough to identify.

It was just as Kim Sŏndal had said. Blackie and Spotty hadn't been seen at home for a good two days. The village heads were indignant—that damned mad dog had infected their dogs right from the start and now it had lured them away. And they were fearful as well. And—the villagers didn't know this, because Kannan's grandfather had told his family to say nothing—Kannan's family's dog had also been gone the past two days.

During those two days, a number of villagers reported hearing dogs growling, both in the daytime and at night, from the mountain-side behind the tile-roof houses. The headmen again were indignant, realizing they should have hunted down that damned mad dog and killed it.

On the third day, the brothers' dogs finally returned, one after the other. Kannan's family's dog also returned. Blackie and Spotty immediately found some shade and lay down on their stomachs. They panted, drooling tongues hanging low, then closed their eyes and fell fast asleep. They looked wasted from their two days outside.

The brothers were watching over the transplanting in the re-claimed paddy when the farmhand arrived with the news.

"Good enough," said the brothers. "About time we got rid of them."

They set out for home, the farmhand and Kannan's grandfather in front.

Kannan's grandfather approached Blackie bare-handed. *That old fellow's in for some trouble*, thought the older headman and the other onlookers, keeping their distance. The old man stroked the dog's head. The animal opened its sleepy eyes, then closed them and began wagging its tail in delight, sweeping it back and forth across the ground like a broom.

"And this dog is supposed to be mad?" Kannan's grandfather said, returning to the village head's side.

"Well, it's a good thing if it's not," said the headman. "But when you see it drooling, when it can't keep its eyes open, you know it's only a matter of time—we'd better get rid of it before it's completely rabid."

"Mad dogs aren't supposed to have an appetite," said the farm-hand. Why not try to feed Blackie? In the kitchen he prepared a mixture of steamed rice and water in the feed basin. When he brought the food out Blackie put his snout near, but after a token sniff he closed his eyes.

"There—what did I tell you?" said the village head.

There was a reason Blackie was acting that way, said Kannan's grandfather: he'd been doing stud work the last few days.

Up jumped the headman. "With that mad dog!? That's even worse. Get the rope," he ordered the farmhand. "The Dog Days aren't far off," he muttered. "We'll get rid of the dog and have ourselves a Dog Day party to boot."

Kannan's grandfather had to give in. The farmhand tied a noose and passed it to the headman, who secured it around Blackie's neck. The farmhand took the other end and jerked the dog toward the gate, drew the rope under the threshold, and pulled it tight from the other side. Caught unawares, the dog yelped frantically, but it was no use.

Hearing the yelps, Spotty came out to look, and all the dogs from the neighborhood at the foot of the mountains to the west emerged onto the road and started barking. Blackie's eyes blazed blue. He clawed at the ground and finally at the threshold of the gate. This was what the headman had seen every time a dog was slaughtered, but this time the fire in Blackie's eyes was unusually blue. However you looked at it, he repeated to himself, the dog was mad. Excrement spurted from the dog's bowels, and then the animal gave one last great twitch and went limp.

Now to the younger brother's house. As if sensing his fate, Spotty began a slow retreat into the yard, making it a chore to snare him. The farmhand had to act more swiftly to tighten the noose around his neck. And so Spotty met a similar fate.

The older brother's wife brought out a large kettle and propped it off the ground beneath the chestnut tree in back of their house for boiling water to remove the dogs' fur. Meanwhile, the brothers conferred, then sent the farmhand off to Dolmen Village, near the pass to the north, to invite the village head and Pak Ch'oshi.

As the butchered dogs were cooking in a soy-paste stew, the three men returned. The Dolmen Village headman had slicked-down hair parted to the right. Pak Ch'oshi was a pudgy man who wore the traditional horsehair cap and an unlined ramie jacket that resembled a pair of dragonfly wings. The guests contributed two half-gallon bottles of *soju,* which the farmhand had toted on his shoulders.

The drinking commenced immediately. The men fished out the dogs' innards, already cooked, to snack on over a couple of rounds.

The host removed his jacket.

"Strip down and get comfortable, men. It's time to let loose."

The brothers had decided not to mention that the dogs they were eating were rabid. It wouldn't be much fun if the guests lost their appetite.

"Now this is what I call getting a head start on the Dog Days," said the Dolmen Village headman as he removed his jacket. The host's younger brother did likewise.

Pak alone demurred—he never removed his jacket, even at drinking parties. And when he paid a visit without wearing the traditional topcoat, as he had that day, he felt he'd committed a breach of etiquette. And so after the first polite suggestion to remove his jacket, no one mentioned it again.

"How about a repeat performance out our way when the Dog Days start?" asked the Dolmen Village headman. He gazed at Pak as if to say, "You'd better join in the fun then."

Pak nodded once.

The Dolmen Village headman continued to stare at Pak.

"Kilson's family have a dog, you know. And they're planning to sell it. Kilson's sick with food poisoning, and they need the money, so the dog won't cost much. Pretty scrawny, because they don't feed it very well, but it's good sized."

The head beneath the horsehair hat nodded once more. It was as if Pak thought the Dolmen Village headman could speak no wrong.

Meat from a foreleg was served, then meat from a hind leg. Kannan's grandfather was kept busy stripping the bones so the others could eat while they drank.

Evening came earlier to the highlands, and before they knew it the long twilight of early summer was settling over them. The first bottle of *soju* was sprawled on the ground, mouth gaping, and the second bottle had assumed its place on the table. By now everyone was quite drunk.

Under the influence, the older brother went so far as to admit that the dogs they'd slaughtered that day were rabid. But the meat of a rabid dog was a tonic, so the guests were to set their minds at ease and eat up.

"*That's* why it tasted so good," chimed in the Dolmen Village headman. "Let's eat till our belly buttons pop out." And with that he loosened his waistband, exposing his navel—as he was wont to do on such occasions.

The younger brother asked the two visitors if they could find him a puppy. As was his habit, he kept passing his hand back over his stubbly hair.

The Dolmen Village headman responded first. As a matter of fact, his in-laws in Temple Hollow had a bitch that was about to pop, so not to worry. It was a good breed, he added.

"Make sure you save me one," said the younger brother. When it was grown, he continued, they'd slaughter it and have another feast.

Everything sounded fine to Pak. He continued to nod, smiling a smile of utter contentment. Perspiration had dampened his white ramie jacket. The torsos of the other three men glistened with sweat and dogmeat fat. Gradually all of them blended into the evening shadow.

The farmhand lit a kerosene lantern and hung it from the chestnut tree. The oily, sweaty torsos and the Dolmen Village headman's slicked-down hair came alive, flickering in the light. Sitting bleary-eyed around their low table, each man passing his empty drinking vessel to the next and filling it, stripping meat from bones, then slapping their necks and chests when bitten by mosquitos and other pests—they resembled a pack of animals.

"Let's limber up the vocal cords, boys," said the Dolmen Village headman. Thick tongue and all, he was the first to launch a tune. The younger brother then took up the challenge, still in control of his voice, and the others followed in their turn, all except Pak, who was content to keep time tapping his knee. Sitting in the dim glow of the lamp on this early summer evening, the men sounded like a band of howling beasts.

Which was why, among the people who would gather in the corner of Ch'ason's family's yard at the foot of the mountains to the west, Kim Sŏndal had always been able to draw a laugh by saying that the singing accompanying a dogmeat party was actually the howling of the slaughtered animals. Tonight too, Kim set the others laughing. There you could hear Blackie, and now Spotty, he said as the Dolmen Village headman and the younger brother traded songs. And whether it was the jokester Kim or the laughing villagers, any feelings they may have had for the dogs were subordinated to the same thought: if only they could taste that meaty stuff—when was the last time they'd savored it? Late into the night the lantern remained in the chestnut tree, like an animal's eye glaring in the dark.

The next day the brothers visited the families who lived at the foot of the mountains to the west. Someone had seen, besides their own dogs, another dog following the mad one. Whoever's dog it was, he had better get rid of it now. And remember, the brothers said—if the owner knew his dog had followed the mad dog and was concealing that fact, the day it became known would be that man's last day in this village.

Understandably, Kannan's grandfather did nothing about the family's dog, Yellow. Five days passed, then ten, but Yellow didn't turn rabid. Meanwhile the villagers at the foot of the western mountains put their mill to use for the first time in a long while, sweeping up the dust and hulling barley. Whitey seized this opportunity, and whenever the mill was used she would visit at night and lick up whatever chaff the broom had missed. Because this was the season for rice weevil infestations, the brothers constantly hulled small amounts of rice as a precaution, so their mill was an even better source of chaff.

Two months later, Yellow still wasn't rabid. The villagers near the mountains to the west harvested and hulled the early millet. For the poor among them, a nicely cooked meal of rice mixed with this millet was one of the year's supreme delights—how could food be so nutty, so tasty? A bowl of it would call to mind the old saying that young-radish kimchi eaten with early millet will draw milk from a virgin's breasts. How true, these impoverished people thought.

In the meantime, Whitey continued to visit the mill at opportune moments in search of food, and there she would sleep. She kept out of sight of everyone, and seemed to rest a bit easier. But she made sure to leave for the hills early in the morning, so that even Kannan's grandfather wouldn't spot her.

But then one day, word spread that the mad dog had been sleeping in the mill. Ch'ason's father, bound for the western mountains to find a tree limb he could make into a crossbar for his oxcart, had seen something emerge from the mill and run off. A closer look revealed it to be the mad dog. And even in the predawn darkness he had seen it wasn't alone. Ch'ason's father saw well in the dark, and the villagers took him at his word.

Hearing this news, the village heads visited the families at the foot of the mountains to the west. The wild dog would have to be ambushed that night. (The brothers no longer referred to it as a mad dog, for if it were truly rabid, they told themselves, it wouldn't have eaten anything and eventually it would have bitten off one of its own legs and died.) And if it were carrying young, they added, that would mean it had mated with a jackal—in which case there was no better tonic than the meat of the pups, so after they'd slaughtered the dog they would take only the pup fetuses and leave the rest of the meat for the villagers. After this pronouncement, they went back home.

At nightfall the brothers returned. The villagers had gathered in Ch'ason's family's yard, and the brothers made sure each was armed with a stick or a backrack support. Kannan's grandfather was among the group. He didn't think Whitey had changed, but if in fact she'd been sleeping in the mill next to his house, then she'd doubtless been consuming his scant supply of nightsoil. No way could he allow that, and he decided the time was ripe to slaughter the dog. And, like his neighbors, he knew this was a rare chance for meat.

The night was far along when Ch'ason's father returned from his scouting mission to report that the wild dog had just gone into the mill. The villagers tiptoed there, each already anticipating the taste of meat. The brothers remained at a safe distance, watching carefully.

The mill had two openings, and the villagers surrounded each one. They looked inside, and sure enough, something was moving in the dark, a light-colored animal. Clearly it was that damned Whitey dog. They crept inside a step at a time and closed ranks. As the animal was gradually forced backward, part of it lighted up—the eyes, like the eyes of a wild dog. The villagers tightened their grips on their weapons—Kannan's grandfather among them. The circle narrowed by one step. The dog whirled about once, as if the blue flame of its eyes were seeking an opening to escape. And then Kannan's grandfather realized that the flame emanated not from Whitey alone but also from the pups inside her. So what if it was an animal? How could they kill a creature carrying young? he wondered.

"Get it!" someone shouted. The next instant, those on either side of Kannan's grandfather rushed forward and swung their sticks down. At the same time, the old man saw a blue flame slip past his leg.

"Who let it out?!" said an outraged voice.

"Who was it? Who was it?"

Emerging from the grumbling, the farmhand stuck his face up close to Kannan's grandfather's chin.

"It was Grandpa here."

"What happened?" came the older brother's voice from off to the side.

"It got away," said the farmhand.

"Got away?!" shouted the brothers simultaneously.

"Who let it out?!" asked the older brother, his irate voice carrying nearer.

Kannan's grandfather walked outside to his home next door.

"These old goats'd be better off dead!" barked the older brother a short time later, his voice carrying into the old man's house.

One day about a month later, when autumn was gone for good and the people of Crossover Village were busy gathering winter firewood, Kannan's grandfather set off for Fox Hollow. This place across the mountains to the west had long been known to be rugged, and most woodcutters avoided it. There the old man could quickly fill his backrack with fuel. After an easy day of gathering, he was on his way back home when he came upon a brood of animals at the side of the path. He startled, thinking they might be tiger cubs, but quickly discovered them to be a litter of sleeping puppies. And there was Whitey herself gazing his way from a distance. She was nothing but skin and bones.

Kannan's grandfather approached the puppies. There were five of them, and they looked a good three weeks old. But then the old man received another jolt. There was no doubt about it—among the sleeping pups were a miniature Yellow, Blackie, and Spotty, all in the same litter. Well, it was only natural, wasn't it? A smile formed on his rugged face with its bushy salt-and-pepper beard, and he made up his mind that he wouldn't tell a soul what he'd seen, not even his family.

One summer when I was an eighth or ninth grader, I was visiting my mother's family in Crossover Village, and there I heard this tale, at the end of one story or another, from Kannan's grandfather, Kim Sŏndal, and Ch'ason's father as they were taking a work break beneath the weeping willow near the well at the foot of the mountains to the west. Kannan's grandfather was the main storyteller. The tale unfolded, and since it had happened two or three years earlier, if the sequence was wrong or someone's recall was faulty, the others would correct him, and if one of them left something out the others would fill it in.

After Kannan's grandfather had seen the pups, he'd exercised caution so that no one would suspect, and it was his pleasure alone to see them when he went to gather fuel. Though his family didn't have enough to eat, he would secretly gather the remnants of their vegetable porridge and feed the pups. When they were old enough to eat solid food, he brought one of them home, explaining to his family that he had gotten it from someone at such-and-such a place. A second one he took in his arms to neighboring Koptan's family. He said he had gotten a third puppy from someone in Temple Hollow, which he could reach directly from Fox Hollow; a fourth one from someone in Sŏjet-kol; and in this way he ended up accounting for all five of them.

At the end of the story, Kannan's grandfather said that the dog now living with his family was Whitey's great-granddaughter. And because Whitey herself was of a good breed, practically all the dogs in Crossover Village were either her great-grandchildren or her great-great-grandchildren. Even the two village heads had been given pups from his dog, which would make them Whitey's great-great-grandchildren. A broad smile lit up the face of the old man, whose bushy beard was by now the color of frost.

When I asked whatever had become of Whitey, Kannan's grandfather turned serious. Rumor had it she was shot by a hunter the same winter he had found the pups. Whatever her fate, he never saw her again.

I wished I hadn't asked.

March 1947

Lost Souls

DEATHLESS

Low gray clouds draped the sky. Another breezy day that was cooler than it should have been for spring, thought Lucky Nose.

He began to load the salt bags onto his donkey as the animal finished its feed. A good fifteen miles lay ahead of them that day.

His mother-in-law emerged from the kitchen, the corners of her eyes crusted with sleep.

"Will we see you on your way back, Son?"

"Probably not. I've got folks in Basin Village and Magpie Hollow waiting for me."

"So you do. You know," she said hesitantly, "it's an awful long way for her to come with a baby. Why don't you tell her not to bother?"

"All right, I'll do that. Anyhow, you know we'll be taking you in with us next year."

Lucky Nose cinched the cord that held the salt bags fast to the donkey.

Last night he had told his mother-in-law that Sŏbun, her daughter, would visit during the upcoming Yudu Festival.

If only she could! the woman had thought. Already two years had stolen by since Sŏbun had gone to live with the salt peddler. Initially, it was agreed that the couple would return for her in the autumn. But then Lucky Nose had gone to see a fortune-teller in preparation for building a new house and was told it would be risky for someone to move in with them. Last spring had brought a further delay: according to Sŏbun's fortune for the year, bad luck lay in the northeast quadrant, and if a newcomer were to arrive from that area, even if it was her mother, it would cause Sŏbun to go blind. And so the woman had told herself that as long as no harm came to her daughter in her new surroundings, it wasn't such a terrible thing not to be able to see her for a piddling year or two.

She had married off her only daughter to Lucky Nose the salt peddler, preferring to send her to an unfamiliar urban area, where clothing was readily available and food abundant, rather than subject her to a hard life in this backcountry mountain village. She would be content as long as her daughter was doing well. And then her son-in-law had arrived yesterday. According to the mother's fortune for this year, Lucky Nose had said, bad luck lay in the southwest quadrant, and if she journeyed in that direction she would die. But everyone's fortune boded well for next year, so he and Sŏbun would be sure to come for her then. And since his last visit, Sŏbun had produced a fine-looking baby boy with the fairest skin you could imagine. Finally Lucky Nose had told her about Sŏbun's plan to visit during the Yudu Festival. Hearing this, she felt as if she had caught a momentary glimpse of her daughter and grandson, and she had to blow her nose to keep back the tears. But after mulling over this prospect for most of the night, she had decided that the hundred-odd miles from that place he called Chinnamp'o was too far for a mother and a nursing baby to travel, and had changed her mind. She had endured the absence of her daughter until now, and could do so for another year.

Lucky Nose finished loading the donkey and gave it a swat on the rump with his whip.

"Have a safe journey," said the woman. Her son-in-law was every bit as precious to her as Sŏbun. "And remember, I don't want you sending the baby and his mother here."

"All right."

And then, without so much as a backward look, Lucky Nose urged the donkey on its way. He cleared his throat and spat, then turned up his nose with its round red tip. *Hmph! Might as well forget about that little darling of yours,* he silently retorted to the woman. *It's been a long, long time since I sold her off to that whorehouse in Pyongyang.*

The year or so he had lived with Sŏbun, starting in the spring two years ago, hadn't been very pleasant. And she wasn't much of a looker, so the money he'd gotten for her had barely covered what he'd invested in order to take her from her mother. *Hmph! Girl was ugly as a lump of soybean malt! What else could I do with her? Hmph!* Again and again he turned up his nose with its round red tip and snorted. The nickname Lucky Nose had come from that well-shaped, healthy-looking feature of his.

These unpleasant thoughts of Sŏbun soon dissipated, and into his mind drifted the image of Koptani in Basin Village. She had a charming face, as her name suggested, and already the previous autumn her chest had filled out into a nice pair of mounds. This spring she must have blossomed even more.

The cool spring breeze whistled through the dense stand of pines that flanked both sides of the road. In the spaces where big rocks separated the pines, the azaleas were at their fetching peak.

The donkey stopped at a bend in the road, stretched out its neck, and hee-hawed. At the sound of the resulting echo, it pricked up its ears, craned its neck again, and hee-hawed once more.

Listen to the damned thing—it's got its own spring mating call. Lucky Nose gave the donkey's rump a good-natured tap with his whip. Now it was the jingling of the bell hanging from the donkey's neck that was echoing in the valleys. Lucky Nose pushed back the brim of his well-worn hat. He felt a pleasant warmth radiate through him.

This time I'm going to take that little skirt back with me, yes I am. Her father half-agreed to it last fall, didn't he? Once I get her home, the rest will be easy. I'm going to settle down with this one. Age forty is looking me in the eye and it's time I put down some roots.

And in fact he had already rented a shop in Pyongyang where he planned to sell salt wholesale.

Got to take Koptani home with me, yes I do. Got to work on her father first, but this time her mother needs some buttering up too. The mother's bound to be more concerned about the daughter's well-being. Well, if I put my mind to it, I shouldn't have much trouble with that backwoods broad.

A grin appeared beneath the round red tip of his nose, and he began absentmindedly to croon a stanza of "The Yangsan Region": "The Taedong swirls and flows, from Yangdŏk and Maengsan to Pubyŏk Pavilion—hey, hey, yah."

Yangdŏk was a remote spot about seventy-five miles from Pyongyang, a third that distance from Sŏngch'ŏn, and a good seventeen miles from Changnim, the nearest town. In this and the more remote villages, the only way to get salt for your side dishes was to raft down the Taedong toward Pyongyang in summer, or else wait for the peddler who packed in salt on the back of a donkey in spring and autumn.

This was the case with Basin Village. It consisted of a grand total of six dwellings—which for a backcountry mountain village wasn't that small. The houses were tucked into a bend in the road where a dead pine stood, stripped bare by the elements.

Spring and autumn, the villagers anticipated the salt peddler's arrival. When the donkey finally ambled around the bend, the first person to see it would cry out, "Here comes the salt peddler!"

No words were more welcome, none more gratifying. Doors swung open and out came toddlers, babes in arms, everyone. All gathered in the courtyard of Koptani's house, where for as long as anyone could remember, the salt peddler would unload his cargo and lodge.

On this particular day Koptani was the first to spy the salt peddler. She emerged from the shed, where she was fetching millet husks for the swill she would boil for the pigs, and there was the donkey trotting into sight at the bend in the road where the skeletal pine stood.

But instead of announcing the salt peddler's arrival she hurried into the kitchen, her heart fluttering. This wouldn't have happened if Lucky Nose hadn't asked her father for her hand the previous autumn.

"Hey, it's the salt peddler!" shouted Pottori from next door. Koptani detected a note of triumph in his ringing voice.

She heard the neighbors gather in the yard. At first the jingling of the donkey's bell had been so distant that she wasn't really sure she'd heard it. But now it was clearer and louder, and with it came the raspy voice of Lucky Nose asking in his P'yŏngan accent how everyone had been.

Koptani's heart jingled like the donkey's bell. She couldn't bring herself to look outside.

While the men exchanged greetings with the salt peddler, the women returned to their houses to collect the items they would barter for salt.

Lucky Nose unloaded the salt bags, sat down beside them, and produced matches and a cigarette from his pocket. He lit the cigarette with a flourish. To these people, smoking involved dried pumpkin and tobacco leaves, a pipe, and a flint; striking a match to light a ready-made cigarette was stylish indeed.

The women reappeared with armfuls of hemp fabric they had woven during winter.

While Lucky Nose smoked his cigarette he rehearsed the ways he would find fault with the rolls of hemp. "This roll's too narrow," he might say. Or, "The color's no good." Or, "The weave is too loose." He could then obtain the fabric dirt cheap and resell it later for a profit.

But Lucky Nose had more on his mind than bartering as he examined the women and their goods. Where was Koptani? She should be here with these women. Was she sick? Had she already been married off? He wasn't in a position to ask right now, and this annoyed him considerably.

Lucky Nose stubbed out his half-smoked cigarette and stood up. He went through the motions of haggling with the women, and finally it was Koptani's mother's turn.

"How's everyone, Mother?"

Already he had begun addressing Koptani's parents as "Father" and "Mother."

"Can't complain. Except our Crazy Hair's in bed with a fever these last few days."

"Well, I'm real sorry to hear that."

That explained Koptani's absence, he told himself.

Pottori's mother came forward next. She had less fabric than the other women. She was a slothful woman, and the meager amount of hemp she did weave was of poorer quality than the rest. So her family usually bartered the pelts of animals her husband had trapped. But the previous winter the husband had caught only a wildcat and some rabbits, and it was these pelts she now offered Lucky Nose after receiving salt for her fabric.

"Auntie, do you really expect salt for this stuff? A cat's fur is worth more than this."

"We couldn't help it. There wasn't much snow last winter. Come on, just a quarter bushel more, and we'll make it up to you next time."

"Auntie, listen to you! There's no such thing as 'next time' in my business."

"You think we're going to die on you? Come on, scoop me another quarter bushel. Tell you what—we'll trap a fox for you this fall, a beauty. I've got my eye on one. It's a female, at least thirty years old, and you can make a fortune selling the privates. Want to know why? Because whoever gets them, all their dreams will come true. If a woman has them, then her husband will end up pussy-whipped even if he's a big-time skirt chaser. And if it's a man, then any woman he hankers for will crawl right into bed with him."

This woman had always been known for her brazen manner.

"What idiot scheme is she jabbering about now?" her husband said. He spat and turned away.

The others burst into laughter; it wasn't the first time they had heard such talk from the woman. They enjoyed listening to her banter with this man from the outside world whose face had become familiar to them over the past seven or eight years.

Lucky Nose laughed with the others.

"Well, if they're so precious, why not keep 'em yourself?"

"For what? Getting old and dying? That's all *we* got to look forward to. But if they're yours, Mr. Kim, your business will prosper, and any young lady you fancy will crawl right into bed with you."

Lucky Nose again joined the villagers in laughter, but this time his was a sardonic laugh. There was something in Pottori's mother's words that hinted at Koptani and himself.

"Well, all right," he said in a placating tone, and to silence this shameless woman he scooped her another half peck of salt. "But you'd better keep that prize yourself in case your husband starts playing around in his old age; else you'll have a problem of your own."

Next was the wife of the elderly village head, accompanied by their adopted son, Komi, who in terms of age difference could have been mistaken for their grandson by an outsider. Grandfather Headman, the villagers called the husband, since he was the oldest male among the six households in the village. It had been more than ten years since they had taken in Komi. The boy's parents had passed away in quick succession when he was eight, and the childless couple had ultimately taken responsibility for him. He was twenty-one now, with shoulders broad enough for a man's work, but he still wore the pigtail that marked him as unmarried.

Lucky Nose poured a bushel and a quarter of salt into Komi's bag. Komi picked it up with one hand as if it weighed no more than a feather, and turned to go.

"Hold on, fellow—what's the rush?"

Komi came to a halt.

Lucky Nose had always called Komi "kid," but the young man was too old for that now, and the previous fall the salt peddler had started calling him "fellow." Likewise, he had always regarded Koptani as a fuzzy-cheeked girl, until discovering that she had ripened into a young lady. And it was around that time that Lucky Nose had discovered he could no longer treat Komi as a child.

Yes, it was last autumn, Lucky Nose recalled. On the way here to Basin Village, that rascal donkey of his had developed a limp in one of its hind legs. Thinking something had gotten stuck in its hoof, Lucky Nose had unloaded the donkey as soon as he arrived. But when he tried to inspect the leg the donkey began bucking, and Lucky Nose couldn't restrain it. The men tried in vain to rein in the animal. Finally Komi joined in, grabbing the reins with one hand and the donkey's mane with the other, and brought the animal under control. The villagers goggled at the young man. Lucky Nose too was amazed. "No wonder they call him Komi—true to his name, he really is a bear." Never again had he used "kid" in reference to Komi.

Lucky Nose now turned to the village head, who was squatting off to the side, smoking his pipe with its long bamboo stem and small metal bowl.

"You've been kind to me all along, sir. . . . I know it's not much, but please take some more." Saying this, he added a full peck more to Komi's sack.

The village head put aside his pipe and rose.

"Hold on—that salt's too valuable. . . . What have we done to make you obliged to us? We're the ones who ought to be obliged to you."

"Please. I'm indebted to gentlemen like yourself for allowing me to build up a steady trade over these seven or eight years."

"Listen to you.... I can't tell you how grateful we are that you come here every spring and autumn."

The village head followed up by inviting Lucky Nose for supper. After several protestations, Lucky Nose pretended he could refuse no longer and accepted the invitation.

Lucky Nose organized the remaining bags of salt, then left for Koptani's house with a cloth bundle. He arrived to find Koptani's mother squatting beside the kitchen door, removing the chaff and other foreign matter from her portion of salt.

"I brought you all some fabric—silk for a jacket for you, calico for a coat for Father, and Japanese silk for a jacket and skirt for Koptani. Nothing fancy, I'm afraid."

And that wasn't all. Lucky Nose had brought a hand mirror and a jar of face cream for Koptani as well.

Koptani's mother gaped at Lucky Nose, searching his face for an explanation. Her own face, weathered to a purplish hue by wind and sun, was tinged with uncertainty.

"Mother, don't think twice. I've started a wholesale shop and I'm going to kiss this darned peddling business good-bye. I've put you to all sorts of trouble over the years, and this is just my way of saying thank you. Don't think twice.... Do you mind if I wash up?"

He took from his pocket a bar of soap wrapped in paper.

After a moment Koptani's mother collected herself and managed to call toward the kitchen, "Koptani, find the washbasin and fill it for Mr. Kim." Her voice trembled.

The swill for the pigs had boiled by now, but Koptani continued to stir it with the wooden paddle. Her heart was pounding. Something about having to face Lucky Nose frightened her. But her mother had told her to prepare water for the guest, and so she located the basin and the gourd dipper. Suddenly she remembered something. She put down the dipper and instead used a round, wide-mouthed basin of unglazed clay to fill the basin. Once before, she had used the dipper for this purpose and it had come back from the salt peddler smelling of soap. For days afterward the rice and the drinking water had given off a nasty odor that she couldn't get rid of. It had been very annoying.

Koptani kept her head bowed as she emerged with the water, but she could sense Lucky Nose's gaze sweeping over her forehead. She hurriedly set down the basin, then disappeared back into the kitchen.

Well, look at how the girl shies away from men, Lucky Nose thought. *She's growing up. And she's starting to fill out around the hips. . . .* With a feeling of satisfaction he lathered and washed his face not once but twice.

Night fell quickly in the valley. The silhouettes of the hills were already indistinct because of the low clouds, and the shade soon thickened into creeping shadows.

The onset of evening was the noisiest time of day in this back-country village. You could hear the chirping of birds returning to their nests in the hills, the fluttering of their wings, the cooing of mountain doves. Even louder was the cawing of magpies. And then there was the breeze blowing through the pines, seeming to carry the dusk along with it.

Lucky Nose and Koptani's father were sitting on the ground under the eaves smoking hand-rolled cigarettes. Lucky Nose repeated what he had suggested to Koptani's mother a short time ago—that this would be his last time around as a salt peddler, that from now on he would sell salt wholesale and make a thriving business out of it. But there was no way he could run the operation by himself; he needed a fellow to help out. One by one he made sure Koptani's father understood these particulars. This time Lucky Nose wasn't lying.

Meanwhile, Koptani's mother emerged from the kitchen with a bowl of feed for the donkey. Lucky Nose jumped to his feet and relieved her of it. This was a disappointment. He had hoped it would be Koptani, so that he could accept the bowl from her as in the past. But now that Koptani was a mature young woman, she was keeping her distance from men, he reckoned.

While Lucky Nose stood watching the donkey feed, Komi came from the village head's home to tell him supper was ready.

Lucky Nose had been waiting for this opportunity. Ever since starting on this trip he'd looked forward to a quiet chat with the village head. Which was why he'd given the old man the full measure of salt. When he had received a supper invitation in return, he'd made a show of being obliged to accept, but inwardly he was delighted.

"Try one of these, fellow." He offered Komi a cigarette, so satisfied was he that his plans were being realized.

"I don't smoke," Komi said without looking back at Lucky Nose.

"Oh? I do believe I've seen you smoke before?"

"I don't smoke."

Lucky Nose couldn't quite understand Komi's sulky tone of voice.

Poor sucker must have gotten a scolding from the old man, he thought. *Well, you don't have much of a life to look forward to—work yourself to the bone here in the hills and die a broken-down wreck.* Comparing himself with Komi, Lucky Nose felt quite the fortunate man.

A castor-oil lamp was burning in the village head's house. Lamps would never be lit this early in a backcountry village, and if they were, resinous pine knots would be used for fuel. But for the sake of his guest the village head had lit the lamp—something he generally reserved for important occasions.

"Come on in. Nothing fancy here, but I guess you know that."

A small meal table for two was brought in. The villagers had made it from pine boards. They had also fashioned the wooden dishes containing the seasoned wild greens and the acorn jelly. Only the brass rice bowls were store-bought, and they had developed a patina by now. Corn mixed with hulled yellow millet was the main dish. Lucky Nose, the guest, received a larger portion of millet than his host.

"Dig in, now. It's a tough job making the rounds out here in the sticks."

"You've really gone out of your way for me."

"Well, I know you eat a lot of rich food in Pyongyang, so perhaps a meal like this isn't so bad. . . . Ever hear about the fellow who went to Pyongyang and had himself some rice for the first time? Stomach couldn't tolerate it, and did he ever get sick!"

The old man's mouth opened in a wide grin. Pine-knot smoke had turned the white of his beard a dark yellow.

Lucky Nose pretended to eat his fill, as the village head had urged. He could have finished his bowl, but he left a small amount uneaten, as a gentleman would.

After the meal table was removed, Lucky Nose offered the village head a cigarette. He debated whether to have one himself, but thought better of it. To smoke in front of one's elders or superiors would betray a lack of etiquette.

"Nice and sweet! Like it's got a touch o' honey."

Lucky Nose responded with a belch, then began talking again about the salt business he was establishing.

The village head couldn't quite understand what his guest meant by "wholesaling" salt. All he knew was that this fellow Lucky Nose seemed to have become a rich man.

"I'm happy things are working out so well for you, Mr. Kim. But it looks like the folks around here will have a hard time finding salt from now on."

Before Lucky Nose arrived on the scene, an elderly salt peddler had made the rounds. But for some reason or other he had stopped coming. One of the villagers had gone as far as Changnim in search of a replacement, and there he had found Lucky Nose. The old man was reminded of all the trouble this other villager had gone to.

"No cause to worry. I aim to hire some peddlers, and I'll pick out the best of the salt and have one of them deliver it to you." This was a genuine offer.

"That would be wonderful."

At this point, Lucky Nose felt comfortable about speaking his mind.

"By the way, Grandfather Headman," he began. And in a more confidential tone: "There's something I'd like to ask you about."

The village head gazed at Lucky Nose, wondering what this fellow could possibly want to discuss with him.

"It's about Koptani. Has she ever taken sick—you know, real sick?"

Not knowing the reason behind this question, the village head continued to gaze at Lucky Nose before replying.

"Why would she be sick?"

"Her face, I mean. She's kind of dark complected—doesn't look very healthy."

"Oh, that. It's the sun. You won't find many people with fair skin in these parts."

"So that's it," said Lucky Nose, though he knew well enough.

"Actually, she was fair-skinned to begin with, so she's lighter than the rest of us."

"Her parents said Crazy Hair was sick in bed, and I thought Koptani might have caught something too."

The village head searched Lucky Nose's face, wondering why he was bringing this up. Then he remembered the precious cigarette burning near his fingertips, and he drew on it several times.

"You know, I've got a notion to take her for my wife. I'd like to hear your opinion on that."

The village head was about to take another puff, but the salt peddler's words brought the fingers holding the cigarette to a stop in front of his lips.

"What? You mean to tell me you're not married?"

"That's right. Take my pleasure from making money, I guess. Haven't met the right woman, either."

"What do you want with a girl from a mountain village?"

"Please, please. I've thought about that. First of all, the girls out here have pure hearts. And a girl who's had to put up with a hellish life will treat her husband like a god. Isn't that right?"

"I agree with you there."

But no matter how he looked at it, the two of them were a mismatch in terms of age, the village head thought as he stuck the cigarette butt in the bowl of his pipe and drew this time on the stem.

As if he had foreseen this objection, Lucky Nose spoke up again.

"I don't feel quite right talking about myself, but the truth is, a man like me with a few years under his belt knows how to care for the little woman."

"I see, now that you put it that way," said the older man, bobbing his head.

"Well now, could I ask you to speak for me to Koptani's folks? Better a man in your position, instead of the one who's directly involved."

"This is a match I'd be tickled to help out with."

Lucky Nose got back on the subject of wholesaling salt. He intended to make it into a large business, but there was no way he could go it alone—it would be swell if someone like Koptani's father could lend a hand.

Koptani's folks stood to reap the benefits of raising a daughter like Koptani, the village head realized. They wouldn't want to turn up their noses at a golden opportunity like this.

The night was well along when Lucky Nose left the village head's house. The moon—more than a crescent, less than half—shone faintly through a veil of thin clouds. The breeze had died down, and in every direction all seemed buried in the still of the night. A cuckoo called from a distant valley. To Lucky Nose the fleeting call was like something from a dream. A bird heading for its nest grazed his shoulder and disappeared into the darkness.

Lucky Nose was pleased with himself. Everything was going his way, he thought as he approached Koptani's house.

But then he noticed a shadow in the gloom near the back corner of the kitchen. He tiptoed forward. If it was Koptani, he would have a word with her. The thought excited him. He might even take her by the wrist. If you did that to these mountain girls, they wouldn't disappoint you in the future. He had done so two years earlier with Sŏbun, and from then on he had the girl at his mercy. He inched forward, fueled by these thoughts. But no: it was Koptani, all right, only she wasn't alone. He pressed himself against a pear tree.

"So, what's it going to be?" came the insistent, low-pitched voice of a man.

There was a pause, and then Lucky Nose heard Koptani's voice, also muffled. "I just don't know," she said anxiously.

"What do you mean, you don't know? That damn salt peddler's over at Grandpa's right now, and it sounds like he's fixing to take you away. Is that what you want, get yourself dragged off by him?"

Lucky Nose's heart pounded harder. The son of a bitch who was feeding Koptani this line was none other than that good-for-nothing Komi.

"What do you really feel like doing? Huh?"

All Koptani could do was whimper feebly.

"We have to get out of here—tonight. It's the only way. Like I said, if we can get as far as Tongt'anjibol, we can take up farming—rice or whatever. I've looked into it. Let's just go, tonight."

Koptani's faint sobbing was the only response.

"You haven't changed your mind about me, have you?"

Koptani's sobbing abruptly stopped.

"Tell me the truth. You haven't changed your mind, have you? . . . Well then, let's get out of here."

Koptani remained silent.

"Try not to worry about your mom and dad. We'll go first, and when we're settled they can join us. You think I like the idea of running away from my grandparents, after they raised me like their own boy? It breaks my heart. But we can take them in with us too."

Still no answer from Koptani.

"We'll leave at the first crow of the rooster. When you hear it, come outside. I'll come by for you. Now don't forget."

Koptani began to whimper again. "I just don't know," she quavered. "I don't know what's right."

"Of course you do. Just make up your mind and do it my way."

"Do we *have* to run away? What if I don't marry the salt peddler?"

"What are you going to do, say no to your mom and dad? Don't be silly. We have to get out of here tonight. If we don't, we'll never see each other again."

Koptani's anguish briefly burst forth in sobbing.

"I just don't know. . . . Everything's so scary. . . ."

"Not if you make up your mind. I was scared too when I first thought about this. Not now, though."

More faint sobbing from Koptani.

"So buck up, and when the rooster crows, come outside. I'll be waiting for you."

At these words, Koptani's whimpering stopped.

"No, it's no good here. . . . What if someone has to go to the outhouse and sees you? It's all right now because Mom and Dad are inside talking about you." And then she spoke more distinctly: "Instead, cover yourself up with one of those straw mats in the front yard, like you did before." Resolve had crept into her voice.

"All right. I'll see you when the rooster crows—don't forget."

Lucky Nose, unnoticed behind the pear tree, was swept by conflicting emotions. But then the trace of a smile formed beneath his nose with its round red tip. He had hit upon an idea.

Inside, Koptani's parents had lit the pine knots that fueled their lamp.

"Dear, any way I look at it, it scares me, sending her off to town," the mother said yet again, hunched up next to Koptani's bedridden brother.

"I know," said Koptani's father. "Like they say, a privy rat belongs in the privy, and a barn rat belongs in the barn. But you know, now that I've had a chance to look over this salt peddler, he seems all right. Sure, there's an age difference, but that's good for Koptani— she'll get more affection from him because of it."

"Well. . . ." Koptani's mother searched her husband's face. "As far as I can tell, a fellow like Komi would do just fine for her."

She had wanted to tell her husband this for some time.

She had a good enough reason. About this time last spring, Pottori's mother had dropped by one evening and told her a story: she had gone up in the hills behind the village that day to gather some wild greens. Suddenly a roe deer had jumped out from a cluster of kiwi vines. Transfixed by the sight, she had watched as a startled roebuck then leaped from the same cluster and bounded off. Hearing this story, Koptani's mother had said, why not have Pottori's father set a snare for the animals? But with a knowing smile, Pottori's mother put her lips to the other woman's ear. "Actually they weren't deer; they were deer people. One of them was a Koptani deer and the other was a Komi deer. . . . This morning I asked if Koptani wanted to go gather greens with me, and she said she had to weave some hemp cloth. Maybe she was doing her weaving in those vines," she said with an insinuating smile. This had set Koptani's mother to thinking about her seventeen-year-old daughter. At the same time, she had taken a closer look at young Komi's behavior toward Koptani. Sure enough, there was more to their relationship than met the eye. For example, whenever Komi had come to help in the fields, hadn't their Koptani heaped his rice bowl full? From then on, everything seemed to indicate that Komi would become her son-in-law.

Koptani's father had thought likewise. If he were to pick a son-in-law from the immediate area, Komi would be the obvious choice. He realized that he had Koptani to thank for Komi's willingness to work from first light until late in the evening whenever he came to help in their fields. And so his mind had wavered ever since the salt peddler had emerged as a potential husband for his daughter.

"She'd be safe marrying Komi," he now said to his wife, "but then she'd just end up like us, working herself to death out here in the middle of nowhere."

"But even if she marries the salt peddler and moves to town.... You can't teach an old dog new tricks."

"That's not always true. There's such a thing as fate." Koptani's father lifted his gaunt face toward his wife. "The peddler says he's started wholesaling salt," he said fervently. "But he can't do it by himself—says he needs someone to help out. And I have a hunch that I'm the one he has in mind. It would probably take less out of me than working these fields, so I could give him an honest day's work. The important thing is, we should get while the getting is good."

There was no more mention of the privy rat and the barn rat.

"I'll never get used to the idea of her living in that awful city...."

"Remember, though, we have to think of him." So saying, he gestured with his chin toward the boy lying on the warmer part of the heated floor.

Koptani's mother could find no reply to this. So they might have to move to the city. Well, as long as her boy and girl turned out well, then all of her present fears and reluctance would amount to nothing.

"I've made up my mind. If the salt peddler speaks up about Koptani, I'll give her to him."

Koptani's mother thought about the fabric that Lucky Nose had given her that evening. Perhaps the material for Koptani was meant for a wedding dress. Suddenly she thought of Komi, and shuddered.

After seeing Komi off, Koptani had returned to the kitchen, and there she overheard this conversation. So it was just as Komi had said: they were going to marry her off to the salt peddler, and it would be useless to try to talk them out of it. For the sake of her parents and her little brother, had she any choice but to become his wife? The palpitations of her heart were replaced by a burning sensation.

Finally, after a long while, from a neighbor's house came the crow of a rooster. Koptani instinctively jumped up from where she had hidden near the stove. She was drawn by something even more precious than her parents and brother—something she dared not lose. There was a place she had to go, and now was the time. But as she pushed open the kitchen door, she heard someone emerging from the adjoining room.

It was her father. The crow of the rooster had set him to wondering why there had been no sign of Lucky Nose. He drew the screen to the guest room and looked inside. No, the salt peddler hadn't returned.

As long as he was up, he thought he might as well visit the outhouse. But as he stepped down to the stone shoe-ledge, a movement startled him. The moon was perched on the ridge to the west, and its faint light disclosed something crawling under a straw mat that lay folded at the side of the yard.

After a moment of uncertainty it became clear to him that the form beneath the mat was a man. His heart quickened. *Komi, that rascal! So this is what he's been up to—thinks he's going to fiddle with my daughter!* The blood rose to his head. He found himself a club.

As he was about to approach the figure beneath the mat, he noticed someone else's shadow moving about next to the donkey. Well, the salt peddler had finally returned from Grandfather Headman's house and was tending to his donkey. *What's going to happen if he greets me and this other guy finds out I'm here?* But then the shadow near the donkey disappeared toward the outhouse.

Koptani's father set down the club and took a piece of rope hanging from the rafter of the shed. He tiptoed toward the straw mat. Just as he reached it, a hand shot out and grabbed him by the ankle. But it was too late. Koptani's father pounced on the mat.

"Don't move, you son of a bitch, or I'll smash your head in—I mean what I say!" he raged in a choking voice.

He rolled up the mat and its occupant and began carefully to tie it up.

"Son of a bitch," he muttered. "Sure, you're a strong young buck. But there was a time when I could carry a tree as big as a good-sized cow. Worthless son of a bitch—you haven't seen anything yet. We'll leave you like this for tonight—you're in enough trouble already—and in the morning we'll bring you out in front of all the neighbors and teach you a lesson you'll never forget. And I'm going to make sure you never settle your ass here again—son of a bitch!"

On the far side of the hills to the west of Basin Village the light of the moon showed a donkey being urged down a dark path. A young man held the reins. There was no bell around the donkey's neck. A woman was riding the animal.

The man gave the donkey an occasional swat on the rump with his whip. It was a bit awkward the way he handled the whip and led the donkey. Yet he and the woman on the donkey moved with a purpose, making their way along the dark path redolent of pine resin, and on down the hill.

October 1955

LOST SOULS

It was in November of the previous year that Suni had left for Sŏjetkol to become the concubine of a former low-level official named Pak. And it was then that Sŏgi had taken to gazing from the paddy dike out to where the dusty road disappeared around a nearby hill. Suni had left in a sedan chair and someday, Sŏgi told himself, she would return in one.

But the new year arrived and January passed without Suni returning to pay respects to her family. Suni's case was unusual: her role as a concubine was to care for a sick old man. Sŏgi guessed old Pak had taken a turn for the worse because of the cold weather, and this would have prevented Suni from returning.

Nor did Suni appear in early May for the Tano Festival. As in the old days, the villagers staged a wrestling competition and tied a triple-ply rope swing to the old weeping willow at the entrance to the village. But Suni, who should have been among the village maidens as they washed their hair with sweet flag and combed it, the scent of ch'ŏn'gungi all about them, was not to be seen. And so Sŏgi shut himself up at home.

The rope swing was taken down and several days passed. Sŏgi went out again to the dike. But on this particular day he wasn't expecting Suni. Given her absence from the Tano Festival, he held no hope of her returning before the Yudu Festival in mid-June. All the same, Sŏgi gazed toward the nearby hill. His face was noticeably drawn.

For some time Sŏgi had been plagued by a disturbing dream: Suni had returned in a sedan chair. But unlike the chair that had taken her to Pak's house, this one was white. This could only mean that old Pak had passed away. But Suni's sedan chair stopped only a moment at her house, then returned to Sŏjetkol. She had to prepare for the traditional three-year mourning period, Sŏgi assumed. Or perhaps she had returned there to live out the rest of her days as a widow. Sŏgi found the latter thought intolerable, so off he went to Sŏjetkol, where he climbed the lofty wall of Pak's house on a rope made of cotton cloth and stole away with Suni on his back. Sometimes the dream would continue with Suni obediently following Sŏgi. Other times Suni resisted, rolling on the floor, kicking and screaming. Usually he awakened at the point of jumping from Pak's wall with Suni on his back.

Deep down inside, Sŏgi wished old Pak really were dead, and this realization brought with it a sense of shame. Why couldn't he have contrived to prevent Suni from leaving in the first place? It disgusted Sŏgi to see himself in this light.

Suddenly a chilly breeze came up, raising dust devils on the dike. Dark rain clouds swept in over the ridge behind the village, and in no time everything was in shadow.

Sŏgi started down the dike, taking one last look toward the hill as he did so. There, what was that? Coming into sight was a sedan chair—there was no mistaking it. Even from this distance he could see it was the regular variety and not a white one.

A few heavy drops plopped on the ground and then rain was spattering all about. The sedan chair's dark outline blended into the haze of the downpour. Sŏgi remained where he was, peering toward it.

Precisely three years earlier Sŏgi had been caught in a similar cloudburst on his way to the brook for a bath. He took shelter in the lookout shed in the melon patch worked by Suni's family. There minding the shed was Suni. Upon Sŏgi's arrival she stood and looked away. Sŏgi noticed the roundish profile of her chin and the flush beneath her ear. The oily stains near the breast ties of her thin summer jacket loomed prominent. *She's not a little girl anymore.* Already for a year or two Suni had been avoiding his gaze if they happened to meet outside her house or at the village well. But not until the encounter in the shed did it occur to him with visceral certainty that she was no longer a girl. Adjusting her pigtail ribbon, she climbed down from the shed, shoved some *ch'amoe* melons and a sickle inside so he could eat, and set off toward the village—just like that. Sŏgi watched as she picked a large pumpkin leaf from the path and covered her head with it. But her clothes were sopping wet and they clung to her body, clearly revealing the undulations of her ample figure. Once again his own body reminded him of what he had just realized about Suni.

The mist of the downpour alternately veiled and revealed the sedan chair in its gradual advance. The vehicle passed the old weeping willow, then disappeared among the dwellings in the village.

Sŏgi had stood motionless the whole time, oblivious to the rainwater streaming down his spine and chest.

Old Pak's family and Sŏgi's family had long been on friendly terms. It so happened that the Pak family's fields were located in the village where Sŏgi's family lived. And during the harvest, or at any other time when the Paks found it necessary to come to the village, they always lodged with Sŏgi's family. But Sŏgi himself had had no direct ties with Pak until he began to study under the old man.

Sŏgi's paternal grandfather, Squire Hong, after some untoward incident in the capital, had exiled himself here to Umulkol in the Hadong countryside, to live out the rest of his days in utter seclusion from the outside world. He would take Sŏgi along when he went out to oversee the work in the fields, but otherwise he never ventured forth from his seat in the master's room. Nor was he the sort of man to dwell on such matters as his son's conduct and progress in the world. He seemed to want to make a farmer out of him.

But the son, Sŏgi's father, had different ideas. While he respected his parents' wishes and went quietly to seed here in the countryside, he wanted his own son to turn out more respectably. And so as soon as Squire Hong passed on, Sŏgi's father saw to it that Sŏgi applied himself to studying. Always awaiting Sŏgi in the master's room, where he studied, was a bundle of ash switches.

The year he turned fifteen, Sŏgi left home at his father's bidding to study reading and writing under Pak. He shared a room with Pak's son, his elder by a year, taking his meals and studying with him. Because of all the Chinese medicine the elder Pak had taken in his earlier years on account of his frail health, his hair had turned white even while his cheeks retained a rosy glow. Somehow Sŏgi found these features more intimidating than his father's rebukes or the ash switches.

The incident at the lookout shed had occurred after Sŏgi returned home from his three years of study under old Pak. During that period Suni had become a young woman inside and out.

Sŏgi recalled the times his father had caught him playing with Suni as a youngster, occasions that might result in a whipping. To fuel the boy's enthusiasm for learning, his father liked to offer Sŏgi various goodies after he had finished his studies for the day. Sŏgi had taken the chestnuts, the Chinese dates, the persimmons, and other edibles to share with Suni, and had been discovered by his father. This encounter with the offspring of such a lowly family had earned Sŏgi a lashing across the calves. But now, this was merely an insubstantial memory from his childhood.

After the encounter at the lookout shed Sŏgi had begun to regard Suni with new interest. During the Tano Festival it was Suni more than the other girls who seemed to produce the fragrant scent of sweet flag and ch'ŏn'gungi. The night of the Harvest Moon Festival she looked ever so comely, wheeling about under the moonlight in the circle dance. It was inevitable: Sŏgi waited for Suni and took her by the wrist as she was walking home. Her hand trembled ever so faintly. Sŏgi felt the warmth of her blood. He began to lead her away. For a moment she seemed poised to resist, but then she followed without a word. They arrived, breathless, at the oak grove on the ridge behind the village. The brilliant moonlight was no longer welcome. They searched for a place that was shadier still.

The previous spring, old Pak's son had visited. While he and Sŏgi were out for a stroll among the dry fields, they saw Suni approaching, a round wicker lunch basket balanced on her head. She made way for them by stepping down into a furrow. Pak's son wondered which family she came from. She wasn't strikingly beautiful, he remarked, but he liked her lovely eyes and the clean profile of her ears. She seemed to have eyes for Sŏgi—was it true? Sŏgi had better be careful: her fleshy lower lip suggested that once she had begun to think about someone she wouldn't give up easily.

Sŏgi smiled. "Since when have you been a face reader?"

Pak's son took a quick glance at him. "Well now—you're just as interested in her, aren't you?" he said with a laugh.

"Don't be silly," Sŏgi had responded. But his face had flushed and he had quickly turned away.

Around the time when the ears of barley were ripening to a golden yellow, news arrived that the elder Pak had taken ill. Sŏgi's father paid a visit and returned to report that the old man's chronic backache, dating from a bout of palsy in his youth, had flared up. Day and night the family were taking turns massaging his back.

A few days later Sŏgi was asked by his father to look in on the sick man. It would have been unthinkable to refuse. Confucian precepts required a person to treat king, master, and father as one, and Sŏgi was as indebted to old Pak for his favor as he was to his own father. So he went. He discovered that Pak's face was pale, lacking its attractive flush.

That fall, around the time the Chinese parasol tree outside Sŏgi's father's room shed its leaves, there was a further report on Pak's condition. The old man's back was no longer a problem; instead he had lost all movement from the waist down. Sŏgi called again and found that there was a complication: Pak had trouble keeping warm from the waist down. The old man's complexion had turned sallow; his white hair, once so shiny, was a dull ashen color; blotches had appeared around his hollow eyes.

A well-known doctor offered a remedy: the patient had to be warmed from the waist down, and this was best done with the body heat of a young woman. Pak's family decided to try this approach, and the woman they chose was Suni.

Suni's family had always sharecropped Pak's land, and so in return for their daughter's service they received an acre of paddy. And it was decided that when Pak died, Suni would be given land of her own so that she could live out the remainder of her life in dignity.

And so it was that on a frosty morning in November, Suni climbed into the sedan chair and left for Sŏjetkol. Two nights previous, Sŏgi had instructed her younger brother Kwidong to have her meet him in the oak grove up on the ridge. When she arrived, all she did was weep. What was to be done? Sŏgi wondered. He couldn't very well interfere if Suni was being asked to tend to a sick man.

But as the days passed, Sŏgi began to suffer. Never before had he felt compelled to see Suni's face every day, and now that they were apart he yearned for her. He could have gone to Sŏjetkol, some four miles away; he could have gone two or three times a day. But he never did, not once. For there he would encounter the forbidding gaze of Pak's son, even if he pretended to be visiting the sick father. More intimidating still was the prospect of the awkward behavior he would most certainly display in Suni's presence. In this troubled state Sŏgi awaited the day when Suni would return.

His father urged him to take the state civil-service examination in two or three years' time. Sŏgi stayed up late, his books in front of him, but all his eyes did was search for some distant place. And when he went to bed the dizzying dream would return. Sŏgi realized for the first time that he would never again encounter a woman as precious to him as Suni.

This was Sŏgi's state of mind when he witnessed Suni's return.

Suni spent the night with her family, and the next day, shortly before lunchtime, she visited Sŏgi's family.

"Well, look who's here? I heard you were back, and I thought of visiting you myself. Please, make yourself at home."

Sŏgi, studying in the master's room, detected the note of delight in his mother's voice. He had reckoned that Suni would come calling that day. But it wouldn't be seemly to leave his room just then for the person he so longed to see.

Again he heard his mother's voice: "How is the old gentleman these days?"

"About the same," came Suni's soft voice.

"I guess it's not an overnight kind of malady, is it? I don't envy you. Your face shows the strain."

Suni remained silent.

"When must you go back?"

"Tomorrow. If I'm away even a day. . . ."

"Of course. It's not like other maladies."

Sŏgi heard a rustling from the other room; it sounded as if Suni was getting up.

"I'll say good-bye now in case I don't see you tomorrow."

His mother urged her to stay for lunch, but Suni felt obligated to return home.

That evening Sŏgi cautiously sought out his mother in her room.

"Mother, could you give me some money?"

The abrupt request puzzled her.

"I'd like to take a trip—could you spare some money?"

"Where to?"

"I thought I'd stop by Grandpa and Grandma's. . . ."

Sŏgi was referring to his mother's parents, who lived in the city of Chinju.

"What do you need money for, then?"

"I thought I'd head for Seoul afterward. I need a change."

Sŏgi's mother took a closer look at her son. His oval-shaped face had always been attractive, but now his cheeks were hollow, making his eyes seem larger.

"You haven't said anything, but I've been wondering if something's wrong with you."

He was fine, Sŏgi replied.

The boy's studies must be wearing him down. Perhaps this would be a good time to let him go off on his own for a change. But the decision was not hers alone to make.

"Have you talked with your father?"

"I just told him I'd be visiting Grandpa and Grandma."

If her husband had given Sŏgi permission to visit his grandparents, then there shouldn't be a problem sending him off to Seoul on his own afterward.

"When were you planning to leave?"

"Tomorrow."

"And when will you return?"

"First I'll go and see what it's like, and then maybe I'll stay for a while."

His mother fished out the money bag she kept hidden deep in the wardrobe and gave him fifty silver pieces and fifteen brass coins to live on. And so he wouldn't have to hoard this money, she made him take some of her wedding jewelry as well.

*　　*　　*

That night Sŏgi arranged through Kwidong for Suni to meet him at the oak grove. He had been absorbed in thought the entire day. He was prepared, if Suni did not appear, to hide the next day where the road to Sŏjetkol left the village, and take things into his own hands.

The night was far along when Suni finally arrived. Her only thought was to see Sŏgi and cry her heart out.

The outstretched hand that took her wrist was strong and reassuring. Before she could burst into tears, he led her off through the oak grove. They came out where a road crested on a height of land. What Suni saw now in the light of the moon frightened her: Sŏgi was dressed for a long journey.

From the pass they could go in one of two directions: northeast past Sŏjetkol to Samch'ŏnp'o, more than twenty miles away, or southwest seven or eight miles to Hadong. The road was a rugged backcountry track that was some distance from the main summit of the Chiri Mountain massif.

Sŏgi chose the road to Hadong. The moon had a bluish tinge. Almost full, it inched its way toward the horizon. Suni was all giddy with anxiety. Now she would have to follow Sŏgi wherever; now they would be pursued.

Startled birds took wing from the woods beside the road. Almost without realizing it, Suni wasn't holding Sŏgi's hand anymore. The flapping wings of the birds and the bluish tinge to the moon no longer frightened her.

Before sunrise they were within sight of Hadong, and there they set about changing their appearance. Sŏgi loosened the pigtail that marked him as an unmarried man and made it into a topknot, then donned the traditional man's overcoat he had been carrying. Suni combed and redid her hair and tidied her clothing.

They lodged for several days at a peddlers' inn, and with the help of the proprietor were able to find a place of their own to live.

For work they decided to try fishmongering. Inexperienced as they were, they were constantly cheated, but miraculously they found at the end of each month that their losses were minimal. This was almost more than they could have hoped for.

Winter passed and the ground began to thaw. One day Sŏgi returned home to find Suni's face filled with anxiety. After a moment's hesitation she sat down beside him and said she had noticed a young man staring at her as she was doing laundry at the village well. Certain she had seen the man before, she grew apprehensive and rushed to finish the laundry before returning home. She sensed the man had followed her.

Around sunset four days later they had a visitor. Suni opened the door a crack and started. It was the same man.

Sŏgi went outside. He recognized the young man as a distant cousin of Pak's.

The young man asked Sŏgi to follow him and Sŏgi felt compelled to do so. He had secretly dreaded this day, which he had known was inevitable.

After walking some distance they arrived at a path running through a paddy. Awaiting him there were several young men from Pak's extended family, among them his son.

"I thought I'd never see you again," said Pak's son. He was dressed in mourning. "And then a few days ago my cousin had some business here and he discovered you. Once I knew where you were, I had to do something."

His tone was polite, but without the feeling of intimacy that had characterized their conversations when they were friends.

"You knew my father didn't take that woman as an ordinary concubine. He didn't use her for his pleasure; he needed her because he was sick. What you did was no different from stealing a sick man's medication."

Sŏgi's gaze was drawn once again to the son's mourning outfit. Pak must have passed away. This bothered Sŏgi, but he realized he couldn't undo what he had done.

The other young men began to clamor for revenge:

"Rip his head off!"

"Break the bastard's legs!"

"I understand how you must have felt. But for human beings there is such a thing as duty. That woman came to our house as my father's concubine, and no matter what anyone says, she was his woman. And doesn't that make her my stepmother? What you did was wrong. You disgraced your teacher's wife and your friend's mother—that's what it amounts to."

The young men showered Sŏgi with more curses.

Pak's son continued:

"I wanted to put the whole affair behind me and never see you again. That way I could prevent rumors from spreading and avoid soiling our families' reputations. But when I found you were here, my duty as a son forced me to act. I think you can understand."

The young men swarmed closer and heaped more abuse on Sŏgi.

"Off with his topknot!"

"Cut off his nose!"

Sŏgi tried to brace himself for what would happen next. Following Pak's cousin to the paddy, Sŏgi had resigned himself to the prospect of physical attack. But he had never anticipated the horror of having his nose cut off. He had to get away. But the next moment he realized it would be useless. These vengeful young men would spare no effort to track him down, and when they found him, Suni would suffer as well.

Before Sŏgi could think of an alternative, Pak's son spoke again:

"Cutting off your topknot accomplishes nothing—it would only grow back. And a man has only one nose, so that won't do either. Instead I'm going to cut off one of your ears. From the time you were a boy, my father tried to drive home to you the Confucian moral precepts, but apparently they didn't sink in. Since your ears seem to serve no useful purpose, I'll take one of them off."

So saying, Pak's son produced a knife from his waistband.

Sŏgi recoiled, but the young men closed in and held him fast. Resistance would just make things worse. Better to let them have their satisfaction. He closed his eyes.

Off came Sŏgi's right ear. Pak's son tossed it into the paddy.

"This is the end. There's no reason for you to see me, and I'm of no mind to see you ever again. One last thing: you're a burden to me, staying in this area. I want you out of here. Go someplace where I don't have to hear about you anymore."

Sǒgi had already decided he could stay no longer in Hadong.

Sǒgi spent a sleepless night. Quite apart from the burning pain where his ear had been, the question of where he and Suni would go next kept him awake. Around daybreak he finally dropped off to sleep, but he was soon awakened by the sound of a door opening and shutting. Suni, who should have been beside him, was gone. But it was too early for her to have been preparing breakfast.

Sǒgi opened the small door that led down to the kitchen. Suni's white form drifted into view in a dark corner.

Sǒgi hurried down in time to see a porcelain bowl fall from Suni's hand. He heard it shatter.

"What are you doing?"

Suni heaved a great shudder, unable to answer.

Sǒgi stooped and located a piece of the bowl. It was coated with a sleek liquid, which he rubbed between thumb and fingertips—lye.

"You little fool!" He angrily shoved Suni away from the shattered bowl. "What the hell are you doing?"

Suni collapsed in a heap. Her shuddering seemed to concentrate in her back, which began to heave rhythmically as she broke into tears.

"It's all because of me," she sobbed. "Why don't you go back home today?"

"Don't be silly! If you don't like this life we're living, then you should go someplace where you'll be comfortable."

All Suni could do was cry.

"What are you crying for? Don't you like that idea? If we sell everything we have we could raise fifty *nyang*—that's enough for you to go and live wherever you want."

Suni quickly crawled to Sǒgi and embraced his legs. "No, I'm not going anywhere." She rubbed her tear-streaked face against his knees.

From Hadong Sǒgi and Suni moved to Yangjitkol, a cozy little village a few miles southwest of the town of Sach'ǒn. There they bought an acre of paddy and an ox.

Nearby lived a poor farmer whom everyone called Went-and-Did-It-Again for his numerous offspring. Sŏgi allowed him to use the ox for his own paddy in return for plowing theirs and doing manual labor for them.

Naturally Went-and-Did-It-Again was surprised to see that Sŏgi was missing an ear. But then he noticed Sŏgi's hands.

"Will you look at those nice white hands—I'll bet they've never done a day of farmer's work!" he said, his mouth dropping open in amazement to reveal a set of longish teeth.

Automatically Sŏgi stuck his hands inside his waistband.

When it came to putting in a day's work, Suni held her own. And she was always welcome when the neighboring farmers needed temporary help. But Sŏgi stayed at home, concentrating on their own paddy. An able-bodied boy could have outworked him. At weeding time Sŏgi could initially do half a row to everyone else's full row, but later in the day he could barely finish that half row while others did three or four rows. The work was too taxing, and Sŏgi began to moan in his sleep.

Suni couldn't bear to see him like this.

"Why don't you stay home and look after the ox or something?"

Sŏgi would hear nothing of it.

"What! Do you think I'm a boy? That's a job for children and old men."

Next it was heat prostration, which kept Sŏgi in bed several days with the flu. Afterward Sŏgi noticed his sunburned skin flaking off.

"Goodness," he said as he worked at the skin peeling from his shoulders, "I'm like a little boy. Well, a crab has to molt in order to grow. Maybe it's the same with me."

Suni didn't have the heart to laugh at this jest.

By the time they finished threshing the grain from the autumn harvest, Sŏgi's pale forehead had taken on a coppery hue and his soft palms had callused.

Sŏgi and Went-and-Did-It-Again loaded the ox with grain and set out for the market in Sach'ŏn.

The other man noticed Sŏgi's roughened hands. "They aren't nice and soft anymore. Too bad. They were so white, just like powder."

But Sŏgi felt thankful that he didn't have to hide them anymore.

Went-and-Did-It-Again produced a short pipe from the back of his waistband, filled it with leaf tobacco, and lit up.

"A farmer's hands are like the hooves on that old ox. When we get real busy, the nails wear down and don't have time to grow. I think we ought to have some kind of covering for our hands, like the shoes on that old fellow."

Sŏgi produced his own pipe. He had started smoking not long before. But he still handled the pipe clumsily, the strong leaf tobacco made him cough, and he couldn't inhale the way other men did.

"You know, I just can't figure you as a farmer. Whatever made you want to do it?" Went-and-Did-It-Again had long been wondering about this.

"Can you really draw a line between people who are cut out to farm and people who aren't?"

"Sure, why not? Seems to me some folks are born to be farmers." Went-and-Did-It-Again inhaled deeply on his pipe.

"Well, we've been farmers since my grandfather's day," Sŏgi said as he watched the smoke exhaled by the other man.

In a certain sense Sŏgi believed this. He remembered his grandfather acting just like a real farmer as he went about supervising the farm work with Sŏgi in tow.

And after three years of farming, Sŏgi looked and acted like a farmer.

It was winter—a time of respite from the busy farm work. One evening after dinner had been cleared, Sŏgi said to Suni, "Look at my fingernails. When I see them growing like this, it gives me the itch to work."

By now, Suni could smile at the sight of Sŏgi's toughened hands. And sometimes he unwittingly brought her to laughter. It had all started one day when Suni happened to watch him handling his pipe. Producing the pipe from the back of his waistband, filling it with leaf tobacco, lighting it with the flint—in each of these actions he was the very image of Went-and-Did-It-Again. Sensing the reason for her laughter, Sŏgi had turned to Suni and showed off by puffing away more deeply. Such was the life they had settled into as the years slipped past.

In their fourth spring of farming, a baby boy was born to them.

That autumn, as in previous years, Sŏgi loaded the ox with grain and set out for the Sach'ŏn market with Went-and-Did-It-Again.

Sŏgi had negotiated a price for his grain and was about to leave when a man approached him and bowed deeply. Sŏgi recognized the man as an elderly servant of his parents.

"Young master. . . . Goodness, what's happened to you?"

The man tearfully related to Sŏgi that he had come looking for him at Sach'ŏn the previous market day, five days earlier, after learning that a man resembling Sŏgi had been seen there. He then confessed he hadn't recognized him at first—the young master had changed so much! Finally he explained the purpose of his visit: Madam was critically ill; they should leave for home at once.

Sŏgi entrusted Went-and-Did-It-Again with the ox and set out immediately with the servant.

Along the way Sŏgi asked when his mother had fallen ill. It was not so long ago, he was told, but for two or three years prior to that she hadn't been eating properly. It occurred to Sŏgi that he might have been the cause of her illness. But what could he have done differently?

They made the trip quickly, arriving just before dusk at the hill in front of the village.

Here the servant asked Sŏgi to wait, saying he would return shortly. With no further explanation he disappeared down the hill.

Sŏgi began to understand. It probably wasn't his father but his mother who had sent for him. And now the servant would be telling Sŏgi's mother that her son had arrived, and would await further instructions.

Sŏgi noticed that his family's chimney was the only one producing smoke; the other families must have finished supper. Even from that distance he could see figures moving between the women's quarters and the master's quarters. It appeared that his mother's illness was indeed critical.

In the evening shadows Sŏgi could see ripe red persimmons among the bare branches of the Chinese parasol in front of the gate to the master's quarters. He recalled from his youth the familiar sound of his grandfather coughing as he tapped the ashes from the bowl of his long pipe—and the voice of his mother calling him too softly for others to hear.

There had been an evening—was it spring? autumn? He remembered only that the mornings and evenings had been chilly then. Once again he had been whipped by his father for playing with Suni. He went behind the chimney in back of the house to cry. He had no idea how long he remained huddled there. He felt as if he were melting in the heat from the chimney and began to nod off. Then he felt his nose tingle in the chill air and woke to realize that the fire had been lit for supper. He rose and discovered something flickering in front of him. A tiny spider was descending on the thread of a web it was weaving. And he heard his mother call him softly from the front yard. Sŏgi gazed at the flickering spider web, not answering. It felt good just to stand there listening to his mother's voice.

All he could think of now was that his mother was calling him from her sickbed. He shouldn't be waiting here. He kept rising only to squat down again, paralyzed by anxiety.

The servant returned, his face streaked with tears.

"We're too late. Madam has . . ."

"Has what?"

"Madam passed on early this afternoon."

It had all happened so quickly. Sŏgi was too stunned to cry.

The servant for his part began weeping again.

"I asked the master if you could—"

"I know, I know!"

Sŏgi realized his father was loath to allow the sinful son to see his departed mother. It was just as well, he thought. After all, he hadn't returned to see her while she was alive.

"Since you've come all this way, shouldn't you get a good night's sleep here?"

"I don't think that's necessary." Sŏgi turned and set off. The servant followed. "You can go back now," said Sŏgi. And then something occurred to him. "How is Suni's family?"

"They're all right. They returned the land they received from the senior Pak, and now that Kwidong can do a man's work he's taking care of the farming."

The servant continued to follow.

Sŏgi stopped. "You're holding me up—I want you to go back."

The man reluctantly stopped. "It's not easy for me to say this," he said hesitantly, "but the master asked me to tell you—he doesn't want you in the Sach'ŏn area any longer."

"I understand," said Sŏgi, his voice trembling.

"I just don't know what to think about all of this."

"Don't worry. Now off with you."

Finally Sŏgi was alone on the darkening mountain road. His legs were unsteady and he plopped down, feeling as if the grief he had suppressed was about to explode. But the tears never came.

Sŏgi and Suni decided to move to the foothills of Chiri Mountain. They loaded their ox with seed, staples, and farm tools and departed.

Went-and-Did-It-Again was at a loss. Four years earlier this fellow had drifted in, the most unlikely looking farmer you could imagine, and now he was disappearing elsewhere just as winter was approaching and, what was more, leaving him all his paddy land. How to explain it?

Sŏgi would tell no one where they were going, not even this man to whom he had drawn close over the past four years.

The day Sŏgi and Suni arrived at Chiri Mountain they began felling trees, and eventually they were able to build a hut. Nearby they found a rocky slope, an area suitable for fire-field farming, and burned it. After clearing the stumps and rocks, they planted barley. In all of this they put to use their four years of farming experience.

Night and day they saw the ridges of Chiri Mountain, heard the mountain freshets, the wind, and the calls of bird and beast. And sometimes when they least expected it they would hear the patter of centipedes as long as your hand is wide, crawling along the walls of their hut.

They picked mushrooms and gathered acorns. There was the occasional visitor foraging for medicinal herbs, and they were all too happy to put aside their work and keep company with this person for the rest of the day.

Winter arrived and the herb pickers stopped coming. During the long, long nights the wind and the cries of the animals sounded all the more fierce.

The following spring, when the nights were still frosty, they sowed the unplanted areas of the rocky slope with cold-resistant crops such as potatoes, corn, and millet.

The supplies they had brought with them and the acorns gathered the previous fall sustained them until they harvested the barley, which they had husbanded with care. To supplement these foods there were pine trees whose edible inner bark they could peel, and an abundant supply of mountain greens such as bracken fern, bellflower root, aralia shoots, *tŏdŏk*, and aster shoots.

They managed to obtain fabric for clothing and condiments for their food. Before the arrival of the herb pickers early in the spring they picked their own herbs, then bartered them for such commodities as salt and cotton cloth.

The first ripe ears of barley were small, but when they clipped them and rubbed away the husks, they saw that the kernels had filled out nicely.

They sat down to their first meal of cooked barley. Before they ate, Sŏgi offered a spoonful to their little one, who was old enough now to be reaching for food.

"We'll have to plant a lot more barley this fall."

"Where will we ever find the time and the energy?"

"If we put our minds to it, why not? That little fellow comes first. We'll just have to work more land."

Sŏgi looked down at the baby trying to mash the barley in its mouth. A smile lingered on his face for the first time in a long while.

"I suppose you're right," said Suni. With a beaming smile, she pretended to give their son a playful pinch on the cheek.

The potatoes, corn, and millet were small as well, but they were plentiful enough.

And now it was Suni saying, "Next year we'll have to plant more corn and potatoes."

One day Sŏgi went far up one of the valleys and returned with his narrow-mouthed basket full of wild grapes.

"Look at the little bugger's eyes—just like these grapes," Sŏgi said as the three of them ate. He held one of the grapes next to the baby's eye for comparison. "What do you think?"

"His eyes look like those grapes? Darling, really! It's the grapes that resemble his eyes."

They both laughed.

And so the little one came to be called Grape Eyes.

The sound of the wind and the animals' cries no longer bothered them. Nor did the long centipedes seem as frightening.

That fall they burned a different patch on which to grow more barley. And the following spring they planted even more potatoes, corn, and millet.

Summer arrived and floss appeared on the ears of corn. One day around sunset Sŏgi was resting in the hut while Suni gathered water at the spring below. Suddenly, a scream from Suni rent the air. Sŏgi ran outside barefoot. Suni was beside the spring, clutching silently at the air in the direction of a large wolf as it disappeared into a thicket some distance away. In its mouth was the baby. With a sickening feeling, Sŏgi grabbed an ax and set off after the animal.

Sŏgi could see the wolf loping away in the distance, but he couldn't gain on it. He shouted and shouted, his cries bringing echoes from all over the mountain. The wolf's only reaction was to look back; it gave no indication of releasing its prey.

Time ceased to exist for Sŏgi. It was dark before he knew it, and he lost sight of the wolf. As he thrashed through the woods, his fiery gaze met the gleaming eyes of animals. Sŏgi charged at those eyes, flailed at them with his ax. But instead of the wolf his ax found a tree trunk or glanced off a rock with a shower of sparks.

And then there there were no more gleaming eyes to be seen. The short summer night had given way to dawn.

Face, arms, shins, the soles of his feet—Sŏgi was everywhere sweaty and bloody. He returned to find Suni in a state of shock, still huddled beside the spring.

Suni never returned to that spring. The sound of the wind, which had become a regular presence in their lives, now threw her into a fright. When the wolves howled she blocked her ears—she said it was their baby crying—and quivered like the leaves of an aspen. Sǒgi would take the ax and run off into the woods like a man distracted.

The two of them seemed suddenly to have aged. The wrinkles in their faces deepened; flecks of white appeared in their hair.

They could no longer bear to stay in the hills, so they left for the coast.

Along the way, at Tansǒnggol, they sold the ox.

"Beast looks ready for the glue factory," said the broker. He opened the animal's mouth. "Only eight years old, and it's a bag of bones!"

In truth, the animal, like its master, was suddenly old and bony.

They agreed to the broker's price and continued on to Samch'ǒnp'o. There they boarded a ferry for T'ongyǒng.

They had no special reason for choosing T'ongyǒng—except that Sǒgi recalled how much Suni liked the taste of abalone, scabbard fish, and such when they had lived in Hadong. So why not give coastal life another try? For a seaside town Samch'ǒnp'o would have sufficed, but they wanted to go farther so as to avoid, as much as possible, attracting the attention of anyone they might know.

The ferry to T'ongyǒng was a sailing vessel of modest size. There were only half a dozen other passengers.

The ferry put out to sea and the boatman, after trimming the sail, began striking up conversations with the passengers.

"Where you from, uncle?" he asked Sǒgi in an amiable tone.

The "uncle" took Sǒgi by surprise. The boatman seemed no more than thirty, and therefore close to Sǒgi in age.

"Up in the hills," he answered reluctantly.

"And you're on the move, eh? You must have had a rough go of it there," the boatman said, inspecting Sǒgi, who was all too conscious of his missing ear and his generally wretched appearance. "You have some connection in T'ongyǒng?"

Sǒgi stared at the water ahead, his silence telling the boatman that there was no one there to welcome him and Suni.

"No matter what they say, for a farmer, farming is the thing. From the time I was a boy my father used to tell me, 'Son, pine-eating caterpillars don't eat oak leaves, and sea gulls can't live on the mainland.'

And that's why he told me not to worry as long as I took good care of this here boat and made a living from it."

The ferry arrived, and Sŏgi and Suni found lodging near the dock in a locality called Haep'yŏng.

Sŏgi brought home the seafoods that Suni enjoyed so much, but mostly the two of them kept to themselves.

When they had exhausted most of their money, Sŏgi took to the shore and helped with hauling in the communal fishing nets. In return he received a share of the catch.

Eventually most of their jewelry was sold. Finally Sŏgi was at his wits' end and decided to ship out on a fishing boat.

The day before he left, Suni sold the sole remaining item of jewelry Sŏgi's mother had given him—a silver ring. With the proceeds she bought Sŏgi a pipe and tobacco. For lack of tobacco, Sŏgi had given up smoking during their time in the hills.

The day that the boat was scheduled to return came and went. Two more days passed and still the boat did not appear. This was very strange, for there had been no sign of rough seas.

The families of the fishermen kept a daily vigil at the dock, but Suni remained long after the others had left, watching Mirŭk Island, across from the dock. Its outline seemed to grow ever more somber.

On the third day after the boat's scheduled return one of the crewmen appeared. The boat had run into thick fog and broken up on a reef, the young man reported. By a stroke of luck he had grabbed one of the timbers and a passing boat had rescued him.

The wails of family members enveloped the dock. But no tears flowed from Suni's eyes.

The following day the family members went out to sea with the young fisherman. They had given up on finding survivors but held out hopes of retrieving the bodies. Suni joined the others. In the course of those several days her hair had turned noticeably grayer.

They located the reef but found no trace of the boat, nor the bodies.

There was nothing to do but return. But as the boat turned back toward land there was a splash. Suni had jumped overboard. Her body was never recovered.

Something occurred to the young fisherman: "I couldn't figure out what made her husband tick, either. He kept saying his tobacco tasted different than it did on shore—asked how long it took for tobacco to taste the way it ought to when you shipped out. And he kept saying he wanted a couple of live cod to take home."

To the left of the path that ascends Mirŭk Island, across from Haep'yŏng Dock in T'ongyŏng, there sits a small, round, moss-covered gravestone that reads, IN MEMORY OF THE VIRTUOUS WIFE OF HAEP'YŎNG. The simple story of that woman and her husband can be heard even today from the people of T'ongyŏng: many years ago, a man and a woman drifted into town and settled near Haep'yŏng Dock. They kept to themselves, and no one seemed to know their family names or their ages. They had an unusually harmonious relationship. And then one day the husband, to provide for them, went out to sea on a fishing boat and the vessel broke up. Learning of this, the wife located the place where her husband had been lost and threw herself into the water. The following day a passing boat discovered two bodies floating on the surface. The corpse of the wife was embracing that of the husband.

November 1955

From the water, practically all you can see of the island called Cheju is a huge mountain. Passengers from the mainland first see it as a faint purple blotch on the horizon. "Look—Cheju!" they exclaim. In truth, Cheju appears less like an island than a large mountain with two linked summits, the higher one to the right. For Cheju is a volcanic island formed by this mountain—Halla Mountain.

Not surprisingly, then, most of the island's fishing villages and farming hamlets are right at the shore, clinging to the foot of the mountain. Only the town of Cheju gives the impression of being on flat land removed from Halla's base. Look closer, though, and you'll see that this side of the island is where Halla slopes most gently. Directly behind the town is a hill and then a notch, another hill and notch, forming a fluted ridge all the way to the base of Halla's main summit.

On a normal day the main summit is wreathed in clouds or mist. On a mountain so large and lofty you might think that water flows down its creases. But this is not the case with Halla, so fresh water is always scarce on Cheju. You can often see children going about with water jars in a bamboo basket strapped to their back. If they come across water, all they have to do is scoop it into the jars.

Sŏgwip'o is the sole exception. Like Hallim, Mosŭlp'o, and the other seaside villages and hamlets, it clings to Halla's lower slopes. But because it's closer to the mountain itself, the water you wouldn't find elsewhere is abundant. Descending in clear, clean braids from the mountain gorges, it trickles and rustles around the back corners of houses and alongside the courtyards. Ultimately it collects at a rock wall to the rear of the village, providing a place for the men to take sponge baths, and then, at a low outcrop facing the sea, it forms a small waterfall that produces a fine spray.

It was in the summer of 1951 that Chuni and his mother moved from the town of Cheju to Sŏgwip'o. Chuni had always been a fussy eater. His mother wondered if this was why his neck was white as a girl's even though he was already past twenty. In addition, his skin was sensitive to water. Previously they had lived in Seoul, and when the Northerners retook the city in January of that year, he and his mother were told it was easiest for refugees to leave by boat. But the vessel they boarded at Inch'ŏn had moored at Cheju rather than their expected destination of Pusan. And in Cheju the first thing that bothered Chuni was the water. Drinking it had caused him several times to break out in a rash, and to get rid of it he had to rub his flesh raw with rock salt. His mother interrupted her daily chores to find sources of water recommended by the villagers, but even then she always boiled it before allowing Chuni to drink. For a good six months they had lingered in the town of Cheju, awaiting word from Chuni's uncle, who had left Seoul before them by truck. Their plan was to return to the mainland as soon as they heard from him. But in spite of all their inquiries to other refugees, they were unable to learn his whereabouts. They couldn't set out blindly for the mainland in search of him, so in the meantime they decided to move to Sŏgwip'o in the hope that a change of water would be good for Chuni. Chuni's mother had also heard that Cheju had more than its share of hunchbacks and cripples because the island's water lacked sufficient iron, and that's what ultimately convinced her to make the move. The water in Sŏgwip'o was better, several people had told them. Before moving, she sold those belongings of hers that would fetch a good price.

The day Chuni and his mother arrived in Sŏgwip'o, it was brisk and clearing after several days of heavy rain. Their bus passed villages surrounded by stone walls two or three times a man's height, constructed during the Cheju Rebellion a few years earlier, and Chuni recalled from a recent report that guerrillas had been sighted in a hamlet in eastern Cheju. It was almost midday when the bus reached Sŏgwip'o. Chuni was confused. Was this sleepy town the place they had heard about? The bustle of Mosŭlp'o, visible earlier through the bus window, was nowhere in evidence. Nor was there an imposing stone wall surrounding the town. But the next moment it occurred to Chuni that here was a place where he could get a good rest before he and his mother moved on. He felt even more certain of this when he looked down to see a rivulet passing right in front of his feet. The sight refreshed him as nothing else had for a long while.

The water was clear and clean—not muddy—in spite of all the rain. Chuni removed his socks, dipped his feet in the water, and gazed out to where small breakers were cresting in the sea. The ocean was a deeper, clearer blue than any he had ever seen. Looking inland, he saw Halla Mountain. Clouds streamed from its summit, making the northwest sky overcast, while above Sŏgwip'o, to the southeast, the azure sky was like a lake.

Chuni spent most of his time outdoors, wearing a straw hat for protection against the sun.

At the southern edge of town sits a one-story building with white plaster walls and a tin roof. There, buttons are made from the shells of clams, conch, and abalone gathered from the nearby seashore. The shells of Sŏgwip'o are supposed to have the finest texture of any shells on the island. Next to this small factory is a heap of shell fragments discarded during manufacturing. For some reason the factory wasn't operating, and Chuni never saw any activity inside. The building was hedged with sweet oleander, whose pale pink blossoms were at their peak.

If you walk around to the other side of the factory you come upon a small breakwater. Directly before it is Firewood Island, a small piece of land so close you can almost reach out and touch it. Trees ring the islet, which is otherwise flat. Just beyond it is even tinier Mosquito Island, a graceful curve between ocean and sky, and the southernmost part of Sŏgwip'o. Unlike its sister, Mosquito Island is crowned with a few trees, and rock beds form its circumference. The passage between the two islets is narrow, the current swift. Even the *haenyŏ*, or diving women—called *chamnyŏ* by the people of Cheju— dare not venture too close.

If you turn back from the end of the breakwater and follow the pumice-covered shore, another smallish island—Grove Island—comes into sight across the water. It might be about the size of Firewood Island. And like Mosquito Island, it is topped with trees and rocky along the shore. Grove Island is known for its medicinal herbs and for a variety of bellflower root with white flowers. For Sŏgwip'o's diving women, the most popular spot for foraging is off this island.

In May, when it's time to pick seaweed, they converge there from every direction. You can see groups of them—all belonging to the divers' guild—not only from Sŏgwip'o but also from Pomok, the nearest village, and the villages of Tonghong, some two and a half miles away, and Pŏphwan, five miles distant—all gathering in the waters about the island.

Chuni and his mother had arrived in Sŏgwip'o at a time when the local people were especially busy with farm work, so the diving women had yet to appear in full force. Still, Chuni could see half a dozen of them every day diving and surfacing in the waters near Grove Island. He heard their distinctive whistling, noticed the way they dove, extending their legs straight up in the air like a boat's mast. Sitting on the shore, he watched the women dive and tried to guess where they would surface. But it was generally a different place where they shot up, whistling. Next he'd try to guess how long they would stay underwater. Like the divers, he held his breath, but in some cases he would have to take in air three times before the diver surfaced.

Next, Chuni would visit the small waterfall. If it got too hot for comfort, he went behind the town to the place where the men took sponge baths. They called this kind of bathing *chaguri*, but Chuni had no idea where this word had come from. Ever since arriving on Cheju, in fact, he had heard quite a few words for the first time. The verb endings were sharp and harsh, compared with those of the standard dialect, but not enough so to prevent him from guessing the meaning of the words. Other words, though, were incomprehensible at first. For *twaeji*, "pig," they used the word *tosaegi*; *tak*, the standard word for "chicken," became *tok*; *talgyal*, "egg," was *toksaegi* (they even had a different word for "chicks"—*ppingari* instead of *pyŏng'ari*); *manŭl*, "garlic," was *k'oktaesani*; *muu*, "radish," was *nomppi*; *sŏngnyang*, "match," was *kwak*; *mŏnji*, "dust," was *kudŭm*; *ch'ŏnyŏ*, "young woman," was *pibari*; *noch'ŏnyŏ*, "old maid," was *chaksan pibari*; and so on. As for the place where the men took sponge baths, he heard it referred to as the *chaguri* bath and assumed it was a traditional indoor public bath—until he found that it was out-of-doors.

The bathing area itself is a pool some five or six yards in diameter. The near side is bounded by dark, round rocks that have been rolled into place any old way, and the bottom of the pool is covered with pebbles. The deep part of the pool, such as it is, doesn't reach an adult's navel. Still, the place has a couple of unique features that make it particularly appropriate as a summer bathing area. The pool is clear and chilly, and the water that pours over the rock wall that screens it in back is always clear and clean—and much colder than the water in the pool. The first time Chuni ventured under this cascade, he shot out of the pool at once, shuddering all over. The goose bumps and the chattering of his teeth lingered for some time. He had returned after that, had gritted his teeth and waded in, but had never been able to last under the cascade to a count of ten.

Finally the day came when Chuni, after splashing water on his face and dipping himself into the pool as he usually did, counted all the way to thirteen beneath the cascade. Then he retired to the rounded rocks on the near side of the pool to bask in the sun. He had been sunbathing there nearly a week, but his skin had scarcely any color to show for it. He just didn't seem to tan easily. His rounded shoulders and his back were tinged with pink, but the skin under his arms and on the inside of his thighs remained pale, almost translucent.

In Sŏgwip'o Chuni and his mother rented a house from a middle-aged couple and their grandson. Their son had been killed during the Cheju Rebellion after being drafted into the Volunteer Army. According to the woman next door, the daughter-in-law had then given birth, but had abandoned the boy soon after his first birthday, before she had even weaned him. A rumor circulated that she was sharing the bed of a man in Sŏngsanp'o, but the grandparents made no effort to find her and raised the boy themselves.

They were a taciturn couple who survived by working a patch of land and raising a pig and a dozen chickens. On market day the wife, following Cheju custom, took the eggs to town in a box-shaped wicker basket and sold them. It appeared that she did most of the farm work as well. This included grinding up clam shells to feed the chickens and cutting grass for the pig. The master's sole duty, it seemed, was to look after the grandson. When it was naptime he took the little fellow outside, laid him in a basket in the shade of the

bead tree, and rocked him to sleep. To Chuni the grandfather's rock-
ing seemed forceful enough to wake a sleeping baby, but instead it
put the boy right to sleep.

The master had time to spare and he sometimes took Chuni fishing, not so much to add food to the table as to keep himself occupied.
When the tide went out they lifted up rocks on the shore, and out
came the lugworms. These creatures, thinner but firmer than earthworms, were bottled together with a sprinkling of salt to kill them,
then used for bait. Grove Island was where they liked best to fish.
They rented a boat, found a spot on the island, and threw in their
lines. You could forgive Chuni since he had never fished before,
but the master himself was quite clumsy, and so their catch never
amounted to more than a few mackerel and *sulmaengi*. From time to
time, though, Chuni had another diversion: he could watch the diving women. The distinctive whistle and the surface dive with legs
straight up, which he usually saw from a distance, were now happen-
ing right in front of him.

One day, after their usual meager catch, Chuni and the master
had taken a nap on the crest of the islet in a grassy area adorned with
white balloon flowers, then set out for home. Along the way they
noticed someone behind them. They turned to see one of the diving
women, her shoulders still wet, a kind of shawl draped over her torso.
In her net bag were abalone and conch, which she would eventually
sell. Chuni suspected she was aware that he always came home from
fishing with little to show for his efforts. She must have decided he
might like to buy some of her catch to make up for it. The abalone
and conch were certainly large enough, and they looked appetizing.
Chuni had always preferred seafood to meat, and since arriving at
Cheju he had insisted that his mother not buy meat, especially pork.
For the pigpens on the island were located below the privies. All you
had to do was approach a privy and the pigs would roll their eyes and
poke their snouts toward the hole in anticipation of a meal. More
than once this prospect had sent Chuni fleeing from the toilets, his
business unfinished. He made up his mind that pork would never
touch his lips again as long as he lived. Fortunately, the fish to be had
on the island were of good quality. And the fish of Sŏgwip'o, because

of its clear water, had a tender, delicate appearance and a fresh taste. Chuni that day invited the young diving woman to follow him home, and there he bought several abalone and conch.

Chuni and his mother could now buy fish without stepping outside their door. The young diving woman brought them what she had caught and they bought whatever they needed. Sometimes she visited daily; other times, perhaps when she caught little, she missed a day or two. Besides abalone and conch, she brought a fish called *pukpari* that looked like a perch but had a slightly larger mouth and was mottled with reddish orange. These were fish you speared, she explained. There was another fish they speared—the *tagŭmbari*. It also resembled a perch, but its mouth was even larger than the *pukpari*'s. Its spines were light blue, its belly silvery white. These two fish, even after being speared, would continue to flop on the cutting board.

Almost without realizing it Chuni and his mother began referring to their source of seafood simply as the *pibari*, rather than using the standard words for a young, unmarried woman or a diving woman. They couldn't tell from looking at her just how old she was, but they had no doubt she was unmarried, and she couldn't have been much more than twenty. One day she did something different: after selling Chuni and his mother a *tagŭmbari*, she had turned to leave when suddenly she produced a good-sized abalone and placed it in Chuni's hand. Chuni accepted it on the spur of the moment, but then he wondered whether it was proper to have done so. On the other hand, he and his mother had bought a fair amount of seafood from her, and perhaps this was her way of thanking them. But in that case it would have been more appropriate to give the abalone to his mother when she paid for the *tagŭmbari*. Chuni looked with new interest at the *pibari* as she walked away. Her firm body and the copper sheen of her skin appeared in a new light. Chuni suddenly realized his face felt warm.

The following day Chuni followed the master of the house back out to Grove Island. He set the line, but for a long time there was no action. Suddenly the bobber was pulled underwater. Chuni was looking elsewhere at the time, and the master had to alert him. The instant Chuni took hold of his rod, he could tell he had hooked something big. The rod bent every which way. The master rushed to Chuni's side and helped him steady the rod, and they carefully reeled in the line. And then Chuni found himself sitting on the ground in a state of shock, the rod tossed aside. For attached to the line was a human head. The head, he now saw, belonged not to a corpse but to a living person. The head emerged from the water, then the body, coming up the small bank along the shore. It was a diving woman, and none other than the *pibari*. The hook was caught in her mouth and blood seeped between her lips. Ignoring the master, she looked at Chuni, her black eyes set between equally black eyelashes glaring at him. They weren't sleepy eyes, yet they didn't sparkle. She removed the hook from her mouth, and then a faint smile formed on her bloody lips. Finally she turned and dove back into the water, her legs forming a graceful mast before disappearing beneath the surface. Chuni was speechless. He couldn't help cowering at that scolding look she had given him. But when he saw her turn away with the faint smile he realized it had been no accident. She had taken the hook in her mouth as a joke. He felt his face flush. He looked out toward the water and already the *pibari* had emerged near a group of diving women off in the distance. The sound of her whistling carried across the water to him.

The master of the house, scowling at the brazenness of the *pibari*, gathered his fishing gear. Chuni did likewise. But for some reason he couldn't think completely ill of her behavior. For the drenched, sparsely clothed young woman with the hook in her mouth who had appeared before him and then returned to the water reminded him of a huge fish. And even though that fish had jumped back into the water, Chuni was left not with the disappointment of losing a fish but with the thrill of reeling in one just hooked.

On their way home Chuni heard a story that shocked him. Perhaps because his landlord had found the *pibari*'s behavior so intolerable, this man of few words launched into the tale as soon as they set off in their boat for Sŏgwip'o. The *pibari*, he told Chuni, had killed her own brother. Her family had always lived in Pŏlmong, a village a mile or so east of Sŏgwip'o. During the Cheju Rebellion her brother had gone up into the high country with the partisans. The authorities decided to liquidate them. About that time, the brother's wife was found dead at the foot of Halla Mountain, killed by an unknown hand. She was survived by her two young children. On a subsequent night, when the liquidation campaign was about over—the authorities estimating that some thirty partisans remained in the high country—the *píbarí*'s brother had appeared at their house. And that was when she had killed him, shooting him with his own rifle as he emerged from the outhouse. It was the landlord's theory that she had been outraged at the death of her sister-in-law and the helpless situation of the little ones, and blamed him for the plight of their family. Or perhaps the brother had come down for plunder and the *píbarí* had acted out of fear of what might happen to the family as a result. The landlord added one more thing: for a while, people had praised her for what she had done, but inwardly they found it repulsive and they avoided her.

Chuni found the story plausible. It would explain why the landlord and his wife never greeted the *píbarí* in spite of her frequent appearances at their house, and why the landlord, so mild of temperament, had been intolerant of her maneuver with the fishhook. Chuni suddenly found himself visualizing a *pukparí* or *tagŭmbarí* flopping about, spear wound and all. He couldn't rid his mind of this image.

Late one afternoon Chuni was on his way home from a dip at the *chagurí* baths when he encountered the *píbarí*. It seemed too early for her to be returning home. She remained where she was, looking expectantly in his direction, and Chuni realized that she was waiting for him. She wore traditional unlined cotton summer clothing—pants that ended at the knee and a short-sleeved jacket. In one hand she held the gourd float and net bag she used when diving. Her eyes were the same as always—not sleepy, but lacking a sparkle. He had to say something to her, he told himself. But then it occurred to him that as long as she was waiting for him she should speak first, and then he could respond. And so he walked on by, avoiding her gaze. She didn't move aside for him, nor did she say anything. He quickened his pace, and as he did so he wondered if perhaps he had become afraid of the *pibari* since hearing the landlord's story. But there was part of him that denied this.

At home Chuni's mother placed before him some sliced raw abalone.

"The *pibari* was here—she seemed to be looking for you. Too bad you were gone—she might have given you something extra," she said with a smile. She couldn't hide her delight at the improvement in his health since they had arrived in Sŏgwip'o.

Chuni told himself to ignore his mother's jesting. Still, why had he behaved like such a dolt in the *pibari*'s presence just now? His face burned.

It was a few days later. The climate on Cheju is such that even at the peak of the summer heat, refreshing offshore breezes come up as the sun begins to set, and in the morning the cool air creeps over you just like in autumn on the mainland. But on this particular day the heat persisted into late afternoon, and Chuni went to the *chaguri* bathing area. It so happened that most of the regulars had left, and all he could hear was the water pouring over the rock wall. Soon the townspeople would finish their supper, and when dusk began to fall, the womenfolk would occupy the bathing area. As he always did, Chuni entered the pool, washed his face, dipped himself in the water to remove the sweat, and then stood beneath the rock wall. Again today, he had to retreat not long after the count of ten. He was not quite out of the pool when someone else jumped in; he looked more closely, and saw it was the *pibari*. Startled, he squatted in the water to cover his nether parts, then waddled out. Without bothering to soak first, the *pibari* went straight to the rock wall and stood under the water. Chuni seized the moment to get up on the bank and throw on his clothes. After buttoning his short-sleeved shirt, he glanced back at the pool. The *pibari* was still standing under the waterfall, modestly covering her groin and chest. Almost by reflex, Chuni started counting. When he reached twenty, a shiver began to creep over him and he gave up. He started back home along a side path threading among the rocks, but before very long the *pibari* was beside him, wringing out her sopping wet hair. Wouldn't Chuni like to see some orange trees? she asked

without preliminaries. There were quite a few of them in her village. Chuni knew the island was well known for its orange trees,
but he hadn't yet seen them, either in the town of Cheju or in
Sögwip'o. Even so, he didn't immediately respond to this frank
proposal but looked off instead toward the western sky. She would
walk him home if it were dark, she added. Without waiting for an
answer, she started off.

Like the other seaside villages, Pomok, where the *píbari*'s family
now lived, occupied the verge of the mountain. Just offshore was
Grove Island. After walking a mile or so, they arrived at the shore.
Explaining that this was the village where she lived, she pointed to
an orange grove beside the settlement, shaded by the mountain. The
rows of trees had dark green leaves, and the light green fruit, no bigger than a baby's fist, dangled from the branches. Weren't the summer oranges supposed to be larger? Chuni asked.

A girl came running toward them from the village. She was barefoot and Chuni guessed she was six or seven. Deftly the little thing
avoided being pricked by the vitex shrubs that were spread about the
area. The girl came up to the *píbari* and babbled something to her. It
turned out she was the *píbari*'s niece. By listening carefully, Chuni
was able to understand that a horse to be sold on the mainland the
next day had run off. The *píbari* told Chuni she would return shortly,
and proceeded toward the village with her niece.

Originally, Chuni knew, horses had run free on Cheju, to be
rounded up once or twice a year. But the experience of the recent
rebellion and then the outbreak of war the previous year had convinced people to take their horses in at night. It appeared the little
girl had been tending the horses that evening and had discovered
one of them missing.

Chuni sat down. The waves broke against the not-too-distant
shore at regular intervals. But even without this regular sound, Chuni
could tell where the ocean was. He could tell by the direction in which
the vitex shrubs bent. These shrubs have round, thin leaves with the
well-developed cuticle characteristic of seaside flora, and white fuzz
sprouting from their backs. Their small but abundant deep-purple
blossoms resemble an annual. These pitiful-looking dwarf shrubs

mature while hugging the ground and pointing away from the ocean because of the offshore winds.

Before long the girl ran up to Chuni and handed him two of the light green oranges, then ran back the way she had come. The two of them together weren't even a handful, but already they had the fine nap and the dimpled surface of a ripe orange. He sniffed one orange and then the other, and as he listened to the breakers, dusk began to steal over the area. The houses and orange trees gradually faded from view, along with the flickering outlines of people that Chuni occasionally saw. And then the land and water blended together. The moon appeared on the horizon, a thin, distant crescent.

Chuni heard someone approaching out of the dusk from the direction of the village. At first it sounded like a herd of people. But the moonlight revealed only the *pibari* and a pair of horses. The *pibari* approached Chuni, stroking the neck of one of the horses. "We're selling you on the mainland tomorrow." And then she drew that horse up behind the other horse. In the dusk, Chuni could make out dapples of white. Why had the *pibari* brought these horses? He had no idea. Suddenly the horse to the rear whinnied and mounted the other horse. Chuni flinched. In the dusky light of the moon the two huge bodies became one. The *pibari* turned to Chuni and took his wrist, then ran off with him in tow, leaving the horses to themselves. Arriving at the shore, she threw off her clothes and rushed into the water. She called to him. Chuni hesitated, bewildered, conscious only of his burning face. The *pibari* emerged from the water, came up to Chuni, pulled his shirt apart, and undressed him, the buttons popping loose and falling to the ground. The two oranges dropped from Chuni's hands and his fair, white skin was revealed in the dusk. The *pibari* searched Chuni's body with greedy hands. Chuni wanted to free himself, but a stronger force held him back and to that force he yielded. Her hands grew more insistent, and Chuni noticed a faint smile on her lips. He felt her hot breath as she nibbled on his neck. Relaxing beneath the weight that clung to him, Chuni tumbled to the ground. The bristly vitex pierced his flesh, but he ignored the pain. The distant sliver of moon whirled in the sky, seemed to drop before his eyes, then returned to its place.

Every night that moon filled out more, before returning to its crescent shape. And every night Chuni met the *pibari* there at the seaside.

One night when the moon had waned almost to nothingness, Chuni returned from his nightly rendezvous feeling ill, and the next day he kept to his bed. He had a slight fever, and his joints ached so that he couldn't stir.

His mother was the more upset. Since they had come to Sŏgwip'o, with its change of water, Chuni's rashes had disappeared and he had regained his health. How delighted she had been! But now he was flat on his back. She had a hunch about her son's nocturnal doings, but was reluctant to scold for fear of irritating him. It had always been that way. As a youngster Chuni had loved dried squid. He couldn't go to sleep unless he had a couple of them beside his pillow. Once he ate so much of it that he practically fainted. The doctor had told his parents never to bring dried squid home again. But Chuni would pester to her wits' end, and when she returned from shopping, there in the folds of her skirt was a squid, concealed from her husband's eye. And now, mother that she was, she couldn't bear to confront her son as he lay sick in bed. So she decided to take out her frustrations on the *pibari*. She began buying seafood elsewhere. She'd bought everything from her until now, but she felt the *pibari* had taken advantage of her and the seafood she was passing off these days was no good. Of course, there was no substance to this complaint. Before long Chuni's mother had stopped mentioning the *pibari* altogether.

But the *pibari* continued to visit, bringing abalone, conch, or *pukpari* she had caught that day. She would observe Chuni in bed, keeping her distance, then leave for home, her catch unsold. Always her eyes were the same—neither dull nor sparkling.

Chuni for his part seemed to disengage his mind after the fever and joint ache set in. It seemed as if the events of his recent life had happened to someone else. Despite the *pibari*'s almost daily visits, he felt little interest in her. But as he nursed himself back to health with the medications his mother journeyed to the town of Cheju to buy for him, his fever gradually eased, the weariness in his body dissipated, and it was only a matter of time before he grew nostalgic for the *píbari*. One day he asked his mother to buy a *pukparí* from her. Dismayed though his mother was, she couldn't deny her son's request. Chuni then asked her to fetch some water from the ocean. Into a large bowl of this water he placed the fish. Bloody from where it had been speared in the spine, it pursed its mouth open and shut, fins and tail working vigorously. How impressive, Chuni thought. But it wasn't long before the fish began to keel over. With an effort it righted itself. But presently it tilted again, and as the minutes passed it tilted farther and farther. Chuni had seen enough: he asked his mother to take the bowl outside, and he refused to eat the fish for dinner.

Two weeks passed, and one day when Chuni had recovered sufficiently to go outside and brave the wind, a letter from his uncle arrived. When Chuni and his mother had lived in the town of Cheju, every time an acquaintance left for the mainland they had asked the person to inquire as to the uncle's whereabouts. And finally the uncle had made contact with them. After fleeing Seoul he had planned to settle in Pusan, he wrote, but circumstances had forced him to stop in Taegu. There, a "federated" school had been established, and it appeared that classes were now in session. Chuni and his mother should join him there. All along Chuni's mother had been wondering from one day to the next if they would hear from the uncle, and as soon as the letter arrived she packed up, telling Chuni they would leave on the first bus the next morning.

That same day, for the first time in a while, Chuni put on his straw hat and set out for a walk beside the button factory at the southern tip of town. The factory still hadn't resumed operation. In these lonesome surroundings, the flowers of the sweet oleander bushes had passed their peak.

From the bank he looked out toward Firewood and Mosquito islands, and as he walked back toward town along the pebbly inlet he looked out at Grove Island. As before, several diving women were at work, disappearing underwater and then surfacing with a whistle.

The braids of water that flowed through the village looked clearer and colder now. The waterfall looked like a real waterfall. He visited the *chaguri* bathing pool but had no urge to take a dip. The mere sight of the water cascading over the rock wall that bordered the pool like a folding screen sent a chill through him. He looked up to see the tip of Halla Mountain's lofty summit distinct against the brilliant azure sky. The sun gently prickled the back of his neck. Thus had summer turned to autumn while Chuni was sick in bed.

Chuni turned in the direction of Pomok Village. This in fact had been his destination when he left his house that morning. He had to see the *pibari* one last time. The days were shorter now and Chuni walked slowly, and by the time the Pomok seashore came into sight, the entire village was draped in the mountain's shadow. The fruit on the orange trees beside the village was more noticeable, bulging clusters in the shade. Now as big as a grown-up's fist, the oranges had taken on a yellowish tinge. Chuni decided to wait for the *pibari* where the vitex spread along the shore, and there he sat. The surge and ebb of the breakers sounded at regular intervals.

Figures descended toward the shore, trailing a herd of horses. The animals seemed tame and easily led. Chuni inspected the group of villagers, wondering if the *pibari*'s niece was among them. And then a woman came into sight leading a horse dappled with white into the village. She rested one hand on the horse's back and stroked its belly with her other hand. It was the *pibari*. And that dappled horse whose belly she was stroking was certainly the horse he had seen that first night. The *pibari* must have taken the day off, Chuni thought. Or else she had returned early after a poor catch. Chuni rose to his feet. There was the niece, holding a long set of reins. She spotted him first and told the *pibari*. The woman looked up and approached without hesitation. Chuni sat down again.

The *pibari* greeted Chuni warmly, taking his hands in hers. Had he recovered from his illness? she asked, rubbing the backs of his hands. The black pupils within the dark eyebrows were the same as ever—neither dull nor sparkling. Chuni felt his face flush as he told her he was leaving on the first bus the next day. And then something unexpected escaped from his lips: Wouldn't she like to join them? He hadn't meant to say this; the words had leaped from his mouth. But after a moment's reflection he realized he really didn't want to leave her behind. If he implored his mother, she couldn't very well refuse. The hands that clasped his tightened as he repeated his proposal: "Let's go live on the mainland." For a moment the *pibari* looked at Chuni with those eyes that were neither dull nor sparkling. She shook her head. And finally she spoke. However much she wanted to follow Chuni, something inside her would not allow her to leave for the mainland. So she had made up her mind that when the day came, she would see Chuni off without a word of protest. What Chuni heard next was at first shocking, almost incomprehensible. The reason she had killed her brother wasn't what people thought—the fear that his tainted background would be the downfall of the other family members. The brother was her favorite from childhood. And it was she who risked every danger to secretly ferry food and clothing to him in his mountain hideaway. Then one night he came down from the high country, saying that his only hope was to escape to Japan. But he fell ill, and it was all he could do to get around; he simply couldn't subject himself to further hardship. She urged him to give himself up. For a time he looked into her eyes, and then he set down his rifle and went into the outhouse. It was then she knew: it was by her hand that her brother's body would return to the Cheju soil—that was his wish. From that point on she felt something inside that prevented her from ever leaving Cheju. Bringing her story to a close, she told Chuni she would think of him whenever she saw a horse leaving for the mainland. And with the same hand that had stroked the dappled mare, she stroked her own belly several times, then embraced Chuni's neck.

September 1956

VOICES

They were dragging him down a mountain, pulling him by a rope around his neck. Tŏkku didn't recognize the mountain, saw only that the terrain was incredibly rugged.

Jagged rocks and tree stumps gouged his chin, his chest, his knees. And then he was flipped over and it was the back side of him being gashed and scraped. Soon there would only be shreds of him left. He would surely die if they kept dragging him like this.

"Let go of me! I'm not dead! I'm still alive!"

But they continued to drag his bloody carcass down the rugged mountain slope.

When there weren't enough troops to remove bodies from the battlefield, laborers might be assigned the job, and they would drag the bodies off by a rope around the neck. Tŏkku had been at the front some three months the first time he witnessed this. A forty-eight-hour pitched battle had just ended, a battle in which a height of land had changed hands no less than nine times. Tŏkku had sunk back against a boulder, overcome by a hollow feeling that was partly the relaxation of tension and partly the exhilaration of surviving. He always felt this way after intense fighting.

The sun had risen over the summit of a neighboring mountain. The wind breached a gap in the mountains and swept over him, carrying the odor of gunpowder and blood and the moans of the wounded. He was hardened by then to these smells and sounds, was used to them, in fact.

As he rested against the boulder in the direct rays of the sun, his eyelids had grown heavy. Normally, drowsiness was more of a worry to the men than hunger. They couldn't help dozing off even when they were marching toward enemy positions. They were like sleepwalkers, waking one moment and nodding off the next. Nodding off and waking up—this had been Tŏkku's routine since arriving at the front. Back on the farm he'd been able to sleep through the most furious storm.

Finally Tŏkku had dozed off, only to lurch awake at a sound. He flinched at the sight that greeted him—a body lying at his feet. It wasn't the corpse itself but the rope around its neck that had shaken him. When they pulled the rope and the carcass caught on something, the neck stretched out. The upturned eyes glittered in the lovely morning sunlight. The mouth was half open, the chin bouncing up and down with the movement of the body. Tŏkku jerked his head away.

Beside him, Sergeant Kim had burst into his distinctive high-pitched laugh.

"You coward—haven't you ever seen a body before? Bet you never knew how convenient a neck can be—all you do is tie a rope around it and you can drag people dead or alive. A neck is just right for tying a rope around, and once you knot the rope, it's not about to come loose. And a neck can stretch and shrink, so whoever's doing the pulling has something to work with if the body gets caught on something. Look—it got snagged again. See how the neck's stretched out?"

Tŏkku hadn't been able to look.

Sergeant Kim had been right: Tŏkku was something of a coward. His first action at the front had left the crotch of his pants soaked. And the first time he had seen the corpse of a comrade he had burst into tears—but more out of fear than sorrow. To Tŏkku a trench felt like the inside of a tomb.

People adapt to most anything, though, and over time Tŏkku saw so many corpses that nothing shocked him anymore. A severed arm, an unconnected leg, guts looped over a branch, swaying in the breeze—whatever the sight, he would pass a hand down his belly and savor the joy of still being alive. And by now the callus on his trigger finger had thickened. What was it, then, about the corpse with the rope around its neck that had upset him so? Maybe it was the realization that the eyes and chin of a corpse weren't so different from his own.

In the trench that night he had whispered to Sergeant Kim that if he were ever badly wounded the sergeant should finish him off. So saying, he quietly passed a hand along his neck.

Sergeant Kim had responded with his short giggle. "Sure, as long as I have some ammo left."

Some time later, at the conclusion of yet another fierce battle, Tŏkku had seen a laborer dragging a corpse by the neck. In a fit of rage, he struck the laborer with his rifle butt.

Sergeant Kim had uttered his giggle and thumped Tŏkku on the shoulder.

"Don't get so worked up, soldier. I've gotten mad like that myself. I even shot one of those fellows in the leg once. But then I thought about it—what difference does it make if they put the rope around your neck or your ankles? Just count yourself lucky you're not crow bait in the first place."

Ultimately Tŏkku had accepted this. At home on the farm he had to haul rocks and logs and such. Dragging bodies on the battlefield was no different, he told himself.

And then, during yet another fierce battle, against a large enemy force for control of a ridge, Tŏkku had been struck down by a stray round. The bullet entered through the eyeball, but fortunately at an angle, fracturing the orbital bone before exiting. Time seemed to stand still, and then close by he heard Sergeant Kim. He had never been so glad to hear that giggle.

"Sergeant Kim, I'm dead. My head's gone."

Again the giggle. "If your head's gone, then what happened to your mouth? You're still talking."

"I mean it! My head's gone! I can't see!" Tŏkku had shouted.

Blood flowing from his left eye had covered his sound right eye.

The sergeant had brought his mouth close to Tŏkku's ear.

"Relax, soldier—the only thing missing is one of your eyes. Now, you asked me a favor, remember? I just happen to have a bullet left— how about it?" This time he burst into an even higher-pitched giggle.

"No!" Tŏkku had screamed. "No! No!"

Two months later Tŏkku had been discharged.

And now here they were dragging him by the neck down a rugged mountain slope. Little was left of his chin and his knees. There was no more of his back or his skull to gouge open. And he could no longer feel pain. He was dead—there was no doubt about it. Still, he wanted to know what son of a bitch would take a man who was still alive and drag him by the neck with a rope.

With an effort he lifted his head and groped for the other end of the rope. And that was when he received a shock. The man bent over pulling the rope was Tŏkku himself.

"Hey, let go, damn it! It's me—Tŏkku! Can't you see? What happened to your good eye?" And then the Tŏkku pulling the rope vanished.

Thank god, thought Tŏkku. But the rope kept dragging him. Something the size of a man's fist had attached itself to the other end and was rolling down the slope, pulling the rope behind it. Tŏkku looked more closely; it was a bloody lump of something. The rolling lump grew like a snowball. And the larger it grew, the faster it pulled the rope. From the size of a fist it grew to the size of a large brick, and then a large pumpkin. A cliff loomed ahead. This meant death. With a final supreme effort he shouted, "Help me!"

The shout startled him awake.

He was at the foot of the hill behind his village. The evening sun was slanting across the ridge of the mountain to the west. Its outline was clearer than when it was directly aloft; it looked larger now, and more crimson.

Tŏkku had returned home after his discharge, his empty eye socket hideously shrunk and misshapen. But there was something else about him that startled the villagers: he was a changed man.

Tŏkku had been as diligent a farmer as you could find. He never borrowed an ox except to turn up the earth of his dry field and paddy, at which times he called upon Samdol's father, who lived a couple of houses away. Otherwise, whether he was fertilizing, harvesting, or doing some other chore, he packed everything on his back. Whatever work one man alone could do, he did himself. But despite his large frame, there was something meek and tight-fisted about him. Once, when he was raising a pig, a neighbor's pig got sick and died overnight. Thinking that swine disease was going around, Tŏkku immediately sold off his own pig for less than half the market price. He learned later that contaminated feed had killed the other pig. Even so, he stood by his decision and he never again raised a pig.

Another peculiarity was that he never bought liquor or tobacco. It wasn't that they didn't agree with him. If he happened to attend a celebration at one of the neighbors', he would empty bowls of *makkŏlli* until the skin around his eyes turned red. It amounted to this: if it was free, he drank it. In this respect he tended to be stingy.

The autumn before Tŏkku was drafted, he was taught an expensive lesson. He was on his way home from the market, where he had sold some unhulled rice, and he stopped at a drinking house along the way. He had in mind not just a quick bowl of *makkŏlli* but also the soybean-paste soup that customers were served along with their drinks. To this soup he would add the ball of steamed barley he had packed before leaving home.

He was just about to drop the hardened ball of barley into the steaming bowl of soup when he heard someone call his name. He looked up to see a face gazing at him through the glass door to the back room. It was Yongch'il, a man who hadn't been seen in the village for some time. Tŏkku couldn't very well ignore him, and he forced a wan smile. Diligent farmers such as Tŏkku didn't need to be any more friendly than that with dissolute gamblers such as Yongch'il.

Yongch'il threw open the door to the back room and invited Tŏkku inside, where it was warmer. The day was gray and overcast, and where Tŏkku sat it was cold enough to make him shiver. Still, he told Yongch'il he was happy where he was.

"Oh hell, you're stubborn as a mule. Get in here. I'm telling you, it's cold out there."

This display of goodwill convinced Tŏkku, and he stepped up into the back room with his meal.

Sitting across a small drinking table from Tŏkku was a young man he had never seen before. In the warmth of the room Tŏkku's thoughts returned to his bowl of soup and barley.

"Not so fast—you can eat that stuff any time of day. First warm yourself with some of this." So saying, Yongch'il passed Tŏkku his drinking bowl and filled it for him.

Tŏkku didn't always eat three proper meals a day. In winter, when the days were short, he took only breakfast and supper. Today was special: he had planned to treat himself to lunch because of his trip to market. And besides, a meal suited him fine on a cold day like this when his stomach was growling. But he had to admit that the thought of a drink had also crossed his mind. And so, pretending he couldn't resist the offer, he accepted the bowl from Yongch'il and drank.

It was *yakchu*—fresh clean *yakchu* and not the thick, bland *makkŏlli* that folks drank out here in the boondocks. He sampled a chunk of the raw octopus that the others were having with their drink. It was sleek and chewy, and very tasty. Never before had he eaten raw octopus.

The young man now offered Tŏkku his bowl. Tŏkku declined, saying the first one had warmed him up just fine. But the other continued to hold out the bowl. A peculiar smile came to his face, only the lips moving, the other features, eyes and all, dead still. Again the smile. *Go on, take it*, he seemed to be saying.

Tŏkku told himself it wouldn't do to accept a bowl from one man but not the other, and finally he took it and drank. He felt a prickling sensation growing in the pit of his stomach, followed by a warm glow. Those are the times when drink goes down most easily. And now Yongch'il was offering Tŏkku yet another bowl, saying the latecomer had to drink three bowls in a row.

"Say what you want, liquor's the thing when it's cold out. All the quilted clothing in the world won't help if you don't line yourself on the inside too."

Tŏkku considered. When country folk drank and one person bought a certain amount, the common practice was for the next person to buy the same amount. If he were now to gulp down what the others offered but fail to reciprocate, it would be awkward. And so he drew a deep breath, made sure his money belt was secure about his middle, and said, "I'd better get home while it's still light out." He turned back to his barley and soup.

"Will you listen to this?" said Yongch'il. "He wants to go home. You miss the little woman's butt, don't you?"

Tŏkku was caught off guard. It hadn't been a year since he had taken a wife, and he had yet to experience the connubial bliss that newlywed men were supposed to feel. He merely felt thankful that his wife was a thrifty household manager.

"What's wrong—afraid I'm going to stick you for the drinks?" Here Yongch'il struck a nerve. "Relax. Who do you think I am, anyway? Is

old Yongch'il ever out of money for booze? Come on, don't be a
pussy. Drink up and give me back my bowl."

As timid men will do at a time like this, Tŏkku attempted an excuse: "No, it's just that . . ."

He was about to protest that a couple of days earlier he had drunk
too much and his stomach was still unsettled. The fact of the matter
was, he had attended a birthday celebration for Samdol's father two
days ago, where he was treated to two soup bowls full of *makkŏlli*. And
he would have liked an equal amount more, but Samdol's father, always stingy, hadn't offered and Tŏkku had gone unsatisfied.

In any event, Yongch'il was not persuaded.

"It's just what? Come on—your friends are better than the little
woman, and your drinking friends are the best."

Finally Tŏkku accepted the bowl. And then he passed it back,
empty, to Yongch'il. Twice the empty *yakchu* kettle went out to the
kitchen and twice it came back full.

Tŏkku's face began to redden—not just the skin around his eyes but
the tip of his nose and the rims of his ears. He grew talkative, as people
of few words are wont to do when they're under the influence. And the
more timid a person is, the more he brags. The villagers could say what
they wanted, Tŏkku now declared, but no one could live it up like
Yongch'il. As long as he was an able-bodied man, he too wanted to live
it up just once, and then he could die without regrets. He'd worked
himself to the bone farming, and what had he gotten out of it?

"Yongch'il, my friend, we live in the same village—let's get to know
each other better. It's just like you said—a friend's better than the
little woman. Or like they put it in the old days, sell the wife and buy
a friend!"

The young man punctuated every sentence of Tŏkku's with the
twitch of the lips that was his way of smiling.

When they had finished their third kettle, Yongch'il suggested
they take a break. He then produced a fistful of paper money and paid
the bill. Tŏkku had never seen such a green profusion of thousand-
wŏn notes. Yongch'il must have cleaned up at gambling, he thought.

Yongch'il and the young man withdrew to a closetlike room. Tŏkku
followed and found the two men spreading out a blanket on which

to gamble. In no time the blanket was heaped with thousand-*wŏn* notes.

Tŏkku looked over their shoulders as they played. Surreptitiously he undid his money belt, extracted a ten-*wŏn* note, and placed it beside the thousand-*wŏn* bills on the blanket. In gambling parlance, he was "investing" in one of the players.

The young man gave his little twitch of a smile, picked up the note with two fingertips, and flicked it aside. The smile this time was contemptuous.

"Better stay out of this," Yongch'il followed up, as if admonishing a youngster.

Tŏkku was feeling the alcohol and couldn't help taking offense. So, they were looking down on him, were they?

He placed two hundred-*wŏn* notes on the blanket. And for the next round, three. And then five. He began to feel expansive. Occasionally the money he bet would return to him, doubled.

But as the night wore on and he began to sober up, he discovered that his money belt was almost empty. He grew fretful and broke out in a sweat. The hand that held the money trembled like someone shivering in the cold. Why had he ever started in the first place? But repentance had come too late—his pockets were empty now.

He wished he were dead. He wanted to die right there where he sat.

Yongch'il ordered more liquor. When it arrived, Tŏkku, without waiting to be offered, poured himself a bowl and gulped it down. Again he wished he were dead. He wished he could drink until he passed out and then never wake up.

But alcohol works in strange ways. Even while his stomach was warmed by the bowls he drank, his emotions cooled. *Be a man,* he scolded himself. *If you're going to gamble, can't you afford to lose a piddling amount of money? What about that guy who lost everything gambling? He's still alive, isn't he?*

Tŏkku looked up and gazed in turn at Yongch'il and the young man.

"Make sure you keep that money safe."

Spoken like a gambler. If they didn't squander the money they had won from him, he would win it back someday. He rose deliberately.

They asked him to stay until daybreak, but he wouldn't be swayed, and out he went, wanting to put up a brave front. From the market street to his village was a good five miles. As he walked through the cold, moonless night he realized he'd made an expensive stop at that drinking place. "So what?" he muttered. What was wrong with having some expensive drinks for once in your life?

The cold air soon sobered him. The image of his wife rose before him; she was most likely waiting for him. She would ask about the money. Well, he'd spent it drinking with a friend. No, that wouldn't work. But hadn't that no-good Yongch'il told him that a friend was better than the little woman, and a drinking pal was best of all? And if Tŏkku was such a friend, then was it right for Yongch'il to have cleaned him out? *Might as well pull a knife and rob me*, he thought. And who the hell was that asshole with the sly smile? How could he have let himself be taken in by those sons of bitches? Regret settled in his heart.

His throat was choked with sobs. But the tears wouldn't come, frustrating him all the more.

Reaching the entrance to the village, Tŏkku knocked on the door of Auntie Wart's drinking house. The door opened to reveal the woman rubbing her sleepy eyes.

"Mr. Cho!" Her voice registered her shock. "What are you doing up at this hour?"

"I was coming back from the market and I got robbed."

"My goodness, what a terrible thing to happen. Come in, come in."

"A couple of guys jumped me, they must have knocked me out. When I came to, they'd taken every last copper I got for my grain."

"Heavens! Well, it's good you weren't hurt."

"Give me a bowl of *makkŏlli*, would you?"

He drank that bowl and then another.

"I'll pay later if that's all right." True to form, Tŏkku was happy to postpone payment.

"Don't worry about that, just get yourself home. You can imagine how long she's been waiting."

Despite the *makkŏlli*, Tŏkku for some reason felt wide awake. He'd have to tell his wife the same story about being robbed—what else could he say?

But this excuse and every other one he framed in his mind seemed flawed. He should have brought that money home at all costs, even if it meant risking his life at the hands of robbers. Again he wished he were dead. As he entered the twig gate to his home, he had an urge to strangle himself with his money belt.

The soy crock in the yard caught his eye. He'd guzzle the stuff until it killed him. He rushed to the crock and scooped a gourdful. But by the fifth swallow he was on his knees vomiting. Everything came out, including what he had eaten at the market. All he could think of was that he had wasted a gourdful of soy sauce.

For three days he kept to his bed, sick at heart if not in body.

He became a laughingstock among the villagers. "Got enough soy sauce to last the year?" they would ask. Tŏkku, red-faced, would say nothing.

But the Tŏkku who returned from the army was nothing like Tŏkku back then.

The villagers had raised money, and they welcomed him with a party the day he returned. Tŏkku managed not to overdrink, but he had something to say: on the battlefield, the dead were no different from a chunk of wood or a rock you might see alongside the road. And so the sight of a corpse wasn't so awful; in fact, it didn't faze him at all.

When the villagers registered surprise at this, Tŏkku responded with a short, high-pitched laugh in direct imitation of Sergeant Kim. While Tŏkku was recuperating in the army hospital in the city of Taegu he had received word that Kim had died in action. Whereupon he had adopted the sergeant's giggle. And now, surveying the crowd as he giggled, he added, "Long as you're alive, you should eat what you want and do what you please."

As if to translate these words into action, Tŏkku proceeded virtually to take up residence at Auntie Wart's drinking house. And when intoxicated he would say things he wouldn't have said before; he even flirted with her.

"Auntie, how old are you?"

"What's gotten into you? If you really want to know, I'm thirty-seven."

"What rotten luck. If you were five years younger, I'd settle down with you."

"Are you out of your mind?"

"No. It's just that I've fallen in love with that wart under your ear."

Auntie Wart scowled at him but managed to hold her tongue. *Can a person change that much for the worse?* But she didn't want to be too hard on a man who had just returned from the army.

And Yongch'il for his part dealt differently with Tŏkku than he had previously. First of all, he now held Tŏkku a notch higher in his estimation. He himself, through some mysterious means, had been able to avoid every draft notice that came his way. A wastrel and gambler second to none in that area, he couldn't quite bring himself to stand tall in Tŏkku's presence once the soldier was back home. Instead, he wished to follow as much as possible in Tŏkku's wake.

The two of them took to visiting the Mokp'o House, a good-sized tavern in a larger village the next valley over. It was run by an aged woman from the city of Mokp'o and always featured at least one loose barmaid from Seoul. The young crowd fervently wished they might someday have a drink poured by the hand of this particular barmaid. Yongch'il was already ensconced there, and with Tŏkku in tow, would stay up all night drinking. Naturally, it was Yongch'il who paid.

The two of them also frequented the drinking house near the market.

"None of that weak *yakchu* today," Tŏkku would say. "Let's make it *chŏngjong* instead."

This clearer rice brew was brought to them nice and warm. And for a drinking snack they wouldn't settle just for raw octopus; they liked such succulent fare as grilled meat or ribs to grace their table as well.

When the young man with the twitch for a smile joined them, Tŏkku had no qualms about shouting him down: "Wipe that sneaky smile off your face!"

Thereafter the young man was ever cautious about smiling in front of Tŏkku.

Not a day passed that Tŏkku's good eye wasn't bloodshot from drinking and gummy with discharge. Three rounds of drinking took precedence over three meals a day. To all appearances he had fallen in with a dissolute lot.

And then a shocking rumor made its way back to the village: Tŏkku had gotten into a fight near the market and had knocked a man's teeth clean out of his mouth. And he had gotten away with it.

On the day in question, Yongch'il and the victim had been gambling in the back room of the usual drinking house. Tŏkku, mellow with drink, was observing. Most of the money had passed to Yongch'il's side of the gaming blanket when suddenly the other man snatched the cards from Yongch'il's hand, spread them out, and shot to his feet. Grabbing Yongch'il by the collar, he accused him of cheating from the outset. Punches and kicks followed, and soon the two of them were rolling about. Yongch'il's opponent was a tough man to subdue, and Yongch'il on his own might have had to submit. So finally Tŏkku had aimed a quick kick at the man's face as he sat on top of Yongch'il. The man flew backward and spluttered, spitting out a couple of teeth mixed with bloody froth.

The men were taken to the local police station. But because Tŏkku was a disabled veteran and had acted under the influence of alcohol, he was released without much of a fuss.

Tŏkku and Yongch'il reclaimed their drinking table.

"That other time you played me for a sucker too, didn't you?" said Tŏkku.

Yongch'il produced a sheepish smile. "Let's not talk about the past—men don't do that," he said, sticking a handful of money in Tŏkku's pocket. "If it wasn't for you, he would have beaten the shit out of me."

"And that's why it's good to have friends," Tŏkku said, trying to sound manly. "Besides, we're drinking pals and neighbors too."

This was the life Tŏkku had lived since his discharge during the summer, and he kept it up until the spring thaw of the following year.

Tŏkku would have been the first to admit that most of the time he was palling around with Yongch'il he had been living off of his friend. Not that he himself had spent nothing. Of the modest sum of traveling expenses he had received upon his discharge, not one copper had gone to the support of his household; instead, it had all been cast to the wind. If he and his wife hadn't dipped into the grain that she had harvested by herself from their measly plot of land and sold a half peck or so as necessary, they wouldn't have survived.

His wife had continued to be a frugal household manager. But she was not one to bawl out her husband or find fault with his every misdeed. That he had survived the perils of the battlefield and been delivered back to her was more than she could have asked for. How thankful she was that he had lost only an eye rather than an arm or a leg, and so was still able to do farm work. Besides, she wanted to believe in her husband: he wouldn't always be the way he was now. So when he returned after a night of dissipation, she prayed he would eventually mend his rough ways, just like she had patched his tattered army uniform.

It had seemed Tŏkku would ride his high horse forever, but he was not quite the same after his fight near the market. In the army, the loss of a tooth or two was nothing to men who could dispatch bullets at will and kill with little effort. It was kill or be killed.

Tŏkku realized he hadn't knocked out that man's teeth because of a threat to his life. But as long as he was under the influence he could actually feel proud of what he had done. *Yongch'il, you no-good, I'm different from you,* he would tell himself. *You swindled me out of that money I got for my grain. That's not something I'd do; you wouldn't catch me emptying someone else's pocket. I respect my friends among the neighbors.*

But when he was sober and thought back on it, that fight weighed on his mind. If he were in that other man's shoes, he'd be mad as hell. Unknown to others, he was afraid of encountering the man again. And so his visits to the marketplace grew less frequent. He began to revert to his former meekness and his cowardly tendencies.

Closer to home, he could no longer frequent Auntie Wart's drinking house. His tab had reached the point where she refused to serve him. And by now there was no more grain, or anything else at home, to sell. He and his wife were reduced to two meals a day of barley gruel, and even that was more radish leaves than barley.

Already the villagers were fertilizing their fields for the new crop. But Tŏkku was reluctant to set himself to work. The callus on his trigger finger had disappeared, but it was not the lack of toughened hands that discouraged him from working but rather the life he had led since his discharge. He had somehow come to think that his neighbors might feel awkward witnessing a disabled veteran having to farm for subsistence.

About this time, Yongch'il returned after a considerable absence. Immediately the two men began hanging around again at Auntie Wart's. If you don't drink for a while and then take it up again, you become intoxicated more quickly. Before Tŏkku knew it, the corners of his eyes had reddened.

"No matter what people say, this is the best," he said. "Down the hatch, and all your worries wash away."

"What about your wife?" Auntie Wart broke in.

"I've got my booze, and she's got this," he said, pointing toward his crotch. "What else does she need?"

"That's right," Yongch'il chimed in. "And a tit for a baby, and shit for a dog."

"No problem there. I got no kid and no dog."

Auntie Wart was reluctant to interrupt the blithering of these two customers even though they were acting like bums, but she felt compelled to remind Tŏkku, "Mr. Cho, you're going to be a father soon."

"Right—I'm going to snap my fingers and the little bastard'll pop right out," he said. "Heads it lives, tails it dies."

In spite of his bluster, Tŏkku had always felt ill at ease about his lack of children. A neighbor had once mentioned that Tŏkku's ancestors had never been blessed with plentiful offspring. When Tŏkku was drafted into the army, he wished he had at least one son to return to. And now his wife was in her eighth month. These days she was taking in sewing. He could picture her sitting in their room, the upper part of her heaving with every breath she took. Although Tŏkku couldn't get her out of his mind, his chaotic life made it easier to set these worries aside.

As he returned home from Auntie Wart's that night, Tŏkku told himself he had better do some serious thinking once and for all.

Various thoughts had been accumulating since his discharge, but there was no specific question he could make sense of and act on.

He felt the urge to urinate and did so in the yard. Suddenly he was hit with a realization: if he was going to urinate, the decent thing to do was use the urine crock. At that moment, this thought stood out more clearly than any other.

From then on, Tŏkku began to apply himself, little by little, to household matters. He wove straw sandals; he went up in the hills for firewood; he even began to think about borrowing an ox, since it was time to plow the fields.

And then three weeks ago something very unseemly happened in the village. The elderly woman who lived in the Chinese Date House at the foot of the hill behind the village lost a brood hen. She was sure she had seen it in the morning, but toward sunset when it should have come home to roost, it had failed to appear. Neither weasels nor wildcats had ever been seen about the village, which meant the hen must have been stolen. Secretly fingers were pointed at Tŏkku. The neighbors began to keep a closer watch on their chickens.

Around this time Yongch'il had returned to the village after another of his absences, and he and Tŏkku were drinking at Auntie Wart's.

"Tŏkku, my friend, I had you figured wrong," said Yongch'il. "You're quite the sly fellow."

Tŏkku asked what he meant.

"You've been sneaking over to the Mokp'o House," Yongch'il continued. He kept batting his eyelids in a knowing way. "What's it like now? Do they have a new girl from Seoul? That last one, her mug was kind of cute but her body was no good—she could have used more meat in the butt. What about this one—decent body?" And then Yongch'il lowered his voice. "A boiled chicken goes good with a few drinks, eh?"

Tŏkku finally caught the drift of this last remark.

"Listen to this crap." *I'm not going to defend myself every time you say something—I'm not like you!* he told himself.

But a short time later when Tŏkku stepped outside, his right eye bloodshot from drinking for the first time in a while, he shouted in the direction of the village, "Hey everybody—keep an eye on your cows too, not just your chickens!"

And then the previous day, Yongch'il had returned from yet another foray. He and Tŏkku were reunited at Auntie Wart's. Ever since the theft of the brood hen, Tŏkku had lapsed back into idleness.

The night was getting far along when the two of them left, drunk.

"I am damn angry," said Yongch'il, who went on to explain that a disreputable character had shown up at the market with a wad of money, and Yongch'il had been unable to fleece him. Before he would gamble, the fellow said, he needed to see if Yongch'il had any money.

"Here's this big fish, and I can't reel him in—it's ridiculous. A wad of money looking me right in the face. So I come over here to borrow some money from Samdol's father. But the old fart just looks at me like he's bitten into a lemon—doesn't say a word."

Drunk as he was, Tŏkku wondered if his friend had lost his mind. No way Samdol's father would lend a copper to a gambler like Yongch'il. And Yongch'il should have known that. Had he actually lost some money to this guy, and was he now so frantic he was trying to cover his losses? It somehow seemed that the distressed look Yongch'il wore tonight was different from his usual expression—something was bothering him for sure.

But Tŏkku felt no need to reveal these suspicions to Yongch'il. Instead he replied, "You know that old fart—he's as tight as they come. I tried to borrow some barley from him and he told me to get lost."

Three days earlier, Tŏkku had asked Samdol's father—one of the more affluent farmers in the village—to lend him a *mal* of barley.

"Come back after you've thought about that soy sauce you wasted," the other had shot back. The implication was that he wouldn't consider lending the barley until Tŏkku resumed the ways of a frugal farmer.

Idiotic bastard! thought Tŏkku. *Just you wait and see, you old fart! I'll never again ask to borrow your ox, and if that means I don't plow my fields, then so be it!*

"Shit!" said Yongch'il, who had hoped Tŏkku would stand in for him and ask Samdol's father for the loan. "The pigheaded old fart—he'd be the last one to help someone out in a pinch."

"You're right," Tŏkku chimed in. "The cussed old bastard—he's such a skinflint, he won't even go peacefully when he drops dead."

That night a fire broke out at Samdol's family's house.

Tŏkku had just returned home and sprawled on the floor when a clamor erupted outside. Tŏkku's wife hurried out, then frantically rushed back in.

"Honey! There's a fire at Samdol's!"

"Hmm? Fire?" Tŏkku replied in a sleepy voice.

"Yes, a fire! Aren't you going to help?"

"Why shouldn't the damned house catch fire?" Tŏkku snorted. "It's not made of tin, is it?" And with that he turned away.

The next morning Tŏkku's wife observed her husband carefully. As luck would have it, only the ox shed at Samdol's family's house had caught fire. And because the fire had been spotted by a family member emerging from the outhouse, the ox had been led away unharmed. But to Tŏkku's wife, the extent of the damage was not the issue. Rather, she wondered how the fire could have started in the first place. Samdol's family seemed to think it was because the ashes from the evening fire had been disposed of carelessly, but this was difficult for her to believe. There was no doubt in her mind that the fire had been set, and no matter how she looked at it, she had to suspect her husband. There was something fishy about his attitude the previous night. All the neighbors had rushed out to help fight the fire, but her husband, living practically next door to Samdol's family, hadn't even stuck his head outside. And that wasn't all. "Why shouldn't the damned house catch fire?" he had said. How could he talk such nonsense! The more she thought about it, the more her heart was troubled. It was too much for her. She would rather have had him swilling liquor and loafing around. It had been all she could do to put up with the whispers among the neighbors about the disappearance of the brood hen belonging to the elderly woman in the Chinese Date House. And now this.

"Honey, we can't live here anymore."

"Why not?"

Tŏkku, hung over from the previous night, looked up from his watery gruel of dried radish leaves, his bloodshot eye glaring at her.

"I'm too ashamed to go out in public. And scared."

"Eat up, woman, and quit your fussing."

Tŏkku's wife hadn't touched her spoon to her gruel.

"Whatever made you . . . ?"

"What are you talking about? Samdol's family's house? So what if that damned shack of theirs burned down?"

"How can you say such a thing?"

"They ought to be thankful their ox wasn't roasted."

"Really, I never thought you'd turn out this way. First the hen at the Chinese Date House. . . ."

"Damn bitch—how long are you going to keep this up?"

Tŏkku jumped up, intending to go to Auntie Wart's for a drink. In the process he accidentally tipped over his bowl of gruel. In a fit of anger he kicked over his wife's bowl as well.

"Look at you! Is it such a bother to get some gruel down your gullet?"

"Bitch! I ought to wring your neck!"

Tŏkku lashed out with his foot, accidentally kicking his wife in the belly. She curled up in a ball, moaning. He had not intended this.

It's human nature not to want to own up to a mistake in front of others, especially if you're a timid sort, and Tŏkku was no exception. Leaving his wife to wail in pain, her face ashen, he disappeared outside.

"Why don't you all just drop dead!" he muttered.

Yongch'il was already at Auntie Wart's having some hangover soup. His face was sooty and there were red marks on his forehead and neck. It looked as though he had turned out to help fight the fire along with everyone else.

Their eyes met, and then simultaneously they looked away from each other. Without a word, Tŏkku sat down beside Yongch'il and poured himself a drink.

Just then, Samdol's mother rushed in.

"Here you are, just like I thought. You'd better get yourself home— your wife's calling you."

Whereas Samdol's father was coarse and blunt, his mother was on the gentle and compassionate side. After the earlier episode when Tŏkku had returned empty-handed from his attempt to borrow barley from the father, she had secretly taken him some grain. Likewise, she enjoyed doing the dirty work in family crises. She was especially skillful as a midwife, and was called whenever a woman went into labor. It was said that all she had to do was cup her hands in front of an expectant mother and even breech babies would come out the right way. Doubtless she had heard Tŏkku's wife in distress and gone to her aid, putting aside her cleaning up from the previous night's fire.

"Is something wrong, Auntie?" called Auntie Wart from behind the counter.

"Well, this man's wife is suddenly hurting in the belly."

"How could that be? She's only eight months along."

"I know."

Auntie Wart shot Tŏkku a knowing glance. "Don't tell me you're up to no good again, Mr. Cho."

"How could you kick her like that? She's passed a lot of blood," said Samdol's mother. "It's too early to tell about the baby, but I hope the mother's all right."

Tŏkku drank without saying a word.

"Now get yourself up, you. Your wife needs you."

Tŏkku exploded. "Go to hell, all of you! After all the slaughter I saw at the front, what's the big deal here?"

"All right," Samdol's mother tsk-tsked, giving up for the time being. "I'm going to look in on her. You'd better come right along."

Tŏkku drained his bowl of *makkŏlli* in reply. For some reason he wasn't feeling the liquor. Turning a deaf ear to Auntie Wart, Tŏkku continued to pour himself drinks. A quart of *makkŏlli* later, he silently rose and left. A peculiar glaze had come over his good eye.

He too had some words for his wife, Tŏkku told himself. *What more do you have to say to me, you bitch? I'm the one who has something to tell you. And I'll say it before you drop dead!*

But upon nearing his house and hearing his wife's moans together with Samdol's mother's soothing voice, he turned on his heels. He couldn't very well speak his mind with someone else there.

Tŏkku climbed the hill behind the village until he found a sunny place to sit. As the warm sun beat down on him, his eyelids grew heavy. Dog tired, he fell asleep.

*   *   *

Dusk had spread over the hill, and the evening breeze had risen.

Tŏkku passed a hand down his throat, his body shuddering. It wasn't just that he was chilled. It was that horrible dream; it just wouldn't go away. He could still picture that bloody lump tumbling along at the end of the rope. A dream that bad must have meant something had happened to his wife as a result of her hemorrhaging. He felt as if right now, in his wakeful state and not in the dream, he were sliding deep down into a pit.

He started down the hill. He had gone no more than a few steps when he heard a strange sound. Straining to listen, he recognized it as something he had heard upon waking a short time earlier. It was a clucking sound. All he could tell was that it wasn't human.

Tŏkku searched until the sound became a vigorous cackling, and then he knew it was a chicken. There it was, a hen warming its eggs in a nest of last year's dead grass.

Why would a hen be out here sitting on its eggs? The next instant Tŏkku understood. *Damn bird, so this is where you disappeared to!* He shot a fierce glance in the direction of the Chinese Date House.

Once in a while a hen would stray off to lay her eggs, ending up in an out-of-the-way spot. And there she would sit. All the owner would know was that a hen was missing. And sometimes, around the time people forgot about her, the "lost" bird would suddenly appear with a train of twenty or more chicks.

"The old bag!" Tŏkku snorted. "She had to go and blame someone!"

He continued silently to harp on the missing hen and to shoot looks at the Chinese Date House. He felt like running over then and there and giving the old woman a piece of his mind. And then he had a thought.

He reached out, grabbed the hen, and wrung its neck. It soon became still, without so much as a flap of its wings. Sergeant Kim was right—a neck is such a convenient thing. And how little the hen weighed. But there was enough meat to snack on for several rounds of drinking. He gathered the eggs and put them in his pocket.

He thought of his wife: *You bitch—you thought I stole this chicken.* . . . *One of these days, before you croak, I'm going to give you a piece of my mind.*

Into the drinking house he went.

"Where have you been?" said Auntie Wart. And then she saw the hen. "Where did you get that?"

"You really want to know? I paid for it a while back and I just now took possession.... Where's Yongch'il?"

"He left right after you did."

"Too bad. Clean this bird and boil it up for me." Tŏkku handed the chicken to Auntie Wart. "I think I deserve a drink."

Auntie Wart noticed the bird's belly, which was missing some feathers.

"Wait a minute—did you take this hen from her nest?"

"What if I did? It's not going to kill me if I eat it. Don't worry, I didn't steal it. Come on, cook it up. I already paid for it, and then some.... Oh yeah—and boil these up, will you?"

He took several eggs from his pocket and handed them to Auntie Wart.

"Haven't you been home yet?"

Tŏkku didn't know what to say. What followed next was what he had feared.

"Mr. Cho, I don't know what you've done lately to deserve this, but your wife just delivered, and even though it's premature it cries just like a full-term baby. You don't know how lucky you are."

Tŏkku gulped once, his throat hot. Could this be true? But he couldn't bring himself to express these sentiments.

"It's no big deal having a baby—the hard part's raising it."

"Mr. Cho, you'd better start acting like a father."

"Put those eggs in the pot, will you? And pour me a bowl of *makkŏlli*."

There was now a different reason for him to want a drink.

"Today's special, so I'll let you pay later. But this is the last time."

It was indeed a special day, Tŏkku reflected. An unintentional mistake that morning had set him trembling inside, but here his wife had delivered a premature baby without incident. Suddenly he felt relaxed. Wouldn't it be fun now to be able to show Yongch'il this hen belonging to the old woman from the Chinese Date House?

"Where do you suppose my pal went? Down to the market?"

"You know," said Auntie Wart, "when he left, he was mumbling to himself—'That Tŏkku's just plain scary.'"

"Scary? Is that what he said?" He giggled automatically. *Well, so I am. I'm scary. And if you're the one who set that fire, buddy, then you might find my mouth scary too. And that means you're not going to want to show yourself in this village again, buddy. But you can rest easy—I won't say a thing.* He gulped his drink.

"Hurry it up with those eggs, Auntie!"

Auntie Wart began to peel one of the boiled eggs.

"Good lord, what is this!"

She dropped the egg and shrank back a step.

Where the eggshell had separated Tŏkku could see a completely formed chick, with yellow down and reddish feet all curled up. Were the eggs that old? Tŏkku then realized it had been a good three weeks since the disappearance of the hen.

Auntie Wart cracked another boiled egg, then put it back down.

"Where'd you get these eggs?" she asked, tsk-tsking in disapproval. "They're ready to hatch."

"I paid for them, I told you. And I better eat them—they'll be good for me." Tŏkku produced another giggle. "I guess you wouldn't know this, Auntie—on the front line, there's nothing a man won't eat if he's hard up."

"Give me one of those eggs from your pocket."

Tŏkku did so.

Auntie Wart held up the egg in front of him. "Look, you can see the chick squirming inside."

Tŏkku wasn't surprised, knowing they'd been laid three weeks before.

"And listen—you can hear it cheeping too."

Nothing so unusual about that, either. Almost absentmindedly he began to produce the remaining eggs from his pocket, one by one.

"And this one's pecking. . . . It's ready to hatch," said Auntie Wart.

Tŏkku wondered why the woman was chattering like this.

"Pour me another drink, will you?"

"Look at these chicks—I can't believe it. . . . Maybe we could find a hen for them. They need a bit more brooding."

There's a woman for you. How tenderhearted.

Tŏkku felt another giggle coming, but it stayed inside him. There was nothing surprising in what Auntie Wart had said, but something in the way she said it had struck a chord.

The next instant something began squirming inside Tŏkku, pecking at his chest, a faint, whisperlike cry that grew in volume until it became the cry of his newborn baby, and along with it, a peculiar, insistent terror he had never felt before, emanating from the small egg in front of him—the egg he thought he had paid for.

February 1957

AFTERWORD

Aside from his signature story, "Sonagi" (1952; usually translated as "Shower" or "Cloudburst"), the short fiction of Hwang Sunwŏn (1915–2000) has suffered from popular and critical neglect. This may not be surprising, given that Hwang published more than 100 stories in a career extending from the 1930s to the 1980s, in an educational environment in which literature tends to be commodified and compartmentalized for easy digestion by students. Thus, apart from the occasional story anthologized in a middle- or high-school reader, Hwang's output in this genre, arguably the most sophisticated and accomplished in modern Korean literary history, is not especially well known among general readers in his home country, especially in comparison with the works of household names such as Pak Wansŏ, Yi Munyŏl, Hwang Sŏgyŏng, and Cho Chŏngnae. Moreover, in a literary culture whose scholars and critics (often one and the same) have tended to prize fiction that directly engages with the many upheavals of modern Korean history, Hwang is often pigeonholed as an exemplar of a distinctly Korean lyricism and romanticism. On that basis he does not compare well with writers judged to possess a "historical consciousness," who use literature as a means of socializing a younger generation of readers to the harsh realities involved in Korea's transition from a traditional agrarian economy to (in the case of South Korea) one of the most high-tech nations in the world. He is seen by many as a bit old-fashioned.

Readers of the stories in this volume, though, will hear an author who is not only a gifted storyteller but also strikingly contemporary in terms of his thematic concerns, sophisticated worldview, and multifaceted narrative style. This book comprises three of Hwang's eight story collections, works written in the 1930s, 1940s, and 1950s, respectively. Composed in the late 1930s while the author was a student at Waseda University in Tokyo, the thirteen stories in *The Pond* (Nŭp) show early indications of Hwang's eventual mastery of the short-story form, especially his storytelling skill, the variety of his narratives, and the dualities in his worldview. Some of the tales are modernist narratives set in the city of Pyongyang (and in one case, Tokyo), others are starkly realistic sketches set in the countryside, and still others are surreal portraits that hint at Korea's anomalous position as a colony of imperial Japan from 1910 to 1945. A precocious fictional voice relates conflicts within the family and between the sexes, describes a colonial society in the process of modernization, and offers glimpses of a sovereign nation emasculated by colonization. *The Pond* first appeared in book form in 1940 as *Hwang Sunwŏn tanp'yŏnjip* (Hwang Sunwŏn story collection), at a time when publication in Korean was becoming increasingly difficult in colonial Korea. Although Hwang was only in his early twenties, he was already a published writer, having issued the poetry collections *Wayward Songs* (Pangga) and *Curios* (Koltongp'um).

The Dog of Crossover Village (Mongnŏmi maŭl ŭi kae) was published in Seoul in 1948, the second of Hwang's story collections to be published but the third in order of composition, after *Wild Geese* (Kirŏgi, 1951). Hwang wrote these seven stories during the chaotic post–World War II period that in South Korea is termed the Post-Liberation Space (*Haebang konggan*), a name that attests to the sudden removal of the Japanese colonial overlords after August 15, 1945, and all of them except the short "My Father" (Abŏji, 1947) reflect the turbulent social and political circumstances of those years. Hwang himself had only recently, in 1946, moved with his family to what is now South Korea, leaving forever his centuries-old ancestral home in the north (a fate shared by hundreds of thousands of Koreans). An empathic and curious writer, Hwang in this collection proved that he could write realistically about contemporary problems and, more important, about the people affected by those problems—without sacrificing his trademark command of narrative and dialogue or his insights into human psychology. That is to say, each of the *Dog of Crossover Village* stories is more than just an account of a contemporary issue. "Booze" (Sul, 1945), the first, is about a struggle among Koreans for control of a distillery recently abandoned by its Japanese owners, but it is also about the unraveling of a good man attempting to remain decent amid an increasingly frenzied scramble for position in post-Liberation society.[1] "Toad" (Tukŏbbi, 1946) is a grimly realistic portrayal of the desperate housing shortage in Seoul shortly after Liberation as hundreds of thousands of refugees streamed back from Manchuria, Japan, and elsewhere, but it also shows us the ordeal of a man compelled to compromise his principles in order to feed his starving family. Hwang, who upon resettling in the South with his family lived in the Samch'ŏng-dong neighborhood described in this story, was surely sensitive to the plight of his fellow refugees. "Home" (Chip, 1946) portrays the new landowning class in post-Liberation South Korea and the conflict occasioned by their social mobility in a traditionally class-conscious and hierarchical society, but it also examines the psychology of addiction—in this case, addiction to gambling. "Bulls" (Hwangso tŭl, 1946) deals with a peasant uprising against the Korean constables who served the Japanese colonizers in Korea, but it is also a coming-of-age story related by a naïve narrator who knows that his father and the other men of the village are engaged in something dangerous and is compelled to follow this herd under cover of darkness as they advance on the county seat. "To Smoke a Cigarette" (Tambae han tae p'iul tongan, 1947) highlights the difficulties of Korean residents of Japan who attempt to resettle in Korea after Liberation, as well as the weakening of interpersonal relationships as people migrate from the ancestral village to the big city, whose denizens grow indifferent to the suffering of others (the protagonist's concern for the difficulties of the returnees from Japan lasts about as long as it takes him to smoke a cigarette). The title story (1947) is usually taught in Korea as a story of the ultimate survival of Koreans amid adversity (represented by the progeny of Whitey, described at the end), but it may be read just as usefully as an allegory of Korean fears of outsiders (whether the Japanese colonizers or the more recent occupants, the USSR and the United States, who divided Korea at the 38th parallel upon Liberation in 1945 in order to accept the surrender of Japanese forces in Korea) as well as a case study of stigmatization as a means of social and political control. The aforementioned "My Father" is atypical of the collection in that it looks back in history—to the March 1, 1919, Independence Movement in Korea—more than it does to contemporary issues, but it shares with the other stories a distinctive (in this case autobiographical) narrative.

Lost Souls (Irŏbŏrin saram tŭl), the sixth of Hwang's story collections, was published in 1958. Previously, between January 1956 and May 1957, the five pieces therein had appeared in literary journals.[2] Among Hwang's eight volumes of short stories, *Lost Souls* is thematically the most unified. The primary focus is moral transgression and the fate of an outcast in a highly structured society. The stories take place variously in the hinterlands of the Korean peninsula, on the southeast coast, and on the volcanic island of Cheju. Three are directly connected with the Korean War, the catastrophes of which Hwang and his fellow countrymen had only recently survived. Two concern elopement, one of them—the title story—unfolding with all the certainty of Greek tragedy. As always, Hwang's storytelling skill and ear for speech are everywhere in evidence. In "Deathless" (Pulgasari, 1955), Komi and Koptani defy their parents' wishes by eloping. In doing so they are committing a moral transgression that will likely result in their estrangement from their families and their ancestral village. Here Hwang is setting the stage for the title story of the volume. Just as Hester in *The Scarlet Letter* must wear a scarlet *A* for the rest of her life, Sŏgi will be forever marked by his missing ear as he and Suni begin an outcast life in which they are driven farther and farther from their ancestral home; not even nature welcomes them. The protagonist of *"Pibari"* (Pibari, 1956), a young diving woman on Cheju Island, is one of Hwang's most complex female characters. This *pibari* (the word is Cheju dialect for *ch'ŏnyŏ*, "maiden") is an outcast for two reasons: her act of fratricide and her sexuality. In "Voices" (Sori, 1957), the last story, moral transgression is centered not in a single person but in war. Tŏkku, the protagonist, becomes hardened to violence and death while serving in the Korean War, his trauma paralleled by physical injury—the loss of an eye. An industrious farmer before the war, he becomes drunk and irresponsible afterward and before long is a virtual outcast in his village, feared (as is the *pibari*) by the same neighbors who earlier welcomed him home from the battlefront.

Hwang is both a modern and a traditional writer. He is modern in his familiarity with Freudian theory, literary modernism, and contemporary trends in both Western and East Asian literature (he read contemporary Japanese authors in Japanese and especially liked

Shiga Naoya, and read authors such as Lu Xun, Ernest Hemingway, and Albert Camus in translation). He is traditional in his storytelling technique. Hwang made no secret of the debt he owed his elders, at whose feet he heard many a tale as a boy ("The Dog of Crossover Village" may have been one such story), and he acknowledged as well the veterans whose accounts inform his novel *Trees on a Slope* (Namu tŭl pit'al e sŏda, 1960) and his several stories that take place against the background of the Korean War.[3] Among Hwang's several narrative approaches, the one that perhaps best reflects the performance of the traditional storyteller is his use of indirect speech, utilized to especially good effect in the title story of *The Pond*. Also distinctive is his tendency to reserve the use of first-person narratives for the autobiographical stories, such as "My Father," that constitute about one tenth of his short-fiction oeuvre. Finally, it should come as no surprise that Hwang was a careful writer, observing a regular schedule and not infrequently returning to a story to edit and revise for second publication (the ending of "The Dog of Crossover Village" as it was first published in March 1948, in the literary journal *Kaebyŏk*, differs somewhat from the ending of the story as it appears in Hwang's *Collected Works*, published in the early 1980s[4]). The result is a bracing experience for readers who prefer their fiction short, and especially for readers of modern Korean fiction in English translation, which until very recently has tended to showcase works with compelling themes but not necessarily commensurate narrative skill.

The translators wish to thank the editors of the following, in which earlier versions of four of the stories in this volume appeared: *Shadows of a Sound: Stories by Hwang Sunwŏn*, published by Mercury House ("Mantis"); *Asian Pacific Quarterly* ("The Dog of Crossover Village"); *A Man*, published by Jimoondang ("The Dog of Crossover Village" and *"Pibari"*); and *Korean Literature Today* ("Deathless").

NOTES

1. Hwang, often waggish when asked to discuss his stories, told me that he wrote this story because he liked to drink (interview with Hwang Sunwŏn, April 3, 1997).

2. Of these five stories, one, "Mountains" (San, 1956), is not included here. The translation appears in *Land of Exile: Contemporary Korean Fiction*, rev. and exp. ed., trans. Marshall R. Pihl and Bruce and Ju-Chan Fulton (Armonk, N.Y.: M. E. Sharpe, 2007).

3. *Trees on a Slope*, trans. Bruce and Ju-Chan Fulton (Honolulu: University of Hawai'i Press, 2005). See the afterword to this volume, "The War Stories of Hwang Sunwŏn."

4. The texts used for the translations in this volume are those in *The Collected Works of Hwang Sunwŏn* (Hwang Sunwŏn chŏnjip) (Seoul: Munhak kwa chisŏng sa): vol. 1, *The Pond* (Nŭp) and *Wild Geese* (Kirŏgi), 1980; vol. 2, *The Dog of Crossover Village* (Mongnŏmi maŭl ŭi kae) and *Clowns* (Kogyesa), 1981; vol. 3, *Cranes* (Hak) and *Lost Souls* (Irŏbŏrin saram tŭl), 1981.